"A whip-smart, whirlwind novel of noir ɑ
cynicism and romance. Lutz's sterling p
this unique page-turner about the friend
good and the amoral, magnetic narcissist who come͙
story." — Steph Cha, author of *Your House Will Pay*

"An instant, finely wrought story of friendship, ingenuity, and blithe evil. Lutz has the seven deadly sins nailed and rethought for our 2020 world. You've got to dig this book!" — James Ellroy, author of *L.A. Confidential*

"What a pleasure, to sink under the comedic spell of Tom Lutz's debut novel! The perfect book for a dreary day — a gleeful, twisty tale of an unlikely friendship. I'd put it on the shelf between Tom Robbins and Martin Amis, if a place can be cleared there." — Janet Fitch, author of *The Revolution of Marina M.* and *Chimes of a Lost Cathedral*

"A highly literary and always engaging twenty-first-century noir. *Born Slippy* confronts contemporary questions about the relativity of evil that no one can dodge."— Chris Kraus, author of *I Love Dick* and *After Kathy Acker*

"A smart and propulsive wild ride from the genteel mansions of Hartford, Connecticut to the more louche corners of Asia. Lutz's debut is a technicolor noir, a smart, literary and literate thriller — like the love child of Elmore Leonard and Graeme Greene. Original and deft and not to be missed." — Ivy Pochoda, author of *Wonder Valley and Visitation Street*

"The kind of novel a globetrotting Graham Greene might have written had he lived to trot around our contempo, gone-to-hell globe — now divided into neo-imperialist sociopathic zillionaires, and the rest of us. *Born Slippy* is smart, dark, funny and, best of all, what used to be called a real page-turner. You'll love this book." — Jerry Stahl, author of *Permanent Midnight*, *I, Fatty*, and *Old Guy Dad*

BORN SLIPPY

BORN SLIPPY

a novel

Tom Lutz

Published by Repeater Books

An imprint of Watkins Media Ltd

Unit 11Shepperton House

89-93 Shepperton Road

London

N1 3DF

United Kingdom

www.repeaterbooks.com

A Repeater Books paperback original 2020

1

Distributed in the United States by Random House, Inc., New York.

Copyright © Tom Lutz 2020

Tom Lutz asserts the moral right to be identified as the author of this work.

Cover design: Johnny Bull

ISBN: 9781912248643

Ebook ISBN: 9781912248650

Printed and bound in the United Kingdom by TJ International Ltd

To Laurie Winer, firecracker

2013

The blast was felt for blocks. The concussion, the shattering glass, the rip of steel, the roar of falling concrete. The thick, evil odor lasted for days as crews dug through the rubble and gathered debris-encrusted body parts. Passers-by choked on the dust. Frank, when he first saw the images online, felt like he had been there, like the explosion was memory, not a photograph.

He had seen the building, the Credit Lyonnais branch in Taipei, only once, months before, during a brief, very distracted visit to see Dmitry, who was the head of their office there, or head of the region. It had been his first time in Asia. They had stopped in front of the building on Frank's way out of town, that was all.

But when the *Taipei Times* website came up on his normal breakfast internet rounds, he immediately recognized the "before" picture. He felt shredded, felt the guilt of all survivors, obsessed with the cruel idea that he could have prevented it.

Which was ridiculous, he knew.

Only Dmitry could have.

Something had caught up with him, Frank thought later that day — Dmitry's voracious rapacity had finally met its match. He didn't know how, or who, but he knew its karmic inevitability. *Al Jazeera* turned up some shaky video the next day, accompanied by the idea that radical Islamists were responsible, which Frank thought unlikely — Dmitry had, by his own account, made many enemies, lots of them much closer to home. The video showed smoke blowing out of what had once been ten or twelve gleaming stories, now not much more than a maw, spewing black and noxious billows.

Did he see it coming? Like sharks and chum, like the Three Stooges with a ladder, like falling in love where you shouldn't — Frank knew as well as anyone how stories start and how they end. This fiery mess, or something like it, was bound to happen. He had been expecting it for years.

He blamed himself, if not for everything, then for not doing better. After all, he was the one who pretended to be Dmitry's conscience. He was the one not paying attention, the one who had forsaken his duty, the one who had reneged on the implicit bargain he had made those many years earlier, without telling anyone, without telling Dmitry — without even telling himself. He was supposed to fix Dmitry. But he didn't. He was inconstant.

He was, after all, the one who fell in love with Dmitry's wife. He'd set some kind of bomb, too.

Frank Baltimore had first met Dmitry Heald on a building site in the Connecticut hills a dozen years earlier, when the eighteen-year-old Dmitry had come to America — in his Liverpudlian accent it sounded like *Ameriker* — trailing whatever dusty innocence he might still have had, looking for a little work, wanting to earn some quick money and then wander around for the rest of the summer doing a low-rent grand tour, reeling through the Big Lonesome West, as he always called it. Then he'd fly back to England for university: Leeds or Reading, Frank could never remember which, and didn't know what the names meant, where they were on the status hierarchy — Ivy League-ish? Loserville? Frank had never gone to college. He had tried once, failed, quit. He had a chip on his shoulder about it, he knew.

He was a kid himself back then, having just turned twenty-six. Like many people approaching thirty, he was haunted by a sense that time was short, that he might remain an irredeemable failure into the flaky, moldy decrepitude that lurked around the bend. The house he was building was his big break, his move up from what he had always called a remodeling business, even though he had been nothing but a glorified handyman. This new house, nestled in the woods at the advancing edge of Hartford's northwestern insurance-executive suburbs, had been his move into actual contractorland. He never made billions, like Dmitry did, but in the end he did all right. And, he said to himself, looking at the mayhem on his computer screen, he did it without killing or maiming anyone, either.

PART ONE

2000

The house in Connecticut was on a deep flag-shaped lot — the driveway being the pole — running out a forested ridge. A month before Dmitry showed up, the plot had nothing on it but a thick weave of new-growth birch, fir, hemlock, ash, and pine; Frank chain-sawed a dirt-rut drive, thrilled that the client agreed to leave the rest of the woodland untouched — a lot of people in the neighborhood made monstrous, wasteful lawns, but this guy had at least some ecological restraint.

He subcontracted a backhoe driver and concrete guy. They worked fast, and over the next ten days the foundation was set and — with the help of Jillian Gustafson, a large humorless carpenter — an immense, 60'x30' rectangular deck appeared, a foot-deep platform of perfect braced joists and sublime subfloor you could drive a missile launcher across, with a single hole for the basement stairs. All neat and clean, square and level, it capped the foundation, bolted and pristine, ready for the rest of the framing. The day they finished, as Jillian was packing up her tools at 5pm sharp, like always, Frank said something about it being a thing of beauty.

"Thing of beauty?" Jillian asked, uninterested. Nine times out of ten, you say something is beautiful, people will agree with you, just to be sociable, Frank thought — especially women, who aren't, as a tribe, afraid of talking aesthetics like men are. But Jillian avoided standard feminine behavior like she was achieving some political milestone each time. She was good and professional, steady, and knew things — how to use a transom, for instance, thank god, because he didn't — and more than that, he found something about her tough-guy pose reassuring. He'd never been any good at male bluster, at the backslapping sports talk, and working with her made him more comfortable in his own skin. He liked that she called him by his last name, like guys do. It had always seemed affected to him when he did it in the past, but somehow she made it OK. He called her Gustafson and felt solid.

"Yeah, I call it beautiful, I do," Frank said, into her doleful stare, volume trailing off, his enthusiasm waning. She stood there, giving him nothing.

And then, almost inaudible, maybe slightly peevish, he added, "Beautiful."

It wasn't Jillian alone, he knew that. He had yet to meet anyone who shared his love of framing, those squared-up house bones, their artistic perfection.

"Listen, Baltimore," she said. "Can you write me a check tonight?"

She was from the Midwest and looked it, like a minor Willa Cather character, all muscle and mild disapproval. She was a better craftsman than Frank, and she was taller and broader too — a big tough carpenter who was religious about her union-mandated breaks.

"You sure you can't stay on?" he asked. "Even for another week?" She had told him when she started that she could only work for a few weeks, that she was on her way to the Greek islands with her girlfriend. "Please?" The economy was good, and Frank was having real trouble finding carpenters. He had lived all his life in the Massachusetts hill country, and a few years earlier people there would have jumped at a job like this. But now nobody was hard-up enough to come down. The economy was booming, everyone had work, and the fact that Frank was from out of town didn't help. Paul — his partner in the project — was useless; he was new to the area too, and the sole working-class person he knew was Frank. Frank had found Jillian through the lumberyard and checked with them every day for a replacement. No luck yet.

"Can't do it," she said.

Frank looked up and noticed a kid walking down the lane, lumbering out of the woods like a sated bear, at a pace he would soon learn to hate, with a goofy grin and a few red zits on his very white English face, his dark hair in its permanent dishevelment.

"Hey," he said. He was 6'1" or so, maybe 6'2" given the slight slouch.

"Hey?" Frank asked.

"That's right, isn't it?" he said, sounding like John Lennon, still grinning. "That's how you say it here. *Hey*, and then you chuck your chin like this, right?" He pointed toward Frank with his chin a couple times, and then once at Jillian. "Hey," he added to her.

"Hey," she said back, without looking. She walked over to her truck, threw her toolbelt behind the driver's seat.

Frank knew who the kid had to be — Dmitry, the son of friends of friends. His parents had each written Frank a letter filled with polite harrumphing, pleading to give him a job. Thinking about them reminded Frank that nobody likes begging.

"My check, Baltimore?" Jillian said, coming back.

"I can up your hourly, you know," Frank said, reaching into his truck to get his books. "Time and half if you give me another week to find someone."

"We've been over this. No."

Jeez, Gustafson, Frank thought, you could sound some slight note of empathy, it wouldn't kill you, a tiny smidgen of regret that you're leaving me in a jam. Nothing. He leaned over the table saw — it doubled as a desk — and opened his checkbook.

"*Been over this.*" Dmitry said. "I like that."

They both looked at him.

"Looks like my timing is perfect," he said, pulling out a box of Marlboro reds and lighting one up.

"You're Dmitry, right?" Frank asked, though who else could he be?

"Hey, yeah, no, really," Dmitry said. "That's another Americanism."

He was smiling at Jillian. She was frowning at him. Frank's friends in the hills of Western Massachusetts, Dmitry's quasi-relatives, had suggested he would be a good worker, but his parents had been less convincing, and something seemed off about the kid. He was doughy and heavy-lidded, and maybe sinister, watching Jillian like he was a bloated mosquito just landed on her sleeping arm.

Frank copied the amounts for pay and taxes from her last check stub. He didn't have to calculate her hours. Jillian worked, hell or high water, a straight forty.

Still grinning, Dmitry asked her, tipping his head sideways toward Frank: "So what's he like to work for, between us?"

She made a point of looking away into the woods. "Fine," she said, and found an itch to scratch on her shoulder.

"Well I must say, you aren't much of a talker, but you are a great strong woman, aren't you?" he said to her, but she ignored him, not about to be baited.

"Baltimore?" she said. He finished recording her check, ripped it out, and handed it to her.

"Really strong," Dmitry said. "Want to Indian wrestle some time? You know, the one with the legs?" She turned and gave him a casual, well-worn glare.

"Thanks," she said to Frank, walking away. "Good luck," she added, maybe in reference to Dmitry. She got in her truck, and before she pulled out, she rolled down the window and said, "Hope you make your boat." He had told her about his dream — building a sailboat and sailing around the globe — but she had never before given any indication she had heard him. It was nice of her to say. She rolled her window back up and drove off. She didn't look back.

Trog had come to see him about hiring Dmitry, a week before it was time to head to Connecticut to start Paul's house. Frank had been working in musty Turner's Falls, a town that was exactly what would happen if you built a movie set of the perfect New England hill town, with a picturesque river running through it, and then let the paint peel off, the metal rust, and half the wood rot. Lately, though, newcomers were arriving, sprucing up some of the churches, refurbishing a rundown factory building for retail shops, getting the old water wheels running again. Frank was building an old-fashioned well-house for some newly arrived weekenders, a miniature, rough-board Currier & Ives thing with a cute wooden bucket they could hang a plant in. Cheesy, Frank thought, city folk getting rural with a fake well-house — the pail was nonfunctional. But the money was good, and he was working alone, his preference. He was sucking on a soggy sandwich and finishing Henry James's *The Turn of the Screw* when Trog pulled up in his ancient VW bug.

Frank's college-educated friends had told him James's prose was too difficult, and at first it was, but once he realized how it was put together, he could relax and enjoy it. He was just figuring out that *The Turn of the Screw* was not about the governess; it was about the cook. There were no ghosts, no corruption. The cook wanted to drive the governess mad, because the governess had her eyes set on the man whose niece and nephew she was supposedly protecting. The governess was a spectacular failure — the cook won — and the nephew ended up dead. The irony was not lost on him that Trog was asking him to do something for his nephew.

"How's it going?" Frank asked without inflection as Trog grunted his way out of the VW. Trog was round-faced and round-bodied, bald on top with long stringy side hair, a wild grey beard, and an oversized, misshapen potato of a nose. He looked like a cross between an angry, gone-to-seed David Crosby and a nineteenth-century Polish syndicalist bomber.

"Struggling," he said, as he always did, looking for a prompt to rage against his legion of tormentors. When Frank said nothing, he moved on. "You have any coffee?"

"No, just what's left in my cup."

"Huh," Trog said, in his customary put-upon grumble, handing Frank two envelopes. "My nephew Dmitry — you know, this kid I told you about? — well, his parents sent a couple letters for you."

Both letters were already open.

"You read them."

"Yeah, nothing interesting, really."

They were addressed to Frank, c/o Trog and Catherine.

"Federal offence, you know." Why people put up with him, the bilious old goat, Frank didn't know. He was opinionated, grumpy, irritable, and full of conspiracy theories. But it was a small town. You put up with each other. And with time, you grew fond, or if not fond, familiar.

Trog eyed the thermos like he knew Frank was lying about the coffee, one eyebrow hiked up, stroking his anarchist's beard. Frank looked at the letters.

> *Dear Mr. Baltimore:*
>
> *Dreadfully sorry to intrude, but since his gallant Uncle Trog and intrepid Aunt Cathy had suggested the remote possibility, I dare write this excessively presumptuous impudent missive, which you are well within your rights to consider all mouth and no trousers, or, as we used to say in the Midlands when I was a kid, "all my eye and Peggy Martin." I wouldn't blame you if you found my parental ramblings as daft as a brush — nonetheless, I do hope you won't* [something crossed out] *find it amiss to give some consideration to affording my Dmitry some small role, any kind of noddy work at all, in your operation.*
>
> *Yours, etc., George Heald*

Frank thought, OK, first, that explains Henry James's inability to get to his verb, and second, were all those imbecilic idioms some attempt at jocularity?

The mother's letter was both less Byzantine and less successful at being careful.

> *Dear Franky (if I might),*
>
> *I know our dear friend Catherine has mentioned her "nephew" Dmitry will be looking for some suitable employment while across the pond, and if in fact it all works out to your benefit, I wanted to thank you in advance for your kind thoughtfulness. I think he would be of some help to you. For some years now there has been no telling when he might actually arrive anywhere — the lads will have their head! — but he probably will show himself sometime in May if he isn't derailed en route. I hope it isn't terribly cheeky of me to hope to someday return the consideration…*

That implied Frank might someday come to England, which had never occurred to him. He found it reassuring when she suggested that this Dmitry likely wouldn't show up and decided not to worry about it. While Frank was reading, Trog was declaiming against some indignity foisted upon him by the local authorities, and he listened half-heartedly. Trog's old stories — about wandering around Morocco in the 1970s, getting chased by international police and rival hashish runners — were fabulous, but his current litany of complaints less so. The rants sometimes formed an oddly soothing background noise, though, like muzak, filling gaps in whatever actual conversation was happening.

"So you like these people?" Frank asked.

"Yeah, why not?" Trog said. "Known them forever."

"And you know the kid?"

"Nah, but he doesn't work out, you let him go." He looked with disgust at the cutesy well-house, and then up at the out-of-towners' manse. "These fucking new people and their bullshit."

"Work's work," Frank said.

That had been the last he'd thought about the nephew.

"Well!" Dmitry said, with a clownish wink, as Jillian's truck pulled away. "She seems like quite a lot of fun!" Henry James aside — yeah, Frank knew he was born in New York, but he was a Brit in every other way — and maybe a half-dozen other novelists, Frank wasn't a fan of the English. Aristocrats. Snobs. Not that he'd met that many of them. "*Nostromo*," Dmitry said, reading the cover of the paperback on the desk-saw. "What does *tromo* mean?"

"Have you read Joseph Conrad?"

"Not that I know of," he said.

Although Frank couldn't say why, he found this mildly reassuring. And Dmitry had found his way to the middle of nowhere, Connecticut, which meant he had some resourcefulness and clearly wanted the job. Maybe he wasn't as flaky as his mother's note suggested. Besides, Frank needed the help and wasn't allergic to wiseasses.

Dmitry looked down at his index finger and picked at a hangnail. "I may as well tell you, Franky," he said, still with the grin, looking back up. "I'm going to need your help."

"Not Franky, Frank. I know, you want a job."

"Yes, but more than that. I want to learn as much about Ameriker" — Frank started to think he might be exaggerating his accent at times, but maybe not — "as I can while I'm here, so I'll need you to catch me up on the local customs and mores or I'll never learn, all the flora and fauna and folklore and legends and whatnot — you say *whatnot* here, right?"

"Have you ever swung a hammer?" Frank asked.

"No, I'm forced to admit that I have not, Franky, although I have swung other things."

"Frank."

The sun was getting low.

"Frank?"

"Yes, not Franky, Frank."

"I'm sorry, *Frank*, but really, think about it: me mum and dad, me auntie and uncle, and their kids, and your Tracy: everyone calls you Franky. I feel like I know you as Franky."

So Dmitry knew Tracy, Frank thought. Of course he did. It was a tiny town up there.

His ex lived in the house they had rented, up in the hills a few miles from the Vermont border, the house she lived in when they met. She had a baby and a toddler then, and was twenty-six to Frank's nineteen, so she struck him as impossibly mature, totally out of his league, a woman to his boy. In retrospect, he found it almost criminal, like those female high-school teachers who sleep with their students — the young guy doesn't stand a chance. Not that he complained. He was the first to admit that he was absolutely fucking in love. At twenty-six, she was all mystery and oracle and wisdom, and meeting her gave him an immediate incurable longing. That never changed. The craving started and never stopped. Maybe, he thought, he should read some more Jung, and let him explain it, because she did represent some eternal female principle to him, as if she lived at an unbridgeable mythic distance from his own tortured, puny psyche. Hence the longing.

But when Dmitry brought her up, it pissed him off. He was working long, long hours to pay everyone's way — paying for the kids, even though they weren't technically his — since she still didn't have a job. But when he suggested she might bring the kids down to Connecticut, she reminded him they weren't *his* kids. And true, biologically, they were not. But emotionally they were. Lulu was only a month old, Kennedy two when they got together — he was the father they knew. Tracy said it was all in his head, that he barely told them he loved them, that he was emotionally constipated, out of touch, incapable of true bonding. But he couldn't imagine being any more full of love for them than he already was — he told them in all sorts of ways, and he was convinced that the kids knew it, knew how protective, how possessive, even, he felt toward them. He told them he loved them sometimes too, he did, just didn't tell them every other minute the way Tracy did, and which he thought was kind of creepy. The image that came back to him, sometimes more than once a day, was a camping trip they all took to a state park on Long Island Sound, sleeping in two cheap little tents, one for him and Tracy and one for Kennedy and Lulu, cooking on a propane stove, the girls running on the beach all day, still in the plastic bucket and shovel years, he and Tracy like a real couple, real parents. If he spent too much time thinking about it, he would weep, but he wasn't blind. He could see that all along Tracy was looking at him sideways, wondering if she should settle for him, if he was ever going to grow into a man she could really love. He watched her appraise other men, but he refused to dwell on that. He pushed the image of Tracy's wandering reluctance aside, and remembered the way being with them all lifted his chin, filled his chest, and dampened his eyes. He remembered the pride. Was that real, or was he just pretending to be a father? He liked to think it was real.

He looked up to find Dmitry observing him, amused about something.

"So. You've never done any construction at all," Frank said.

"I've constructed plans and I've constructed alibis and I've constructed criticism, Franky." He turned serious. "But hey, no, really, my plan is this: I work for you for precisely one month, thirty days straight, ten hours a day, at ten dollars an hour, which will give me three thousand dollars exactly, with which I can buy what we call a land yacht but which you call a motorhome and drive it to California and back, stopping along the way, meeting toothsome girls, having adventures, buying an American baseball jacket, chewing peyote with Indians, executing love affairs with suburban housewives, rustling cattle, cataloguing the aforementioned flora and fauna and whatnot —"

"Who said anything about ten bucks an hour?"

"*Bucks*," he said, like he loved this word too, feeling it with his lips. "*Bucks*. Well, me auntie and uncle said so, said that's what carpenters make here in the good old US of A."

"But you're not a carpenter. Unskilled laborers make five. If you turn out to be useful I can make it six."

Dmitry crushed his cigarette butt with his shoe and pulled out another.

"You're going to pick up that butt, right?" Frank said. "They take decades to decompose." He walked back to the foundation to resume cutting studs. He wanted to get more of the first-floor exterior wall up before it was too dark.

"Ah, Franky, you see the wages of truthfulness?" Dmitry said, following him. "I should have lied to you. My sterling honesty about my lack of experience has cost me fifty percent of my income."

"But if you had said you knew what you were doing, I would have said, OK, go ahead and make me a dozen thirty-nine-inch two-by-six-by-six headers and their jack studs, per plan, and then what would you have done?"

"Look for a dictionary?" Big grin.

"So you want to increase your vocabulary for five or not?"

"Ah, Franky, you like words too. That's what Tracy said."

Sure she did, Frank thought. Dmitry wasn't helping himself bringing her up — thinking of her made him feel bereft.

"So you've never used a circular saw?"

"Doesn't even sound possible," he said, squinting like a mathematician contemplating a twelfth dimension. "A circular saw. How would you hold it?"

"Christ."

Frank scoffed, but he found himself feeling warmly toward the kid. He had something — he couldn't put his finger on it, but there was something, some level of contagious bemusement at the absurdity of it all, maybe, some quiet self-confidence, and his humor worked on Frank, won him over. They agreed on five an hour, six after two weeks if Dmitry worked out. Frank gave him a few pointers and safety tips and set him up trimming joists. He utterly fucked up a few of them, and was slower than a tree sloth, but Frank needed the extra set of hands. For now, it was the best he could do.

The house in Connecticut was for a nuclear engineer named Paul, who was vaguely related — their fathers were cousins, he gathered — to Frank's defrocked dentist, a little guy they called Catskills because he had grown up playing saxophone in the resorts every summer. Catskills had a closet at home with a row of tuxedos in plastic bags, lined up like xylophone keys, each one an inch longer than the next, a tux a year from age nine until he was in college, during which span he had gone, as he put it, from being four foot five to five foot four. Catskills was on an extended vacation from dentistry, having abused his script pad a few too many times, and was now just another one of the town's backwoods drug addicts. His income was augmented by running the odd bale of marijuana across a state line or two. On one of his trips to New Haven he took Frank to see Paul, who needed a contractor to build his new house. Since it was Catskills, Frank assumed the deal was somehow shady, but he liked the idea of getting out of town, of putting a little distance between him and Tracy.

"Paul's alright," Catskills said as they walked up to their door. "But be careful of the wife." He was the kind of guy, Frank knew, who constantly railed about the women in his life, past and present, so who knew what that meant? He had his own problems with women, or at least with Tracy, but Catskills was off the charts with his constant misogyny. So, grain of salt.

Paul answered the bell. In his thirties but looking younger, he had the blond, pudgy, All-American look of the young Beach Boys before they met Charlie Manson — round, soft, and pasty. He was too boyish to be handsome and too bland to be cute, with a slightly ferret-like nose and pale eyes a size too small for his face.

"Hey, Catskills," he said. "And you must be Franky?"

"I prefer Frank," Frank said, and Paul's crest fell.

"Sorry," he said, looking pure contrition.

"No big deal. I just prefer Frank." Paul looked immediately grateful, and Frank's first thought was: jeez, it will be ludicrously easy to guilt-trip this guy.

"And so, Frank," he said, unrolling blueprints on his dining room table. "Here are the plans?"

Was that a question? Frank wondered. He looked them over. They were good drawings. A big house, saltbox shaped, traditional. Nice details.

"You drew these yourself?" Frank asked.

"Yes?" he said, tensing up as if he were about to be spanked.

"Nicely done," Frank said, and Paul exhaled. "Very professional. Building inspectors love all the different elevations, all the detail insets. Everything above code. Permits should be a breeze."

Margie, Paul's wife, walked in as he was saying this. Paul, nervous, introduced Frank, saying his name and then taking a quick step back, out of firing range. Clearly she owned the place and she owned Paul. In her thirties too, she might have been pretty if it weren't for her angry jaw and her cruel eyes, whipping around like gale-warning flags at the end of a dock. Her hair was an unexceptional brown but rigorously done, like she had checked it just before she walked in the room. Same with the unremarkable and yet precision-guided make-up, the body neither too thick nor too thin, the clothes that weren't too sexy, too dowdy, too dull, or too showy. She looked like she had read every women's magazine and every girl's manual in the world, eviscerated every wayward instinct, spent exactly the right number of daily minutes on each machine in her gym. All this vigilance and discipline had made her calmly and terminally vicious. One sensed bodies strewn in her wake.

"I'm sorry," she said, but she wasn't, and she said it with a killer's smile, without actually saying hello. Frank guessed it was because he was in the servant class. "I'm glad you like the plans, but we were hoping you would be able to tell us what was *wrong* with them. What needs *improvement*. We know what's right about them."

That stumped him for a minute.

"Kee-reist!" Catskills jumped in the breach. "Give him a minute, Margie, damn!" He was working himself up, getting hyper as he sometimes did. One night they had to throw him in the river to keep him from jumping on people.

Frank looked at the plans again to find a mistake, and ended making something up as Catskills paced. "We could note the glazing on the windows — double, triple, single, whatever. Door thickness. Put in a few more details like that."

"Paul?" she said, like Patton.

"Right?" he said, "will do."

"Triple, right?" she said. Frank was pretty sure she knew nothing about glazing, but that she rightly assumed triple was the most expensive option. She was smart, Frank could see — clearly had them all figured out, knew like a high school basketball coach where each strength and weakness was, knew that she would be disappointed in the end by all of them.

"Right," Paul said.

"I'm glad to see the solar worked in," Frank said. "Do you have to use a state-approved vendor?"

"Paul?" she demanded. She ingested new information like a snake, taking it in whole.

Paul looked at Frank. "Yes? Yes."

"OK, no problem. You have enough square feet?"

"We can always add more," Paul said, glancing at Margie.

She left the room on that, with a *my work is temporarily done here* nose in the air. Catskills was smiling broadly, which didn't make sense at first, until Frank realized that Margie, with her every move, confirmed his worldview about female perfidy.

Her husband's jumpy equanimity returned as she disappeared.

"Sorry about that," Paul said. "But it's always best to agree with her? I'll put the details in about the windows. And the doors?" Frank was having trouble not focusing on the fact that Paul inflected every other sentence as a question. "And I'll do the solar panel calculations again, easy to do. Anything else?"

"What's this beam?" Frank asked, pointing to a side-view of the roof framing.

"Ah!" He was proud of the beam. "This roof line is so long that no standard rafters could take the snow load. Well, I don't really know? That's the way I read the building code. I figured we cut the span in half, support it with this beam?"

"Why not a supporting wall?"

Catskills stood up, too jumpy to take this. "OK," he said. "I'm officially bored enough to blow my brains out. You got a gun here, Paul?"

Ignored, he announced he was getting beers, leaving toward what must have been the kitchen. Paul was explaining his reasoning about support walls and rafter length and room size, and Frank didn't really pay that much attention. He just appreciated that, unlike most of his clients, Paul knew how things worked. He liked that he was an engineer, that he was doing his homework, and that he would worry about the specs so Frank wouldn't have to. They agreed about the decision to frame the outer walls with 2x6 to increase the insulation, the use of Tyvek as a moisture barrier — they were having a little love-fest in the language of techno-banalities, and Frank was thrilled that Paul cared about energy efficiency, so he could build something that did as little damage to the environment as possible, even if it was way too big. Catskills came back with three beers, half of his gone already.

"So you have the money for all this?" Frank asked. Paul wasn't doing anything on the cheap.

"The thing is," he said, excited, "the state of Connecticut is giving me an interest-free construction loan — this program to help poor people own their own homes, building them themselves?"

"OK," Frank said. "You don't seem that poor." Plus, he thought a few seconds later, you aren't building your own house. I'm building it for you.

"You have to excuse Franky," Catskills said. "He's got a kind of Tourette's moralism, but it's always momentary. Once he gets over it he's as venal as the rest of us."

Paul still looked worried. It seemed to Frank he should be. Catskills made a show of downing his beer.

"Is it legal?" Frank asked.

"Yes. I mean I had my lawyer look at all the papers." Poor people don't have lawyers to look over their papers, Frank thought, and Paul could see it in his face. So could Catskills.

"Franky!" he screamed, finishing his beer and slamming his bottle down on the table. "The fuck's your problem?" he added even louder, like his meth had just kicked in. He hopped up, ran at Frank, and put him in a headlock. He often went berserk in this little-guy way, and now he was hanging off Frank's head in Paul's dining room. Fuck's sake, Frank thought, what were they, thirteen? Instantaneously, like some finely tuned bad behavior seismograph, Margie walked back in.

"Eli!" she said, in High Schoolmarm. She was the only one Frank had ever heard use his real name.

"Don't yell at *me*, Margie! Tell *him* to stop being such a little *bitch*," he said, but he let Frank go with one last slap to the head. "I'm getting another beer. Who wants?" Catskills always quickly returned to his own version of normal after running amok, as if nothing had happened. Frank straightened out his hair and shirt.

"Oh, help yourself," Margie said, as if depressed by the fact that men were so reliably disappointing. She turned and left.

"Don't worry, Franky, really," Paul said when they were alone.

"Frank."

"Oh, right, sorry! As long as I am the main worker on it, then we're fine? I can hire other people, it's all legal. We wouldn't want any records of you working more hours than me, though, OK? A salary agreement rather than an hourly rate, no record of your hours or mine?"

He spread out a printout of his cost estimates and Frank looked at it for a few quiet minutes. Paul had used the standard *National Construction Estimator*, which was good, a little high if anything, and he had a total number of labor hours, with a single dollar figure.

"How do you figure the labor costs?" Frank asked. He had a horse in that race.

"Well, this is what I'm hoping? You see the total materials cost here? And figure two laborers at six bucks an hour, forty hours, twenty weeks, that's $7,680. I'll be working forty hours, too, four each day after work, and twenty each weekend, and I thought, maybe, if you worked sixty a week, that would do it — Catskills said you wanted overtime. As you can see, I have labor, materials, and subcontracting coming to eighty-two thousand, and the loan is for ninety? We have to figure some overruns, right?"

"I always add twenty percent." Paul looked crestfallen again. Jeezus, this guy was easily derailed. "But let's say ten. I don't mind sixty hours a week if I'm getting paid for it," he said, "but how much?"

Paul paused. Like he was afraid to say.

"The thing is, if it all goes well," he said, finally, looking up with wide-eyed innocence, "we could sell this for twice what it costs to build? Even more."

They looked at each other, and Catskills, returning with three more beers, was suddenly interested, too.

"I thought this house was for you," Frank said, with a reflexive motion of his chin toward the door Margie had walked through. Paul apprehensively glanced that way.

"Once I explain the profit, and show her drawings for a bigger place, she'll be on board."

"The state won't mind?"

"My lawyer says there's nothing in the loan docs about not selling it. You have to move in, which I can do for a week, but that's it. It will sell better if it's furnished, anyway? This one will be in my name, and by then we'll establish your residency and do the next one with state money under your name. When we sell that one, we'd have enough to each finance our own, or maybe do two at the same time?"

Frank saw it immediately. Over a hundred grand profit per house. Four houses, a half million. Eight houses, a million bucks. This was his shot. He would finally have a stake. He had washed up on the shore alive, godammit, pockets full of doubloons. He wasn't stupid: he doubted it all. But emotionally he had already signed the papers.

"Fifty-fifty?" he asked.

"Fifty-fifty. You do the extra labor? I'm the contractor, take care of the legal, etc."

"OK. And how do I live between now and the big payday?"

"Obviously winter will slow us down, but we can get this first one done in four months, get the next one framed before winter, finish the interior even if it's cold? Then launch the next two next spring. Sixteen or eighteen months from now we each have a $250,000 house *and* that much cash? That's a lot of money."

No, duh, five times anything he had ever made.

"Still," Frank said. "You have a job, right?" Paul put on a coat and tie every day and worked — fairly high up — in an insurance company, one that insured nuclear power plants. Must have made this risk here seem miniscule. "I have to get paid something. I have to live on something. I've got child support." Not court-ordered, but still.

"I was thinking that maybe, if you took, say, $6 an hour like the other laborers, it would look kosher for the state? It's not a very good hourly rate, I know? But you could maybe get by on $300 a week?"

Frank looked at Catskills and cursed him silently, since no doubt that's where Paul got the information about his income. But it didn't matter. He could, in fact, get by on that, if it was steady, and the payoff was worth it. Defrauding the state of Connecticut seemed a little dicey, but that was mostly Paul's lookout; besides, a lawyer was on the job and on paper maybe it did look OK. Ethically, he decided, he was in the clear. If the state was trying to extend the ownership society, well, he was, in fact, a poor person, and he would end up owning his own house. Maybe not in Connecticut, and maybe not this house, but still, he would be fulfilling the spirit, if not the letter of the law.

"Make it $350, and charge it as a project expense. The fifty-fifty happens after that?"

"OK?" Paul said.

"Where do I sign?"

"Nothing to sign. We can start right away?"

In less than two years Frank would have hundreds of thousands of dollars. He was in. He had no protection if this Paul wasn't as innocent as he seemed, but he looked at that soft, ineffectual-looking body, clearly on tenterhooks, and tried to imagine it screwing him over. Didn't seem possible. And what the hell, at worst Frank would be right where he was. With the down time between jobs he wasn't averaging $350 a week lately, and he knew the world well enough to know that contract or no contract, the guy with the lawyer had all the power. Paul was sweating, so Frank stayed silent.

"There's a motel in the town? I can rent a double room there by the month for $300. We can make that a business expense, too? I'll need a place sometimes, I assume, but you can have it alone the rest of the time."

Frank was sick of being a loser. And he had been making all the right moves to get ready for this. He had stopped smoking pot all the time. He drank way less. He was keeping better records. He had gotten more serious about his reading to make up for never going to college — he didn't count the semester he signed up for two night courses and, being high all the time, kind of forgot about them — literally forgot he was going to college. But now he was a new man. He was prepared for this chance.

And Tracy. One unintended consequence of getting sober was that his relationship with Tracy changed. He had known all along that he came up short with her, could see it, see her exasperation with him. But he'd always assumed it was because he was high, or drunk, so much of the time — she loved him, he was *almost* her shining-armored knight, he was just still young and stupid, a.k.a. stoned, and she, older and wiser, was waiting for him to straighten up and be his true, brilliant, reliable, gallant self.

But once he was straight, it was harder for either of them to pretend that he was the guy she was looking for. At nineteen, we all look like we can become anything, but by the time we're twenty-five, our limitless prospects have already massively shut down, and we start to look like what we will become. She saw it and didn't like it. They all but stopped having sex, and without that, there was no escaping her disinterest. She had had a project — fix him, make him less of a loser — but now, the drugs and booze put aside, the man replaced the boy, and she wasn't impressed. She may have even preferred the boy.

Less of a loser, but feeling like more of one, he begged for her love. In the final throes he wept in shame and anger, and this mooncow act made her even more fed up. When he moved out of the house it surprised no one, all his friends having seen it coming and wondering why it was taking so long.

The kids were devastated, Lulu six and Kennedy eight, girls already left behind by their real dad. Although Kennedy had been stoic when he told her, he knew she would fall apart as soon as she was alone in her room, and she did. Lulu was talking to herself in the full-length mirror on the bedroom door, as if reminding herself she existed, or maybe the opposite, lost in whatever fantasy she could grab. The only thing that would make it OK, he decided, the only thing that would allow him to feel like less of a shit, was to make something of himself. This boondoggle with Paul was exactly what he'd been waiting for, the thing that would set him up, make him solid. They could do six or eight more houses, then split the resulting millions and go their own merry ways. He imagined Tracy's eyes full of surprised pride, and, once again, desire.

"I'm in," he said.

From then on he and Paul had two sets of conversations, one when Margie was around that was all show, a big charade about the house they were building for her — did she want it this way? did she want it that way? — and one when she wasn't there, working out the actual business plan, stopping to look at other building lots on their way to the lumber yard. Margie was curt with Frank, and he wasn't sure why, but didn't think it was because she sensed their plan. It didn't even seem personal. Her contempt had been sitting there waiting for him, because of the kind of guy he was, a lost soul. He was used to that, he could deal. And besides, he wasn't going to be that guy anymore. He was going places.

Frank had been thrilled to get rid of his sad little divorced-dad Western Mass basement apartment and eliminate that part of his nut. A week after his first chat with Paul, he put his few pieces of furniture in Tracy's garage, stuck his tools and clothes and some books in his truck, and drove the two hours south to meet Paul at the site. The surveyors had marked where the drive and building pad would go. Frank started clearing trees and Paul went off to work. He came back at six, when they were supposed to check into the motel.

"Look what I found?" he said, unfurling an enormous crusty mass of canvas in a cloud of foul dust, holding his arm out like Vanna White showing off a prize. "A tent!" Faded army green with brownish blotches, it looked like it was left over from Ulysses Grant's meetings during the Civil War. It stank of dusty mildew like only thick, ancient canvas can.

"Think about it," he said. "The motel for ten weeks? Three thousand dollars. We put in three thousand dollars of high-end fixtures instead? That's a minimum $50,000 bump in the asking price. It'll be like picking up thousand-dollar bills off the street. Think about it — every night we don't spend $40 on a motel? It turns instantly into $1000. You want to spend $1000 a night on a motel?"

Paul knew, by then, that Frank was a sucker for that kind of reasoning. They cleared a spot for the moldy monstrosity and built a platform with three 4x8s of plywood. The makeshift deck was almost big enough for the rank, asymmetrical, beat-up architectural marvel of a tent. It had a vestibule in front and flapped windows that, with some twigs holding them up, stuck out like awnings. Paul had bought a couple air mattresses, and Frank hung lines for clothes and a utility light.

"We live in here?" Paul kept saying. "Fifty grand. A piece? Sweet."

His estimates could double like that. And Paul never spent a night in it. Not once. His use of "we" was sneaky like that.

Two weeks later, Frank and Dmitry were hanging the second-floor joists, one of those repetitive two-man jobs where you can have a decent conversation, sitting on top of opposite framed walls.

"Trog thinks your father was in the drug business, too," Frank said. Trog had met Dmitry's father Edwin in the 1970s, smuggling hash up from Morocco for the English market — Trog was smuggling hash, at any rate, and he suspected Edwin was as well, although Edwin never copped to it, and had a front as an importer of rugs and kilims and antiques, never letting on otherwise. On the ferry between Algeciras and Tangier, Trog could be mistaken for little except what he was, an American hippie drug dealer, but Edwin might have been a schoolteacher, an archeologist, a mining engineer. One day, the bartender in Trog's local pub in Hackney whispered to him that some very square guy, reeking of Interpol, had been around asking questions. Trog decided it was time to close shop and head back to the hill country of Massachusetts. He packed up his British wife Catherine and a box of books and flew home. He grew a little weed behind his house but was otherwise retired.

"Franky, the simple fact is this: I know nothing about my father," he said.

Having had a tough father himself, the kind of guy who would beat the crap out of you one minute and give you big hugs (and a sermon) the next, and who died young — his anger, Frank always assumed, causing an aneurysm to burst in his brain before he hit sixty — Frank was completely prepared for the *I hate my father* talk. And, frankly, where else do you go after *I know nothing about him?*

"What do you mean you know nothing?"

"Nothing."

"Was he a drinker?" Frank asked.

"No."

"Angry?"

"No, mild-mannered to a fault," Dmitry said. "He is like, I don't know — he's like the clerk at the shop where you buy your bread, or your auto parts salesman, excuse me salesperson, someone you don't really take any notice of, a nonentity."

They pulled the twenty-foot-long slabs of fir into place, their legs dangling into what would be the living room, slipping each board into galvanized hangers, and toed a few 10d nails into the plate and end joist, a task which always took Frank half the time it took Dmitry on his end.

"You're killing me. You're getting paid by the hour," Frank said for the umpteenth time. "I'm getting paid by the house."

Dmitry would then stop altogether, and say, "But, Franky! You own the means of production — for instance you own this hammer — and my surplus labor is going into your pocket." Frank had been telling him about Marx, his latest reading, and proud as he was of his autodidactic accomplishments, he also wondered how much of it he had wrong.

When Dmitry finally finished nailing, they grabbed the next joist and slid it in.

"I mean, he was a smuggler of some sort, right?" Frank said. "That makes him at least mildly interesting. Morocco in the Seventies? That's interesting."

"Perhaps," Dmitry said. But he didn't seem to be really thinking about it. He had lost interest.

They talked some other nonsense for a while, and then, out of the blue, Dmitry said: "I realize now that you are right, Franky, that my father would have been an excellent smuggler, because like any proficient spy he is so ordinary he would never in a million years be suspected or even noticed. You look at him and your eye is immediately drawn elsewhere, not because he's hideous or repulsive or anything, but because he's unable to inspire interest. Look at him a split second and you find yourself contemplating the picnic table next to him, or the yew hedge behind him, or the grass to the left of his shoe, all of which seem more engaging." He thought for a moment, sank a nail. "And if he *was* a spy, it would explain everything…" He trailed off, but then, slipping the next joist in, said, "Yes, that's it, Franky. My daddy is MI6. Hence the fancy electronic gear in the attic."

"Seriously?"

"Deadly serious." He wasn't. "And perhaps this is true of all successful spies; there is no way of knowing whether he is one unless he *were* to be arrested. Then we'd all go on the telly, like the neighbors of serial murderers, and say, *he was always* so *quiet.*"

"Why don't you ask him?"

"Ask him if he's a spy?" he said, with a half laugh, followed by a moment of hesitation. Why he couldn't hit a nail while he was thinking Frank would never understand, and asking would just mean they'd waste more minutes while he explained. "You don't understand, Franky. He's not a man you ask questions. It's not a psychological thing — well, it is psychological I suppose, but not about *my* psychology, and not *his* exactly — even if you intend to ask him a question, one look at him and you realize you can't, any more than you could ask a tree, or a cow" — and here he let out one of his distressingly regular, long-burst farts, the result of eating a pound of Oreo cookies every day — "I mean you *can*, after all, ask him what time it is or whether he would mind passing the butter. You just can't ask him a real question. It's as if some force field surrounds him that transmogrifies every serious query into, *Look like rain to you?* — or no, not even that, that's too ominous: *Right, then?* That's all you can ask: *Right, then?* His answer, ineluctably, is, *Yes, right, then.* I'm not kidding, Franky. Somehow, alchemically, or like an invisible centrifuge taking your words and separating out all their meaning, conversation is drained of content. *Right, then?*" he paused in fake anticipation. "*Right-o!*" They slipped another twenty-foot joist into its hangars. "Don't get me wrong," he added. "He's a perfectly pleasant chap. Perfectly pleasant."

"I don't know," Frank said. "Maybe that's not such a bad way for a father to be, kind of neutral."

Dmitry sighed.

"Honestly, Franky, you have to get over your father, you really do. Yes, he was a little brutal, OK," he said, and added, in his *American guy* accent, "*Hey, really, it's hanging you up, man,*" and then, back in his own voice, "That stuff with your dad. Let it go. I'm so much younger than you and *already* I don't really care about my father's non-entityness. I don't, Franky, it's just that you asked."

Frank was shocked, since most of the time whatever he said seemed to act simply as prompts for further tangential monologue on Dmitry's part, and the last thing he expected was any insight. But Dmitry was right that he spent too much time pitying himself for his tragic youth. His father *was* complicated. He *should* get over it. He was careening toward thirty. It was time to let his dead father stay dead. They were lowering the last joist into place, a natural endpoint for the conversation.

"I don't think I did ask," Frank said.

"Yes, yes, Franky," he said slowly, in the patient schoolteacher mode he reserved for whenever Frank didn't get a joke. "I know you didn't. Try to keep up."

They tacked the last joist in place, stood up and stretched.

Paul was supposed to come after work each day and put in a few hours, but never did. Sometimes he had to work late, sometimes his wife made him come home, sometimes his kids were in a play or a had soccer game or a dentist's appointment. Yes, it pissed Frank off: I may not be much, he thought to himself, but I'm an honest man, and Paul may not have been intentionally lying (except to his wife, Margie, about their business plan), but liar or not, he never came after work, except to check in for a half hour. And he did fairly short days on the weekends too, at most. Since he wasn't much with a hammer, when Frank did the math he figured it only cost the project a percent or two, Paul flaking off like that, but it still irked.

And the upside was that, until Dmitry arrived, he had the tent to himself. From sundown to sunrise he could read unmolested, a utility light hanging from the ridgepole. The setup was kind of perfect for that — no TV, no nothing, alone with his books. Even after Dmitry got there, he managed to read through the guy's snoring an hour or so before falling asleep and an hour in the morning. He always read during lunch and he made Dmitry drive when they went into town so he could get a few more pages in. Struggling through the glorious *The Sound and the Fury* at night, and reading *Beyond Good and Evil* during the day, he was swirling in a world of coincidence — every line he read in Nietzsche seemed to explain Faulkner and vice versa. *Talking much about oneself can also be a means to conceal oneself*, Nietzsche says, for instance, and all those characters in *The Sound and the Fury*, what else do they do? And when he says that distrust and doubt are healthy, that anything unconditional is pathological — Faulkner meant Quentin as perfect proof.

And Frank loved the idea that he was using such a tiny amount of fossil fuel energy. His entire home consumption consisted of a single lightbulb a few hours a night. He bathed in a small pond. He used the woods as a toilet. Yes, his tools used a lot of energy building the house, as did his truck, running to the lumberyard. But that was business. In his private life he was almost fossil fuel free. He was saving the planet every day.

The downside of the whole arrangement, aside from the mess Dmitry made of the tent, was Margie. On weekends she would show up on the site and be a general pain in the ass, like all career-less clients anywhere. He tried to tell himself that she wasn't a real client, that she wasn't going to move in anyway, but it didn't help. She changed her mind and made him rip out perfect work and redo it slightly differently, like a lot of rich people do — make a closet six inches bigger, move a window two inches to the right — but more aggravating was the fact that her default expression was mild disgust, as if no matter what she was talking about, she was, at the same time, noticing that you smelled like a dead possum. Dmitry's arrival helped; she had someone she found even more distasteful than Frank.

He knew it happened in lots of places — migrant farmers' camps, people building roads in the High Pamir, all those guys working the mines in the Andes — but for an average adult American, living in a tent with another grown man is a little out of the ordinary. Even most homeless people don't share their makeshift shelters. It's hard enough putting up with another person when you're having sex with them — to have to live in the same room with their dirty laundry and farting through the night and the rest of it and get no love or sex? Like prison.

And as with prison, he started to recognize a forced camaraderie, accidental bonding. He was almost ten years older than Dmitry, so felt like a mentor, a teacher to his student, and that gave him some satisfaction.

"*Every man has his price, people say*," he read out loud one night, sitting on a crate as Dmitry laid back on his air mattress, cutting his overgrown toenails. "*This is not true. But for every man there exists a bait which he cannot resist swallowing. To win over certain people to something* — you're going to pick up that disgusting crud, aren't you? — *it is only necessary to give it a gloss of love of humanity, nobility, gentleness, self-sacrifice* — *and there is nothing you cannot get them to swallow. To their souls, these are the icing, the tidbit; other kinds of souls have others*."

"Wait, Franky," Dmitry said. "Who is swallowing what?"

"He's saying that we can all get suckered into anything if people appeal to some sense of self, or some vanity —"

"Yes, yes, Franky, but first he says a man's price is a bait he can't resist swallowing, and if he takes the bait, *then* you can get him to swallow anything — it's like an improperly mixed metaphor."

"But the point —"

"Yeah, the point — but what's the icing, the bait they swallow or the stuff they swallow because they swallowed the bait?"

"The bait," Frank said, but then he wondered. Maybe not.

It didn't matter. These discussions, even when he was unsure, made him feel smart.

"What's your bait, Franky?" Dmitry asked.

He thought about it. It was probably the desire to be seen as smart, well read, like he was trying to do right then.

And his boat. His boat was his bait. Or his icing.

His idea had always been, during those years, that one day, after learning how to build staircases and bookshelves, additions and outbuildings for people, how to do kitchens and baths and cabinets, he would be able to fulfill his lifelong dream and build a big wooden sailboat for himself. He could live on it. He could go down the coast to Florida, up to Canada, again, fossil fuel free. The fact that he might never put the money together, that he knew nothing about boatbuilding, that he had yet to bend a board or use fiberglass, that the entirety of what he knew about sailing was based on an hour on a Sunfish in Lake Hopatcong when he was ten: these things didn't at all diminish his enthusiasm. His boat — that was his bait. And the money he was going to make with Paul. And the love of a good woman. And a new truck with an extended cab. And — what wasn't his bait?

"I think," Dmitry said when he didn't answer, "it is exactly what Nietzsche said: the gloss of humanity, nobility. That's what you want. You want to be Gandhi or Martin Luther King. Not *be* them, actually, but receive the adulation they got. That, and your ocean-going sailboat. And pussy."

"Pussy!" Frank scoffed.

"Oh, yes, Franky, you think you hide it, but you are an insatiable pussy hound. You can't see a woman and not think about it."

"That's not true," he said. "Margie, Tracy — the list goes on and on."

"Yes, but *that* list is not very long, is it — it's two — and we both know those two women scare you, and neither will have you. You've got no moral high ground there. I'm surprised you haven't had an accident when you drive, the way you stare at even the most marginally attractive women walking down the street."

"Like you don't."

"Of course I do! But I know the value of pussy in my — what did you call it? — my hierarchy of human needs, Franky."

"That's not what Maslow's talking about."

"Well I think it is — in fact I'm quite sure it is — what I'm talking about. Or was. Now I'm going to sleep." But true to form he wasn't finished, and after three or four beats he went on. "I wonder if other people have people who read for them. Like literary servants, literary butlers, people who give them little digests of this book or that. It's much more efficient than reading them yourself."

"But you miss so much — reading isn't about efficiency."

"I'm not sure. We can check in two weeks. We'll see who remembers more about *Beyond Good and Evil* — me or you. Or if efficiency isn't the right word, tell me what is: the benefit remains the same, but the cost gets cut almost in half, two people get the benefits of reading and only one has to read. It's remarkably efficient."

"What about pleasure?"

"I'm all for it, Franky."

"The pleasure of reading."

"Ah, but it has to be weighed against other pleasures, does it not? After all, we are, as you say, condemned to reproduce ourselves as workers and manufacture surplus value for our evil capitalist masters — that would be you and Paul — and that only leaves so much time for the pursuit of pleasure. And '*Time*,' I believe Quentin Compson's father tells him, doesn't he, Franky, '*Time is man's misfortune*'."

He was an excellent student, and had an uncanny memory for these bits Frank would read aloud out of pure exuberance.

Much later, after everything that happened, Frank no longer found much pleasure in the Great Books — he suspected they mocked him, that they, in a way, had written his own downfall, his own eventual exile. But back then he was elated by them, thrilled when he read one, and thrilled again when he read the best parts to his tent-mate or anyone else who would listen. Dmitry didn't get the time quote exactly right: "*Man is the sum of his misfortunes,*" Mr. Compson says. "*One day you'd think misfortune would get tired, but then time is your misfortune.*" Amen, Mr. Bill Faulkner, Frank thought, although he supposed Dmitry's version was more *efficient*. Dmitry had berated Faulkner for another logical inconsistency, because elsewhere Mr. Compson says that

"*Only when the clock stops does time come to life.*" Dmitry had a complicated argument about why both statements can't be true, something to the effect that if they were, we could avoid all misfortune by watching the clock. And to top it off, Dmitry said, Mr. Compson was a pompous ass.

Maybe.

Not that it matters, in the long run.

Despite Frank acting as Dmitry's teacher part of the time, they were basically fraternal. They spent almost every hour of ten weeks together, eating, sleeping, talking, working, drinking, going to the strip club, eating, talking, sleeping, working. They got confessional, on occasion, telling each other stories they didn't often tell, even if they were somewhat plagiaristic, as Fitzgerald says, the dramatis personae borrowed from central casting and the plots marred by obvious suppressions. They had shared some of their dreams, however shopworn, however often they had been checked out from the local dream library before. They dissected their family lives and romantic histories. They got philosophical, speculative, utopic, dialectical. They got to know each other.

They were young men, eighteen and twenty-six, and therefore both still quite confused about sex, or maybe just Frank was. As in all male intimacies, there were vast, unmentioned continents, unspoken-for and unspoken-about territory. And at the same time, as in all male intimacies, they could sometimes indulge in unexpected, bitter honesty.

"My older sister, Franky," Dmitry said, as they were falling asleep on their respective air mattresses one night in the moldy canvas tent, reeking by then of their dirty laundry, "was the constant companion of my puberty. As I was first sprouting *mons pubis* hair, she was there to point it out to me, and then — you can imagine, Franky how thrilling this was for a twelve-year-old boy — she offered as a comparative study the observation of her own sparse, fourteen-year-old curls. As my erections grew more — because I know you value a certain amount of sexual *politesse*, Franky, I'll just say, as they grew more insistent — she showed me a number of things that could be done with said erections. When I experienced my first orgasm, it was under her hand, as it were." Frank didn't say anything, and Dmitry looked at him sideways. "We live in a society that frowns on such things, Franky. One might even say that they are taboo."

"Duh."

"Yeah, no, really, duh. And yet you do not react with the disgust which, we are told by the anthropologists and ethnologists, the thwarting of such taboos should engender." He was being parodic, speaking in some caricature of academese, some burlesque of learned discourse. Making fun of the way Frank talked about books, in other words. "Why do you think that is?"

"Freud says childhood sexuality is normal."

"Ah," he said, mocking Frank's evasiveness. "But this wasn't normal, was it, Franky?" He paused, then went on. "As we got older, I began to find it all quite confusing. She would come home from a date and tell me how in love she was with Micky or Jake, and how magnificently they had just made love to her in their car, or in the woods, and how wonderful it made her feel, and then she would grab me, find me aroused, and mount me. She would be especially wet at such times, Franky, and at some point I came upon the only reasonable and necessary conclusion available to me, the conclusion that me own sister was a bit of a hussy, perhaps even a bit of a who-er." This was supposed to be funny, and he tried to toss it off lightly, but he couldn't avoid betraying, Frank thought, a deep sadness.

Then again, whether this was revelation or bullshit, he couldn't say. He knew nothing. He sure as hell did not see Dmitry's future coming, could never have guessed in a million years that the Strange and Fantastical

Life of Dmitry Heald, the whole stupendous, horrific, glorious mess, would turn out to be what it catastrophically turned out to be. He never thought he'd have any reason to deeply regret it all, to shudder whenever he reviewed the gory tale of their friendship.

But there it was. There he was. Playing whatever part he was destined to play.

2002

If you had asked Frank, at the end of that long summer, if he'd ever see Dmitry again, he would have said absolutely not. Dmitry had proven himself not just a lousy worker and a horrible slob, but a full-out criminal, and he had fucked over Frank in a half dozen ways — and, well, long story short, Dmitry was back in England, so chances were slim to none they'd run into each other. Frank had never been west of Pennsylvania or east of Rhode Island, so how would he end up in England?

When they finished the house in Connecticut, Paul and Margie moved into it instead of selling it, and that was Dmitry's fault, too — he had completely tanked Frank's relationship with Paul, everyone's relationship with everyone, and by the time he left, all was fucked, and Paul wasn't about to be reminded of the debacle every day by working with Frank. Paul's excuse was that his wife had forced his hand, made him keep the house because she "fell in love with it" — and of course she fell in love with it, since it was tricked out with the best plumbing fixtures and surfaces money could buy: expensive tile, overpriced cabinets, the latest granite countertops, more bathrooms than a family could ever use. Paul never paid him anything, the scumbag, beyond the starvation wages he charged to their joint venture to feed Frank's busted family and keep him in American cheese sandwiches for five months. When Frank ran the numbers, he ended up with a considerably lower hourly rate than he paid Dmitry. He knew that Paul was angry with him, that he blamed him for Dmitry's various crimes, and that it gave Paul a certain amount of satisfaction to screw him out of his half. Frank walked away with a pile of credit card debt and Paul walked away with a house now worth a million dollars. And *Paul* was mad at *Frank*. Chief John Ross had it right, Frank thought: we never forgive our victims.

Frank did see Dmitry again, though, just two years later. Frank was on an upswing, his business improving. The house he built for Paul was beautiful, and it got him other jobs. For those, he had a lawyer do the contracts and had everything spelled out, and the one housing sector that didn't freeze up after 9/11 was the high-end stuff like he was doing. He made decent money — it wasn't the big money he hoped to make with Paul, but he could see a path to eventually getting there without him.

Before Dmitry's junior year *at university*, as he said it, he came back to the States, in the summer, to take the Green Tortoise — a hippie alternative to Greyhound, a $2 hostel on wheels — across the country. Frank knew he should still be pissed at Dmitry, but the pain of the various betrayals was dimmed by time and prosperity. Everything had already changed so much. Only two years, but they were long ones. He never forgave, Frank thought to himself, but he always seemed to forget. Over time, he found himself remembering the good parts — his sense of being an intellectual mentor and moral conscience — not the bad. He did the same with Tracy too, only remembering the upside. Maybe that's the way people were. Maybe that was why they put up with each other.

"The Green Tortoise," Frank said, and it sounded a bit derisive, as they walked into the kitchen of his apartment in Avon.

"Don't be such a snob, Franky," Dmitry said, throwing his duffel bag on the floor.

"I am not a snob."

"Well," he said, "For a non-snob you do quote quite a few glitzy writers." He looked around the apartment. "This is a step up from the old tent, eh, Franky my boy?"

"Yeah, really," Frank said. "No thanks to fucking Paul in either case."

"Well!" Dmitry said, opening the refrigerator and grabbing a beer, handing Frank one. "Let's not go there right this minute!" He meant let's not talk about it ever. "*Anyways*," he said in his American accent, "do you realize how expensive prostitutes are in the United States of America, Franky? It turns out that in those four days when Matty and her two friends from the Green Tortoise were living in the land yacht — and let's not talk about *that* right this minute, either — I did the math, and I had roughly eight thousand US dollars' worth of sex."

"Her two friends."

"I didn't tell you about them? Well, I suppose we didn't talk about much of this, did we... Sally was a waitress from Jonestown, New York, and was a tiny girl, but had the most ridiculous, really quite large, really quite exorbitant knockers, hard as boulders. She must have been five feet tall at most and she had a breathtakingly miniscule vagina. I could barely get a finger in it much less my cock, although lord knows I tried. Mary was the opposite, a really tall girl — and it was all in the legs, the longest legs I've ever seen in my life — in my memory, Franky, even though I know, rationally, this can't be true, I can still feel those incredibly long thighs resting on my shoulders, and they seem to each be a three-feet long or more — is that even possible?"

Ach, god, I don't miss this kind of talk, Frank thought, don't miss it at all. Margie was right, he really is just a pig. Frank caught Dmitry looking at his nauseated face, and he seemed to actually enjoy it.

"Can I borrow this?" Dmitry said as he grabbed a tape measure from the tool belt hanging on a hook near the kitchen door. "Just like old days! I never could remember where I put mine down, could I! So let's say she was the same length to the knee as me, about two feet, the same from the belt to the top of the head," he held the tape measure so that it ran over his nose to his belt, "or about two-eight — if she had a three-foot thigh she would be seven-feet-eight-inches tall, which she was definitely *not*. The three-foot thigh is an aberration of my memory, what T. S. Eliot called an objective correlative, right?"

"No, that's not what it means," Frank said. But then he thought, well, maybe — he wasn't sure.

"We had several days of what was for me an absolute paradise, with everyone pretending nothing was happening, the girls all very lovey-dovey with each other, everything very discreet and me as happy as a man can be, the Neapolitan ice cream of sex every day. Except that, as I found out, not everyone was pretending: Mary didn't, as it turns out, actually know I was boffing Sally and Matty as well, nor did Sally know, and so when it all was uncovered so to speak there ensued a great wailing and rending of garments and gnashing of teeth. A lot of great make-up sex, until Mary and Sally found out I was having make-up sex with both of them. Matty was the imperturbable cucumber she always was, but eventually we had to drop off the other two at a bus station."

"And the point of all this is?"

"I think it should be obvious, Franky! I developed an idea about the kind of women who ride the Green Tortoise, based on a quite delectable sample, and if history repeats itself, which we know it does, the entire trip will be effectively free."

"You had to come here for this? There are no women in England?"

"Well, Franky, I have found that unlike in their home environment, women, when traveling, are much more like men, ready to roll the dice. Women at home have all this pressure from their girlfriends to land the big game, you know, put the head on the wall. Naturally they don't want to marry every eligible man they meet, but they are determined to make us act like *we* want to, and parade us around to their family and friends, and make us change our clothing and hairstyle, while all the while, and if they were to be honest, they would have to admit it: not only are they planning to dump us for various infractions as soon as our trophy-tour is over, but they decided what the dumpable infractions were the night they met us. They enter the fray marvelously well-armed.

Women who are traveling have no audience for their trophies and so they are, like we are, ready to fuck and suck and make a pleasant night of it." He took a sip of beer. "Ah, I forgot how easily distressed you are, Franky, by such talk."

"Which is what you want to do, distress me, right?" Frank said, which stopped him for a moment. "The thing that distresses me is how much more cynical you've become."

"Yeah," Dmitry said. "Right…" He stretched the word so it sounded like a version of *riot*. "You getting laid at all, Franky? I suspect not. You don't want to get pulled around by your nose-ring by a flock of vile hens, either, I assume — not to mix my barnyard metaphors. *Thus*, if we want to get some *trim* — a laudable American addition to the idioms, becoming more apropos every day as shaving and waxing conquers the last outposts of territory formerly haired — the only way to get it is to buy it, which is where I began: it's expensive, and you're even tighter than I am, so I can't imagine you dropping a couple hundred dollars a bang on a regular basis. Then you dress this frugality up as moral reprehension. You ought to take a little trip on the Tortoise one day. It'd do you good."

Frank had busied himself putting together some dinner from the fridge and chose to ignore this, knowing Dmitry would start off on something else right away, which he did. Frank let him monologue his way into the night, and they managed to avoid any tricky subjects, because what would be the point? Dmitry had changed his major from physical therapy — yes, Frank thought, funny — to business, had transferred to another university Frank had never heard of, and reported himself to be quite a success.

"The thing about university, Franky, is that basically you only have a couple of elementary chores in each of your courses. The first is to make your professors feel fantastically smart, and the second is to make them think you want to be exactly like them. Most students think you parrot back whatever they say, but since professors are flattered like this constantly, they are jaded, and their higher vanity makes them look for proof that they have taught you not just *what* to think but *how* to think, a stupendously high standard, really — how can they all do that? Three or four or five of them a term? So you pretend to vigorously disagree with some minor point they have made while ceding all the major ones slavishly — your apparent struggle and error, which you let them correct, convince them they are having an effect.

"Then you hint you want to do research in field *x*, because whatever their vanity about teaching, their narcissism about their research is massively stronger. Most of them will explain that you need decades of training before daring to attempt the awesome and intricate feats they manage, which is perfect since your path is greased forever by the offer, and you didn't want to do the research, now, did you? They tell you to write a term paper that would be nothing more than a summary of their latest white paper, but they never remember what they told you to do three or four months down the road, so you can hand them anything. I've given the same research project to every one of my business professors, simply inserting very recent data each time, so they never suspect it's an updated version of the one from the preceding term."

"That's godawful, Dmitry," Frank said, having slowly heated. "Imagine what that sounds like to me. I'd love to go *to university*, I'd love to have that kind of chance, and you're just fucking off? Cheating your way through? Christ, what a waste! Don't you care at all, don't you want to learn anything?"

"Whoa! Franky, boy! What a torrent from you! If I remember correctly, you, yourself, remember not a single thing from your wantonly brief time at university." This seemed to Frank a low blow. "That aside, you needn't worry. I *do* want to learn, and the research I show them is research I'm actually doing — building data in an always evolving and actually quite useful project, unlike most of theirs. I'm learning the Asian markets. I've decided it would be a gigantic error to settle for being a capitalist pig when I can, with not an iota's more effort, be an imperialist pig."

Faulkner said Harvard teaches you how to drown yourself and Sewanee doesn't even teach you what water is, Frank thought, and so who knows: maybe British universities teach smartass nihilism. They managed not to talk about the motorhome disaster or about the debacle with Margie or his pimping in Connecticut or his other crimes, not that time or the next. Frank knew, after a while, what Dmitry would say if he ever did confront him with them. "Risk," as he put it much later, apropos of something else, after he had made his first fortune, "risk is the essence of our world, Franky," and his risking of lives certainly didn't end that summer. Far from it. "Risk," he said with that fucking grin. "Makes the world go round."

Among the lives he risked, eventually, was Frank's.

2004

Two years later, after he finished his degree, Dmitry came through again. When he called, Frank was still working in the Hartford suburbs, on another custom house, and he was surprised to find himself happy to hear from the kid. He felt an odd pride that Dmitry valued their relationship. Something in him *wanted* to be upbraided for his lack of morals. Behind all the bluster and bullshit, he wanted to be a better man, to be more like Frank, to be less of a prick. He made fun of Frank's scolding, but why else would he come back for more?

That much he found explicable. But why did *he* want to see this lout? What was in it for him? He knew that, even while being disgusted by stories of Dmitry's derring-do, he was taken in by them, and he had to admit that he wished, with some small part of himself, that he could march through life without giving a fuck about anyone else, grabbing whatever laurels and pleasures and monies presented themselves, wryly commenting on the foibles of lesser mortals, having sex with multiple women free of the slightest regret. In the novels he read, people like that all came to grief, but Dmitry somehow never did.

Dmitry usually presented himself in his stories as the bemused mastermind, the self-contained, unflappable marionetteer. Frank wondered if this was why we love stories of dashing bad guys — Butch Cassidy, Jay Gatsby, Tom Ripley, Becky Sharp, Gordon Gekko, Tony Montana — they get away with it all, at least for a while, and do and get whatever they want. Who wouldn't like that fantasy?

Dmitry told the story of his career in student government. He ran for president, hiring a bunch of underclassmen to pull down the posters of the other candidates and throw them in the trash. "In politics, Franky," he said, by way of explanation, "name recognition is very important." He also managed to have the power shut down at the student radio station when competing candidates were scheduled for interviews.

"When I became student union president, Franky — and it's a big deal there, a real job with a real salary and real power of a sort, you have a budget for student affairs, concerts, lectures, that sort of thing — there are so many favors to give out it's almost *Italian* — I had but one goal for my presidency, and I'm sure you will think this is somewhat petty, but it was to last out the full term." No student union president had ever lasted an entire year without being recalled, and he wanted to be the first. He studied the crises that got past presidents in trouble and decided that the only way to stay in office was to manage the risk, to be prepared for the scandals that arose. The only way to accomplish that was to create his own crises, manufacture his own scandals.

As they were sitting in an upstairs bedroom of an unfinished house he was building, Frank had an unsettling sense of déjà vu, generated perhaps by the smell of fir sawdust and the taste of warming beer.

"About a month and a half into my reign," Dmitry said, "a man was coming to campus from Denmark who was a famous champion of pederasty, the head of the Danish Man Boy Love Association, and predictably a group of students was protesting, marching around with banners proclaiming *Just Say No to Pedophilia* and other such tin-eared sloganeering, writing editorials to the newspaper condemning the visit. Of course, equally predictably, another group nattered on about free speech and unfettered inquiry, yadda yadda, as that great comedienne of yours who punches men in the chest says, and so I wrote an editorial for the student newspaper which, if you read it fast, Franky, sounded like I was not only in favor of letting the man visit, but of men everywhere diddling little boys up the bum. There was immediate uproar and demands for my resignation, the beginnings of a recall campaign, but I had peppered the editorial with sentences expressly designed for rebuttal purposes. I had written *if Rosser* — this was the Danish pederast — *is correct, then man-boy love is not only acceptable, it is necessary for the progress of philosophy and enlightenment, while his opponents can only say that if he is wrong, untold harm will be done.* So when the idiots went on and on attacking me for disgracing the office, the university, and human decency, I published my rebuttal, which I had written at the same time as the editorial itself, using this quite impressive list of phrases, like *untold harm will be done*, quoting myself selectively to prove that my critics were quoting me selectively. Which they were, of course. Selective quotation is the essence of contemporary politics, Franky. And you can quote me on that, just not the rest of this." Big goofy grin.

"So the recall failed." Frank cracked them each another, now tepid, beer.

"Same with the scandals about military research on campus and the one about animal experiments. All these brouhahas — isn't that a marvelous word, Franky, brouhaha? From the Hebrew by way of French, meaning *the cry of the devil disguised as clergy*; isn't that fantastic? — anyway these squabbles occurred with great regularity. But my real stroke of genius was realizing that the most powerful political forces on campus were the dorm presidents, elected officials on the student government payroll. They controlled money, handing out patronage jobs of various kinds and putting on concerts, parties, that kind of thing — and as everywhere, patronage plus pandering equals popularity. Every deposed student union president had been replaced by one of these dorm presidents, often rallied around by the rest, and as soon as the dorm presidents join any recall effort, the jig is up — *the jig is up!*" he added in his American gangster accent, finger-guns at the ready.

It had been a long day, so Frank started to head down the stairs toward his truck, confident Dmitry would follow and keep talking.

"The dorm presidents have one and only one onerous job — you've become much better as a carpenter, haven't you, Franky? nice balustrade! — and that onerous job is delivering the student newspaper to their respective dorms: getting up early in the morning, schlepping an ancient cart across campus, often in the rain like miserable pack animals, and distributing stacks of newsprint to each floor of their dorm.

"In my first meeting with all of them I said, *Look. You people work extremely hard for your constituents*, which wasn't at all true, except for the newspaper delivery, *and so*, I told them, *I am going to use some of my presidential discretionary funds to have the student paper delivered, freeing you from a burden that, let's be honest, does not represent the best use of your considerable talents*. They all straightaway agreed, giddy with good fortune. No more early mornings, no more tramping in the rain! And I *had them by the short hairs*" — this again in the gangster accent — "because everyone knew that this was why they got paid, and that to let someone else do it, on other student government funds, amounted to fraud. And, yes, I couldn't use this information without destroying myself, but neither could they. Mutually Assured Destruction, the doctrine that allowed both capitalism and communism to flourish for half a century."

"Hm," Frank grunted.

"Yes, I know! And there was a fringe benefit," he added. "Whenever the newspaper had a piece critical of me or my policies, I had my lackeys take half the circulation to my garden and burn it. By the end of the year I had an *enormous* pile of ash back there!"

"Hm."

"I know you don't like me to call them lackeys, Franky, but that's what they were. I was *your* lackey when we were building the house for Paul."

"You were not a very good lackey."

"No, I was never a very good lackey," he said. "Too slow. I had no ambitions in the building trades, and it showed."

No kidding, Frank thought. They got in the truck and headed back to his apartment, accompanied at first by Dmitry lecturing him about how crazy it was to buy a new truck for a business the size of Frank's, that even the briefest glance at amortization tables would demonstrate this. He then continued with the tale of his history-making presidency.

The campus feminists, it turned out, were too much for him — delicious irony, Frank thought. With only a month left in the school year, Dmitry had attempted another fake crisis and they saw through it. He was clearly losing the battle in the newspaper, and the recall petition was gaining steam. He went around to the dorms and held town halls claiming that the dorm presidents — who he knew would avoid him like the plague he was and not show up — were on his side.

"I knew they'd never have the gumption to contradict me after the fact, and as we know, denials never work. In any case, my strategy worked. The recall narrowly failed, and I achieved my goal. I lasted out the term."

He told this story brimming with the great glee of victory, replete with pride in his own cunning. This was four years and one college education after he had left both Frank's personal life and business in shambles. Dmitry's pieces had now all clicked together, and the future man stood revealed. As they reached Frank's apartment, a step up from the last one Dmitry had seen, which he noted with a characteristic combination of gee-whiz and mockery, Frank thought about all the talks they had had, back on the building site, about Nietzsche — in those years, he found any opportunity to quote the idea that truth was nothing but the interpretation of whoever happened to be in power, and he remembered Dmitry trying to talk him out of that, arguing for the validity of science, for truth with a capital T. Frank loved Nietzsche's idea that Christians thought themselves morally superior as compensation for their own lack of power, and that thus, in other words, his father, the Christian guy, who thought he was the last moral, upright man in a world going to pot, *wasn't*. And at the same time, he took solace in thinking that even though his father thought he knew everything, knew what was right for everyone, he was wrong about that too: as a powerful person, a white man in America, he *thought* that whatever he happened to think was true was the truth, but it wasn't. This whole edifice was not Frank's grandest logical achievement, he knew, since these two ideas were diametrically opposed — it made his father both powerless and powerful — but at the time he found deep satisfaction in it, as if it were two strikes against the man.

Dmitry had, instead, taken another lesson from it all. He had freed himself from both absolute truth and from conventional notions of morality. As Frank watched the now-adult Dmitry rumble off to the extra room for the night, he remembered his cavalier unleashing of three tons of metal down Frizzell Hill, heedless of anyone or anything in its path, and realized that he had known even back then, already, that Dmitry was beyond good and evil. He was already a problem.

2006

Two years later, like clockwork, Dmitry was back, having been kicked out of the London School of Economics. By that time, Frank's business was in good shape — booming, in fact. He had put together enough capital that, with a little short-term bank financing, he could build spec houses on his own. He was in the high-end market twenty miles from Margie and Paul, in the next small town being swallowed by Hartford insurance-executive creep. He never lacked for rich customers insulated from any minor ups and downs in the economy, and he was pulling in serious money, charging most of his expenses to his own little company so they were tax-free, paying himself a salary, and getting a huge chunk of change whenever he sold another beauty. No clients in his hair — he sold them all finished, so if they wanted something changed they could do it when they owned it, and he'd recommend someone else do it — which of course got him those men's gratitude and great prices on subcontracting. He was salting away funds for the kids' college tuitions, even though they were getting less and less interested in him. Lulu, now twelve, had admitted the last time they talked that she didn't really remember them living in the same house as a family. She liked him well enough, he could tell, but he didn't exactly feel like family to her. When she said that, he watched her stirring the slushy he had bought her, on a Saturday in the fall, her brown curls bouncy with youthful energy, piles of crazed maple leaves behind her, like the piles he used to make for her to jump in, and, well, he managed to stop from weeping by squeezing his tear ducts with a thumb and finger. Kennedy was more attached, but at fourteen she considered any deflection of her attention from her friends to be a complete nuisance. He could imagine the day they both would wonder why he kept calling and coming to see them. *Anyways*, as Dmitry said, he was managing to build a little portfolio, and they wouldn't have to worry about college, and he no longer feared the end of the month. Not bad for five years.

None of that compared to the money Dmitry managed to make while he was still an MBA student. He came through the States on his way to a job in Asia, itching to tell the tale of his brief inglorious career as a graduate student, to display the new Machiavellian notches in his belt, and all Frank could wonder was — why? Maybe Frank was where he parked his conscience. Maybe he wanted someone to tell him to be less of an asshole. But does telling someone to stop being a narcissist ever work? That would make counseling the easiest profession in the world.

Frank picked him up at the airport in Hartford in a vicious Connecticut thunderstorm, and as they drove under a sky black at four in the afternoon, tree branches snapping off in the gale winds, electrical lines down, he couldn't pay close attention to what Dmitry was saying. The gist was that he was a star in his MBA program until the scandal broke, the scandal that got him expelled in disgrace weeks from being awarded a degree. At that point he had already been recruited by HSBC, the immense multinational investment bank, had signed a contract with them to start as a trader in their Hong Kong headquarters once he graduated, and, quite surprisingly, Frank thought, that offer had not been withdrawn post-scandal. He was to start in June, and being suddenly free from any further school work, he had come to take another ride on the Green Tortoise rolling free brothel and then fly from San Francisco directly to his new life. He was moving with a single duffle bag. "Franky, you don't *bring* suits to Hong Kong," he explained.

Even as an undergraduate, Dmitry had been concentrating entirely on Asian markets, and at LSE he put together a newsletter, a compilation of data on equities, commodities, and real estate futures, that he began to sell to people in the financial industry. The newsletter and its market information were not cheap — a ten-thousand-pound a month subscription — but he managed to sell it to quite a few people, at least in part because some early adopters made piles of money following his advice and word got around, but also because it was printed on London School of Economics letterhead, which he had stolen from an office on campus. "I didn't actually perpetrate fraud, Franky, I didn't sign the offer *Dmitry Heald, Professor of International Marketing, London School of Economics,* or anything like that. I didn't claim any affiliation with LSE, I merely let people assume, because of the letterhead, that I was head of something called the London School of Economics' Asian Markets Study Group, which of course didn't exist. When I signed the letter *Dmitry Heald, Director, Asian Markets Study Group,* I was telling the truth, since that was the name of my balefully short-lived company, AMSG. Or should that be banefully, Franky? I can never keep them straight. I think it's balefully."

A frantic longhaired mutt streaked across the road and Frank braked too hard and slid. Every driver seemed distracted — some people lose one hundred percent of their common sense in a storm — and Frank was glad to finally pull into his neighborhood.

"Undone by success! My newsletter was so brilliant, Franky, that the *Financial Times* decided to do a story on it and sent a reporter to the London School of Economics looking for the aforementioned Professor Heald, head of the school's Asian Markets Study Group, only to find, without much effort, that no such person or position existed." Frank couldn't take his eyes off the road to see if it was sadness or pride he was hearing in Dmitry's voice. He pulled into his drive, punched the automatic garage door opener, and sailed in.

"Wow, Franky, top flight! American ingenuity foils Thor's hammers! The Automatic Garage Door, Number One in Customer Satisfaction! Nice." They parked and got out. "So *anyways*, I was, as one might assume, hauled before the Dean, forced to sign an agreement to pay back almost all of the four million dollars I'd made, and then instantly expelled. Tell me if I'm wrong, Franky, but one or the other, don't you think? Make me sign your paper, give back the money, and then give me their precious degree, *or* kick me out and I keep the money. But both? Am I wrong?"

They got inside and Frank threw Dmitry's bag in the spare room and took a piss. When he came back Dmitry was looking in the refrigerator.

"Whatever you want."

"Thanks, Franky! How about these steaks? Should we fry them up?"

It figured. Frank went out on the fairly well covered and yet still devastated side porch and checked the gas grill. It lit.

"So you had to pay back *almost* all the money?" he asked as Dmitry followed him out.

"This is a big country, isn't it, Franky, with big weather." The wind would once in a while take a thin swath of rain and slap them with it. Frank turned the gas up as high as it would go and waves of rain sizzled and evaporated against the side of the grill. "Yes," Dmitry went on, sadly. "My first millions. It seemed incredibly unfair." He took an uncharacteristic pause. Frank threw the steaks on, salted and peppered them. "It was *really* good data, Franky, and a *lot* of people made *a lot* of money using it. The idea that I should now give them each back their piddly hundred or so thousand dollars US — it really rankled me. I wouldn't mind compensating LSE a fee for the use of their logo, something reasonable, but to give it all back — well, all of it they could trace, about three quarters of it — seemed exceedingly unjust. The fraud was an advertising fraud. The data was good. Believe me, there are quite a few fraudulent businesses out there doing this kind of work, with an enormous amount of fraudulent data, but that's not what this was! It was merely a quasi-deceptive marketing device. It was advertising! Advertising is more or less deceptive always, isn't it?"

He looked appropriately chastened for three seconds, and then physically brushed off the front of his shirt and smiled. "Half my customers re-subscribed after they took their money back — AMSG now with its own letterhead, as a subsidiary of LSE: London School Economics, Ltd, yes, you guessed it, sole proprietor, D. Heald. They bought in again, at an even higher subscription rate — proof positive that there was no fraud, right?"

Frank flipped the steaks.

"You can answer, you know, Franky — yes, such questions are at least partially rhetorical, and I know you have a policy of not *encouraging* me — despite the fact that you do, of course, in all sorts of ways, don't you? A few supplementary conversational *uh-huh's* and *hm's* and the like would really be perfectly normal and would make the whole thing seem like more of a conversation, don't you think? Did I see a beer in there?" He started back into the kitchen saying, over his shoulder, "You can pull my steak any time, Franky. It looks good and raw."

Frank spent the rest of the night, after a few glasses of wine, sarcastically uh-huhhing and mm-hmming every remark Dmitry made. He thought it was funny and knew it probably wasn't. As they ate, Frank found himself wondering whether, accustomed to making and losing millions as he was, Dmitry might have managed to buy a bottle of wine. Maybe that's why he was cranky.

"So did anyone ever steal Asian Markets Study Group's stationary and sell their products with it?" Frank asked.

"Ah, I see what you are doing here, Franky, trying to teach me morality by putting me in the other guy's shoes — perhaps not even aware that Dean Giddens of the London School of Economics wears nothing but Tanino Crisci or John Lobbs at a thousand US dollars or even two thousand a pair. Very Savile Row, Mr. Giddens is. But point taken. I will say that I would hope, in that case, yes, to be compensated, but I would have no interest in humiliating the culprits or destroying them — unless they were very direct competitors — and I am certainly not a competitor to LSE, the school." He paused to look at Frank. "What is it, Franky? — you have on that stern, Jehovan look."

"I'm wondering whether you are just putting on a stiff-upper-lip show, or if you really have no remorse whatsoever."

"Remorse is an interesting emotion, isn't it, Franky? Do *you* feel remorse, ever?"

"Sure," he said. "Of course."

"When?"

He failed to come up with something, but then again, he couldn't remember a time when he *didn't* feel some vague regret.

"I'm not sure exactly when, but I'm sure I have."

"Precisely," he said, as if Frank had admitted the opposite. "It's interesting because there can't be any evolutionary benefit, can there? Fear, hate, anger — the brain-stem, primitive leftovers of our amphibian forebears, old self-defense mechanisms, all so understandable. And love, good for all our mammalian and herding duties. Disgust keeps us out of gastronomic and other danger. But remorse? What is it good for?"

"It's good for making people decent to each other! Jesus, Dmitry, what do you want, a world of self-interested sociopaths?"

"Isn't that what we have?"

"So Gandhi was a self-interested sociopath," he said. "Martin Luther King."

"*That* is a very interesting idea, Franky. And, yes, at some level they both were."

"You think Gandhi and Martin Luther King were as amoral as you."

"Who can say? How could one possibly measure relative levels of amorality? The fundamental goal of philosophy, Franky, is to teach us to see beyond our socially constructed blindness, to pierce the veil of bourgeois ideology — at least this is what I learned at the knee of my teacher as a young grasshopper in our famous Civil War tent, and I believe that is very close to a direct quote from you, the aforementioned teacher, and it is also exactly why Messieurs Gandhi and King are so revered. They showed us how immoral our notions of morality always become."

Frank sat there like an idiot, instead of saying what he should have, that to compare Dmitry's duplicitous marketing to Gandhi's empowerment of a subcontinent and King's of a people was more obscene than ludicrous. Instead, he sat there like the wine-sodden philosophical dunce he was, wondering if there was some truth to it.

"I'll let you mull that one over, Franky, while admitting that, still, when all is said and done, I did learn one invaluable lesson from the whole affair."

He waited for a prompt from Frank, who was foggy with wine, a little slow on the uptake.

"Uh-huh?" he managed.

"Never, ever, ever, *ever*," he stretched out a preposterous dramatic pause, "*ever* get caught."

Oh, brother. The rain continued its thousands of little wallops on the street.

"I'm surprised that your new employer isn't upset."

"I'm sure they aren't thrilled."

"So they know, but they're going to hire you despite it all?"

He smiled.

"Egads, yes!"

He looked at Frank as if for the first time seeing their roles permanently reversed: Dmitry the man of affairs humoring Frank the dewy naïf; Frank bluffing, Dmitry judging but holding back slightly with a kindly, corrupt mien, wondering whether the truth were too brutal for the likes of his former teacher.

"You have to understand, Franky," he said. "It was very good data."

2007

A year later, Dmitry was rich, and they met in Los Angeles.

"Well, not rich, really, Franky," he said, when he was accused of it. "But I have been having some success, yes."

Frank had come to California following a journalist he met at a party in one of the houses he had built. Patricia was a theater critic for the *Wall Street Journal*, and she was in town to review something or other. He had fallen in love. He wasn't sure how or why, but he fell hard. She was a little wisecracking firecracker and had been hired away from the *Journal* by the *Los Angeles Times* to be their chief drama critic. He found her endlessly impressive, someone actually involved in the world of writing and culture he had admired from afar. Maybe because the deadline of her move to LA loomed, and that made her seem safe, or maybe because she made merciless fun of his bad haircut, or maybe because she wouldn't sleep with him, even after a few dates, him running down to Manhattan — he wasn't sure why, but he knew he was a goner. He was far from alone in admiring her; she wore her skirts short and her tights black and had a wicked sense of humor, could handle more shots of vodka than most guys, and although she wasn't a classic beauty and she didn't really flaunt her body — those black-sheathed legs aside — there was something about her. Men were always a little surprised, after a few minutes, to find themselves intrigued. They wouldn't have noticed her as she entered the room — she wasn't loud or showy, she was small, a couple inches over five feet and trim, didn't turn that many heads, but she had a way with an outrageous one-liner, and she would lob them in, lots of them, tossing them over the boundaries of polite conversation, and then step back and enjoy, like a connoisseur, the successive dropping of jaws. If they had a brain in their head, the women wanted her as a friend and the men lusted for her. Or vice versa if they were gay. When Frank finally did have sex with her, a month or so later, just before she left, it was hot and fun and sweet, and he was desperately hooked.

A few weeks after she left New York for the job in LA, Frank decided it was a good time to visit his friend Dwayne. They had been best friends in high school, but Dwayne had become a devotee of one of the Maharaji guys — he could never keep them straight, but he thought it was the teenage one — and had moved to California to be the guru's musical director. Dwayne had been in the band and orchestra in high school and in the rock bands that played their dances, and now he recorded New Age CDs and lived in a little house in Culver City with his wife, also a follower of the Maharaji, and their two kids. He was a beautiful guy, really decent and warm and thoughtful, and although Frank was usually allergic to religion, Dwayne was a walking advertisement for his. He was happy, kind, fun, didn't proselytize, and for some reason, except for a couple flecks of grey in his hair, looked exactly like his high school yearbook picture.

Frank didn't want Patricia to feel like he was stalking her, or presume too much, so he stayed at a motel near Dwayne's house, and then, the next day, arranged to meet her for dinner downtown. Much later, he realized that her surprised laughter when he said he might move to Los Angeles was not the jubilant endorsement he took it for — and maybe if she hadn't left right away the next day to cover some play in Seattle, they would have had enough time — *Frank* might have had enough time — to learn, before it was too late, that she wasn't, as they say, that into him.

Dmitry, in a pure coincidence, had called him from New York, and when he found Frank was in LA had added a stop there on his way home. He took a room in a cheap motel in the dead zone of Olympic Boulevard near the 405, presumably because he liked the seediness of it. They met that night at a ramen place on Sawtelle. Dmitry, off on his usual monologue, said he was making bales of money — "not the little rectangular bales, Franky, the great big round ones." He had an Australian girlfriend who worked as a trader at Credit Lyonnais, a Chinese girlfriend who worked as an executive at Bank of China, another "local girl," as he called her, a secretary, that he had set up in an apartment, and there were "establishments" where he regularly brought clients and thus got "exquisite service." All of that took care of his weekdays. He spent most of his weekends in Bangkok, Manila, or Ho Chi Minh City, playing golf during the day and whoring at night.

"And yes, I know what you're thinking, Franky, all this must take quite a bit of effort and planning, especially when you throw into the mix the fact that the maids can sometimes get a tad demanding and the sixteen-year-old schoolgirl who gets in my car on Thursday afternoons so I can go down on her. All in all, a very full, logistically complicated life, and one that took many, many months to cobble together."

Frank, queasy, knowing Dmitry would mock anything he said and up the ante, said nothing.

For some reason that Frank could never pinpoint and came to extravagantly regret, he wanted Dmitry to meet Dwayne. He told himself it was because Dwayne lived right around the corner, and was such a perfect exemplar of a conscious, conscientious existence, that it would do Dmitry good to see what an ethical life looked like. Dwayne would be good for Dmitry. Then again, he may have wanted Dwayne to see the interesting people he knew, how worldly he had become, that he knew people from England and Asia — well, one person from England and Asia.

Two more dissimilar people may never have encountered each other, except perhaps Cortés and Montezuma, and even they didn't have to stand awkwardly in Dwayne's living room after the introductions were over. Dwayne's wife was out somewhere, thank god, and he had tucked in his young son when they arrived, so it was just Dwayne and his thirteen-year-old daughter who stood before them, the two of them equally unversed, it seemed, in standard social usages — the girl, Emily, was actually his wife's daughter by a former marriage, a very sweet kid whose father was from Uttar Pradesh or somewhere, with bright, intelligent, nearly black eyes. Frank did the introductions, since Dwayne, by his own description a Brian Wilson-level recluse, couldn't manage it. Unaccustomed to playing host, no one knew to say *have a seat, want a beer?* or anything. The four of them stood there, smiling.

Dmitry decided the room was in need of regaling.

"I was about to begin telling Franky a funny story on the way here," he said, "about a little weekend outing to Vietnam not long ago with a friend. We had gone to play a little golf and do, well, some other things — no sense being so jumpy, Franky, I am not going to divulge our entire itinerary, since there's a young lady present — but there *was* one night during which — how to put —"

"Maybe we can save this one for later, Dmitry," Frank said.

"Oh, Franky, don't worry."

"No, *really*."

"Dwayne, don't you find that Franky worries entirely too much?"

Dwayne shrugged. "I, well — in high school he really didn't worry at all," he said, trying to lighten things up. God bless him, Franky thought, he's trying to make a joke to Satan. What he said was both true and not true: in high school Frank didn't worry about grades, or teachers, or getting in trouble, because he was always in trouble. But he was as anxious as hell in general. Maybe with the pot nodding him out back then people couldn't see it. His father in alcoholic rages, his mother — this he only realized later — almost comatose with undiagnosed depression, he was the walking wounded back then, the marijuana he assumed was active rebellion had in fact been inadvertent medical intervention.

"I can do this, Franky," Dmitry said. "Utterly PG. Don't be concerned. This young lady — what's your name again sweetheart?"

"Emily," she said, halfway between repelled and fascinated by this odd, enormous person with the funny accent. She never took her eyes off him.

"And how old are you?"

"Thirteen."

"Precisely. And Emily you are exactly the kind of thirteen-year-old girl who knows quite a bit about what she does know and knows absolutely nothing about what she doesn't, isn't that true?"

Emily looked at him for a moment, and then she and Dwayne looked at each other.

"The thing is," he went on, unmaneuverable as ever. "We had rented two motorcycles, and we weren't particularly good drivers of the things to begin with, and what with our golf bags strapped over our shoulders we were considerably wobblier, not to mention that, speaking of wobbly, we had had a few beverages, and when I say beverages, Emily, I do mean the demon rum, something which you will never, ever partake of until you are eighteen — or is it still twenty-one here among you Calvinists?" he looked from Dwayne to Frank, got nothing, perhaps because neither of them could say what a Calvinist was, exactly, and went on, " — and then you will have a dainty glass of sherry or perhaps a tiny Cabernet with your meal, but no more, not like your stupid Uncle Dmitry," — Dwayne visibly winced at that appellation — "and stupid Uncle Dmitry had managed, by this point in our saga, to imbibe a couple of pints of that horrid Vietnamese gin — I truly believe it is dredged from the bottom of some industrial pit, it is vile stuff that not even the Thais will drink, and they will drink almost anything; I have a friend who says they would drink their own mothers' urine if it was dashed up with a little caramel coloring and had a whiskey label slapped on it —"

"OK! Emily, time for bed," Dwayne said.

"I apologize, my dear Emily," Dmitry said, "for that friend's horrid metonym, and of course it goes without saying —"

"Yes, good night!" Frank added. "Great to see you, Emily, and I apologize for my friend's language."

"Language?" Dmitry said. "Urine?"

"But, Dad!"

"Yes, *but Dad!* indeed," Dmitry went on. "Truly, don't worry, no more bodily fluid references — and so there we were, Emily, loblollied on our scooters, nearly knocking people over on the street, inadvertently crashing through the potholes with our golf bags, risking life and limb, and then it started to rain — not a prodigious rain, not the kind that even drunk people would know to get out of, but a light drizzle, a bit refreshing in our state, and I believe we started laughing, because, I'm sure you don't realize this, Emily, but a motor scooter gets outrageously slippery in the rain, and we were now become unpaid comedians, slipping and sliding around in the mud, golf clubs flying everywhere, and all the people on the street — this is Ho Chi Minh City, Saigon to you, where people are, well, let me put it this way: the *French* think they're rude — and they were laughing at us, at the spectacle of these two stratospherically drunk and uncoordinated Englishmen flailing about in the rain, and we were laughing like mad people along with them. You see, not to jump ahead too much, the moral of the story is one shouldn't drink and drive — Dwayne? Franky? You will agree with that, yes? *Anyways*, as we thrashed about we espied, down a little side street, the unmistakable signs of a certain kind of drinking establishment — again, how to say — a bar that specialized in a certain type of entertainment, with a cast of, um, well, now we're getting into territory that perhaps —" and to their surprise, he paused, turning his gaze from Emily to Frank and then to Dwayne. "Dwayne, have you had the talk with Emily yet about ladyboys?"

Up until that moment, Dwayne had been torn. He was such a sweet guy that although he dearly wanted Emily out of ear-range, he simply had no experience interrupting people. Now he moved into action.

"OK, Emily, bed, now," he said, a hand on her shoulder.

"But, Dad! Franky's friend is here! And there's no school tomorrow!" It was a Friday night. Not much of a disciplinarian, Dwayne, as it turned out — he relied on his wife at moments like these — so, fatally, he hesitated, and meanwhile, of course, Dmitry kept going.

"Oddly enough, that isn't integral to the story. What happened was that we went over to the stupendously seedy bar —"

"Excuse us, please, I'm sorry, Emily's going to bed." Dwayne put his arm around her and steered her out of the room.

"— and we were so paralytically drunk — is that a word, Franky? Paralytically?"

"But Daddy, I have to get a drink of water," Emily said, twisting out of his arm and escaping across to the kitchen.

"The fact is that these ladyboys could have been beautiful courtesans or could have been lads in English schoolboy outfits, for all we would have known the difference. We had another pint of rotgut — there's a great American word for you, eh, Franky? *rotgut* — and arranged for two of them to drive us back to our hotel on our motor scooters, finally and belatedly aware that we were incapable of keeping upright anymore, and then two more said they wanted to come, too, and we were, as you say," and here he broke again into his gravelly Americanese, "*ready to party*, so we said sure, why not. And thus there we were, now another bottle of so-called gin toward oblivion, three to a motor scooter and a golf bag apiece, sloshing forbiddingly and yet comically across the city, making a motley scene and I'm afraid a rather blue racket, and miraculously arriving safely."

Dwayne was pushing Emily toward her room, and it finally dawned on Frank that he wasn't really helping. He grabbed Dmitry's arm.

"Really, Dmitry, hold on a minute, will you?" he said, quietly, and he thought, convincingly.

"No reason to, Franky old boy, we're almost done," he said. Emily was leaning as far back as she could, digging her heels into the carpet, Dwayne pushing her gently but forcefully along like she was a handtruck without wheels, she smiling at Dmitry and encouraging him with her open face to continue, and lord knows what, exactly, she was making of the story, maybe Frank hoped, just liking the slapstick. "So we get to the hotel, and you can imagine, the two of us blotto and dripping wet, looking like we wandered out of the garbage dumps of Manila, our muddied golf bags making a disgrace of the lobby, with four extremely, *extraordinarily* tarted-up boys in tutti-frutti miniskirts and ripped hose, and I swear, Franky, it wasn't until that moment, seeing things through the eyes of the young girls at the front desk, that I noticed that they *were* in fact ladyboys, and not your standard Vietnamese prostitutes at all!" At this he started to sing, "*She was a lipstick boy, she was a beautiful boy…*"

Dwayne had Emily in her bedroom and shut the door.

"And then there was a great hubbub, since, well, I suppose you'd have to say it was a far more innocent time than our own, Franky —"

"When was this, again?"

"About two months back, it's a figure of speech, for comedic purposes. As I was saying, we couldn't see our way clear to a tranny-boy slap party, so we told them to leave, which, being whores, they were disinclined to do without remuneration. *Don't* look so severe, Franky, Emily's gone — you'll notice I didn't mention prostitutes until she was behind doors —"

"Yes, you did."

"*Anywho*, we said we had to get money from our room safes and that we'd be right back. We went with every intention of getting them something but promptly passed out on our beds. I have no idea how long they waited. Obviously they were gone by breakfast." He looked over at the closed door. "Whatever could possibly have become of your friend Dwayne?"

When Dwayne came back, he looked so pained that Frank made as quick a getaway as possible. He didn't want to be there when Dwayne's wife came home — she was the kind of woman Dmitry would have tortured, even if he didn't do it on purpose, even if he did it the way he tortured most women, and a lot of men, just by being himself. They went to have dinner with the journalist, back from Seattle, and Frank expected the worst. Dmitry, though, was much less obnoxious, which little hint of discretion demonstrated considerably more couth than usual. He waited until she went to the bathroom to evaluate her as *a comely little Jewess*. He, she said later, as Frank walked her back to her car, was *a truly terrifying swine*. She hated him.

"It isn't like we're going to be neighbors," Frank pointed out. "He lives in Hong Kong."

She looked at him funny.

"Yes, I know," she said finally, opening her car door. "He lives there *for the pussy*. Ugh!"

"I see him at most once a year."

"Yes, but, still, that begs the question, doesn't it," she said, getting in the car. "Why even that? What the fuck!" She had a mouth on her. "You are fascinated by him! What sick part of you is there — which, by the way, you have up until now done a very good job of hiding from me — what sick shit within you responds to him?"

What could he say, leaning on her open door? Except that he wasn't sure. He didn't know.

"Sometimes you talk like an idiot businessman, too, you know," she went on, all wound up now, starting the car. "But I always assumed that was all those years in construction, that the *real* you was the guy who rhapsodizes about the beauty of lumber and sailing and quotes Wharton and Cather to me." She looked at him from a new distance. "With Dmitry, though, there's no real human being in there, none. He's nothing but a beast, raw, nasty, *empty*."

Frank tried to defend him, mumbling, and she put her car in gear. Before rolling up her window, she leaned toward him and gave him, yet again, what felt like one of the most loving kisses he had ever had in his life. He clung to that as she drove away, trying not to feel completely doomed.

When he got back to Dmitry, waiting at the rental car, he was convinced that Patricia was right, that Dmitry was nothing but a sexist asshole and a hopeless pig. "And probably a wildly criminal one at that," she had said, "because how else does a person get rich in two years?" And knowing Dmitry, she was right about that too.

"What do you even want, you asshole?" Frank asked when he got in the car, hotter than he meant it, the wine from dinner at cross-purposes with his attempt not to weep at the turn his life with the journalist might be taking. "What the fuck do you want out of life?"

"Ah, Franky it's like old times, you sexually frustrated," with the British accent on the second syllable, "driving me around, lecturing me on my morals, righteously angry like your ancestral Puritan clerics, my perfect guide to America and American thought. It's quite wonderful, isn't it, Franky, the sacred rage?"

"I have no ancestral Puritan clerics. My ancestors were Catholics who came here in the twentieth century from Ireland and Germany and Finland." The Finnish ones probably weren't Catholic, he realized. "Seriously, what do you want?"

Dmitry looked over at Frank and then out his side window, sitting quietly for a few moments, both of them watching the sad, nondescript Los Angeles streets go by.

"The thing is, Franky," he said, finally. "I do know what I want." He waited, his standard dramedic pause. "I would like to retire by the time I'm forty with a house staff of eight."

"A house staff of eight." Everyone wants to retire by forty. "Are you joking?"

"No, I met a man once, in a business meeting, and we were all talking about how in Asia we could all afford endless domestic help, and it's called *help*, Franky, because they really help, they make your life much, much," he made it sound somewhere between *mootsch* and *mutsch*, "easier and *much* more pleasant, and you can roll your eyes all you like, but try it my friend and see if you ever go back to washing your own skivvies or trimming your own hedgerows or driving around looking for a parking place, then throw into the mix that you could rumpy-pumpy with one of the cute little maids now and then, which you could, and then come tell me it's a bad idea, and yes, go ahead, hitch up one eyebrow the way you do — I really wish I could manage that, Franky, that thing you do with the eyebrow, I feel it is *just* what I need to kick my communicative skills up to the next level." Frank, fuming, turned on the ignition and started to pull from the curb, and Dmitry continued. "At any rate, this man said that he had finally hit upon the perfect arrangement to cover all the services the average person like me needs — you know, cooking, cleaning, laundry, driving, and I'd like a little garden, and running errands, and keeping my schedule, let's see, that's one, two, three — I can't remember exactly how it all works, but if you sit down with pencil and paper it comes to eight."

Something about the way he said this, with the slightest tinge of melancholy, suggested he might be hearing, as it came out of his mouth, how horrible and pathetic it sounded, out loud in the dark, glowing Southern California night, families of immigrants crossing the street and homeless tents under the overpasses. Frank realized it wasn't fair of him to take his difficulties with the journalist out on Dmitry — he was right about that — so he let it drop. Perhaps it was his own lonely and lonesome life hitting him, nothing more. Besides, the next day Dmitry was going back to Hong Kong and Frank to Connecticut. As they drove, Dmitry kept repeating a little ditty:

"*Drive boy, dog boy, dirty numb angel boy.*"

"What is that?" Frank asked.

"Franky, you really need to catch up with the times. It was among the most popular songs in the world a decade ago. Underground.

"She was a lipstick boy, she was a beautiful boy."

Frank had no idea what any of that meant.

He dropped Dmitry at his terminal before returning the rental, and standing on the curb, looking in the window he said, "Franky, I'm going to ask you to do something for me."

"OK. It doesn't involve a motorhome, does it?"

"Ouch, but no. And of course you are right to be a little wary of getting into business with me again."

"Oh, brother."

"What I want to do, Franky, is open a bank account in your name, at a Japanese bank, and one at a mainland Chinese bank."

"Why in the world do you want to do that?"

"Well, Franky, please believe me that I do, in fact, have my reasons, and that I will explain them all to you very soon, but there really isn't time right now."

"I have a couple minutes," Frank said, taunting. "Give me a hint."

"I'm not telling you the details for your own good," he said. "But suffice it to say that if anything should happen to me, not having any heirs and assigns, I'd like to leave a little something for you, and this is one way to do it, since I will be keeping whatever reserve I may have from time to time in these accounts. That way, too, when and if the time comes, there would be no haggling with whomever over an estate, and it would all be free of income tax, which is the only way to save nowadays." He winked.

"What do you mean? You're young. Why this now?"

"Franky. A lot of money passes through my hands. A lot. A lot of it stays in my hands."

"Are you in some kind of trouble?"

"These accounts will help me avoid trouble, Franky. They're prophylactic."

"Well, I don't see why you're even asking me. Can't you go ahead and open an account in any name you want?"

"Well, no, Franky, not with these kinds of sums. Trust me on this; I know banking law, and I know it country by country."

"So you want me to go open accounts in *Japan* and *China?*"

"No, don't be silly. I just want to borrow your passport."

"I don't have a passport."

"I know. Get one. FedEx it to me. I'll FedEx it back."

"So you *are* in trouble."

"Perhaps. Trouble is a side effect of being ambitious, and I've always been ambitious. But like I say, this is a way — and again, you'll have to trust me — to keep trouble at bay. You know how important to me you've been, don't you, old buddy? All that advice and lack of consent, all that ball-busting — it had an effect, perhaps not one visible to the naked eye, but it did. And so I'm cutting you in on the spoils, old man. Fifty bucks for a passport, thirty bucks to FedEx it; it will be the best eighty bucks you ever spent. You don't have a retirement account, right? You have nothing saved. This will take care of your old age."

Frank didn't want to do it, knowing it would somehow or other come to grief. Everything to do with Dmitry did. An airport cop was making his way toward them to shoo Frank on, and he put the car in gear.

"I'm trying to see how this could possibly *not* end me up in legal trouble."

"The addresses for statements and the like will be mine; these banks don't require your social security number, the IRS will never be alerted. And the bonus is you can come and visit. I know you want to see the famed fleshpots of Asia, Franky. I know you better than you pretend to know yourself."

Was there any truth to that? He felt himself acquiescing, however slowly, to the request, so maybe there was.

As the cop approached and waved his nightstick at Frank, Dmitry stepped off the curb, saying, "Do it! OK, old friend?" and walked into the Bradley terminal.

A month later, Frank's affair with the journalist was over. He didn't exactly blame Dmitry for things not working, although his boorishness sure didn't help. The truth is, if Frank had been reading the signs a little better, he would have seen all along that she had better fish to fry, a woman like that; he was nothing but a little out-of-town fling before she moved, chosen because nothing would get messy, because he didn't know her friends and they didn't know him and never would, because he was from a different world in the wilds of Connecticut and manual labor — he had been invited to that party as an exotic, a kind of folk artist, crafting beautiful houses with his bare hands, a freak to display to the owners' fancy friends. She had dated him because he was disposable, leave-behindable. So what did he do? He followed her across the country and moved into her new town.

Yes, moved. He knew: what a bonehead.

While she had been in Seattle he checked out the home-building scene, scouted a few lots, and, for the first time in his life, considered the possibility of life without winter. When he'd met her outside her *Times* office downtown, where he'd stopped on his way to take Dmitry to the airport, he told her that he thought there were great business opportunities for him in LA. She shrugged and flipped her head slightly to the side and said, "Well, that would be a big move to make on so little information, wouldn't it?" This he, in his love-addled derangement, saw as encouragement, believe it or not, while she meant it to be the opposite. She gave him a buss on the cheek — she was outside her office after all — and that made him nuts with desire. As Dmitry droned at him on the way to the airport, he was making plans to move to LA immediately. He would soon understand that her kiss the night before had been her real kiss goodbye, the buss on his cheek a sign that, for her, it was over, done, dead. He, heedless, was deaf and blind.

He got lucky and managed to sell the spec house he had finished in Connecticut right away, packed up his stuff in the back of his truck, put his good tools and favorite books in a U-Haul trailer, leaving the rest with his head carpenter, and moved to California. The journalist, appalled when he told her what he had done, made it very clear that she thought it was a big mistake. She met him for a cup of coffee at a trendy spot called Intelligentsia near her house in Silver Lake. Everyone in the place except the two of them was working on an Airbook.

"Do you think that, if we actually *were* a couple of some sort — *if we were* — that it would be wise to move three thousand miles without consulting me?"

"Well, no."

"And don't you think, if we're *not* a couple, that moving three thousand miles while pretending we are is a tad, oh, let's not put too fine a point on it, *deranged*?"

"I'm kind of clutching to the *if* in each of those scenarios," he said, hoping it sounded like a joke when he knew it was unvarnished fact. The shame-heat in his chest was unbearable.

"Oh, Franky," she said, sad.

"Frank."

"It's not too late. Turn around. Go home. Have a good life."

She actually patted him on the head as she left. Christ.

So that was over.

He wasn't about to turn around, though, not about to leave California. Even the next morning, instead of waking up feeling like a miserable, lovelorn failure, he woke to the bright desert sun, walked to one of the thousand breakfast places full of beautiful hipsters, sat with some fresh-squeezed orange juice, and thought, I've got no girlfriend, I've got no job, I'm living in a motel — life is good and I'm home. There's a reason, goddamit, why they call it a *sunny disposition*. He was going to buy a convertible and assimilate. He started setting himself up, found a little fixer-upper he could live in, perched on the side of a hill in Echo Park. He applied for a contractor's license, and around the same time he remembered Dmitry's request and applied for a passport. When it came back he overnighted it to Hong Kong. Because, why not? Dmitry would do the same for him. Maybe. A few weeks later it was returned, without a note.

Workwise he was lucky. He bought a teardown in Laurel Canyon and replaced it with a moderate-sized, fiercely-designed spec house, and the market was inflating so fast he could barely believe the profit. It was what Dmitry called Mafia profit. The drummer who bought it asked him if he knew how to soundproof a room, and, as with everything else in his life, he lied a lie he would turn into truth with time, and said *sure I do*, then ran to the library to figure it out. The drummer owned a little studio in Hollywood, but wanted to be able to play at home without the neighbors calling the police. Frank did the job and the drummer sent him a bunch of other clients. He got very good at soundproofing after that, building and refitting music rehearsal and recording studios and soundstages, that kind of thing. Farcically easy, it turns out. You build extra-wide walls and fill them with sand, then line the inside with acoustic foam.

He became the go-to guy, building little recording studios in the ten-thousand-square-foot hillside homes of famous rock musicians who wanted to jam in the middle of the night, and then building them for the famous actors who wanted to pretend to be famous rock musicians. These people had so much money, and there were so few contractors for them to turn to, that he soon had more work than he could handle. He would quote people outlandish figures to get rid of them, which they would accept without a qualm. Almost always they would want something else, too: a Zen meditation room, a rotating observation tower, a basketball or squash court, or something really kooky, like a gun closet for sex toys or, his favorite, a half-bath done as an oversized replica of an airplane bathroom, complete with the folding door. For parties, the guy explained.

He continued to inflate his rates, and over the next couple years took on a business manager and a few excellent guys as full-time employees, subcontracted all the grunt stuff, and started to reach the point where he didn't have to work all the time. He used to wonder who the hell it was that filled the golf courses every weekday, and all of a sudden he realized that, if he golfed, he could be one of them. He was rich. Not Dmitry rich, not house-staff-of-eight rich, but rich.

Isa, a young woman he met soon after the journalist dumped him, had moved in a few months later — yes, only a few months, but he felt he had no right to call it precipitous after his own jump. She was tough as an ash plank, with sparkling, intelligent eyes, a big heart, and when she finally let him see it, a body designed by his id. She was working a job in an office downtown and not happy about it, but she was happy with him. When they clicked, he adored her and she adored him, and sex felt like Adam and Eve. She was smart, she was clever, she was kind, she loved him, he loved her.

He had more or less arrived. He started drawing pictures of his ideal boat and looking into what it would take to build it. The logistics, the special tools, the price of parts, a warehouse space with a big enough bay door to get it out — it seemed less and less likely that it could be a weekend hobby, and he decided he'd have to use a yacht builder. Then, the more research he did, the more he realized that, like sneakers, it no longer paid to build them anywhere but Asia. So he put the how-to books back on the shelves and started shopping the websites and dreaming up voyages, sketching them on his charts for Isa, and she played along. The days slid by. All's well, he often thought to himself. All's well.

2000

They had lived like gypsies on the lot in Connecticut, building Paul and Margie's house, sleeping in the tent, washing up in a pond on the far edge of a large city park next door. They worried that people picnicking a couple of football fields away might notice that they were bathing — it would be strange enough to see two grown men half-submerged in the park's pond, much less lathering up their hair — but they waited until dusk when it was almost always empty, and were far enough away from the underused tennis courts and picnic tables that, in the gloomy evening light, no one could see what they were doing. Frank half-hoped someone would complain, a cop would come and make them stop, and Paul would be forced to get them a motel room. They shaved using a little mirror nailed to a stud in what would become the kitchen and ate out of a mini-fridge.

In the morning, the sun would force them out of the tent. Like clockwork, Dmitry would start his day with his ritual question as he lumbered off with his roll of toilet paper.

"Does the pope shit in the woods, Franky? Let's go see." That Paul didn't get a fucking port-a-potty for the site Frank later racked up to neither of them having done a project like this before. Paul knew nothing, Frank not much more, and of course Dmitry less. It was easier to use the woods than come to this most obvious conclusion, one that every other building site since the invention of the port-a-potty had come to. It wouldn't have surprised Frank if Paul or the even more miserly Margie *had* thought of it and decided against it to save money. Paul went home every night and took a civilized dump in the morning, so yeah, probably.

Once you got over the original disgust, and after the balancing act became second nature, it was pleasant enough, like camping. You didn't want to go wandering off at night if you could help it, in part because some of them (Dmitry) didn't always bury things as well as they should, but also because they were building on the edge of a ravine, which would, when they were done, give the back windows a terrific view, but for now could make night crapping treacherous.

Each day they worked until sunset, which meant 9 o'clock or later in the middle of the summer, then shivered into the murky pond and did their ablutions before heading to the local bar. The town was well on its way to becoming a fancy big-house suburb of Hartford, but on Main Street it was still the little hick burg it had always been. Lucille's, the tavern, a typical, mildly run-down neighborhood dive in the middle of the central block, had a pool table and strippers most nights, dancing without a pole on a tiny low-rent stage with dingy lights, a sign of how working-class the neighborhood had been before the new people started moving in.

Sometimes Frank felt miserable when they arrived at Lucille's, felt like they were participating in the degradation of these women in their G-strings, like he was complicit in some complex shaming ritual, and in those first few minutes each night he thought he could see the misery behind the women's mocking smiles, could see the anguish buried a few layers beneath their practiced good-naturedness, could see the way years of contempt for base male folly had left them despairing that life might ever get better than this. But after a few beers, it all started to seem like a mutual kindness — this brave band of lonely boy-men and the women who watched over their desolation like governesses, this equally brave band of women and the men who pay them with tips and obeisance, who worship literally at their feet. After a couple more beers he ended up feeling like it was the most natural possible arrangement, everything out on the table, open, benevolent, almost quaint.

At that point he was ready to argue with anyone that Lucille's was far less sordid than the creepy new Galleria Mall they had built off the highway, with its surveillance cameras and security guards, less sordid than the Stepford invasion transforming the town into some dystopian futurist nightmare. Compared to that, this little mom-and-pop titty bar was pure heartwarming Americana. In another two years they would shut it down and you'd have to go to the Smithsonian to find anything as wholesome and decent. The strippers were good kids, Frank came to see, very down-to-earth, and they saved his life. He could imagine if the same bar had no little stage, how antsy and jumpy he would have become, sucking beers while talking the same shit with the local buffoons just like him night after night. You can spout and listen to great loads of crap if there is a near-naked woman writhing away in your sight line. Otherwise it could have gotten ugly.

Of course it did, eventually.

He spent time most nights talking to Cyndy, a Midwestern blonde who was as sweet as a candy-striper, and who needed to complain to him regularly about her asshole of a boyfriend — and he *was* an asshole, calling her fat, physically abusive sometimes. Frank encouraged her to leave him, but she wouldn't; she was in love, though she knew it was fucked up. She stopped selling Frank lap dances, and wouldn't take his tips, said she liked his life tips better. They were friends. When they were talking he forgot, for stretches, that she was naked. He had fantasies of saving her from this life.

Lucille's was run by Carmen Vahsen, a short tank of a woman with the square, bitter face of a Mafioso and an inexplicable, improbable, fifteen-inch-high, cylindrical, dyed-black beehive on top of her overlarge — huge, in fact — sixty-year-old head. At some point in the dim past Carmen had been married to the owner, Charlie Vahsen, a man who sometimes sat at the end of the bar looking like Colonel Sanders gone to seed, with a white goatee and a quarter inch of the pink inside his sagging eyelids showing. After they divorced, she had stayed on to manage the place. The split happened some time before Frank was born, and she was still there. Dmitry had a little routine he did with her every night, walking up and bowing.

"You look enchantingly lovely, this evening, Miss Carmen," he would say, or some new variation of same. She stood in front of him, one hand on her truck fender of a hip, the other wagging a finger in his face.

"Don't give me any of your shit, Dmitry," she would say.

"And what, pray tell, do we have on tonight's bill of entertainment?" he would ask, without fail.

"Fuck off, Dmitry, and go buy a beer."

"Splendid suggestion, Miss Carmen!" he would say, "splendid suggestion, my colleague and I thank and salute you." Carmen was not a woman anyone ever saw smile — she wore exasperation like a military campaign medal — but these nightly greetings were the closest she ever got to it.

They'd get a couple of long-neck Budweisers and chalk their names up on the pool board. After a couple of beers, they waxed speculative and philosophical, sometimes during pool games, which meant most of the local guys wrote them off as a couple of weirdoes and left them alone. This in turn made them philosophical.

"Do you ever feel like you're a spectator in your own life?" Frank asked one night. "Not a full participant, just a watcher?"

"No, Franky, but something tells me you do."

"Nathaniel Hawthorne has a story called 'Wakefield'," he said, lining up a fairly easy shot at the 3 ball. "The guy, Wakefield, is a salesman, and once a month he has to go from Salem to Boston for business. It requires an overnight in Boston." He blew the shot. He was much better at the hard shots. The easy ones threw him. "And one day, his wife packs his overnight bag as usual and the guy takes it and leaves, but instead of heading to Boston, he goes to the other side of town and rents an apartment."

"This new girl — have you noticed her, Franky? — has perhaps the tiniest boobs in the history of exotic dancing."

"From then on he watches his wife and family, lurking in the shadows. He watches his wife looking for him to come home. He watches the neighbors go over and talk to her as she gets hysterical because he hasn't returned for a day, two days, a week. He watches her worry for a month or whatever and then put on widow's weeds."

"*Widows, weeds,*" Dmitry said to the tip of his cue as he rechalked.

"Then he watches as his kids grow up, his wife remarries and grows old."

"And that's it?"

"Yeah, I forget how it ends."

"I've got it, Franky, I know exactly what this means."

"OK, what?"

"It means you are going to tell me, next, exactly what this story means."

"Haha, yes. It's about how we all, somehow, can stand outside our own lives and watch them go by, unperturbed and yet melancholy observers."

"Do you *like* tiny titties, Franky? You seem to be staring at her as you hold forth, which if we are talking about being inactive yet melancholy observers of life rather than participants, rather seems to fit the bill."

"But do you know what I mean? This sense of stepping out of your own life?"

"Why would anyone do such a thing, Franky?"

"I don't know, because life becomes stale? Maybe Wakefield needs to get out of his boring routine, but the boring routine is all there really is. Maybe it's because we are alienated, like Marx says, and so everything feels distant — Hawthorne wrote the story around the same time Marx started writing — ha! I hadn't thought of that before. Interesting!" Dmitry lidded his eyes to suggest otherwise. "Or maybe it's that we're always faking it, so that if we opt out of pretending life is what it is, we have nothing. I don't know."

Dmitry bent into a bank shot.

"I think the lack of breasts is erotic because it is different," he said. "On a man, the lack of breasts is not erotic. The presence of them is. Not fat-guy, old-guy breasts: actual, synthetic ones."

Women hated Dmitry, Frank thought, not for the first time, precisely because he was the guy who reduced everyone to body parts. Frank might be occasionally self-deluded, but he was pretty sure he was the opposite. Yes, he could be attracted by this feature or that feature, but he was a feminist, dammit, he was interested in the whole person, he didn't reduce people, he didn't confuse his fantasy life and his real life. His love for Tracy had been total. The fact that he didn't entirely understand her was proof that he was trying. The fact that she didn't love him, he knew, was because he wasn't entirely lovable. But not because he was a misogynist, like Dmitry.

"It occurs to me, Franky, that it comes down to supply and demand, doesn't it — if we saw gigantic bosoms everywhere, they would cease to be desired. We crave the abnormal — bigger than normal, smaller than normal, skinnier than normal, taller, shorter, bigger. And yet isn't it funny that so many people want to be considered normal? We don't want anyone to think we are strange, peculiar, deviant. We want to be normal."

"That's not strange, that's normal."

"Funny. But while we may want to be normal, we don't *want* normal. We want rare. We want exceptions."

A day or two later, Frank stood in one of the framed-up bedrooms on the second floor trying to figure out why all the window openings were an inch too narrow. This was a major problem; the windows had already been delivered, and the openings were not, now, the right size. Dmitry said, "Have you ever noticed, Franky, speaking of things becoming stale à la Wakefield, that it is necessary, for the purposes of masturbation, to recharge one's fantasy material on a regular basis?"

The undersized window openings had Frank in a panic — it meant ripping out acres of framing, a mess, an enormous amount of extra work, a death blow to the schedule. It made no difference whatsoever to Dmitry.

"It's as if the images decompose," he went on, "get dispersed amongst the neurons, and you can't access them any longer. When we get recharged in the normal way, seeing some girl sashaying down the street, watching women on the telly, seeing our next-door neighbor bend over in the garden, we get recharged on the fly, without hardly noticing, right? If we were truly stuck out here in the woods in the dark, never seeing anyone except deliverymen and subcontractors all day, our fantasy life would wither and die. We would try and try to wank, give ourselves blisters, and retreat in despair. Thank goodness for Lucille's. Lucille's is making our world safe for masturbation."

Frank was about to cry. He turned and looked at Dmitry and considered firing him on the spot. It was obvious it was his fault. Whenever Frank sent him on a chore, to cut some pieces of framing, for instance, Dmitry would dawdle over to the saw, put his goggles on, leisurely pick up a 2x4, *maddeningly* slowly measure and mark it, put the tape measure back in his belt, take time to stick the pencil behind his ear, stop and say, for the umpteenth time, "Is it measure once, cut twice, Franky, or measure twice, cut once?" and then measure a second time, work a kink out of his shoulder, bend down to turn on the saw, take forever to line up the stud, push it through as if he were cutting a diamond, then stand, stretch, bend to turn off the saw, take off his goggles, thus dislodging his pencil, pick it off the ground and put it behind his ear, then remember he was supposed to cut four pieces the same length, put the goggles back on, losing the pencil again, starting the entire snail's game over once more, with, if anything, even less urgency than before. Eventually he would wander back, with the gait of an oversized koala, forgetting half the pieces. All the headers were short because Dmitry had cut them short.

He told himself that if he could find anyone else, anyone at all, he'd fire him without a second's hesitation. Gustafson wouldn't be back from Greece for another month. The guys at the lumberyard couldn't help. Their nightly forays to Lucille's, the precise place where you'd expect to find an out-of-work carpenter, turned up nothing. So despite Dmitry's miserable work ethic, despite his being a total slob — the tent was a catastrophe from the minute he moved in — and despite the fact that he moved like an ancient, recalcitrant turtle, Frank put up with him.

2012

"You know, Franky, this is getting ridiculous," he said as they ate a bowl of pho at a little noodle place on Western in Koreatown. "Our relationship has developed a frightful asymmetry. It's time you came to Asia."

It had been a long spell this time, almost five years, in part because Dmitry had, out of all probability, fallen in love. It had never seemed real to Frank, for some reason, the idea of visiting Hong Kong or Jakarta, but why not? Why the hell not? He could do it now, easily afford it. Dmitry had moved to Taipei, and that appealed to Frank more than the other two anyway. Some of his favorite sloops and ketches were made in Taiwan.

"Yeah, hey, really: why have I never done that?" Frank said. "And I'd love to meet — I'm sorry, what's her name again?"

"Yuli, Franky, like Yuli Andrews. But I must say, if I could raise my eyebrow right now I most certainly would."

"What?"

"Why do you want to meet her?"

"Christ, what do you mean, *why*? Maybe I'm just being polite."

"I don't think so." Dmitry looked at him sideways, like a raven trying to decide: bug or pebble? Then he looked across the street at a sushi restaurant.

"Sugarfish," he said. It sounded lewd, coming out of his mouth. "Sugarfish. A truly superb name."

"Have you seen Trog or Catherine?" Franky asked.

"No, Franky, I'm afraid I've fallen out of touch. They seem to have fallen out with me mum, of all people — I don't know nor do I wish

to know the details, which are undoubtedly boring as cabbage soup —
but, you know, people disappear, don't they."

"Maybe."

"Are you in touch with them, Trog and Catherine?"

"No, I keep meaning to."

"Match, set, point."

"I think it's *point, set, match*."

"*Whatever*. My father's still in touch with Trog, from what I glean,
and I'm still in touch with you, but you can't deny that people kind of
float away."

"How are your parents?"

"*Why* do people ask that?" he said, arms in the air, flabbergasted.
"Why on Earth?"

"I'm making conversation, like a normal person!"

"It implies such a low standard for conversation, doesn't it? No offense,
Franky, but really. The fact is I can't see why you should possibly care,
but I see them once a year or so. I don't believe I ever told you this, but
when I made my first big pop, four or five years ago, I did what every
stupid boy who makes a lot of money does and bought the grandest
residence available in my old hometown. It's an ancient Hawthornian
manse, a hundred meters down the road from my mother's little shack,
the house where I grew up. When I was a boy I would look at it and
think about how filthy rich you would have to be to live in something
like that. I really felt that the big stone pile mocked our cheap little
drum, mocked it every day. It became a titanic presence in my psyche
— in fact, I may have even mentioned it to you. Did I?" He hadn't.
"No? Well, surprising, because it maddened me, *made me crazy* as you
Americans say. So as soon as I could, I bought the old thing, and — this
is the best part — I bought a Rolls Royce exactly like the one that used
to park there when I was a wee lad. Except mine is newer."

"You're kidding."

"No, Franky. I suppose you think it's a horrid cliché."

"You bought a Rolls Royce as a lawn ornament for a house you don't live in?"

"Well, Franky, I do live in it, and I drive the car — well, actually, I get driven in the car — every year."

"Every year."

"Well, yes, Franky, and often" — with his accent it was off-ten — "more than once a year. I have to be in London or Paris every three or four months, and I sometimes manage a night in Liverpool on those trips. Then we go back every Christmas to see me mum, practically next door, me, Yuli, and now the boys" — he already had two little sons — "and we usually spend a week or ten days then."

"And you bring your driver, to drive you around in your Rolls."

"No, Franky, we do bring the nanny, but I keep a small staff in England."

"Small staff. Really."

"Hey, yeah, no — I keep a butler and a maid there, although the butler drives and the maid cooks while we're around, and the two of them take care of everything else while we're away, so it's enough. They're perfectly willing to work the extra hours when we're there, since, let's face it, they have it unconscionably light the rest of the year."

He was eyeing the Vietnamese server — he had a way of gazing at waitresses that Frank was sure most of them found abhorrent, but was in its own way admiring, almost tender. This one wasn't sure what to make of him, but was wary.

"Speaking of which," Frank said. "Did you ever reach your goal, the eightfold staff?"

"Very good, Franky, the play on the Buddhist path, very good. I did, and it was the furthest thing from meditative peace one can imagine. I put together my staff of eight soon after I saw you last, while I was still living in Hong Kong, but it was a disaster, truly a disaster. The chauffeur and the chief steward were both in love with the upstairs maid — impossible to blame them, she was an almost perfect little girl from the mainland, with the cutest little Platonic triangle of pubic hair — and there was no end of drama in every direction. No end. The two of them got into fisticuffs, and ended up wrestling and ruining the shrubbery, the gardener went berserk and ran after them with a machete, and the downstairs maid and the cook's helper would get into jealous catfights if I bent either of them over the kitchen table, which I couldn't resist doing, even though I knew it would *lead to grief*, as you say. It was the least restful period of my entire life." He slurped some pho. "I now have a nice tidy house staff of five, Franky, and I'm much" — again, *mutsch* — "much, much happier."

However weird the eight- or five-person staff seemed to Frank, as conspicuous consumption they both paled compared to the phantom staff in England — like characters in an Edwardian ghost story, they waited for the imperialist baron to descend on his semiannual visits.

"And the *pile* in England, it just sits there?" he asked. "Empty the rest of the year?"

"Well, except for the staff, yes. What do you want me to do, rent it out to a rock band or something?"

"Why don't you let your mother live there?"

He looked confused. "But she has a house already, doesn't she," he said. He had never for a second considered it.

"But you said, yourself, her house isn't nearly as nice. I think you called it a shack. Or a *drum*?"

He snorted. "No, of course it's not as nice, Franky, and that's the whole point." He turned inward. "The fact is," he said, with an uncommon pensiveness, "I realize now that I *like* the fact it's empty, that it's sitting there for me. It's as if at any time, if I need to get out of there" — the big sweep of his arm suggested all of Asia — "I have a place to go. It's my refuge. My escape clause. I have it for the same reason you want to build your ten-meter sailboat."

"It's not ten-meter anymore. Now it's a twenty-meter ketch. And I've given up on building it. I want to buy one." And yes, the idea of buying it and sailing it around the world did function as an imaginative refuge and escape. Key word in Frank's case: imaginative. "How many bedrooms does the pile have?"

"Well, there's no particular reason to count them, Franky. Quite a few."

"Your mother's alone now, right? You could give her one bedroom, one bath? Would it make a difference?"

Dmitry looked dark. He rarely brooded, but this conversation had depressed him.

"Franky, Franky, Franky," he said after a moment. "I don't really know why, but I don't want anyone living there except the staff. Maybe it is socially irresponsible, as you like to point out about most of what I do — although allow me to say that the little society of two I employ there would find it extremely socially irresponsible of me to close up the place. And I know it wastes an enormous amount of fossil fuel, and there are vast amounts of lawn to water — there, I've said it all, so you can skip it." He frowned at the floor. "Anyway, I honestly don't know why I'd want to put me mum there, no." He watched the waitress walk past, and that cheered him back up.

"So how's married life?" Frank asked, a lighthearted dig, he thought.

"Were you always this confoundingly conventional, Franky, or has it gotten worse?"

"No, actually, it's a serious question. The last I heard you were running around on sex-and-golf tours and managing several girlfriends and courtesans. I'm wondering how you're managing the transition."

"Well, let's just skip over whether there's been a transition. Still, I get the question," he said. "I was as surprised as anyone that I wanted to get married. Hadn't been on my horizon at all, but I suppose that isn't uncommon."

The waitress walked up and asked if they wanted anything else.

"No, thanks," Frank said.

"Dangerous question," Dmitry said to her, with the full-bore goofy grin.

She put down the check and left.

"In passing allow me to say, because this girl reminds me, you would love Ho Chi Minh City, Franky. The girls are very flat, boyish, the way you like them." Frank let that pass.

They paid and opened the door into the monoxidized heat of midday LA. "But my conversion narrative: Yuli grew up in Jakarta, or on the edge of Jakarta, because her father was a government minister. The best of everything inside the family compound and the best education outside. She went to Yale and Wharton Business, and was recruited by HSBC's Jakarta office before she finished her degree, in the same way I had been recruited, lo, these many years ago. She came home in triumph as the hot new junior exec with bigtime connections."

"So she works for the same company," Frank said.

"Well, she doesn't work for a firm now, does she, Franky? — but by that time, I had also moved companies three or four times. If you're making money, you're getting offers in this business, and I'd been gone from HSBC for years when she arrived. Not that it would have mattered, since the odd bonk between coworkers isn't frowned on there the way it amongst you Shakers; I indubitably would have made a play hell or highwater."

"Play."

"Yes, indeed, thou Heroic Defender of Feminine Honor. When I met her, the first thing she said was *Oh, yes, Mr. Heald, I've heard about you*!

"*Have you now, darling? I said. And what have you heard?*

"*In America*, she said, *the polite usage would be you are a serial monogamist.*

"*That's a damnable lie!* I said, quite forcefully. *A foul and putrid slur, cowardly disseminated by mine enemies! I am, my dear, and I'm willing to prove it to you if need be, a parallel polygamist, albeit somewhat extralegally.*

"The fact that she laughed at this, Franky, I mean really let out a laugh, was perhaps the beginning, but who knows? It just happened, in the way I hear it happens in books. I fell in love. I know I always made fun of you for being so moony about women, but I get it now, Franky, I really do. I'm in storybook love."

And, as in the books, it didn't go smoothly.

Frank had picked Dmitry up at his motel — as always, downmarket and in the middle of nowhere — and as they got back in Frank's truck, parked at a meter on Western, to go the airport, he told the rest of the story. Yuli's highly-placed, bourgeois, Muslim family, as might be imagined, was not very pleased about having a live-in sex tourist as a son-in-law, and Dmitry knew from the minute he met the parents that although the mother seemed nice and addle-headed, the father, the government Pooh-Bah, would be trouble. The father could see what kind of man Dmitry was, and was ready to marshal all his considerable power to get rid of him. In those first wistful weeks of true love, Dmitry didn't care, and he ignored all the pesky obstacles strewn in his path. Within a couple months Yuli was pregnant, and blithe, gleeful, giddy with the news, they announced to the parents they were getting married.

"The minute we told them, Franky — it was on a Sunday in their horrible, stuffy living room in Jakarta, something designed from a picture-book of Windsor Castle, really, all knickknacks and gewgaws — it was clear that we had been living in dreamland. Her mother said, in Bahasa Indonesia — that's the Indonesian language, Franky, although it is actually just a dialect of Malay; a very simple grammar, by the way, but I digress from my digression. The mother says, trembling with fear and looking at her lummox of a husband, *God have mercy*.

"The father says, in an obnoxiously officious tone, as if he were cowing some subordinates at his ministry, *And when were you planning on taking this extraordinary step?*

"Yuli says, *On Saturday*.

"*Yes, on a Saturday*, he says, *but when? Certainly not until next summer*.

"Buying time, he was. *No, sir*, I said. *Saturday. The day after tomorrow*.

"Yuli's mother was in paroxysms, and the father about to blow. I started to say something mature and reasonable, the way you'd talk to a traffic judge — *I am sure this seems awfully sudden, sir, but I strongly assure you that, in the future…* — that kind of thing, but before I could finish, the preposterous, round little man ran over to the mantle, where two stupendous, silly sabers, or scimitars, were crossed, and popping up on a chair, he grabbed one of them — and this is the funny thing, Franky, because while I was standing there, about to be sliced open by an enraged Muslim bureaucrat with a gleaming, four-foot medieval sword, I stopped to think in that bizarre mind-wandering that can happen in a crisis, *What a risibly harebrained colonial remnant, this asinine fireplace, for who could ever possibly want a fire in Jakarta? and where does the word scimitar come from, anyway? Turkish, I think,* as if I had nothing more pressing than to entertain such musings — and then he came crashing toward me, sword above his head, with a nimbleness and speed I never would have suspected, because you have to imagine him Franky, he sits at his big government desk and glowers, glowering has been his only exercise for thirty years, and he huffs getting out of a car. So I hopped over the sofa and turned to face him again, saying, *Sir, really, this is uncalled for!* hoping a little etiquette might spark a short circuit of some kind, but the women were screaming — Yuli's sisters had run in to see what the ruckus was all about — and Yuli was exhorting him, using her best managerial tone, to behave in a civilized manner, which, again, oddly, I found amusing, the civilizing mission and all that, and my smiling redoubled his anger. Like a mother lifting a car off her baby, superhumanly strong all of a sudden, swinging the saber wildly, taking out lamps and an armrest, maniacally chasing me around the room, clambering over the furniture I had started strewing in his path. *OK, get out!* Yuli finally yelled at me. *I'll handle this.* I gave the old man a footballer's head feint and then sprinted out the front door, which slammed behind me. I heard a horrible clang, which I learned later was the scimitar, which her father had let loose, and which had cartwheeled past Yuli to strike against the door and break in two.

"By the time I heard that, though, I was also rehearing Yuli saying *I'll handle this*, and finding it more resigned than assured. I immediately started banging on the door to be let back in. Nobody answered, so I rang the bell and then the phone. The butler finally answered through an intercom and said that Yuli was not at home. *Come on, Lat Sen*, I said, *you know as well as I do that I left ten seconds ago and that she is still there.*

"*I'm sorry, sir, she is not at home. Any message?* And then I realized that he was already taking a different tone with me, incredibly smug. I hung up and waited for Yuli to call.

"But she didn't, Franky. Not that day, not the next. If I phoned, Lat Sen claimed no one was home. I started straggling outside the tall, sloping, white-washed walls, ready to pounce and intercept anyone coming or going from the family compound. The gate would slide open each morning as the father was driven to work, and I would run alongside the car screaming, But *I LOVE her!* while he calmly refused to acknowledge my manic presence through the glass. Finally, two weeks later, Yuli's younger sister, Amarya, overcome with the romance of our dilemma, found a way to sneak out and talk to me.

"She became my confederate, the little nubbins, running notes back and forth, awash with girlish intrigue and blushing fantasy. I wrote missives in which I pledged my undying, unalterable love — these were Amarya's favorites — and Yuli wrote back telling me to calm down, that she had decided how the situation would be rectified. She would get an abortion. She loved me, she wrote, but she couldn't shame her family this way. She couldn't have her father resign from government, although there was fat chance of that, frankly — he would throw Yuli under a train first. She knew her parents would come around, say in a year. Did I love her enough to wait?"

Dmitry was so overjoyed to see some road back that he agreed with everything, and on the appointed day for the abortion, having been given all the arrangements by Amarya, he met her at the hospital and they devoured each other in the examining room until the doctor entered with his nurse. They rearranged their clothes and looked at him, somber.

"He was one of those doctors that look too young for the job, like Doogie Howser," Dmitry said. "*You realize this is a very serious decision you are making*, young Doogie said, using English, as always happened when a European was in the room, while the nurse took Yuli's blood pressure.

"*Of course*, we both answered.

"*You are the father?* the youngster asked.

"*Yes*, I said.

"The doctor looked at me as he would a noxious bug. *And you want to end this pregnancy because why?*

"*It would shame my family*, Yuli said.

"*Because he is bule?* the doctor asked, in Indonesian this time, as if I wouldn't understand even the one word every foreigner learns, the word for foreigner.

"*In part*, she answered, *But also because we aren't married*.

"*Are you in love?* he asked Yuli in Indonesian again, ignoring me, and we both answered *y'a*, thus proving that I understood Bahasa, upon learning which fact, he switched back to English. Funny how people do that. *Well then why not get married?* he said, with that scrunchy face, you know, like he had a little acid reflux problem. But I thought, with true excitement, he's right, why don't we?

"*Because*, Yuli said. *Because my family's honor would be destroyed*. And the doctor said, *Family honor! Listen to you! This is the year 2009! Be serious! Nobody believes this business anymore*.

"I felt like the tape had speeded up and I'd gone from the sixteenth century to the twenty-first in an instant. But Yuli said, *We don't believe it, but my father does!*

"*And because he is a dinosaur you will destroy your own baby?* the doctor said. *I am leaving. You two should get married and have your child*. Then he looked at me like he was reconsidering. *If you decide to go through with this procedure you can make another appointment*.

"I wanted to kiss him. He turned and left, taking his nurse with him, and we sat for a moment in silence. *OK*, Yuli said quietly. *Maybe he's right, maybe we should get married.* And this is the funny thing, Franky, I said *Darling!* like I was in a 1930s film, like I was William Powell, or some character from a Noël Coward play. *Darling!* Why do we turn into stock characters at moments like that, Franky, why?"

Frank knew he didn't want an answer. They had pulled up to the curb at the Bradley Terminal at LAX.

"Well to make a horribly long story short, we agreed it had to happen that very day, her only stipulation was that I convert to Islam, since that, for her father, was non-negotiable.

"I'm not sure if you know this, Franky, but converting to Islam is quite simple. All one need do is say *Allah is great*, or *Allah Akbar*, three times, preferably facing Mecca, although that is not entirely necessary, and then, shazam, one is Muslim. Providing, that is, one is circumcised. As you know, I was not. So there I was, a half hour after coming to the hospital to get my girlfriend an abortion, strapped to a gurney down the hall, having Little Dmitry's head chopped off. Funny, isn't it? Life?"

They got married. Her father died a year later, never reconciling, but never resigning from his post, either. By that time her mother already seemed acquiescent, and after a while none of it mattered.

2000

Paul, oblivious as always, never realized how inept Dmitry was, and Dmitry's sense of humor left him perplexed. After a couple of early headscratchings, Paul gave up and assumed it was all nonsense, which most of it was. Margie, though, had become allergic, and took every chance she could to insinuate that he should be replaced. The first time, standing in what would be the dining room, looking at the view from various angles, she was trying to figure out something to complain about, and Dmitry walked through with some studs for the upstairs closets. As he left he farted, loud and shameless, for a full one-one-thousand, two-one-thousand count.

"Disgusting," she said, furious, as if she were having an actual dinner party when it happened. "How can you stand it?" She locked eyes with Frank, sneered, and shook her head, like she'd found herself reasoning with a strange dog, and walked away, saying more to herself than anyone, "I thought he was temporary."

"He's here another five weeks," Frank said, which made her turn around and come back.

"Can't you use someone who's not such a horrible pig?"

"Bring me his replacement, Margie, and he's gone," he said, confident she wouldn't know where to start looking, and that if she did, he could use a third person anyway.

She shuddered. "I wish this dining room window was a little bigger," she said.

Frank walked out as if he hadn't heard. Her wishes were not his problem until Paul made them his problem. And in this case, he was safe. He knew what the next size up would cost. Paul was whipped, but cheap, and the window was big enough that it had already maxed out any resale value. He would agree to whatever she said but forget to tell Frank, or wait it out and then blame him. Whatever, it wasn't his problem.

From that day on, Margie was never on-site without saying something nasty about Dmitry. "Grotesque," she would say, any time he walked by. He treated her the way he treated anyone whose skin he wanted to get under, faux-polite, overloading her with high-toned manners, smirking the whole time. It drove Margie nuts, being a queen of etiquette abuse herself, and it provided Frank with mild comic relief in his own secret battle with her.

"I've decided, Franky, what I'm going to have embossed on my American baseball jacket," Dmitry declared one day as they sat having depressing sliced-turkey sandwiches for lunch yet again. Frank was in the middle of Freud's *The Future of an Illusion*, occasionally listening in on Dmitry's harangue. "And by the way, Franky," he went on, not needing any response, "I will take this moment to remind you that although you promised to help me find a baseball jacket shoppe, you have taken no steps in that direction whatsoever, a grievous error I feel it is in your power to correct even this very afternoon, perhaps — wait, is embossed the right word? I believe the shoppes that sell these jackets have endless supplies of letters and logos they can sew onto the felt and even onto the leather sleeves, although I prefer, I think, to leave the sleeves in their virginal whiteness, and then, on the red felt back, because I've decided it is to be red, Franky, I want these two phrases, the only two phrases one need ever use to navigate the entire American social terrain, the linguistic equivalent of the unified field theory that has so bedeviled the physicists, the Rosetta Stone of the American language, or the Rosetta Pebble I suppose — one of the phrases will be in a circle, with the top arc reading *HEY YEAH* and the bottom arc *NO REALLY* and then, in the middle of that, in a different font or style, Gothic maybe, yes, Gothic, on three descending lines:

The Fuck
The Fuck
The Fuck

Because with those two phrases you are ready for anything one's fellow or non-fellow Americans might throw at one, or anyone in the world, really. In fact —"

"That's three phrases, not two."

He thought about this for a minute. "No, Franky, it's two, but you bring up a bit of a design quandary, perhaps. As you know full well, the first phrase is *hey yeah no really* and I think it should be clear, as when *FITCHBERG HIGH* is on the top arc, and *FIGHTING MUSKRATS* is on the bottom arc, that it is all of one piece. But for the second phrase, *the fuck, the fuck, the fuck*, do you think I should put commas after each *the fuck*?" He didn't wait for an answer. "*HEY YEAH NO REALLY* can't have any commas, because its felicity as a phrase is all bound up with the fact that the punctuation can go anywhere. More importantly, the inflection can go anywhere. If someone says *My father died yesterday*, which if what you were telling me about Freud last night is true, we all would love to be able to say, still, the proper response is *hey, yeah, NO, really*" — he said this as if consoling a widow, with a long, sad *no* in the middle — "while if someone says, *Excuse me, sir, would you like some free pussy?*" the proper response is *HEY! YEAH! no, REALLY!?* — which you'll notice, Franky, is a perfectly symmetrical set of examples, emphasis-wise," after which he kept repeating it, inflecting the phrase by turns comic, sympathetic, aggressive, noncommittal, despondent. "And when all else fails, and you can't figure out how *hey yeah no really* fits the situation, you say, *the fuck, the fuck, the fuck*."

"Nobody says that."

"*Hey yeah NO REALLY*, they do. *The fuck, the fuck, the fuck* is a direct quote, Franky."

"From who, Al Pacino?"

"You, Franky, yesterday, about the subfloor." The lumberyard was supposed to bring a load of three-quarter-inch plywood on a boom truck and lift it up onto the second floor, but instead dropped it on the ground while they were out grabbing lunch, which meant they had to spend half a day huffing the heavy motherfucking pieces up themselves, one by one. Maybe he did say that.

"You say it all the time."

"The fuck."

"You see?"

"But not three times, just once."

"Franky, you really don't understand humor at all, do you…"

Maybe he didn't. Maybe he had a tragic view of life. They were coming to the end of the framing, and soon they'd sheath it on the outside with plywood and cover it inside with sheetrock. People said to him all the time: it must be nice doing your work, because when you're done a building exists that wasn't there before, material evidence that your labor came to something, you don't just shuffle paper, or manipulate numbers, or sell crap, or talk to people about their problems — at the end of our day we have nothing but a paycheck, while you have the thing right there, in front of you, what you made. When he looked at things he built, though, he always saw some glaring flaw or other, and even if not, they looked like backaches. All done and trimmed out, the buildings and additions just sat there, minor economic miracles, but they never felt like his offspring or legacy or anything. They weren't his.

And they never thrilled him the way bare framing did. The work of framing, the work itself, the three-hammer-stroke sinking of a 16d nail, the wood still a little juicy, was a deep pleasure. Monkey-hanging, upside down, to counter-nail a corner joist, or the Amish barn-raising thrill of walking a new section of wall up into place, or sliding along the ridge plate, forty feet in the air, tacking in rafter after rafter as someone nails them through the notch below — that's pleasure. That's happiness. Looking up, as the sun sets, and seeing the perfect, planed, plumb wood, and knowing how ludicrously strong it was, seeing the multiply buttressed, yet somehow ephemeral, soon to disappear, sturdy house bones against the dusk: delectable, electric, poignant, profound.

"I have an enormous favor to ask you, Franky," Dmitry said as they were taking their pond-bath one evening during his last week. The late-summer twilight world was flourishing, with lightning bugs roaming, insects and frogs chirping, the sky like distant steel, the black water warm. "I have been researching" — this is what he called going online at the public library for a half hour — "the availability and costs of land yachts in the vicinity. As you know they are beyond my current means, and your short-sighted, untrusting, parsimonious American bankers seem reluctant to loan money to a marginally employed foreigner who plans to leave the country in a matter of weeks." He had gone to the bank, even though Frank told him he didn't stand a chance.

"I told you."

He shrugged and held up his hands, like this was hard to understand or condone. Frank grabbed the soap out of one of them.

"Therefore," he said. "I have a business proposition for you."

"No."

"I propose that you invest $7,000 in my travel company, with a guaranteed return at the unheard of rate of fifteen percent per annum."

"Dmitry, first of all, I don't have $7,000 dollars, and *what* travel company?"

"Ah, Franky, I knew you would smell a good deal when you saw it! Let's *cut to the chase* as you like to say."

"I never say that," he said, ducking under to rinse his hair, taking his time, hoping to miss some of the pitch, but Dmitry waited until he surfaced.

"I was using the collective *you*. Like all good capitalists, Franky, your investment will consist not of your own money, but a bank's. You take out a loan for $8,000, the collateral for which will be a land yacht I have had my eye on. It is worth $9,500 according to the most reliable source, the *Kelly's Blue Book*, and it is listed for sale in the *Hartford Courant* for a mere $8,000. An identical model is for sale in the Boston *Globe* for $9,500, and that one has 10,000 more miles on it — proof positive that the *Hartford Courant* proposal is quite good value. I will take our land yacht to the West Coast and back, picking up hitchhikers for a moderate fee along the way which will subsidize my petrol expenditures, and I will return here in precisely six weeks, sell the yacht in Boston for $9,500, and return to you your $8,000 plus your interest of fifteen percent per annum, prorated to the six weeks."

"No." Frank had stepped out and was drying himself. As usual Dmitry was taking twice as long.

"Don't you realize, Franky, that the entire business world — ie, the entire world — lusts after the grail of a fifteen percent return on investment? Except, I should say, pharmaceuticals and certain financialization schemes, which do somewhat better."

"A. Fifteen percent of $8,000 is like a thousand dollars — prorated to six weeks makes it what, 100 bucks?"

"$132," he said.

"B. There are other costs — insurance, tax when you buy it, the ad to sell it, registration fees, repairs, servicing, who knows what all else, and maybe you can't sell it at all. Forget it. It's a terrible idea."

"You are right to mention the other costs and the risk. I would of course also reimburse you for the insurance."

"Reimburse me?"

"The money-making machine will be in your name, you'll need to put it on your insurance. It will only cost $143 for six weeks."

"How do you know that?"

"I called your agent, said I was your assistant, which technically I am. The risk, though, Franky, is very minimal. I have over $2,000 now, which means it would need to sell for a mere $6,000 for you to get your investment back."

"Stop calling it an investment! You're going to give me $132! That's like taking me to dinner!"

"You are right to bargain, Franky, because you see that I am set to make much more than you, though it is all your capital. You're right to demand more."

Dmitry was so intent on conning him that Frank saw an opportunity to hurry him up. He started walking back up the hill, and Dmitry hopped to it, drying himself as they walked, and continued apace, unremitting. "So I propose this: I will pay all expenses, foreseen or unforeseen, and we will split any profit fifty-fifty. If I am right, that will net you more in the neighborhood of $750, or a spectacular seventy-five percent per annum. Really closer to eighty. We're talking Cosa Nostra interest here, Franky, Russian petro-mafia returns." He looked genuinely pleased with himself.

"No," he said. "Try Paul if you want." And that was it for the night. They went to Lucille's and Frank ran the table for a while. He wondered, when he saw Dmitry talking to the other patrons, if he was trying to find another backer. He probably was.

Later, Frank was amused to think of how old he felt at twenty-six, but it isn't eighteen, and after a while he couldn't manage to work twelve hours every day and then make the trip to Lucille's every night, so half the time or more Dmitry would drive into town himself. The patrons at Lucille's had always found Frank standoffish, but Dmitry, after he started spending nights there without him, had become completely integrated, and when Frank did go, the place seemed busier each time, with guys from the lumberyard who never used to come showing up, the produce guy from the Safeway, even some young businessmen still in their suits, the first flank of the yuppie invasion Frank and Paul's business plan depended on. Dmitry knew them all by name and wandered out back with them to smoke joints, he assumed, or do lines. Frank was strictly on the beer and wanted none of the other stuff, but Dmitry usually had red eyes by 10pm.

Then Frank got absorbed by *The Ambassadors* — Henry James's comic masterpiece in which each of the ambassadors sent to rescue an American scion from the evils of Paris gets sucked up in turn by the Frenchness of it all, necessitating the next wave of ambassadors. He skipped Lucille's all week. Dmitry seemed to leave earlier and stay out later every night, so Frank assumed he was seeing some woman. Well good for him.

By Sunday Frank had a few last pages to read, and knew he'd want to get off the site, at last, so Dmitry hitched a ride into town with Paul and Margie as they left at 5 o'clock. Frank would come in for a late drink. Around 10pm or so, he got to the end of the novel — the hapless hero Strether defeated, having made a point to "have gotten nothing for himself," and Gostrey lovelorn — and as he drove to Lucille's, buzzing with James's big book, he wondered whether he was capable of some grand act of renunciation like Strether's.

But then he thought: what if there was no audience? Strether has Gostrey to witness it, and James's readers. That makes grand gestures easier. Is it really renunciation if you're lionized for it? And, the opposite, is it renunciation if nobody knows about it? He was renouncing all sorts of things right then. After all, he renounced any claim on Tracey or her daughters, although he was still doing all the divorced dad stuff, calling the girls every other day. Sometimes they answered. Sometimes they seemed to want to get through the call as soon as possible and get back to whatever it was — TV, friends, games — they were doing. He was OK with getting nothing much in return. But was that renunciation, or just accepting his fate?

He walked into Lucille's, and Carmen gave him the hairy eyeball, shaking her head in disgust, which maybe meant nothing special. Dmitry was in the back talking to one of the suits. Frank grabbed a beer and walked toward them. Two big biker dudes, in central casting bandanas, leathers, sunglasses — I mean really, at night? In Connecticut? — moved to stand in his path.

"Help you son?" the one that looked like a professional wrestler said.

"No, thanks," Frank said, and started to give them a wide berth and go around.

They moved in his way again.

"You new here?" the one that looked like a movie extra said.

"No," he said. "You are." What was this — bikers looking for a fight in Lucille's?

Dmitry came up between them and put his arm around Frank's shoulder, steering him back to the bar, saying "Franky! Lucille's has missed you!"

"What gives?" he asked as they grabbed a couple stools.

"You mean Benny and The Jet?"

"That can't be their real names."

"Of course not, Franky. They're harmless."

He launched into some tale or other, and Frank noticed Cyndy was on stage. Maybe this is a form of renunciation, he thought, a denial of the flesh, just looking. The whole thing, hearing but not listening to Dmitry's monologue, interacting but not bonding with the locals, the girls pretending to feel sexy when they didn't, it was all a big orgy of renunciation. Thinking so made him blue.

"You ready to go?"

"Franky, you just got here!"

Frank tried to explain Jamesian renunciation, but Dmitry was preoccupied, even a little jumpy, maybe coked up. He drove Frank back to the site and returned to Lucille's, not ready to call it a night. Frank flopped onto his air mattress, jerked off thinking about his favorite stripper, and went to sleep.

In the wee hours the bleary-eyed Dmitry got back. He was even further toasted than usual, with inflamed pot eyes and more than a little drunk. He kicked his shoes off inside and caught his shoulder on the middle pole of the tent, then bunked his head into the utility light hanging from the ceiling and laughed: definitely wasted.

He took his wallet and keys out of his pockets, sticking them on the little nightstand they had tacked together from scrap. The wallet was extraordinarily fat. It fell off the stand and, fastidiously managing his balance, Dmitry leaned over, picked it up, put it back, and patted it.

"You probably shouldn't be doing this," Frank said.

"It's victimless crime, Franky, it really is."

"Not if you kill someone it isn't."

Dmitry thought about this for a stoned minute.

"Oh. You mean the driving."

"Yeah. What did you mean? And is all that *money* in your wallet?"

"Ah!" he said. "I thought that was what you were referring to. I thought you'd got wind of my little venture."

"Venture."

"I do believe I am a little snozzled, Franky."

He had fallen while trying to take off his pants and giggled, rolling onto his air mattress with an exaggerated burp and a sloppy fart.

"You stink," Frank said to the nasty air, a simple, undeniable statement of fact, and he didn't mean much by it.

"Yes, Franky, although *I notice it not myself* — is that Shakespeare?"

"It's not Shakespeare, it's not anything. *What* venture?"

"Isn't it remarkable that we can't smell ourselves? We are the people closest to ourselves after all, we should be able to smell us better than anyone." He glanced over at Frank slowly — it took him a moment to zone in and focus — and saw that his diversion wasn't working. "My little venture. Well. I've been providing a minor service for some of our local friends."

"We don't have any local friends. What kind of service?" without inflecting the question up — sounding a little like Margie.

"*You* don't have any local friends. I have quite a few now. They love me because I help them."

"Help them what."

"Well as soon as we started going to Lucille's, Franky, it struck me, as I'm sure it struck you, that given all the risibly horny men at the bar and all the professionally slutty women, there were colossal entrepreneurial possibilities. One night Nick Bobetsky — you know him, right, the big plumber?" Frank wasn't sure, but Dmitry didn't care. "*Anyways*, he said to me one night, watching Kristine dance, *God, I'd like to pound that!* and I said *How much? How much would you pay to pound that? I'll arrange it.* I had no idea if I could, of course, but he said, *Fifty bucks, I'd pay fifty bucks to pound that*, and I said, *Come on, now, Nicky me boy, look at her! Double down and it's done*. And he said, *OK, a hunnert*. So on her break I asked Kristine if she would do Nick for fifty bucks and she agreed. Word got around fast that I had done this for him, and now I've got so much business I rented a room on a weekly basis at the King's Knight Hotel, and I manage a few trysts a night. I don't always make a hundred percent profit, since given the nature of the thing the business plan is very fluid — no pun intended — and I now have the motel expense, although I figure that at only about eight percent of revenue. All said and done, I've made roughly a third of what I need for my land yacht already, so in another week or two I'll be ready, more or less on schedule" — shed-jew-el — "to *hit the road!*"

"You fuck!"

"What, Franky?"

"You're a pimp!"

"I suppose I am, from one perspective. But I don't have a purple fur or a Cadillac with steer horns on the hood, and I don't beat up any whores. I facilitate. Pimp seems mighty strong."

Could he be this stupid?

"It's fucking *illegal*. You know that it's illegal for me to hire you without a work permit to begin with. You get busted, I get busted, Paul gets busted. The fuck. What is wrong with you?"

Frank got up and walked out into the night, hot, fists and teeth clenched, and walked off to take a piss. The night air was cooler than the tent, but still sticky. Dmitry followed him out, the ungrateful asshole.

"And the women!" Frank said. "Did you give a moment's thought to how degrading this is? Don't you care about their dignity — that they'll live with the fact they've done this for the rest of their lives? That they let some fucked-up misogynistic boy pimp them out?"

"A pimp completely manages his whores, Franky, demanding a percentage of all their income, telling them what they can and cannot do — I don't do any of that. I just act as Cyrano for my lovelorn swains, and take a letter-writing fee, as it were."

"Like that makes fuck-all difference."

"Franky, Franky, face it! This knight in shining armor routine of yours is so out of date!" He'd sobered up quite a bit. "These women don't need you to save them, they are sex-positive sex workers, unashamed and proud to be bringing down twice the money they were making weeks ago. Besides, there's nothing to worry about, there's no getting caught, everything's cash, the room, too, cash under the table, rented under the name 'Fatty Arbuckle.' I know everybody involved. There's no problem, no latent problem, no bombshell waiting. This is not one of your American TV cop shows — no one is going to be wearing a wire, no undercover surprises. What we have here are some losers who want to have a hump and some very hardworking, obliging ladies. They use me because none of *them* want to get busted. The men give me money, so they never have a transaction with the girls, and the girls never directly accept money for sex. I'm like everyone's plausible deniability, one-stop procurement and money laundering. It's genius. Even if the cops staked out the motel, and set up surveillance cameras, which let's face it, the local constabulary is hardly capable of, the tapes would show no crime, no evidence. Just some marginally attractive women having sex with some considerably less attractive men. That, too, happens all the time. And in that equation, there's always money involved, even if sometimes in the form of dinner or cocaine."

"Shut it down or I'll call the cops myself."

"Aw, Franky! I can cut you in. Or arrange some free cooze."

Maybe that's what he offered the Biker Brothers to run interference.

"Cooze is such an interesting —" Dmitry went on, still selling.

"Don't even *start* with the fucking etymology. Shut it down."

Frank went back into the tent and lay on his back, still adrenalized, looking up at the green canvas ceiling. He wasn't sure what he was so mad about. He imagined the cops coming and dragging him out of the tent, charging him with conspiracy to commit prostitution — is there such a thing? — hiring illegal immigrants, defrauding the state, maybe vagrancy for living in the tent. Probably shitting in the woods is illegal in Connecticut too.

But he knew none of that would happen. He felt something else. Oblivious, yes — how had he not noticed? Betrayed, maybe? Yes, betrayed — he had thought they were baring their souls to each other. Thought they were — he didn't know, but what the fuck was this thing if Dmitry was lying to him, treating him like just another yahoo?

A minute or two later, trailing fresh cigarette smoke to accompany his bar-crud, beery stank, Dmitry came into the tent, flopped on his air mattress, and was snoring in seconds. Frank was up late.

In the morning, Dmitry was cheerful.

"There is, you know, Franky, a way to get me to close up shop. Take out that loan for the motorhome. You know that most people don't choose prostitution, they're pushed into it by economic circumstance, like myself." He thought this was clever and funny. It was neither. Still, Frank had to think about it — some of the women dancing at Lucille's *were* stuck with kids and no help.

"OK, I have a plan," Frank said. It struck him that human life goes on precisely because every morning things surprise us again, like we've all got a touch of Alzheimer's, the whole world new and awaiting interpretation, and for some reason that morning, smelling the sawdust and coffee, having his first smoke, looking at this monumental, sun-splashed work of art they had made, a mild wind coming across the ridge, he was ready to find life full of promise again. "I'll take out the loan, but only *if* you shut down the hooker operation *and* you work for two more weeks. I'll keep your pay for this week and the two extras in escrow, and we'll settle up after the thing is sold again."

"*Excellent,* Franky! You won't regret it! Deal!"

Frank had no confidence that Dmitry would stop pandering, but at least he had done what he could. They went that afternoon to the bank and then to a junkyard to see the motorhome Dmitry had his eye on. The junkyard had a batch of nasty old heaps out front, a few grime-covered balloons and bleached-out pennant flags strung among the beaters as if trying to imitate an actual used car lot. The owner was less unguent than a used car salesman, but as hardboiled and grease-stained as any junkyard man. The place made Frank feel even less sanguine; he had somehow assumed Dmitry was buying from a private seller. This establishment did not strike him as an arena of pure, honest dealing. The motorhome itself was unpromising, too, a boxy, trashy, corrugated mess, every screw and piece of trim sending a trail of rust stain into the washed-out brown and beige siding. It had seen quite a few better days.

"I know you don't believe me, Franky, but we will turn a profit on this crate," Dmitry said as they finished signing all the papers in the distributor- and carburetor-strewn office. "We *will* make money. You *will* come out ahead."

"You know that every scam ever perpetrated throughout human history came with that assurance."

"Yes, Franky, but so has every excellent business offering. It's what you call *the narcissism of small differences*, isn't it."

"No, it isn't," he said.

"Well I'm sure one of your philosophers or another can explain it — the same phrase meaning two opposite things."

He wasn't listening. He figured he was safe enough, moneywise. The three weeks' pay would cover the insurance and few payments, and if Dmitry absconded and nobody ever saw him or the crate again, he could report it stolen and let the insurance company pay off the loan, since everything was in his name. He still felt like an idiot, but not a panicked idiot.

"It doesn't matter," Frank said to himself.

"Don't say that, Franky. You know if you find the right quote to describe it you'll feel fine about everything. What about Emerson and the hobgoblins?"

Was he fucking with him? Frank had started walking back to the van, but stopped and turned to face him. The junkman was already back in his little shed office, about to celebrate gouging them with a little dance, Frank assumed, or call his friends in the beat-up car business — *you'll never believe…!*

"That Emerson quote is about consistency, not contradictory meanings. And *foolish* consistency at that," he said, "Nothing to do with this." But then he couldn't help himself and muttered under his breath as he turned back toward the van: "Blaise Pascal: *Contradiction is not a sign of falsity, nor the lack of contradiction a sign of truth.*"

"See that?" He called after Frank. "Don't you feel better?"

"Would you please get back," he said, getting in the van. "And do a little fucking work?"

There was a fringe benefit. They parked the battered thing on the concrete pad poured for the garage, and began to live in it, using its bathroom and shower instead of going to the pond, making their meals in its kitchen. Dmitry insisted that Frank take the big bed in the back, while he slept in the loft over the front seats. Frank started to think maybe he'd keep it when Dmitry got back, live in it himself until this house was done, and the next one, sell it later. They ate their meals in the dining room, with a nice view off the ridge, and even though there was a slight noxiousness drafting from the blue-chemical toilet while they slept, it was a big jump up, odor-wise, from the tent. Really living.

Until, that is, Paul and Margie came up on Saturday.

"What is that horrible thing?" Margie asked, and, being a witch, her brief magical incantation transformed their palatial yacht, their luxurious sanctuary, back into the shabby eyesore it was. She walked around it, then stood tapping her foot — her trademark move — finally stooping down to look under it.

"Oh my god!" she screamed. "It's leaking!"

They all got down and looked, and there was a thin stream of blue liquid running across the concrete, caused by a slow drip from the sewage tank. Frank grabbed a cement-mixing tray to catch the drips, sliding it under.

"No way," Margie said.

"No way what?" Frank said.

"No way you're leaving that disgusting thing on my garage floor."

"Dmitry," he said. "Bring the hose over and flush the floor down, OK?"

"Hey yeah no really," he said. "And Margaret, please allow me to express my most profound apologies for this horrid defacement of the beautifully virginal concrete surface of your future garage floor. Had I had even the slightest of premonitions —"

"Dmitry, would you give me a fucking break?" she said, quietly, and hung her head. They all looked at each other. She never swore, and she never backed down. Had he actually broken her?

"Get the hose," Frank said.

"Right, *jefe*."

"And get that thing off the pad," Margie said, still quietly. "Now."

She turned, silently demanded that Paul look her in the eye, and as soon as he did, she turned and walked away. Paul then looked at Frank imploringly.

"Yeah, yeah, I'll move it," he said.

He started it up, backed it off the pad and left it in the middle of the drive, which was the most level spot around. He vowed that if she griped about it being there he would get a motel room and charge it to the project. Fuck it.

Dmitry dawdled back trailing the hose, singing some silly British sea shanty, smiling broadly. He seemed to get more fun out of driving Margie crazy than he should.

"Rinse it quick and then finish the soffits," Frank said.

"*Jawohl, mein Kommandant*."

Frank started back up the ladder to finish putting in the roof vents when Paul returned from whatever kowtowing he had been doing to Margie.

"Franky and I," Paul announced to no one in particular, "are going to Menard's to get the roof fan I ordered." News to me, Frank thought. "Anybody need anything?" He shouted loudly enough for Margie — who was somewhere inside the house, no doubt finding more work she wanted to tear out and start over — to hear. He waited a three-count and got in his station wagon — his brand new station wagon, by the way, which couldn't help but make Frank think buying a used one and a few nights for them in a motel would have been the more considerate gesture. He blamed Margie for this, too. Margie would never have agreed to a used car. He came off the ladder and got in the passenger seat.

"What's this about?" Frank said. It was a twenty-minute ride to Menard's, but he figured they might as well get started.

"Margie is having a real hard time right now, Franky?" he said as soon as they were out the drive.

"Who isn't?" Frank asked. And then a second later: "And when *isn't* she?" A hard time. She didn't have a job, their kids were all in school, they had plenty of money — what was so hard? Paul was good at waiting out any comment he didn't want to respond to, so they were silent for a minute or two.

"Seriously, Franky. Frank? I really need you to be nice to her," he said after that. "If I'm going to get her to go along with selling the house?"

"If."

"You know? I mean, it will help if she doesn't hate you?"

The percentage of statements framed as questions went up when he was agitated.

"If…" Frank mulled it over. "Wait, she hates me?"

"No, she doesn't hate you." He thought for a minute. "But she really hates Dmitry? Isn't there any way you can get him to lay off her?"

"Probably not," he answered, thinking that if Paul had been putting in the hours he said he was going to maybe they could let Dmitry go. Thinking about that made him come to a boil again. "You said, *If we sell the house*."

He waited thirty seconds, the whole time looking like he was about to speak, opening his mouth, then closing it again.

"I thought Dmitry was leaving this week?" he finally said.

"I got him to stay for two more."

"Oh, god…"

They pulled into the Menard's parking lot and started walking the mile into the store.

"What do you want, Paul? You want to take a couple weeks of vacation time and fill in for him?"

"I just wish…" he trailed off, and it hung there. Frank wasn't about to help him out by saying anything.

They picked up their few items and drove back to the site, Paul very carefully threading his gleaming Buick down the lane through the trees. The house came into view and it really did look good. Impressive, stately, a classic-lined beauty. It was shaped like a Cape Cod, but outsized, so it had that thing Kant talks about; it somehow fell into two opposite categories at the same time, tiny like a beach cottage and yet enormous; modest like those old Cape Cods from the 1930s and yet ostentatious; old-fashioned and yet new-fangled like a McMansion. Kant says that this kind of doubleness makes things sublime, and this house was becoming sublime. The suburban sublime. He didn't bother sharing this thought with Paul.

Off to the right, as they drove closer, partially obscured by saplings, they saw the door of the motorhome open and Margie come out, hastily, eyes to the ground, tucking in her shirt. She didn't look over her shoulder at us, and skirted around behind the house. Then the door opened again and Dmitry came out. He was putting his t-shirt back on, carrying his tool belt. He looked up to see the car, then immediately looked away.

Holy shit.

Frank hoped for a second that Paul hadn't noticed. But he glanced at him, and his face was so slack it looked like his skin might fall off.

Jeezus.

Frank hated Margie, but he felt bad for both of them. Paul was a weakling but not a bad sort. Margie? Wow, Margie. He needed to think through all the possible ramifications of this. He walked around the rest of the afternoon in bafflement.

Paul and Margie, surprising everyone, stayed around until the first intimations of sunset, Margie doing the books and pretending nothing was wrong, Paul looking like he would burst into tears any moment, spending nine out of every ten minutes looking for his tape measure. Usually he only spent five out of every ten.

"What the fuck, Dmitry?" Frank said when they finally left.

"What?"

"For starters, *Margie!?*"

"She's quite hot, you know, Franky, for a woman her age."

"Oh, God, she is *not!*"

"You're blinded by your distaste for the rather horrible kind of person she is. But she's not in bad shape, and she has that angry smoldering *je ne sais quoi* of the improperly fucked."

"You cuckolded my business partner. You fucked his wife practically in front of him."

"Yes, but *you* didn't, Franky. You ought to win some points back there."

"Ah, fuck you, Dmitry," he said and walked away. It's not all fun and games, you little twit, he wanted to say, it's not all a big laugh party, these are real people. But he was too depressed to even bother.

He went into the motorhome to take a shower before heading to town for a drink. *If* Paul sells the house. Fuck. *If.* If he doesn't, this whole stupid summer, barely seeing the kids, them getting more remote with each call, living like an animal in the woods, homeless, frill-less, spending every second on this great scheme — all of it would be for naught. *If,* he thought under the piddly showerhead in the tiny, yellowed, moldy fiberglass enclosure, banging his elbows against the flimsy walls, the water going hot and cold — how did he ever think, for a second, that this stupid fucking shower was a kind of luxury? — if he doesn't sell it, maybe Frank would be living like this for the rest of his life, living in Dmitry's corroded land yacht, watching the progress of the mildew, drinking in front of low-rent strippers, playing out some sleazy, two-bit, dumb-ass version of *The Rockford Files*.

All those hours he'd spent designing his own house in his head, rooms for everyone and everything. Designing *his boat!* Pipe dreams. Dead.

He came out of the shower to see Dmitry sitting in the kitchen, his work boots up on the table.

Pig.

"Yeah," Dmitry said sadly, his smirk, his constant goading companion, finally gone. He added, with hurt in his voice, "Really."

Frank stood staring at him, at his aberrant frown.

At least, he thought, for once he is contrite. It doesn't change much. But it's something. Fuck.

PART TWO

2013

It all seemed so long ago, the building site.

Five years into his life in Los Angeles, he was in clover, so when Dmitry sent an email saying it was a good time to visit him in Taipei, a few months after he'd seen him in the States, he jumped at it. It was unusual for Dmitry to reach out like that, so he had to assume there was trouble.

One of Frank's projects had dried up — a guy who was already spending money from his next film, but whose next film had a habit of disappearing before it got made, had put off building his home studio once again — which freed up some time, and the other projects were humming along without him. He and Isa were in one of their semi-annual fights about whether they were going to get married and have kids, and maybe some time to cool down was a good idea. He told Isa Dmitry needed his help, grabbed a cheap last-minute ticket, and left the next day.

Landing at Taipei International, his first time out of the country, was a letdown. The gleaming airport was ultramodern, and it could have been almost anywhere, except for the Chinese characters on the ads for Armani and KFC and other international brands. He wasn't sure what he expected, but it looked considerably less Asian than the average American Chinatown. As he came out of passport control a man in a chauffeur's suit and hat was holding a Credit Lyonnais sign with *Franky Baltimore* on it. Very funny, the *Franky*. Dmitry had sent the company car. Nice. Not particularly personal, but nice. As he was driven into town, the scene out the window could have been anywhere. Forced to make a guess he might have said Ohio.

He knew it was Taipei, not Beijing, but he somehow assumed the streets would be crammed with bicycles like every picture of China ever published in *National Geographic* when he was a kid, not like an oversized Cleveland full of Chinese people. His hotel was the one thing that gave him a little buzz of being a stranger in a strange land. The Grand Hotel sits on the city like a huge, bright red wedding cake. Built by Chiang Kai-shek right after he arrived from the mainland escaping Mao, it looked the way Frank thought a Chinese grand hotel should — the enormous lobby lofted by red lacquered columns, gold-leafed metal chandeliers with red tassels hanging down, red carpet everywhere, all the staircases and counters and planters massive, sweeping. Dmitry and his companions, when he met them later, wrinkled their noses at the mention of it. Apparently it was a tourist trap. Well, Frank was a tourist. It was pretty grand.

He joined Dmitry in the evening for a business outing, the car picking him up again. Dmitry apologized for forcing him to come along, but said he was committed, and Frank might find it amusing. A new man was joining the Taipei office, another Brit, and this was his welcome dinner with the rest of the bankers. Don't worry about your clothes, he said — and Frank hadn't been worried until then — bankers there don't dress like London or New York, everything is more relaxed.

The rest were standing in the bar at Ruth's Chris Steak House when Frank and Dmitry arrived, waiting for a table, drinking. In the nature of chains, the Ruth's Chris was exactly like every Ruth's Chris everywhere. The guys were all speaking English, and Frank felt like he was across town rather than halfway around the globe. They were all young, the bankers — the selling side, one of them told him, is a young man's game; by the time you're forty, you have to semi-retire to buying, or maybe it was vice versa, that buying was the young man's game, Frank wasn't even sure what was being bought and sold. The only Asian among them was a Korean kid born and raised in Nashville with an accent to match. All of them, except the new guy, were in short sleeves.

They were there to welcome this odd new colleague, perhaps twenty-seven or twenty-eight years old, sandy-haired with pretentious glasses, wearing clothes that were way too big for him, a too formal and clownishly untailored floppy suit and tie, like a kid wearing his father's clothes. But Dmitry, as the head of the office, was the real center of attention, the other guys either mildly sucking up to him or unconsciously combative, both modes increasing as the night wore on. More sedate than usual, Dmitry wasn't drinking at all and was uncharacteristically quiet. At Lucille's Dmitry had sucked beers at a very normal, three-hour-march-to-oblivion pace, smoked countless Marlboro Reds, and talked a mile a minute, but here he was doing none of that. He had decided, he told Frank later, that he needed to give up either drinking or whoring, because the combination got him in trouble, and since he would never give up whoring, the drinking had to go. He explained that because knowledge is power — "as you taught me so effectively back in the woods," he added — everything said in such circumstances can and will be used directly or indirectly against you, and so saying as little as possible is the only reasonable strategy. Not for the first time, Frank wondered if he should have been a teacher; every time Dmitry mentioned something he learned from him, he was filled with overweening pride. At the bar and during dinner, the conversation was often about *the pussy*, all the bankers agreeing this was what had drawn them to Asia. One of them demurred, said he was drawn by the culture at first. Everyone turned and looked at him and stared until he added, *and the pussy*, after which they all laughed somewhat mechanically. Most of them were married to American or British women, or single. They were unremittingly boring. Frank proceeded to get drunk, a process accelerated by the jet lag.

A certain kind of British man had always pissed him off — the aristocratic, Oxbridge-accented sneerer, the overprivileged windbag. It awakened some almost prelinguistic, deep, pitchfork-and-torch-wielding peasant id, and this new guy was of that ilk: he explained, in the bar, that his suit was loose because he had recently lost five stone, and Frank couldn't remember how many pounds that would be, but his suit suggested a hundred. He hadn't had time to get a new wardrobe before coming out to Taipei — and he called it that, *a new wardrobe*, a phrase that in his posh accent was absolutely insufferable — but he was planning to hop over to Hong Kong first chance and get properly fitted — yes *hop over* and *properly fitted*. Then, at dinner, he said he had just lost five stone and hadn't had time to see his haberdasher, but was going to hop over to Hong Kong and get properly fitted first off, and then after dinner, at the whorehouse, he said it all again, slurring it and forgetting what he was saying halfway. Frank wanted to throttle him.

Calling it a whorehouse gives the wrong impression. They had left the Ruth's Chris and taken a fleet of waiting cars to a newish steel high-rise. The elevators whooshed them up to the twenty-sixth of some fifty floors, and they were met in a corporate wood and glass reception area by two prim, pretty, business-suited women who bowed to Dmitry and showed the eight or ten of them down a hallway into a good-sized room with a rectangle of couches surrounding a large, low coffee table. Mirrors on the walls and moderately elaborate crystal chandeliers gave the otherwise bland space a little sparkle and made it hard to gauge its size. The coffee table was set up with platters of meats and hors d'oeuvres, ice buckets and bottles of whiskey, ashtrays and water. Several of the guys warned Frank off the meat trays, saying they were decorative, that there was no telling how long it had been since they last saw refrigeration. Dmitry and a short, boyish Irish thug with reddish-blond hair set down eight or ten hefty stacks of Taiwanese dollars, one for each of us to use as tips, he explained when asked, all Credit Lyonnais money. The thug seemed to be Dmitry's second-incommand, and he was clearly in the combative rather than ass-kissing camp — by the end of the night he would challenge both Dmitry and Frank to a fight. At 30 TD to the dollar, the stacks of money didn't amount to much, maybe a few hundred bucks each, maybe a little more, but it seemed somewhat profligate as tip money — the food and drink were already there, they couldn't eat the food, and they were all putting the whiskey on rocks themselves. A large TV screen covered one wall, and when it popped on, proved to be hooked up to a closed-circuit camera that roved around the room. Korean pop music played at moderate volume — Frank didn't recognize it, but the Irish guy, red in the face, said "I fucking hate this K-pop!" with such vehemence the two guys he said it to stopped talking. Frank, already too many drinks in, with no idea what was going to happen next, sipped his whiskey unconcerned. The guys were strewn about the couches, a few talking to each other, but most staring at nothing, especially after the Irish guy's outburst, in dazed expectancy.

Without warning, the room went black and then rotating colored spotlights and a large strobe snapped on, causing frantic reflections off the mirrors and chandeliers, while the music tripled in volume and turned into heavy dance electronica. More as if materializing than entering, ten young Chinese women in tiny, shiny dresses and high heels pranced around smiling and dancing. A couple grabbed mikes and started singing along with the music, while the rest made the rounds of the bankers, sitting briefly in laps, smiling alternately shyly and playfully, touching the men's faces, their arms, then flying up to greet the next mini-mogul. After a few minutes of this, maybe on a music cue, maybe a light cue, each guy found himself with a girl wrapped in his arms, and they all watched as part of the table was quickly cleared and one of the women, now in nothing but a G-string, went through a slow, beautiful routine, part standard exotic dancing, part downtown art dance, part some primal ritual, part pure desire itself. The tempo was halved, the lights low, the strobe now more background than foreground, and even the other girls seemed mesmerized as the dancer, lissome as a snake, moved across the table morphing from one tormenting, charming, improbable position to the next, moving her hairless and, save two pert teacup breasts, fat-free body around the table, not teasingly, but promisingly close to each of them, almost weightless, effortless yet taut, the one triangle of cloth between her legs, no larger than a summer moth, somehow constantly pushed beyond the plane of her torso, locked on by a dozen sets of eyes.

With no warning, the room changed once again, as if a stage manager stood behind one of the mirrors, choreographing the whole thing. In a flash or two of the strobe, the whole crew of shiny-dress girls was gone, replaced by a new squad, all in lingerie versions of maids' uniforms, each with a multi-colored feather duster. All were bleached blonde and their faces much rounder than the last group. During the course of the night different cosplay battalions kept coming through, a crew of skinny schoolgirls in pigtails followed by one of zaftig nurses with metallic blue hair, the schoolgirls uniformly short, the nurses uniformly tall. He knew he shouldn't objectify these women, but arranged in these cookie-cutter groupings, it was hard not to think of them as interchangeable parts in a fantasy machine rather than individual people. How, Frank wondered, could they keep finding sets of ten and fifteen all with the same body, give or take a couple centimeters? Each group went through three or four set-pieces, sometimes with two or three girls dancing on the table, the others snuggling, sometimes doubling or tripling up on the men.

Frank saw that the bankers were handing bills to the young women, either randomly or based on some perceived perfection, and so he started handing out tips as well. Every once in a while one of the men would get up, grab a fistful of cash and leave the room with one or more of the girls. The Irish guy, red in the face, snapped into focus in front of Frank at one point, saying, "What the fuck are you doing here?" Frank thought it was male camaraderie, which made him nervous, although later he could see that the guy was trying to pick a fight with him — he was just too drunk to notice.

"I'm an old friend of Dmitry's," he said, loud, over the music.

"I know that, you old sod!" the Irishman said, giving him a shove that laid him out flat on the couch. Three girls came over and expertly disengaged them, one nuzzling and giggling into Frank's neck, two distracting the Irish guy.

As Frank watched two stewardesses in microskirts do an intertwined dance (you couldn't call them flight attendants, they were so clearly fronting an out-of-date, stewardess-era fantasy), Dmitry appeared near his ear. "You know, you can pick anyone you like and they will take you to a room. Do you like to have your bum licked, Franky?" he asked, somewhat rhetorically. "These girls will lick your bum for you." He managed to sound less lewd than appreciative. Either out of faithfulness to Isa, or because Dmitry was right and he had some lurking reserve of American Puritanism, or (and in retrospect it was probably this) because he was too drunk and frightened — in any case he said no, no. Were these two girls even dressed as stewardesses? Who knows, maybe those were Taiwanese metermaid outfits. This was the first time he had ever been in Asia. What did he know?

He woke up in the Grand the next day with no memory retrievable between the stewardesses and his stumble into his hotel bathroom at noon. Splayed on the bed, half-sleeping, in pain for the next hour, he started having little flashes that suggested he had let the new guy know he thought he was a putz — he seemed to remember yelling at Dmitry, over the music, *Putz! That's an interesting word! Putz!*, and the new guy, also drunk, trying to focus on him, wondering why he was yelling *putz!* while scowling at him, as if Frank had become the Irish guy. Based on the lapses in his memory and the horrible headache still poking through four aspirin, he assumed there were other things he should be embarrassed about.

Dmitry was picking him up at two o'clock, and they were to stop off and meet his wife and kids, and then go to his latest hobby, an Ultimate Fighting club. It seemed crass, somehow, to go drop in on his everyday family life with all these images of profuse dissipation floating through his head, but there was no way out of it now. He stood under the water trickling out of the showerhead, changing temperature every few seconds like the old motorhome — the bankers were right, the hotel sucked — and tried to wash the night away. He wasn't successful. In the bathroom mirrors he looked disgustingly white, old, and huge, almost fat, nearly oafish. An evening with an endless parade of ninety-five-pound eighteen-year-old girls, he learned, wasn't that good for his body-image. He would need to avoid mirrors for the rest of the trip. He got dressed and went down to the lobby.

Dmitry's driver was standing near the concierge desk with a hand-lettered sign that said *FRANKY*, and Frank followed him out to the black BMW. Dmitry was sitting in the car, reading the paper.

"I hope you don't mind I sent Ralph in after you, Franky. There may be a few businessmen in the Grand I'd really, *really* rather not see." Once he said that, Frank flashed on a couple moments the night before, at the steakhouse, when Dmitry seemed to be looking over his shoulder. "Bad shower, right?"

"Terrible. Are you in trouble again?" Dmitry's eyes shot up.

"You are always so perceptive, Franky." He said something to the driver in a language Frank didn't recognize and slid the window closed.

"Why do you call him Ralph? He tells me his name is Prabam."

"A little joke between my wife and me. When I was first in Jakarta I couldn't remember anyone's name — Ralph has been with me since Jakarta — and so I gave all the servants Anglicized names meant to amuse her. Doesn't he look like Ralph Kramden? As to the other, I may be in a bit of hot water, I may not. Time will tell, although I guess I'd have to admit the water is already quite warm." He looked, for the first time, but only for a split second, truly worried. "Still, let's forget about all of that for now and go bask in the bosom of me family."

"Does your wife — I'm sorry, what is her name again? — know that you go to places like that, last night?"

"Her name is Yuli, and you have to understand, Franky, things are different here." He looked at Frank for a minute as if deciding where he should start his explanation. "It is the custom of the country. Her father goes to places like that, her uncles, her teachers, her co-workers. We never mention it — part of the bargain is that these things are never thrown in one's face. Occasionally her gynecologist will have to tell her that I've been up to something, and we have a little row, and then we move on." This made Frank nauseous and left him dumbstruck. Not that it mattered to Dmitry. "And Yuli and I have sex every day, Franky, rain or shine, when I'm in town. So she really can't complain."

"Lucky her."

"Yes, indeed. The thing is, Franky, you know all my secrets, and I want you to, and although I won't tell you everything this time, I will eventually — I'm of course talking about business now, not sex — and I might as well tell you that I may, indeed, need you, at some point, to help me, to do me a service or two." He looked at his American friend, as if sizing him up all over again, shook his head slightly, and went on. "I have money in very many places. I told you what happened to me in the last crash, so this time I've diversified so widely it might perhaps constitute overreacting." In the last Asian financial turndown, he lost all of his considerable fortune, having made, he said, "a rookie mistake" and kept all his assets in one currency and all his debt in another. The values of the two currencies flipped and it wiped him out. It took him two years to build his millions back up. A different world he lived in. "I have money onshore, offshore, metals stashed here and there, trading accounts everywhere, some in my name, some under other names, some, in fact, under yours."

"Mine."

"Yes, Franky. You remember the account I opened in your name. Well, now that I have Yuli and the boys, I'm glad I can trust you to see to their needs from the monies there. If something were to happen to me, you can easily make sure that they are well cared for with what you'll find there in a safe-deposit box — it's in your name at a bank in Tokyo — I mean, don't get me wrong, there is plenty right here, legal, and plenty of insurance and everything else, but you know, I'd count on you to see that they had everything they deserved, if, by some improbable concatenation of events the House of Heald comes tumbling down."

"A bank in Tokyo."

"Yes, Shinjuku. Do you know Shinjuku? It's the place with all the neon. Bank of Tokyo, Shinjuku. Say it."

"Bank of Tokyo, Shinjuku."

"Password: bornslippy."

"Bornslippy. That crap song — I've heard it now. Why are you talking like this? How bad is it?"

"Up! No time now, here we are!"

The car had stopped. They got out and took the elevator up to his apartment, up to Frank's unforeseen enrapturement.

Dmitry's place was nice enough: a floor in a leafy building outside the city bustle, the kind of thing that would be a pretty good attorney's apartment in Manhattan, although it didn't seem the scale of a place with a house staff of eight, or anything like the ancestral manse in Liverpool with its uncountable bedrooms. The elevator opened onto a large foyer with an oversize pot holding a tropical plant with orange flowers. When they arrived, a butler answered the door, wordlessly took Dmitry's attaché and keys, and quietly left.

They entered a living room strewn with a few kids' toys. Seconds later Yuli came into the room. She was Indonesian and had a beauty that left Frank quite speechless. Her eyes were large and dark, with little specks of gold, shockingly alive with intelligence and something more than intelligence, a kind of shamanistic knowingness. Her smile managed to express infinite warmth and yet, at the same time, to give no ground. The combination overwhelmed him with a sense of the woman's power, with what seemed to him immediately and ever after a self-mastery and competence and acuity almost superhuman. It felt more like being ushered into the presence of an ancient deity than meeting the wife of an old friend. Her features were achingly fine, and the color of her skin, Frank thought, was not a surface phenomenon, but something that smoldered, radiating from a deep dermal level, in a shade it would take an infinite number of oil painters with an infinite palette to ever capture, more gold than tan, more cream than coffee. She was dressed simply, in a Jackie Kennedy large-collared, white, men's-styled blouse and lithe Capri pants, suggesting a body that would seem almost fragile if she wasn't so obviously vigorous. He realized with a start how smitten he must look and felt embarrassed. But he was smitten. Acutely. Painfully. He mumbled "Hello." He could barely stand to look at her, except in the briefest of glances.

Dmitry filled the time with chatter about Yuli's mother, who was recovering from an operation, his own schedule — he was going to take Franky to his gym, and then he needed to stop in his office — and blah, blah, Frank wasn't listening. Yuli pleasantly took in what Dmitry was saying, occasionally throwing Frank a mild, polite smile that just floored him, he still wasn't sure why. Maybe because she seemed so flawlessly autonomous, and so, well, sublime: ethereal and earthy, colossally vital and astonishingly calm, her every gesture perfect, unbroken. It wasn't true, what people said, that there were only the pursuing, the busy, and the tired, because she seemed to be none of those. He knew, because Dmitry had told him, that she was brilliant and accomplished. And he knew that she was fearless, that she had risked being shunned by her family to be with him. He knew, hopelessly, that he knew nothing.

He stood in her living room tongue-tied. He thought forever after how implausible, how remarkably demented even, his tumbling into obsession was, how little evidence he had for the impossible conclusion he had reached, the conviction that standing before him was the complete, perishable incarnation of his every ideal. A nanny, also Indonesian, appeared with the two boys, and Yuli introduced her and them. The boys were over a year apart, the younger three, the older four and a half, but the same size. The older, Peter, took after his mother in coloring, size, and the fineness of his features, the younger, Rodney, enormous for his age and very white, was a mini-Dmitry. They had perfect manners and stepped forward one at a time to shake Frank's hand and then step back. Dmitry promised to take them for ice cream when he got back.

"Because the desire for ice cream is what, Petey and Rodnicks?" Dmitry asked.

"A human universal!" they said in unison, the younger's version a bit garbled.

"*Atta boyz!*" he said in his gangster accent, and they looked pleased with themselves, turned, and left the room with their nanny.

Yuli held her hand out to Frank and thanked him for coming, leaned in for the slightest, polite buss goodbye, more European than Asian, and smiled directly at him.

"I see what you mean," she said, clearly to Dmitry rather than to him. What? What had Dmitry said about him? Whatever it was, somehow she seemed to know him, impossible given these few moments, and know him in a generous way, like she saw some version of him that had yet to be realized. What a blockhead he was being!

Did he say anything? He didn't remember. He didn't remember leaving the house, or what scenery passed as they rode to the gym. On the way there, Dmitry talked about the various people in his fight club, the rules of the sport, strategy, but most of it he didn't hear, still hypnotized by the fact of Yuli. He registered that Dmitry and his friends were all training to compete in actual Ultimate Fighting matches, a brutal combination of wrestling, boxing, kickboxing, and brawling in which the only rules are no biting and no gouging, a sport Frank had been introduced to during Dmitry's last visit to the states, when they had gone to a bar, a Hooter's, no less, to watch a pay-per-view championship bout. That was when Dmitry had first started fighting himself.

"Why?" was the obvious question, and Frank asked it. He assumed Dmitry gave an answer, but it didn't matter: Frank was at sea, floating on an eternal image, adrift in some hypnotic fantasy — if someone had slapped him and said *snap out of it!* he would have been at a loss to explain where he had been. He could still smell her scent, still feel the slight brush of her perfect cheek against his as she said goodbye. Even the idea of men smashing elbows into each other's faces — which was legal in Ultimate Fighting — could not encroach upon this fragrant, tender world.

Prabam dropped them outside yet another unremarkable office building, and they took an elevator up twenty floors or so — all of Taipei seemed distributed vertically — and walked down a nondescript hallway to a door on the left. Not for the first time it occurred to Frank that he was getting no real sense of the city, that he was forever stepping off of elevators into blandness — except for his meeting with Yuli. They entered a gym-sized room smelling of its vinyl-and-foam floor mats and old sweat. He watched Dmitry and two other guys, one Danish, one Dutch, get instruction from an Australian expat, mostly about wrestling. Dmitry was doing very well in his local competitions, he told Frank during a break, and was hoping to compete internationally. His current goal was to retire from finance within three years and do nothing but fight. "It turns out, Franky, that I can take a really massive blow to the head without losing my concentration, and this gives me an incredible, *incredible* edge in competition."

The object in ultimate fighting, he had explained as they watched the televised match, was to get your opponents to "submit," and the way you did this, most of the time, was to hyperextend one of their limbs. Just before a knee or elbow actually popped out of its socket, the pain is so intense that even the toughest guys, the hardest cases, will pat the mat to signal surrender, submission. Getting an opponent's arm or leg into the proper hold to snap their joints was difficult, since defensively, it was the main thing everyone concentrated on avoiding. The trick was to daze them with blows to the head, so that you could get the wrestling advantage that would give you, in turn, the proper death hold. Or so he understood.

The day's training focused on spin moves for escaping holds, followed by some skirmishes, the four of them switching opponents after each 120-second sparring session. Frank kept time for them. Dmitry wrestled the way he worked construction, methodical, slow, almost plodding, and before the grapple he would stand in front of his opponent, hunched over, his arms hanging low like a gorilla's, swaying back and forth. He was strong, and he slowly brushed aside the darting hands and legs of the faster guys as he worked to snare a limb and crank it back centimeter by centimeter.

"There are two basic ideas, Franky," he explained as everyone packed up to leave, the others all nodding in agreement. "Maximum strategy and maximum exploitation. It is exactly the same as business. You make sure you have the right strategy, which, when it boils down to it, means primarily two things — although I predict you will say it is three or more — one, having the right offensive and defensive posture, and two, having the right array of tools." He was right, Frank would have said that was three things. "And then you exercise Maximum Exploitation, which is no more and no less than discovering weakness and attacking it. Good businessmen are good strategists. Great businessmen are great exploiters. You can teach strategy — Bernard here has taught us a little more today. But exploitation is a gift, a talent, an intuitive, almost artistic thing." He finished tying his shoes and stood up and smiled.

"You see, Franky, I know you love it when I talk shite like that," and he and the others laughed, although Frank wasn't sure about what.

It *was* all very odd, and Frank couldn't help thinking that despite the fact that Dmitry had the most dazzling wife in the world, without doubt still had a few mistresses stowed around town, had his men's club (he took Frank there after his fight club and did the baths for an hour, each of them getting a remarkably thorough massage, professional in the oldest sense of the word, from two young women each in private rooms; Frank's two were very confused when he asked them to stop) — yes, despite his brothels and girlfriends and his sex trips to Thailand and everywhere else, despite all that, he somehow did not feel he had enough physical stimulation, enough touch, enough bodily contact, and so spent a couple hours every other day writhing around on mats intertwined with very active, muscular men who were trying to hurt him.

Very odd.

2000

As the building of Paul and Margie's house in Connecticut entered its third act, about a week after the Great Event with Margie, Dmitry left in the motorhome. The guy at the lumberyard finally came through and found an actual carpenter, a pro, and Dmitry — Frank suspected he had never shut down the pimp operation and had plenty of money — was happy to leave. Paul had been scarce, and Margie had stopped coming up from New Haven altogether, which was more than fine by Frank. The new guy made everything go much faster. They repaired the stuff screwed up by the plumbers and electricians — two tribes that have no respect for framing, trashing whatever's in their way — and finished sheathing it. By the end of August they were doing the exterior trim while a subcontracted team of French Canadians swept through inside throwing up drywall. About a month later, around Labor Day — an unintentional irony, he assumed — Dmitry returned from his cross-country trip.

He had with him a woman he had met in a truck stop in Oklahoma. Matty was from Brooklyn, a dark-haired homegirl, knowing and tough. She had been traveling by bus — on the Green Tortoise — when all the luggage had spewed onto the roadside as they took a corner in the middle of some godforsaken scrub around Odessa, Texas, and nobody realized it for hours, not until they stopped for the night at the truck stop, an hour out of Tulsa. The driver, probably as stoned as all the passengers, had forgotten to latch the luggage doors, maybe even forgotten to close them, and Matty described the scene as they all stood around, looking at the near empty, dust-encrusted luggage area, dumbfounded. There was some talk about calling the state police to see if any of it had been recovered, but since three-quarters of the people had stashes of drugs in their bags — it was a hippie bus line, after all — they were afraid to claim them. They took a vote and decided nobody was going to call. The bus drove to a Wal-Mart and everyone bought a new toothbrush and some underwear.

Dmitry met them as the bus was gassing up the next morning. Given that the Green Tortoise vibe had terminally soured, Matty was happy to abandon it for Dmitry's yacht, and Dmitry was happy to take her aboard, along with her new friends Mary and Sally. Matty was noticeably Italian, with that New York borough accent only Italians have, a photographer, and a good ten years older than Dmitry. Despite being with him, she was a surprisingly mature person. She had dark, cynical eyes, a tiny Betty Boop mouth, wore her jeans low and her shirts cropped, a jewel in her bellybutton, and had an East Coast, lower-middle-class woman's way of looking at you, a way that said *I know what you want better than you do yourself*. Hard to say why exactly she was hanging out with this big lug of callow youth, but she was.

And truth be told, Frank did have a very good idea. Maybe the same reason Margie gave him a roll — although he still couldn't, for the life of him, pretend to understand Margie.

How to say it? In Connecticut back then you still saw, fairly often, those guys with the slicked-back, slightly balding hair and disco-era gold chains, Mafioso-style matching sweats, driving a Corvette or other flashy sports car. Whenever one went by, Dmitry would say, in mock astonishment, "Wow, Franky, that man must have an ENORMOUS penis." This was funny, it always seemed to Frank, because the Italian horn phallic symbols, the fuzzy dice big-ball symbols, the gold-necklaced, open-shirted hairy chests, and the car itself: all advertising the drivers as superstuds, as if the response they wanted to elicit was precisely Dmitry's faux-impressed line. At the same time, as everyone guessed, they were probably overcompensating. Ergo, funny. And whenever Dmitry found something that made Frank laugh he would repeat it over and over again, each time the proper prompt presented itself, until it no longer got him going. This one he heard a couple times a week.

It was also funny, in part, because Dmitry himself had an enormous, a *really* enormous penis. They did, after all, bathe in the same clammy pond every evening, like soldiers in the Punic Wars, and they tended to talk as they bathed, Dmitry's thing hanging in front of Frank every evening like one of those big tubes of baloney in the deli case, yes, baloney — huge enough that you really couldn't help looking — and Frank wasn't very homo-inclined, really, any more than an average person as far as he could tell, it was just that nobody could help but notice. There are other reasons his excessive endowment made an impression on Frank, not least of which was that Tracy had made, in the course of their nastiness, some disparaging remarks about his own equipment, and so — anyway, Dmitry had a big dick, and thus could make big dick jokes without sounding like he was overcompensating.

All of this, in other words, might explain why, Frank thought, the photographer girlfriend was interested. Dmitry's interest had a more obvious cause: she was interesting. She was quite a good photographer, it turned out: he saw some pictures she took of his step-kids, or ex-step-kids, or whatever they were, when she and Dmitry went up to Massachusetts, and they were the best he'd ever seen: black-and-white, maybe a little arty, but she got the kids to look into the camera like they really expected to find something remarkable in there. Dmitry was fond of her, and she of him, and it displayed a side of him Frank had never seen — as if he was actually willing and able to think, however briefly, however fleetingly, about someone else's comfort and well-being.

They spent an evening together, the three of them, before Dmitry and Matty went up north, lolling about in the shell of the house as it was starting to get some interior trim — the French Canadian sheetrock crew having blown through in three days, Frank amazed at how fast they were. And so it was an odd little party, as if they were in the ruins of a mansion with all the furniture gone, like the scene in *Rebel Without a Cause*, a bare light bulb hanging from the ceiling of the gargantuan living room. Matty had some pot and they smoked that, and she and Frank drank too many beers, listening to Dmitry tell stories of the multitude of hitchhikers he picked up. He had made them all — except Matty — pay something for the ride, enough, he claimed, to cover all his gas and make a tidy profit. The stories were funny, since predictably the cast was a freak show — one long-haired, bearded guy who ate nothing but raw onions and kept saying, over and over, *powder-blue suit, sirocco*; a young shaved-headed guy who had enlisted in the army while he was outrageously high, thinking it would sober him up, and when he sobered up ran in horror and was still AWOL; a guy who claimed he was a shamus, and when Dmitry asked what a shamus was, said it was a grifter with a license.

After telling stories about a few of these characters, Dmitry abruptly stopped. Frank realized he hadn't been drinking any beer.

"Alrighty, boys and girls," he said. "Time for bed."

He stood up, gave Matty what looked like a remarkably domestic kiss goodnight until Frank realized his hand was cupped between her legs. Dmitry winked at him over her shoulder, and then lumbered off to the motorhome.

Matty pulled out a little tinfoil spoon of coke.

"Dmitry doesn't like this," she said. "But maybe you do?"

"Yes I do!" Frank said, already woozy enough to agree to anything, wondering, *the fuck am I doing?*

"I always say," she said, pulling out a compact mirror and pouring out enough for a fleet of buffalo. "Variety: spice o' life."

There is always something buzzingly intimate about snorting coke with someone — since you've stepped together into illicit territory, you know that you'll both immediately start blabbering without your normal filters in place, and you also know full well that the speedy spits and crackles of coked energy morph with the slightest provocation into sex.

The provocation in this case started with the otherwise inexplicable *variety — spice of life* comment and continued with a quick series of glances and smiles. It wasn't long before they were fucking on the dining room floor.

She was fun and crazily orgasmic and they kept going at it until some noise outside the window, a crunch in the gravel, made them remember Dmitry. They stopped still, glanced at each other, and she just smiled, shuddering yet again, and in that sex- and coke-addled way, Frank said to himself, *OK, I guess it's OK, I mean, if she's cool with it, I mean she's more than cool with it, I mean it's OK, right?* talking to himself at cokehead speed as if his relationship with Dmitry meant nothing. She actually seemed to get turned on by the danger, by the idea that Dmitry would see them, and had a series of rolling orgasms that only the anesthetizing effect of the cocaine allowed him to get through without coming himself. Finally it was too much, he exploded, twitching like a freak, and she hopped up, walked off without looking back, and joined Dmitry in the rusty yacht.

Frank didn't sleep. He sat around looking out the windows of the place as the sun rose, cycling through what this little adulterous moment meant — did it even matter? Was she really even Dmitry's girlfriend? Didn't he kind of encourage it? If not, was Frank the biggest shit in the world? He smoked a sickening number of cigarettes and drank three or four more teeth-grinding beers.

"Well, well," Dmitry said, waking him as he came into the house. It was late morning, judging from the sun glaring outside: Frank had apparently dozed off on the kitchen floor. "It is time, Franky, to get even."

"Say what?" Frank said, coming to. He had a small coughing fit, choked by the nasty, acrid, coke-laced mucous half congealed down the back of his throat. He stood up, splashed his face, and started the coffee, all of which helped him not look at Dmitry, who, when he did, was smiling, happy the way he always was when things were on the verge of chaos. He handed Frank a wad of bills.

"Here's your half of the profit, as promised." It was at least a thousand dollars.

"You're kidding."

"I sometimes had five or six hitchhikers at a time, Franky. It adds up. And I said we would split everything I got fifty-fifty. Hello, gorgeous," he added, grinning broadly as Matty walked in.

"Franky, you're a bad, bad man," she said, rubbing her head.

Christ.

"Yes, Franky, what did you do to my girlfriend last night? The first thing she said this morning was: *It feels like someone took a crap in my mouth.* Excellent, superb for my catalogue of Americanisms, but otherwise not really nice, and it can't possibly reflect that well on you." One effect of his constant smirking smile was that it always seemed like he knew all your secrets. Maybe he did.

"I'm never doing coke again," Matty said, faux-melodramatically. "Thank god! Coffee!"

She walked past us to the pot.

"She's a complete whore, Franky," Dmitry said, grinning at him.

"Don't say that."

"Gallant, Franky. But if I tell her to suck your cock right now, she will. Would you like me to tell her to?"

Did he know about last night? Is that why he was taunting Frank with such bullshit and that infuriating smile?

"Stop it, Dmitry," she said. "Don't be an asshole, it's too early."

"But Matty," Dmitry said. "I can tell Franky doesn't believe me. Isn't it true you once had five cocks in one day?"

She walked right past him with her coffee. "Dimwit," she said quietly as she headed back to the motorhome. "Dimwitted fucking Dim-mitry."

"I see she's not in the mood to play. This is why drugs are bad for you, Franky. They may enable sex at first, but then they disable you.

Even alcohol. One goes to the bar, drinks enough to fuck anything, and then the next morning one is too hungover to fuck. Best to go ahead and fuck without the booze, and remain ready to greet the new day and all it has to offer. That's why all I do is a little marijuana now and then." It sounded like *mariwanner*. "But to each his own, etcetera, etcetera. Speaking of drugs, do you think that your Marlboro Lights are significantly 'lighter' than my Marlboro Reds, Franky? I'm not sure how smoke can have less smoke in it, but perhaps I should switch if there is a serious health benefit. Have you looked into it or is it just a Pavlovian response to marketing? What do you think?"

The two of them left for Massachusetts an hour or so later. Frank told him not to sell the motorhome, that he'd rather keep it and live in it.

"Of course you would, Franky, although it might complicate our negotiations, since it is my belief and the belief of the venerable *Kelly Blue Book* that the beast is worth more than I paid. I'd prefer to get what I can for it on the open market and send you a check."

"Yes, but you won't have to go through the hassle of selling it, and who knows how long it would take?"

"All right, then, Franky," he said, and he seemed all of a sudden tired, like he couldn't be bothered to negotiate, couldn't even be bothered to explain. "We'll see."

Matty didn't come out again. And then they were gone.

A day or two later Frank was adding a little exterior trim to the first-floor windows, and setting up his ladder under the dining room bay he saw a small pile of cigarette butts in the mud. It had rained the night before, so it was hard to tell when they were from, but he picked up one to check and it was, indeed, a Marlboro Red. He played back the tape of the cocaine night in his head. It had a few blank stretches in it, and it was surprisingly difficult to make the translation from being inside the experience, the sense memory of it, to watching it from outside. It was also difficult to move from his intellectual agreement with Freud about universal perversity to an understanding of his own bit part in this debauched drama. But eventually he had to admit: Dmitry had been watching them. He had a nagging sense he should have an opinion about it.

A week or so later, Tracy called him.

"There's been an accident," she said.

"An accident."

"Nobody's hurt," she said.

He drove up there immediately and saw the wreckage. Dmitry's motorhome had flown off their hill — Tracy and the kids lived on top of the steepest road Frank had ever driven, named Frizzell Hill Road after some eighteenth- or nineteenth-century guy named Frizzell — and crashed through the roof of the Bartons' house at the bottom. If you saw a picture you'd swear it was photoshopped, the back wheels up in the air like the thing had been dropped from a plane, windshield first, straight into their living room. A surreal horror.

The town's one and only cop and thus Police Chief, Horace Snowes, was sitting on the hood of his beater F-150 having the time of his life, the detachable cherry flashing its red light from his roof. Snowes was, in Frank's estimation and just about everyone else's, an annoying nincompoop who wore a pearl-handled revolver in a holster while on duty. Being on duty meant nothing more than wearing the pistol and hassling his neighbor's teenagers whenever he felt like it. The town paid him $100 a month so he could pretend it was a real job. This flying RV fiasco made him happy as a kid at his own birthday party. Something had actually happened. It was his first chance ever to unroll a bunch of crime scene tape. An insurance adjustor was inside the tape taking measurements and notes.

Snowes saw Frank and came over, one hand on his gun like the dork that he was.

"I'm going to want to ask you a few questions about all this here," he said.

"I don't know anything about it, Horace," Frank said. "I just got here."

Snowes started to say something else but Frank pretended he didn't hear him and headed up the hill, which he knew from past experience was the only way to deal with the guy. He was glad Tracy had told him nobody got hurt, because it sure looked like people were dead. Dead in the motorhome for sure, and anyone in the living room dead, too. The thing had rolled down the hill in the middle of the night, Tracy told him on the phone, with no one in it, and no one in the living room either.

He went up the hill to her house, their old house, although self-protectively he rarely thought of it that way. The kids were at school, he assumed, and as he got to the door, he could see Trog, Dmitry, and Tracy sitting around the table he had built, in the kitchen he had built, having coffee. People always seemed to have plenty of time up in the hills to sit around and drink coffee.

He knocked on the door and Trog looked up and shrugged, as if to ask why he wasn't coming in. Well it wasn't his house anymore, was it?

Trog got up finally and opened the door.

"How the hell-?" Frank said, unable to even finish the sentence.

"Oh, don't say hello!" Tracy said. "You want a coffee?" She tried to sound unperturbed, but he could tell she was as shaken by the murderous destruction below as he was. She was already pouring the coffee and was putting in the milk and sugar that she knew he took when it dawned on him. She was fucking Dmitry. Why else was the thing parked there, and him not in it, in the middle of the night?

Oh, well, not his business.

Plus, he couldn't blame Dmitry. Tracy still looked good. Better than Margie, that's for sure. Black hair. Really black. Oddly white skin. Her grandparents were from Estonia.

"Lulu? Kennedy?" he asked, not trusting himself with full sentences.

"They're at Tom and Trish's with Mayela," she said. Mayela was their best friend. More than anything, he wanted Tracy to say she'd call them, or say not to worry, he'd see them later, or — well, anything. She didn't look at him.

"What happened?" he asked Dmitry, quietly.

"It was parked on the street," Trog said. "We don't know if some kids pushed it down or somehow it wasn't in park and it just rolled."

"Yeah," Dmitry said. To his credit the smirk was missing and the monologue turned off.

"It wasn't locked?" Frank asked.

"*Franky!*" Tracy said. He remembered she sometimes replaced argument with inflection.

"You know nobody locks anything here," Trog translated.

"It must have literally flown off the side of the road," Frank said, more to himself than anyone else.

"Yeah," said Dmitry, quietly.

"It's a hell of a grade," Trog said, and it was. This baroque little corner of Massachusetts — the high hills west of the Connecticut River — with its fishnet of cobbled stone walls, its lush hardwoods and hemlock, the houses extended, addition by unmatching addition over hundreds of years, and every fifteen miles the requisite white church, still had a number of gravel paths like Frizzell Hill Road, unimproved for a century or more, steep as a roller coaster. Many a brutal winter day trying to get home, taking a run up that hill spraying snow from his back tires, sliding back down sideways, and trying it another half-dozen times, Frank had had to give up, leave his truck in front of the Bartons' house, and slip-trudge up the exhausting hill home. It was, indeed, a hell of a grade. A stretch of the Bartons' roof could be seen from the bottom of his driveway during the winter, and although once the spring came it was hidden by green, it was almost straight below you as you hit the top of the hill.

"Weren't the Bartons home?" Frank asked.

"They were all asleep in bedrooms," Tracy said. "It was like 3am. It landed in the living room and took out most of the kitchen, but no one was hurt."

"Another couple of feet any direction and somebody'd be dead," said Trog. Dmitry stared at his hands.

They sat silent, the presence of death making Frank aware of his own carcass. He watched his arm raise his coffee mug to his lips from somewhere else.

"They're pretty shook up," Tracy said. "As you can imagine."

"The only good thing," Trog went on, "is that we don't have to put a new engine in the thing."

"New engine?"

"Yeah, you didn't know?" Trog asked him. "Serious rod problems. Dimatteo's Garage said it would be a minimum of four grand to get the thing saleable."

He clocked Dmitry, who was looking out the front window. He pointedly stared at him, but Dmitry wouldn't look back.

Trog decided it was time to change the subject. "I hear it's a pretty fancy mansion you're building down there," he said.

"Yeah, it is," he said. And it was. It would take quite a few motorhomes thrown from the sky to take it down.

They small-talked their way through the next half hour, Trog doing a rant against the income distribution that allowed Paul to build a mansion while farmworkers in California lived in tents. And carpenters in Connecticut, Frank could have added, but he was too preoccupied. After a bit more nonsense, Trog and Dmitry got up to leave. Dmitry was headed to Boston on the late bus, flying back to Britain the next day. Tracy gave them both equally warm, equally chaste hugs goodbye — she was always a pretty good dissembler — and then they all walked out to Trog's truck.

"So if you were leaving today, what were you planning to do, Dmitry? Leave me with the bum engine?"

"No, Franky. I was planning to stay another week. When this happened I moved my flight up." He looked wary now, alert, snapped out of his lethargic apathy.

"But you're leaving us to clean up."

"I called your insurance, Franky, and reported it," Dmitry said. "They will be taking care of everything."

"They didn't ask you to stay, or give a statement, or anything?"

"No. In fact, Franky, you should know — I didn't give my name. I guess they assumed I was you when I called."

They were looking down the hill, down at the disaster, outlined with Snowe's yellow tape.

"So they think I'm the one who parked it on a hill without putting it in park?"

"It was vandalism," Trog said. "These fucking hillbilly kids, snorting meth and opioids, you know how it is. It doesn't matter who parked it."

"OK." Frank knew he should be figuring out what this meant, liability-wise, but he was too stunned. People had almost died.

"The *Blue Book* is still at $8,500, Franky," Dmitry said. "They will send you a check. The difference will pay the deductible."

As if that made everything all right.

"And the Bartons' house?"

Trog answered. "Their insurance guy was down there this morning. He said the two insurance companies will figure it out." Trog was a worldwide conspiracy theorist, a person who assumed the CIA, the KGB, the interlocking multinational corporate directorate, the Chinese, and the Mafia were all in cahoots, that they were all out to fuck us, the little guys, and that they were about to turn the Earth into an eternal fireball any day now. At the same time, although the entire world was careening toward cataclysm, his own little corner of it was always looking up, doing great, about to bloom forth: he was a universal pessimist, a familial optimist. The economy was always heading for the toilet for everyone except CEOs and Blue Chip coupon clippers, but he, personally, against the odds, was always about to make a big score. "The insurance flack said, by the way, that it wasn't the weirdest thing he'd ever seen," he added. "Hard to believe that."

"I'm sorry, Franky, if —" Dmitry said, uncharacteristically fumbling for words, "If, you know, there's any, well, unpleasantness."

"If?"

"I mean for you, with the insurance."

"So just to be clear," Frank said, unable to keep the blooming ire from his voice. "As far as anyone knows, *I* was the one who parked the motorhome up there. This is on me."

"*Franky!*" Tracy said again, this time scolding him as if he was being needlessly oversensitive in not wanting to be blamed for destroying someone's house.

"Well," Trog said. "Legally, the thing is yours, nobody was driving, so like I say it doesn't matter who parked it. I don't think you have to worry, though. They could never prove negligence or anything. So unless one of those cretin kids spontaneously confesses, it's going down as a freak accident. You don't have to worry."

Frank was always much more comfortable when Trog was declaiming against the Republican Party or the New World Order, always thrown off by his silver-lining side. Not to worry? Untold Bartons almost died.

And he was thrown off by Dmitry's guilty moping, too. Not like him to stand there quiet, with his head hanging.

Tracy put a hand on the back of Dmitry's shoulder, as if he was the one who needed comforting. Was it possible that Frank was alone in seeing that Dmitry had pushed the motorhome down the hill himself, that because the engine problem had made it unsaleable, he had involved Frank not just in a freakish liability suit but in an insurance scam — was he the only one? What the hell?

Finally he turned to Trog, and without thinking about it, blurted: "What makes you think it was kids on meth?"

"Who else?" Trog asked.

"He probably thinks I did it," Dmitry muttered.

"Oh, *Franky!*" Tracy again overemphasized.

"Did you do it, Dmitry? Did you push it down the hill?" Frank asked.

"Of course not, Franky." The *of course* was, of course, a mistake. It gave him away as much as the moping.

"Fuck, Franky," Trog said. "It's not bad enough?" It pissed Frank off that they were both covering for him.

"Maybe it was the Trilateral Commission, Trog," Frank said. He was a loose cannon, and felt a need to pass this gaping wound he felt somewhere, anywhere. He knew he should be quiet, but he was leaking at all the seams.

"What the fuck is that supposed to mean?" Trog asked.

"Nothing," he said. "Nothing. I'm the asshole."

They all stood there, the New England countryside spread before them, the quilted fields with treelines as perfect as Lincoln's beard, in odd serene contrast to the four twisted souls, bristling at each other, seething for their own separate reasons. Except maybe Dmitry, who wasn't agitated — he had deflated again and just looked sad.

Like that was good enough.

PART THREE

2013

Frank had had one last chance, on that first, fateful trip to Taiwan, to talk with Dmitry about his dire straits, the day he was leaving, his head full of Yuli and not much more. Prabam drove him to the immaculate Credit Lyonnais building on the way to the airport and Dmitry came out to meet them. He and Frank walked across the street to a Starbucks, where they were handed large lattes the minute they walked in. He must have ordered them from the office. He said something in Chinese to the clerk and they walked back out.

"Don't we have to pay?"

"I bought this franchise, Franky, once I calculated how much I was spending here. It's a fine product, Starbucks. The people on the Green Tortoise all seemed to think Starbucks was the Great Satan, and we would ride around for miles looking for substitutes, which baffled me. I tried to explain that Nescafé was in fact the Great Satan. They had no idea what I was talking about." He was keeping up the banter, but it was obvious he was worried.

"So what's the trouble?" Frank asked and Dmitry looked at him with that assessor's gaze, as if he were not so much reading Frank's expression as doing math.

"Nothing in particular. You have to understand, Franky. When you deal with the sums I do, you necessarily end up dealing with some perfectly atrocious people."

"Criminals," Frank said.

"Yes, and worse."

"Worse?"

"Yes, heads of state."

Frank laughed.

"Well, naturally that works as a witticism, Franky, but it is also true. You know who Robert Mugabe is?"

"The dictator, from Zimbabwe."

"Yes."

"You take care of Mugabe's money?"

"Of course not, Franky, or I wouldn't have used him as an example. But a lot of people just as bad, and almost all of them richer — Zimbabwe has a tiny GDP."

"The generals from Myanmar."

"No comment."

"That guy in Sudan."

"No comment."

"Putin."

"I wish. Now *there*'s an account. But they do it all in-house. If they need a banker they seize a bank. But you get the picture."

He ushered Frank back across the street. Dmitry looked like a different species among the passing Taiwanese, a foot taller and a foot wider, much slower and whiter.

"You don't feel like you're aiding and abetting genocide helping these guys?"

"Well, that's rather dramatic, isn't it? But look, you know that *I* knew, the minute I started to tell you this, that *you* would lecture me, right? That you would launch into a dissertation on my ethics?"

They had walked back to the car, waiting in front of the snazzy glass office building, under the Credit Lyonnais logo. Prabam got out and waited at a discreet distance, ready to grab the door.

"And you also know that I already know exactly what you're going to say, that I know the lecture by heart. So can we please cut to the chase and say, *you are absolutely right, point taken*, and then move on?"

Frank didn't feel that needed a response.

"As you know, the accounts in your name, with money for you and for my family —"

"I don't really need the money any more, the retirement account, I'm doing fine, doing well."

"Yes, that's wonderful, Franky, but we are not talking about that kind of money, not pay-the-mortgage money. We're talking about *owning* a few thousand performing mortgages, that kind of money. Your-own-plane-and-island money. And since there is a possibility that, should the worst-case scenario occur and I disappear —"

"Disappear?"

"Come, Franky, don't play coy. Some of these people have no qualms about killing off an entire ethnic group, much less disposing of a witness to their embezzlement. So it could happen. I am fairly certain that I have enough safeguards in place —"

"Safeguards? Prabam's great, but doesn't seem like much of a bodyguard."

"It's not like that, Franky. This is not the Hollywood version, the lone killer, the foiling of security systems, the car chase. There aren't enough bodyguards in the world to protect you from these people. They'll irradiate your entire town to get you. If they decide you need to die, you die. But I have made clear the retributive exposure that would follow upon my death, what hell would break loose — legally and financially, that is, not Bruce Willis with some big guns. So I think we are all clear, Franky, and do not worry, I'm not asking you to be involved with anything along those lines; I have people in place."

"Gee, thanks."

"But there is always the chance that irrationality triumphs. These people are sociopaths, naturally, and well — like living in California, it makes sense to be prepared for an earthquake."

He was going to say something else, but stopped himself, before concluding: "If there is an earthquake, you take care of the family."

"The family."

"Yes, Franky, I can count on you there, can't I? And don't look so glum! There may be nothing to worry about at all. The only thing, right now, that you need to worry about," he said, making the smallest of facial gestures to the driver, who opened the door for Frank, whereupon he got, semi-automatically, into the car, "is catching your plane."

Prabam had lowered the window while he held the door for him, and as he closed it, Dmitry leaned down.

"I'm glad you came, Franky, to see me in my native environs," he said, and then he turned to go. "Safe trip!"

Prabam got in the front seat, and as he pulled from the curb Dmitry was already disappearing into the building.

Frank felt, what? Foreboding? Mourning, almost. Did he lecture Dmitry that much? Maybe he did. Why? Obviously it did no good. They had been talking about ethics for over a decade now, and he was more glaringly amoral every time Frank saw him. So why did Dmitry keep asking for more, and why did Frank come here? Did some part of Dmitry *want* to be talked out of this life he'd chosen? Did he want moral support and guidance, however much he said he didn't? Or what?

Frank stood up, over the Pacific, massaged his neck and walked toward the restroom. People were watching movies or sleeping, the plane dark. He flashed on a future in which he needed to take care of Yuli and the boys, and in the process assume control over some evil empire of Dmitry's making, running an international cartel from the glass penthouse of that gleaming building, and realized Dmitry was right, that the only way he could think of that kind of life was in Hollywood terms — every image, every notion, every possibility corrupted by cinema and novels, double-crossers and assassins, guns and fedoras, felonious schemes and drugged drinks, suckers and mugs.

The only thing that seemed real was Yuli.

However ignorant Frank was, however mixed up he was about Dmitry and Yuli and the phantasmagoria of high-rise brothels and fight clubs and genocidal fortunes, whatever incalculable combination of temperaments and contingencies and conspiracies were at work, he could look back at that afternoon, meeting Yuli in their living room, as ground zero, as the day his life took a solid left turn into oncoming traffic, as the beginning of his one and only true, hopeless, and endless love. The moment when everything came together, and everything started to fall apart.

Frank had no idea how Dmitry did it, how he managed all those mistresses and sex partners and a marriage. As soon as he got back from Taiwan, he found it impossible to compartmentalize. Isa picked him up at LAX and drove them to Versailles for Cuban roast pork on the way home, and he found it agony to sit across the table from her. She was a sweet person, really, they had had a great sex life for the last several years, and they thoroughly enjoyed each other most of the time they were vertical too. He was constantly surprised by the depth and subtlety of her wit. She learned languages easily, and could throw Spanish around with his workers, making them laugh and yearn, and she could quote French poetry, even say some things in Chinese and Japanese.

For all that, she was a vocationally lost soul. She kept fretting about what she was going to do with her life. She loved every job she had for a week, and then hated it with a passion, convinced that it was taking her farther from the career she was meant to pursue. She just had no idea what that career was supposed to be. This drove Frank nuts, but it was really her problem, not his or theirs, except that she also wanted to have kids. Frank thought of his own mother, stuck at home with her kids, under the thumb of her fearsome, tyrannical husband, frustrated, sickly half the time, absent-mindedly binge-drinking her way to the hospital every year or two. Her problems were not Isa's, he knew, but he had always assumed his mother's depression had something to do with not having meaningful work. She was a big reader, which is why Frank was a big reader. She could have done anything and instead she just languished. And like his mother, and Tracy for that matter, Isa was languishing. It wasn't fair, Frank knew, to project his mother's dejection onto them, but the simple fact was that Isa was unhappy a good half of the time. Unhappy is not fun to live with. Raising kids with an unhappy woman? That seemed unfair to the kids, if nothing else.

Versailles was crowded, as always, and across from each other at a tiny Formica two-top, he immediately missed being in the car: sitting in the front seat, both looking forward, her eyes on the road gave them both a little psychic distance. At the restaurant, there they were, seeing each other. She looked stunning, her ridiculously long auburn hair shiny and luxurious, wearing stuff she knew he liked, offering him the guileless beauty of her eyes. They ordered right away and were brought a beer instantaneously, as always seemed to happen at Versailles. It was like the waiters carried some in refrigerated pockets.

"So your big Asian adventure," she said, not unkindly. "Was it all you hoped?" She had met Dmitry twice. She didn't like him. Most women didn't.

"It *is* different there," was all he managed. I'm an idiot, he thought. She had to notice how evasive that was.

He had met Isa at a blues bar so soon after his journalist decided, unilaterally, not to renew his option that he assumed he was just having a rebound affair. He had been at a nadir, a month or so after he got to town, a little dip in the chart before the business really got going, and the sunshine had started to feel like mockery rather than beneficence, the beautiful people the same way. For a moment he hadn't been sure about LA at all, hadn't been sure he'd stay, hadn't been sure of anything. Isa, as it turned out, wasn't sure of anything either, so there you have it.

She was ten years younger than him, and a serious ten years — when they met he was thirty-two and worried about getting old, she was twenty-two, painfully young, but already on about her biological clock. She had plenty of problems. Her mother, who had been sexually abused by her grandfather, had been a psychological mess, and, to top it off was felled by cancer when Isa was only seventeen. A year later her high school boyfriend died of leukemia and a college boyfriend bought it on a motorcycle not too long after that. She spent a couple years of celibacy dealing with the belief that she brought death to those she loved, which was absurd but nonetheless real, since the feeling overwhelmed every invitation to intimacy. When she emerged from those depths, at least partially, she was met by a series of further disasters: dates who turned into rapists, lovers who turned out to be secretly married in other states, that kind of thing.

When he met her she was a complete enigma. Strong and angry, sexy as hell but untouchable, a flirt who kept you at two arms' length. She was in love with him, there could be no doubt — he had never been the overconfident type, quite the contrary, but it was a simple fact: no one had ever been so enamored of him. And still, despite that, the ultimate sexual seduction was more arduous than he thought possible this side of the middle ages. They would make out on her couch, with her occasionally slapping his hand away, for hours, after which he'd come home and whack off, day after day, until it settled into something of a routine. After weeks and weeks they actually made it into her bed, only to spend night after endless night sleeping together and barely touching, like colonial kids bundling: her stiff with fear and yearning, him so confused and stymied it looked like patience. Eventually all the stories came out and he slowly proceeded, as if trying to domesticate a butterfly, to win her trust.

Finally, months into the thing, they managed sex. After that, she threw herself into his arms and wept on his neck and shoulder, let him know she had never known a man so sensitive, so strong, such a genius, so competent, so talented — mind you he didn't think any of these things about himself, and that was why to have her say them was the most surprising and deeply pleasant experience of his life to date.

It can be very addictive, having someone who thinks you're the bees' knees, especially if that someone is smart and kind with a wicked sense of humor, and once they got past the mess, the sex was heaven. The only real hitch was the kids — not the ones he sort of still had, and who she loved when they met at Kennedy's high school graduation, but the ones she wanted to have herself — and as she sat across the table at Versailles, he knew she was wondering whether he had been cured of whatever ailed him by this trip, whether he was ready to settle down and be a real father. It was a dealbreaker for her, and he had been thinking, for a while, that maybe it was for him as well. Kennedy and Lulu were only eight and ten years younger than Isa, which Tracy and almost everyone else thought was either just short of disgusting or worse than disgusting, but hey, was all he could say, it happened. Now, five years later, the kids were both in college, which he was paying for — and he didn't complain, it was fine, it was part of the deal — and he kept thinking that in three years, no more college, no more support payments, and he'd be a free man. He was seeing the light at the end of that long tunnel, and he wanted to start the next phase of his life, really travel the world, maybe buy that boat after all, get out of the ruts he'd been wedged in all his life: working for a living, the endless attempt at growing up, proving something to Tracy and the doubters, all of that. The idea of starting up the whole big kid machine again filled him with horror — buying cribs, strollers, diapers — Christ, just shoot me, he thought. Plus, if they had two kids now, when was he supposed to sail around the Caribbean or the South China Sea? He'd be in his sixties by the time they got out of college. Game over. Fuck.

So they were headed to a showdown, they both knew it, but they both kept hoping against hope the other one would say, OK, you're right, you win. He had loved nothing more than imagining sailing around the world with her. Two weeks earlier, before his trip to Taiwan, if anyone had asked, he would have said he was in love and wanted to be with her forever, minus the kid thing. Maybe she could work in a preschool or become a pediatric nurse or something and get rid of the jones she had for babies, let them go on loving each other. He could also still think, once in a while: well, if it's that important to her, and I really do love her, which I do, don't I have to plunge in and do it? Don't I have to let her have her babies? He loved kids, he loved being a father, he loved all the ages, and in his weak moments he could see himself giving in, especially on those nights when in the throes of their commonplace passion, profoundly, truly grateful for her sweetness, her brilliance, her love, her body, her cleverness, her generosity, all of it real — he could almost start to weep in post-coital appreciation — then he'd come perilously close to saying OK, let's do it, let's have a kid or two.

"Try to be a little vaguer, Franky."

"Haha. It's a long flight, you know, I'm kind of out of it."

"I'll say, you look like you did the day those two by fours fell on your head — did you get a concussion over there?"

Sitting in front of his Cuban pork at Versailles, jetlagged like only an Asian flight can jetlag you, Isa ribbing him, he was both clearer about things and more confused. He felt like a murderer, like he was killing her dream, and maybe their relationship, for an apparition, a chimera. How did Dmitry manage to go from bed to bed to bed? Frank had barely even talked to Yuli, had spent only moments with her, and yet he already felt like the foul betrayer he only dreamed of being, someday, somehow. How did Dmitry do it?

"It is really different." That was it. The most he could muster.

"Different how?" She knew something had shifted. And when she realized it, so did he. He definitely was not going to start another family in Los Angeles. He ordered each of them a second beer. He told her about the fight club, about the neo-imperialist steakhouse. That Dmitry owned a Starbucks.

"And the missus?" Isa asked, as if in a flash of clairvoyance. "How is she bearing up with the Dmitry-ness of it all?" Whatever she thought or knew, whatever hesitation he was having, he saw that she hated him, Frank, right at that moment, maybe even more than she hated Dmitry.

Soon after he got back, he started to get a few jobs from his regular clients installing the latest security gear, and he could see a whole new lucrative revenue stream appearing. One of his rock-star-wannabe actors — a real prick, actually, a fairly talentless, spoiled brat — had gone on a bender with pills and booze while Frank was putting the finishing touches on the guy's make-believe studio. The actor had managed to get two clueless, adventurous high school girls up to watch him pretend to be a rock star, playing along with a tape of his magnum opus, this cheesy punk number that made Frank's fingernails hurt. Then the actor realized he was too high to even play badly and wandered out to the hot tub with the girls, leaving all the equipment turned on. When the guitar started to feedback, Frank went into the booth and shut everything down.

Half an hour later the girls came running to him, almost naked, hysterical, because the actor had passed out. Frank pulled him out of the loud, bubbling water onto the deck, called a doctor whose name was on the empty prescription bottle floating in the pool, drove the girls down the hill when the doc got there, and didn't tell anyone. This cemented his reputation as a discreet guy, which was a serious boon as he developed the security wing of the business — first job: this very same brat actor decided he needed cameras, motion detectors, the whole shebang, paranoid after his near brush with jailbait jailtime. His friends followed suit. He hired a couple more guys and the business was in hyperdrive. Not Dmitry money, but for Frank, more than enough; he was charging rates based not on his cost and a margin, like in the old days, but based on his clients' fear and checkbooks. He was officially on easy street.

What he wanted, he knew, was to sail, and it looked like soon he would be able to do it. He had had a pathological pit of wanderlust since he was a kid, stoked by reading Conrad and Melville and García Márquez and Hemingway and Graham Greene, but back then he assumed that this was the way imagination worked. It was called a dream because it wasn't ever going to become real. Frank's dream, since that first hour on Lake Hopatcong, was to live sailing from high seas port to port, sometimes on a full-sized clipper ship, sometimes in a schooner, sometimes whatever fancy sloop he saw in the harbor that day. Window-shopping on the internet over the last few years, the reverie had narrowed down to a particular ship — he wanted a sixty-foot wooden ketch — and now a specific place: he wanted to sail it around Southeast Asia, through those mushroom-like islands off Vietnam in *The Man with the Golden Gun,* and around the rest of the Andaman Sea and the South China Sea and the Gulf of Thailand and the Strait of Malacca. He had the charts up over his desk and he would stare at them for hours, plot courses, study the weather and the prevailing winds, calculate how long it would take to sail from Kota Bharu to Jayapura, from Jolo to Balikpapan.

The dream had moved to Asia, but Frank didn't think it was in order to do the things Dmitry did. He might be a little perverse, but not perverse like that. "There's a man in Bangkok, Franky," Dmitry had told him a couple years into his first job in Hong Kong. "I fly over and call him from the airport. I say *Hello, Thaksin, I would like, tonight, let me see,*" and he pretended to be considering some elaborate mental menu for a couple seconds and then talked again into the pretend phone in his hand. "*I would like you to get me a very old guy with, let me see, yes, with a really fat girl, and I would like to see him fuck her. The oldest guy you can find and the fattest girl*. And then when I arrive at my hotel room, Franky, they are waiting by the door, a really old man and a really fat girl. How does he do it? The airport is an hour away, but he doesn't even need the hour. I can call him from the room and say, *Now I would like, Thaksin, a sixteen-year-old Laotian boy and two old wrinkled women, preferably twins from Nepal,* and Franky *within fifteen minutes* they will show up, and within twenty, the seventy-year-old Nepalese twins are performing double fellatio on the Laotian boy. How does Thaksin do it? How *does* he do it!"

But, Frank asked himself, who wants this? Who wants to watch old people having sex with young people? Dmitry, he supposed, on the odd weekend getaway. But not him. He didn't want Dmitry's life, at least not his surreal sex life, even if it made his own existence feel like black-and-white TV, boring, out-of-date, passé. Before his trip, he had decided that life was different out there in the big wide world, and not just different like California was different than Massachusetts. Really different. More colorful, more realistic, weirder. The reality wasn't at all like he had pictured it — which wasn't surprising, since his notions were based on nineteenth-century novels and decades-old magazines — but still, he knew he needed to get out there again, and soon. He needed to sail to Bali, Rangoon, Papua New Guinea and a hundred spots in between.

So it had nothing to do with Dmitry. And yet, if he was honest with himself, he'd have to admit that Dmitry's troubles kept him up at night not because he was worried, but because, if he were to find out Dmitry had disappeared, some not so small part of him would have rejoiced.

He was not, in those days — and it seemed to be hardening into a habit — completely honest with himself.

The old maxim about time and heels is right, and as a couple of weeks went by, he and Isa fell back into their easy way with each other. Things were OK, he inching in her direction, both of them managing to avoid talking about any of it. He was busy, and that helped. They had no money trouble, and that helped too. They eased back into sex together, and that exerted its magic. Life was good, he kept saying to himself, why fuck it up? Especially for an illusion. What kind of future is that?

Then Isa's father came to visit. Herbie was a nice enough guy. Ending up a single father of sorts — his five kids ranging from fifteen to twenty-five or thereabouts when their mother died — he had kept it all together, either developing or maintaining a habitual equanimity, and he was generally known as a mensch. At dinner a couple nights after he arrived he played a different role instead, that of the protective father. They had gone out to eat — by design, in retrospect, so they would be on neutral ground. They went to a little pasta place they liked, Osteria La Buca on Melrose. La Buca had been a tiny six-table hole in the wall, with Mama in the back rolling out fresh pasta and slicing guanciale, and Isa had been so excited about it she invited a friend who was a restaurant critic. The critic raved about the food and the mad rush that followed meant they had moved into the space next door, made it five times as big and dolled it all up. Now it was hard to get a reservation. Frank missed the old place.

"So," Herbie said. "It's been five years now, is that right? Isa said you have an anniversary coming up." He didn't like the sound of that. He looked over at Isa and she was staring at her plate, not dejected, it seemed to him, but conspiratorial, even kind of hopeful.

"Yes," he said, purposely terse.

"Are you two talking about marriage?" He knew damn well they'd been talking about marriage for years. Herbie wouldn't be talking about it himself, with her obvious preapproval, if he didn't know that.

"Yes."

"You know Isa wants children."

"Yes."

"And you don't?"

He looked at Isa again, but she wouldn't look at him. He felt a wave of anger, pissed that she would let Herbie butt in, that they would gang up on him. "I guess it really is that simple," he said, although nothing actually felt simple.

"I mean, I don't want to tell you kids how to run your lives," he said, no less a lie because he delivered it as if he were a nice, harmless Jewish Mr. Rogers. It occurred to Frank that perhaps one reason he and Isa had no problem with their age difference — except for this kid thing — was because she was a little too attached to her father. It also occurred to him that it was backfiring at the moment. "And I hate to say this," Herbie went on, "but it seems to me that if you don't want to be the father of the children she wants to have, you probably need to step aside."

Wow, he thought, that was stronger than expected. She sat there, seemingly no more or less perturbed than she was before. They really had worked this all out in advance.

And then, just like that, things actually did seem simpler. They were making it easy for him, giving him an ultimatum. Everything fell into place, the grey area separated into black and white.

"You're right," he said to Herbie. Now Isa looked at him, finally, strangely calm. She was stronger than he thought. "You're right," he repeated, to no one in particular.

"OK," Herbie said to Frank, and to his daughter, "OK?" Then to Frank again, "So you'll decide?"

"I said you're right, Herbie, what the fuck? You want me to announce it to the restaurant?"

But he wasn't really angry. He was relieved. So he added, calmly, "I'm sorry, Herbie, and thank you, obviously we were stuck. I couldn't decide because I couldn't bear giving you up, Isa. But I will. I can't have more kids, I just can't do it."

"But those aren't really your kids," she said.

"*Anyways,*" he said, imitating Dmitry imitating an American gangster, which he knew, as soon as he said it, was a bad idea.

She looked at him with something less than love, but something less than scorn, too. Maybe it was pity. Maybe it was surprise that he would actually back out. But, and this in turn surprised him, she was fine. He had felt such a responsibility for her, such a fear that if they split, she would clam back up, slam the door on everyone again, get depressed. But no. She'd be fine. She was fine. She could replace him in a week if she wanted to, have her kids, have a great life, a better life. Was he deluded all those years thinking she needed him? He guessed so.

He thought of Yuli.

Not anything specific. She just kept coming up.

The next day, for instance, instead of wondering if he was making the right decision about Isa, instead of worrying about whether he was being an idiot, he asked himself why, *why* would Yuli be with Dmitry? She couldn't share his amorality, she couldn't. Something about her eyes, the empathetic breadth and expertise of that smile — she was the opposite of the unscrupulous conquistador that was her husband. She had made a youthful mistake. That was the only conclusion he could come to.

He was still sane enough to ask the mirror why he was torturing himself. What possible good could it do him? Was he actually wishing his friend dead or in prison? What kind of nasty creep would do that? Not him, he said to himself, not him.

Still, Yuli couldn't be happy, sequestered in that apartment with her sons all the time. She was a banker. She was a professional woman. She must want a wider field to play than the little domestic cage she was in. True, she seemed happy enough, but that may have been social skill, another instance of her interpersonal adeptness, whatever private demons she might be facing. Such a shame. He wasn't sure he could really help her, but he wanted to try.

He'd think all that, and then think: what is wrong with you, you stupid, stupid, delusional putz? Save yourself, numbskull!

Back and forth, back and forth.

Dmitry was in trouble, that seemed irrefutable, but he had invited it into his life, endangering his own wife and kids. At eighteen he was already a Connecticut pimp and an insurance scammer, almost a murderer. His undergraduate banana republic presidency and his fraudulent LSE imposture were all part of the making of a sociopath, the essence of his coming of age. His Asian deals were without a doubt criminal, his dizzying making and losing of fortunes greased by assorted flimflams: how else does a guy make a small fortune, lose it, make a grotesquely large second fortune, lose it again, and then make an even more vast, vulgar, and meretricious one, all by the time he was thirty-one, and do it legally? Frank kept running over their conversations, thinking about the bank in Tokyo, about how ghoulish it was that there was a deposit box somewhere in his name, with what, millions of dollars in it? If Dmitry was in trouble, it had to be either the police after him or whatever horrid criminals he had been consorting with, or both. If there were criminals involved, he kept thinking, were Yuli and the boys safe?

A couple times a day he'd ask himself, *Why are you so obsessed about this?* as if he didn't know.

Meanwhile his actual life lurched precipitously along its wobbly track. Isa moved back east, amidst great, mutual sobbing and abject expressions of regret. They divided up the spoils of their five years, wept bitter tears, and Frank, at intervals as regular as Muslim prayers, called down silent imprecations on Herbie's head, and his own.

And then, bizarrely, Dmitry showed up. Frank got a call one morning with a Las Vegas area code.

"Good morning, Franky!" he said all bright and cheery.

"You're here."

"No, Franky, that's an illusion created by our modern communications system, which allows me to speak to you from a great distance and sound like I am standing right next to you; this marvelous invention is called, euphoniously, telephony. I am not there, I'm in Las Vegas, Nevada." His accent added an R to the end of Nevada.

"Are you coming to LA? Family with you?"

"No, Franky, you sly dog!" Was he that transparent? "I'm alone, training at a dojo here for the last month, getting ready for the world championships next week."

"Sly dog?" he said. "World championships?"

"No comment and yes, Brazilian Jiu-Jitsu Championships, Franky. I will be competing in a number of different categories. They are in a town called Fullerton, California, do you know where that is?"

"Yeah, twenty or thirty miles from here. Close."

"Excellent, Franky. I was hoping you would be my videographer for the event. I've brought a camera."

One thing that had surprised Frank was how solicitous Isa's single girlfriends turned out to be once she was gone. Were they spies, or was it some kind of rubbernecking at the roadkilled relationship? Or — and this is the depressing realization he was leaning toward — was the near-illicit thrill of fucking your friend's ex the allure? However bad he had felt before about his night with Matty, or his bizarre fixation on Yuli, he had to admit it seemed all the more grotesque seen from the other side. It was impossible for him to even think about any of them romantically. He feared he had just made the most harrowing blunder of his life, that he had doomed himself to a life of grievous loneliness and remorse by letting her go, that no one, no one would ever love him again with her care and enthusiasm and intelligence. He knew — he knew, blah, blah, blah — it sickened even him to hear himself, knowing full well that it was entirely his own fault and that it's the same pathetic shit everyone says when they ruin a relationship. But that didn't make it any less true.

And then, always, offstage, left and right, still, Yuli.

One of the girlfriends, Kristine, had wheedled him into going to the farmer's market with her on the Saturday morning of Dmitry's event, supposedly for his own good. Since he didn't really want to do it, he was glad to cancel. He called and explained that a friend had unexpectedly shown up in town from Asia, and was only here briefly, so he'd have to reschedule.

"Is it that Dmitry?" she asked.

"Yeah," he said, nonplussed.

"Man, Isa hated him," she said.

Why do people save up things to tell you after you break off a relationship? What is that about?

"I know," he said. "Well, maybe not hated."

"Yeah, hated," she said. "She said you turned into a dick every time you spent time with him."

"Gee," he said. "I'm sorry we won't be spending the morning together, Kristine. You could tell me about all the other ways I'm a dick." He hoped it sounded like banter.

"It would take more than a morning," she said.

The odd thing is that he really did think she wanted to give a romantic relationship a try with him. And he did think it would take her more than a morning for her to tell him what a dick she thought he was. People are odd.

The competition was in a mammoth gym on the CalState Fullerton campus, with thousands of contestants and fans and staff milling about, thirty rows of bleachers up either side. "The thing about Brazilian jiu-jitsu," Dmitry said, as he signed in for the day's matches at the entrance, "is that there is no striking. You can throw, but the majority of the fight is grappling, groundwork, we call it. My doctor convinced me that blows to my head weren't the best idea, and it turns out I'm marginally better at this, too." He was as keyed up as Frank had ever seen him. "I've been winning quite a few matches. In fact, I have yet to lose. After twelve Federation fights I'm undefeated, including the two here yesterday. That's the International Brazilian Jiu-Jitsu Federation, Franky, *don't accept substitutes*."

The championships had started on Friday afternoon, but one of Frank's few remaining security projects, in Mandeville Heights, needed his attention for the usual reason — the customer was trying to play contractor and screwing everything up. When Frank arrived Saturday, everyone seemed to know Dmitry, some because they trained at his Las Vegas dojo, some from other competitions, some he had met the day before. Matches were starting in the many rings, the men in the traditional keikogi, the broadcloth pajamas and belt that are regulation attire, circling each other or wrestling, a referee hovering and giving points, judges and coaches and photographers and entourages along the edges of the mat. Spectators would occasionally burst into cheers or shrieks in different corners of the stadium. A dozen matches were underway simultaneously. They found the mat where Dmitry's next match was to be and set Frank up with his camera and tripod in some bleachers above it.

Dmitry went down to warm up, and Frank watched the bizarre collection of humanity that had gathered for this event. Old friends and new friends and competitors met with a lot of hand-clasped thug-hugging and bowing. Some of the fighters were obviously big stars in this firmament, and as they cruised through the crowd, people made a point of greeting them, striking up conversations with various looks of awe and reverence on their faces. Dmitry, whatever his status before this, had upset a famous fighter from Brazil the day before, and was a bona fide international celebrity. Frank followed his progress for a while with the camera, zooming in to see people's expressions. The more he watched these men and boys, the more it felt familiar, this mostly-male social dynamic. He had seen it somewhere before, and it took him a while to remember where: a documentary about neo-Nazi groups. Not that these were racists or fascists, though there were a disturbing number of skinheads. In the film, many of the neo-Nazi leaders and followers were quite obviously closeted and conflicted, and toward the end of the film Ewald Althans, the "New Fuhrer" as he was called by some, the thirty-year-old Aryan hunk who had been elected as the head of some international organization, was arrested by police in Germany for soliciting sex from a policeman in a public toilet. A number of these men were looking at Dmitry the way the pimply neo-Nazi youth looked at the New Fuhrer, with love and longing, and the whole rigmarole — not least the rolling around on the mats in each other's arms — started to look more and more like sex through other means.

Dmitry wanted the video for two reasons — his sons liked to see his matches, he said, and he used the tapes for training purposes. He could review missed opportunities, see what he was doing wrong. If he ever lost he would be able to know exactly how and why. Frank filmed him warming up, which consisted mostly of the bent-over arm swaying he had seen him do in Taipei, almost like an elephant in a zoo, very OCD, back and forth, back and forth, his arms almost sweeping the ground like two trunks.

His first match was with one of the skinheads, a guy who probably weighed the same as Dmitry but was almost a foot shorter, practically square, with massive shoulders and a neck the size of a football player's thigh. They greeted each other with a bow, listened to the referee's instructions and then, unexpectedly, Dmitry lay down on the mat. His opponent threw up his arms as if to say, what the hell is this? Dmitry waited, and when the man finally approached to wrestle on the ground, he threw his legs up and around the man's neck, locking his ankles behind his head. The man stood up, trying to break the hold, which lifted Dmitry upside down, with only his head and shoulders still on the mat. The man clawed unsuccessfully at the ankles behind his neck while Dmitry was doing something to the man's knee with his elbow. It was the oddest bit of fighting Frank had ever seen, one man standing almost still except for his desperate arms grabbing at the back of his own head, the other upside down in front of him, also virtually immobile. Adding to the oddity was the peculiar calm Dmitry exhibited, more like a man absentmindedly waiting for a bus than someone in the throes of martial struggle. The scorecards had his opponent up two points, and knowing nothing, Frank assumed Dmitry was about to lose — in Olympic wrestling he would have lost already, his shoulders to the mat now for a solid minute and a half. The seconds ticked on and then, presto, it was over, and he was shocked to see Dmitry declared the winner. The loser gave him an almost tearful post-coital hug and Dmitry, accepting congratulations along the way, joined Frank in the stands.

"What was that?"

"Your legs are much, much stronger than any other part of your body, Franky. It's very simple really. He had such a low center of gravity that I would be at a serious disadvantage in any other position, opening myself to a damaging throw. My only chance was on the ground."

"How did you win if he had more points?"

"He tapped out, Franky. He submitted." He said this last with a degree of serious self-satisfaction he didn't often indulge. "If you can't reach the mat to tap out, you tap the other fighter, usually at the point of most pain, in this case his knee, which I was really, really hurting. I looked to see that the ref caught it and let go."

They moved to set up the camera for his second match, taking place across the gym. As Dmitry went down to stretch and warm up again, Frank sat remembering two early childhood memories Dmitry had shared one night, back in the tent in Connecticut. Both occurred in an apartment in London, where he had lived until he was three, before moving into what was now his mother's house in Liverpool. In one memory he was crawling around the apartment while his mother was vacuuming, and he experienced an overpowering desire to lick the gray and chrome, bullet-shaped machine. He chased it on his hands and knees with his tongue out, and when he caught it, a blue arc jumped from the vacuum cleaner to his tongue with a loud snap, throwing him into a fully conscious, complete paralysis for a number of minutes. His mother screamed, the neighbors rushed in, and then he regained feeling in his limbs and toddled away. The second story he remembered more vaguely, but it was a standard poop-on-the-wall story, except that the wall had just been freshly painted that morning by his mother, who in anger banged him on the top of the head with the porcelain potty bowl.

"Perhaps, Franky," he had said, after finishing the two stories. "Perhaps the combination of electroshock at such a tender age and my maternally-administered concussion are the source — and I'm speaking neurophysiologically, Franky, not psychoanalytically — of my severe dysfunction now as I enter adult life." He was being funny; he didn't think he was dysfunctional.

His second jiu-jitsu match was more spectacular. His opponent had a few pounds and a few inches on him, and it seemed to Frank that Dmitry was not as self-assured as he had been. When they went into a clutch the first time, the man swung a great club of a hand and gave Dmitry a blow to the back of the neck as he grabbed it. A gasp went up in the crowd, and many looked at the ref, expecting a disqualification for striking. Dmitry said later he did, too, that the blow dazed him, but the ref let it slide. A few seconds into the match Dmitry was on his back, his opponent's forearm across his windpipe. It looked to be over soon. But Dmitry was very slowly, methodically, working his left leg up between the two bodies. Even with his face turning red, his oxygen cut off, he remained remarkably calm, as if his adrenal glands had simply been snipped off to float harmlessly through his innards. He managed to wheedle his left foot under the other man's chin — this is what he had been angling for, apparently — and slowly peeled the man back, using both arms to brace the piston of his leg, finally prying the guy off altogether. He stood back up, did his elephant sway and coughed, waiting for the man to come in and clinch again, which he did.

This time, as if he had now made an adequate study of his opponent, Dmitry managed to twist him onto the ground, scissors him across the midsection and start pulling the man's arm back, leaning all his weight against it. He had the perfect angle, the man's arm levered across his own leg, pushing the forearm unnaturally backward. As the elbow became visibly hyperextended, the crowd was squirming in reflected pain, but his opponent refused to tap out, vainly trying to untangle Dmitry's ankles with his free hand. The man was enraged, having been so close to victory only to find himself in this mess, thrashing about and searching for an escape.

Dmitry moved the arm further up his thigh, giving him better leverage, and the crowd moaned in unison as they saw the elbow bend grotesquely backward, something that looked even worse when Frank zoomed in on it with the camera. The man was twisting a knuckle of his other hand into some pressure point on Dmitry's ankle. He had an obscene smile on his face, maybe a smile of pain, maybe of some S&M pleasure, as he continued trying to wriggle out of the scissors lock. Dmitry slowly, affectless, like a ladies' maid tightening a corset, maneuvered the man's arm into more and more calamitous angles and pushed and levered it, causing the crowd to again squeal in distress, and then, as if they had all been waiting for it, there was a POP! The entire crowd screamed, Frank too, and the ref jumped in, patted Dmitry off, and called for medics. Dmitry stood up, bending over his now unconscious victim, more out of idle curiosity, it seemed, than empathy.

"It was quite surprising, Franky, wasn't it?" he said later. "I kept thinking, what is wrong with him? Why won't he submit? His elbow's going to pop! And then, sure enough, pop! Very strange." Dmitry was declared the winner of that match and champion of his age and weight class, and he won several matches in unrestricted competition, too.

"It was really important to me, Franky, to win in the Master class, because in a few years I'll be thirty-five and in the Senior class, and since I never know when I will need to retire from the sport, or at least in its public venues…" He broke off and smiled for a second, then resumed his amiable chatter. "The real champions win in the Adult class, but that only goes up to twenty-nine, and I hadn't started yet at that age, so I couldn't have won it, could I, Franky? Not really."

"You said you were in Las Vegas for several weeks, training," he said. "How did you get so much time off?"

"Well, let's sit down over here, Franky, and I'll look at the film of my man's elbow popping once and then I'll catch you up. The fact is I'm retiring a few years earlier than I planned."

They sat back in the bleachers as the circus continued below and Dmitry watched the film with all the detachment of a scientist tagging tranquilized penguins. Then he turned to him and explained that in the few months since Frank had seen him, things had gone exceptionally well.

"I thought they were already going well," Frank said.

"Yes, but a number of things serendipitously converged, Franky, and I have now reached my financial goals. I determined some years ago the capital I needed to give me a certain income — it would be vulgar to say how much — in tax-free bonds, no market fluctuations, absolutely minimal risk, and, well, let's say henceforth that base is secure. Using even the worst projections for my more speculative monies, my children's children's children will be unable to spend it all. I've just taken my last vacation; I'll go back in for a final tour of duty, wrap up all my loose ends and then retire for good in fifteen months, so that, in my Christological year of thirty-three, I will experience my death as investment banker and have an appropriate resurrection as a man of leisure. I've arrived."

"Last we talked, you were in trouble."

"All part of the same process, Franky. You either make money, or you make trouble, or both if you're good, once you get involved in my kind of business. The old saws — *no pain, no gain; no risk, no reward; no gall, no glory…*"

"I've never heard that last one."

"Yes, William Penn, Franky, the inventor of Pennsylvania and penicillin, in a speech before mine own British Parliament: *No pain, no palm; no thorns, no throne; no gall, no glory; no cross, no crown* — but I was saying that all those old saws are correct, they are built into the economic system. And I have, over the years," he made it sound like he was sixty rather than thirty-one, "been risking more and more thorns and gall, and thus, when I win, I've reaped gargantuan palms and crowns, or, in the vernacular, gobs and gobs of money."

"But you were already rich, right?"

"There's rich and there's rich, Franky, you know that. I was never, until quite recently, *Forbes*-list rich."

"And how did you manage this?"

"Oh, Franky, come now, part of the game is knowing not to take risks when there is no corresponding reward, and given the intimate relationship between risk and information, and given your lack of leverage, you can't afford to know how I managed it, and I will never tell you."

"So this was not entirely legal — that's why you were so worried in Taipei."

"Franky, don't be stupid."

He got up, not mad, with the same kind of nonchalance he had popping a man's elbow out of its socket, but clearly finished with that particular conversation. "Why don't we get some noodles? I'm told there's a Japanese place around the corner."

"You sounded so worried, asking me to help take care of your family," Frank said as they left the gym.

Dmitry stopped, peered at him, thought about what he wanted to say. "Franky there is only so much money in the world at any given time, and to get a lot of it, you have to take it away from people. The money I now have used to belong to someone else, and naturally, they would like to have it back, and just as naturally, some of them, at least, would like to see me die a horrible death, but that's just personal. Oh, sure, there's some new money, always, a few percent growth in population, a few percent in productivity, but the same basic principle applies — other people think they should have my pile, not me, and some of them are scheming to get it. Popping elbows from sockets would be, for some of these people, just a kind of *earlybird special*" — it did sound funny in gangsterese — "on their menu of options. And some governments — they are the scariest, most corrupt criminal gangs in the world, Franky — one of them might find a pretext to confiscate a significant portion of my portfolio. The main instruments they use — the legitimate governments, not Russia or the tinpot crazies nationalizing industries — are laws against money laundering. Nonsense, given that governments are the world's largest money launderers, but that's the subject of a more advanced lecture. Let's go get those noodles."

As they walked away from the gym, the young fighters, like extras in a swords-and-sandals epic, bowed and scraped congratulations to Dmitry.

"And having to retire from jiu-jitsu, or at least public bouts? That's because something, someone is after you."

They entered the noodle shop and sat at a table near the front window.

"Ah, you see, Franky, even when I think something has gotten by you it hasn't — you kept a very good poker face when I made that little slip. In a word, yes."

He seemed unconcerned. They both stared out the window of the noodle shop toward the nondescript Southern Californian street. Across the way one of the hundreds of furniture stores that never seemed to have customers sat next to a Thai massage place with a sagging and tattered, faded yellow, decade-old Grand Opening banner.

"And so you may, after all, need me to look after Yuli and the boys."

"Touching, Franky, touching," he said, tranquil, placid, and something else — for a moment Frank felt he might be the next bug under Dmitry's magnifying glass, the next fly whose wings might be pulled, the next jiu-jitsu match.

Dmitry left the next day. Frank's daily routine, in the months that followed, was more or less distressing. His daily life with Isa was gone forever, and it felt like an open wound. Friends started setting him up on proper dates, rather than pretending to see how he was doing, but he still never felt like his heart was in it. Silly though it might be, it felt sad as hell to be a forty-year-old man going on *dates*. The women his age were all astounding, so interesting that he wondered if being interesting was somehow fatal to marriage, because all of them had a marriage or two in their dossiers. They were smart, professional women with open minds and eyes, and he would leave the first jury-rigged dinner party or restaurant meet-up sure that there were real possibilities. A couple of the women thought so, too, but some important psychic catalyst was always missing, some neurotransmitters not doing their job. He would get fond, and when the women were interested and engineered it, they would end up in bed once, or even twice or three times. But things never got airborne. He didn't know if this was a function of age, but nine-tenths of his impressions seemed only to act as recalls of feelings from the past, and perhaps this was true for these women as well, that he was acting as an understudy for some ghost. Nobody at this age was interested in muffled passion, and so they didn't do the thing younger people tend to — panic about not finding someone else, settle for whoever was around, and wait for long-term propinquity to turn into love. Instead, they would just not so much call it quits as slow down and wander away from each other.

Once he was carried away by a young, spunky girl looking for her requisite affair with an older man, a metallic-black-and-blue-haired, neon-eyelinered, acid-tongued barista who had an art "practice" that sometimes did and sometimes didn't involve a band, and another time a way-too-young bespectacled wild poet from his bookstore. He spent a couple weeks with each of them having great get-to-know-you sex, with all the standard charms such times entail, including that he could pretend to be young again and they could play grown-up. The women spent about ten minutes apiece fantasizing about becoming the mistress of the pretty fabulous house and pool in Nichols Canyon he had spruced up, but then they would realize how thorny it would be trying to tell their friends and family about it and about him. They started wondering how boring it would be to actually live some middle-aged, middle-class life. They wandered away, too. He did nothing to discourage the tapering off.

The problem for him, if was going to be honest, was that everyone he met suffered in comparison to his image of Yuli's brilliance. He wasn't so scatterbrained that he confused this by now airbrushed, colorized, rewritten image with the real Yuli — or at least, he knew he was confusing them. Everyone, in their love life, develops some kind of standards, or at least predilections, and his had developed quite strongly in her direction: she was the only one who seemed to fit them.

He worked much less, doing little more than managing clients and overseeing the labor his employees did. He spent part of each morning with his laptop out by the pool, and after the flimsy camouflage of glancing through the *New York Times* and the *Los Angeles Times*, he would read the English-language Asian papers: the *Jakarta Post*, the *Hong Kong Standard*, the *Bangkok Post*, *Taiwan News*, and the *Taipei Times*. He did this more religiously than he checked his industry pages or pretended to be involved in his investments. At night he read biographies of Pol Pot and Ho Chi Minh and Mao and histories of the Long March and the Cultural Revolution, trying to force his way through *Sumanasåntaka*, the sixteenth-century Javanese epic poem, and reading the novels of Pramoedya Ananta Toer, the only Indonesian novelist translated into English he could find on Amazon. He checked BoatQuest.com and the other yacht sales sites every day, always curious about what was in available in Sunda Kelapa harbor, the old sailing-fleet harbor of Jakarta, or in the various marinas around Taipei. He had kind of fallen in love with the Scorpio 72, a seventy-two-foot ketch built in Taiwan with classic, old-fashioned lines and a bowsprit straight off the cover of some book he read as a kid. They went, used Scorpios, for anywhere from a half to three-quarters of a million dollars. He'd whip up an Excel sheet and calculate whether, if he sold the house and the company, he could walk away with enough to buy and outfit the boat, send the kids a house down-payment apiece, and still have enough to live on the water for the rest of his life. He probably could.

It was a Monday when he sat down to his normal breakfast rounds on the computer, looking forward to his newspapers and boat sites and blogs, and the center picture on the *Taipei Times*' homepage made him catch his breath: a photograph of the once-gleaming silver office building that housed Dmitry's Credit Lyonnais office, with a gaping, jagged hole in the middle and what looked like a half dozen missing stories.

Black smoke spilled out of it and rose into the sky.

PART FOUR

2013

He sprang for business class on Lufthansa rather than wait until the next day, and talk about a different world. It left LAX at midnight, and he had a free Manhattan and a Xanax, then wine with a pretty good dinner, then more wine, then a Baileys, ate another Xanax, laid full out and took a drooling nap, then another Baileys, dozed on and off watching a movie, ate some little petit fours, wandered around stoned in the dark, wrote a draft of a probably useless email with everything he might have forgotten to tell his office manager, maybe had another Xanax and Baileys, fell back asleep with a mask on and woke up to breakfast with model airplane glue for a brain. He continued the self-medication with a Bloody Mary. He was either depressed, or nervous, or mentally ill, or all three.

After a couple hours googling around on the laptop at LAX he had put together the basic facts. No one was taking responsibility for the bombing, and the reports were a little vague about what kind of bomb it was, or if it even was a bomb rather than a gas leak or something else. The explosion happened at 11am, give or take a few minutes, and so the building was full. The police identified some fifty bodies, they had parts of as many as another fifty, and estimates were that there might be as many again vaporized by the blast. The *Taipei Times* listed the presumed dead, including Dmitry. A corporate picture of him accompanied the article, since he was the head of the firm, and Frank couldn't help but think he had been within days of his extraordinarily early retirement. They'd take out your whole village to get you, he had said.

The usual suspects — Islamists, Marxists — were cycled through the speculative machinery alongside a series of competing business interests. Murder was a not an entirely uncommon business strategy in that part of the world, and there had been a number of similar bombings in the last few years in Bangkok, suspected to be perpetrated by security companies attempting to discredit their rivals. None of those, though, had been quite so big a blast, none had killed as many people, and none had involved a major foreign corporation. Unless something more plausible came along, he had to assume that whatever trouble Dmitry had got himself into had cost not just his life but that of more than a hundred innocent people. Maybe being so close to retirement was not a coincidence — maybe whoever it was figured it was their last chance. The idea filled him with something like dread, or guilt, like he was somehow responsible, like he should have warned someone.

On the off chance that Dmitry had missed the blast and was hiding, Frank had g-mailed him right away, but got no response. It was the only contact he had, no home phone and his cell was always different — burner phones to avoid roaming charges, he said, but maybe to avoid being tracked? Like a lot of rich people, he was very cheap about little things, and except for business hated to spend money on fancy restaurants, always preferring the taco trucks in LA or the small fast-food shops in Thai Town. The cheap motels. The disposable phones. Like someone on the lam.

How was Frank going to find the family? His one time at their house he had been hungover and driven there by Ralph-Prabam. The home phone and address were unlisted, and he could find no trace on the internet, even on the pay sites that track people down for you. The Credit Lyonnais phones rang and rang, their answering system, he assumed, obliterated. Their Paris office kept him on hold for a half hour before telling him they had no contact information except for the office, now nonexistent. He thought about emailing the parents in Liverpool, halfheartedly searching for email addresses for them, and was relieved not to find any. He probably would have chickened out anyway. If they knew already, they wouldn't want a stranger invading their grief, especially a stranger who harbored theories of their son's own culpability. If they didn't know yet, he wasn't sure he should be the one to tell them. Either that or he was a coward.

A certain logic suggested staying at home, calling the Taipei police, maybe even hiring someone there to help; find some of Dmitry's coworkers and then Yuli through them. Instead, he was flying to a city he hardly knew, to find an apartment without an address, on a mission as ill-defined as conceivable. Maybe he could find the gym where the fight club worked out, or the brothel, where the madam might know something. Many of the other men from the office, he assumed, would be dead, too, but some must have been out or on the road, and the fight club guys all worked elsewhere. Maybe one of them would know where his house was. Maybe not, though, since he didn't seem to have any real, intimate friends — one of the reasons, Frank thought, that Dmitry kept in touch all those years. Frank was the little drawer where he dropped a few home truths, where he put a few private doubts, the box on the top closet shelf for the old pictures too corny to show anyone else.

Frank *would* find Yuli and the boys, though, he had faith. He'd figure out something.

He had a vague memory of the apartment being east or northeast of the office. He spent some time during the long layover in Narita, once he sobered up, looking at satellite maps, identifying probable neighborhoods, places where the trees were thick enough and the commerce contained enough to fit his fragmentary recollections. He imagined hiring a cab, going around for hours and hours and hours finding nothing, going in circles, and to avoid that he rented a car at the airport. As he pulled out of the parking lot he realized what it meant to rely on Chinese signage and had a moment of panic. Some operatic traditional music was on the radio, which was pretty scarifying, and thousands of motorcycles and scooters whizzed in and out of lanes, so the first few minutes were tough. Then he eased into it, and his route was straightforward: Highway 15, the coast road, east, until it curved around to follow the Danshui River to the first bridge; cross the bridge onto the conveniently named Route 2, which winds its way to the Shihlin District, where, with any luck, there would be a transliterated sign or the GPS on his phone would be working properly. On the Google satellite maps and pictures, Shihlin looked like the neighborhood he remembered, verdant, not too crowded, northeast of the center where the charred remains of Dmitry's office probably still smoldered. If he was wrong about Shihlin, he hoped it was at least in the neighborhood of the neighborhood.

Driving along the coast was thrilling, mainland China fifty miles away in the haze, the small whitecaps registering a good twenty-knot breeze, and he imagined how great it would be to sail across. He had another moment of panic, imagining his boat being boarded by the Chinese Coast Guard — he was jittery and paranoid and out of it, still hazy from the pills and booze and flipping his circadian clock. As he hit the bridge over the Danshui, the traffic got thicker. He crawled along and was glad, since going slow gave him plenty of time to check his maps and GPS and keep track of where he was. He got off the highway and headed into Shihlin at TianMu North Road, nicely spelled out on the sign in English, the GPS jumpy and wandering a little, but eventually matching up with where he thought he was. He consciously tried to appreciate the strangeness and odd familiarity of his surroundings and not be too fretful.

Except for a few outsized buildings, and a few more Chinese-styled roofs, it was much like driving around Monterey Park or San Gabriel, the suburbs of Los Angeles — the same mix of Chinese characters on some big plastic signs, other reading things like "Mister Donut." The drivers — except for the kids on motorbikes — were exactly as deliberate as the Asian drivers in LA. He started doing concentric circles, wavering between the feeling that he was recognizing everything and the fear that he was recognizing nothing. He kept being fooled by buildings that were roughly the same shape and size as Dmitry's, having to pull up, get out and look at a couple of them closely to make sure, but none were right. Then he saw the concrete Chinese Culture University, remembered Dmitry pointing it out, saying "This is a place where they teach people to make culture, Franky, you should get one of these in California," and knew he was close.

A few minutes later, boom. Coming around a corner, he saw it, looking very familiar indeed, and in another block there it was, right in front of him, unmistakable up close. What were the chances? Running up the center of the building was a twelve-foot-wide molded concrete frontispiece, a Taiwanese version of a Frank Lloyd Wright version of a Chinese architectural detail. He didn't remember it until he saw it, but when he did, there was no doubt. He pulled over and parked, and for the first time it dawned on him that he had not, in any way, shape, or form, thought past this moment, except for imagining holding her — he had not an inkling what to do or even think about doing except find her and envelope her in his arms. He walked up to the front door and rang the bell, which was surprisingly and happily labeled "Heald."

No reply.

He backed up to see if he could tell anything from the windows, but he wasn't even sure what floor was theirs. Four? Maybe it was four. He rang the bell again, waited, looking around the very quiet neighborhood. A car or two went by, but nobody was walking. He rang a third time, then went back to his rental car. For all he knew, they were out at a memorial service, or maybe she was getting grief counseling, the boys and their nanny sitting in some waiting room as she got instructions about what to say to them. Maybe she was out food shopping with them, except that chances were she didn't do any of her own food shopping. Maybe they were at a lawyer's office, reading Dmitry's will.

A man came out, held the door open as two others were trying to squeeze a large refrigerator on a hand truck out the front door. A panel truck was waiting on the side street. Frank hopped out of the car, ran up, and grabbed the door as they got the fridge out. He nodded at them and smiled. Nobody questioned or even looked directly at the Euro-guy. He walked in, got on the elevator, and hit buttons three through six. When the elevator stopped at the third floor, he looked out, saw that it wasn't right, then the fourth, again not right, and then on the fifth, he recognized the hallway. The large pedestal stand in the middle held an orange-flowered plant, droopy from lack of water. He felt the hairs on his arms rise. Something was not right.

He walked up to the door and knocked, and like in an old noir film, it swung open slightly. He called in and got no response. He toed the door open further. The apartment was empty.

Completely empty. Furniture gone. Nothing but a couple dozen boxes, stacked and waiting to be picked up to the right of the entrance. The pictures and wall hangings were gone, and he had to assume that the refrigerator had just come from here — he checked the kitchen, and the space was empty. Although it was clear no one was home, he called for Yuli, for Prabam, and poked his head into the other rooms. All were empty, with rectangles of dust where furniture had stood.

The movers were probably coming back for the last boxes, he decided, and went into the furthest room to hide in an alcove. He had no idea why. He could just see the front of the truck out the window. One of the men got in the driver's seat. He put it in gear, and Frank moved to get a better view; the other men got in the passenger door, and the van drove off. Maybe it was full, and they would come back for the last boxes.

This had all happened very fast. He was on the verge of concluding that the move had started well ahead of the bombing — they couldn't have packed and emptied the place this fast otherwise. But before he could think it all through, he started to weep.

Something about the emptiness of the place, the finality it represented, flooded him with the irremediable, irrevocable fact of death. The image that came back was of Dmitry, standing in the shell of the house in

Connecticut, surrounded by framing, yelling hello to an old neighbor, a guy who came by every morning they were on the job, riding a slow, decrepit, anomalous horse. He was ninety-three and deaf as a post, but each day he saddled up that horse and rode through the woods from wherever he lived to see how they were doing. As he approached, Dmitry would yell, *Hallooo! How are you this morning!* all sunny, at the top of his lungs. The old man would shout back, in his screechy, cranky, old man's voice, *What?* cupping his ear with his free hand. Dmitry would gamely, enjoying the ritual nature of the exchange, yell again, even louder, *I said 'HallOOoo! How ARE you?!'* The old man would act irritated then, like Dmitry was purposely mumbling, and every single morning he would shriek, *What did you say? SPEAK UP!* sounding more like the Wicked Witch of the West than a man on horseback. And Dmitry, partly for Frank's amusement, partly just to finish the routine, would bellow, red in the face, *I said, 'HALLOOO!'* hands cupped around his mouth, *'HOW!'* blasting, enunciating every word, *'ARRE! YOUUU!!'* and invariably, the old man would finally process it, and squawk back, irritated again, *You don't have to* shout! *I can* hear *you!* They knew the old man was ninety-three because he told them he had gone to his seventy-fifth high school reunion the week before. *Yes*, he said. *It was just me and four old biddies. And they didn't look too long for this world, either!* He would make some comments about the progress on the house, usually disapproving, and then, before leaving, say, *I'll have to bring my dog over here someday. He's a truly great dog, never a better, you'll have to see, you'll love my dog.* Dmitry encouraged him, saying *Yes, please do, we always welcome visits from dogs*, and the man would scream, *What?!*

One day a car came down the path, a beat-up Pinto, maybe the last one on the road, and driving it was the old man. In the back seat was a huge, ancient German Shepherd that he spent quite some time trying to coax from the car. *He really is the most wonderful dog you'll ever know*, the old man said as they walked over to him. *Come on big fella*, he said to his pride and joy, *Come on, buddy boy*, getting more and more agitated that the dog wouldn't get out of the car. The dog groaned and stuck one leg out. *Come on, now, Scrunchy!* the old man kept yelping, and Dmitry and Frank looked at each other. *Great name*, Dmitry said quietly. After much more exasperated coaxing, the dog had set its two front paws on the ground, without lifting his hindquarters off the back seat. The old man kept up his urging, desperate, about to cry, but this seemed the most the dog was prepared to do. *Hey, yeah, no, really — great, great dog*, Dmitry said, *and he doesn't know us from Adam, why would he want to get out of this nice back seat.* He went over to the dog and pet his greasy, dandruffy coat and exclaimed how wonderful he seemed. *A spectacular canine. A noble beast.* Then the poor old thing grunted and moaned its way back into the car, with Dmitry giving an assist, and the old man, muttering about what had possessed the dog to behave like that, got back in the car, too, and without saying goodbye or even acknowledging them, backed down the driveway and went home. Dmitry really was quite kind, in his way. After the man left, he said, again quietly, *Bette Davis*.

Frank wandered around the rest of the empty apartment, much larger and more elaborate than he had remembered, and except for that last batch of boxes, completely cleaned out. His only hope was that whoever came to get these remnants would tell him where Yuli had gone. He worried that he didn't know a single word of Chinese, and wondered whether he should wait in the hall, or outside, or right where he was. It might be hard to explain how he got in the apartment, but it also might be hard to explain why he was hanging around on the street or in the entryway. He had noticed a service set of stairs leading down at the back of the kitchen — he could wait out front and miss them, wait out back and miss them. If he wasn't there for the last shipment of boxes, how could he ever find Yuli? He decided to wait in the room.

His jet lag was catching up with him, and dusk descending. He poked at the sides of the boxes in the vain hope that one might contain bedding of some sort, but they all seemed to be packed with books or papers or something else solid. He used a box to wedge each door open as he went down the back stairs, ran around the building and out to his car, grabbed his suitcase and came back in. He took out some of his clothes and used them as a pillow, lay down on the floor next to the boxes, and in minutes was asleep.

He woke frequently, turning on the hard wood, once pulling an extra shirt on against the night chill, once wandering around in search of a bathroom to pee, each time returning to restless, spasmodic sleep. In the middle of the dark night the light flashed on overhead with a snap, and he looked up to see Dmitry's driver, who was shocked, and further shocked when Frank said his name.

"Prabam!"

"Sir," he said.

"Where are they?"

The moving men were behind him, and Prabam made whatever calculations he needed to before motioning them to come in and take the boxes.

"Mr. Heald is dead, sir. His building exploded."

"Yes, I know, Prabam. Where is Mrs. Heald? And the children?"

"They have gone away, sir."

"Yes, I can see that, but where?"

"I am not at liberty to say, sir."

"But I am an old family friend, Prabam, I'm here to help."

Prabam remained silent, then bowed as the men took the last boxes out and onto the elevator, and, still bowing, backed out of the room.

"Prabam! Don't do this! Are they in trouble? Do they need help?"

"Please, sir, go home, Mr. Franky," was all he said as he backed into the elevator. Frank watched the doors close.

He threw his clothes into his suitcase and ran down the five flights of back stairs. Circling around the building, he saw the men closing up the back of the truck. As they pulled away from the curb, he let it go a block or so before running to his car and beginning to trail them, leaving his lights turned off.

They headed back toward the airport, and once on Route 2 the early-hours lack of traffic made it easy for Frank to let them get a half mile ahead and still follow. The grey sea felt less welcoming to him in the murky dawn. Just before the airport Prabam's crew turned off onto a service road and passed a series of fenced Quonset huts. As they pulled into what he assumed was a freight hangar, he parked a couple hundred yards away, slid down in his seat, and waited. Some fifteen minutes later the van came back, and he ducked further while they passed. As they disappeared in his rearview he drove toward the hangar and pulled up to a gate. A man came up to his window. He rolled it down and pointed at the hangar.

"I'm sorry," Frank said. "We put one wrong box in that hangar. I'm going to go get it."

The guard tried to process what he was saying, gave up, said something in Chinese, motioned him to stay, and went back into his booth. He got on a telephone and after an exchange, motioned Frank to come over.

He got out of the car and walked up to the booth. The guard handed him a telephone.

"Can I help you sir?" said a Chinese man on the phone, in a voice that sounded like it had just been awakened.

"Yes, this is Dmitry Heald," he said with his best impression of a Liverpudlian accent. "My driver dropped off a batch of boxes for shipment a few minutes ago, and one of them shouldn't have been included. I need to go in and get it, but didn't bring my ID." He wished he had started with the accent, and he scanned the guard to see if he noticed the switch. He couldn't tell. The man just looked worried.

The voice on the phone paused for a minute, maybe just catching up with his own translation. Then he told Frank to put the guard back on, and the guard said something in Chinese, hung up, and walked him into the hangar. He recognized the stack of boxes. They and others were being loaded into the cargo hold of a large, shiny new corporate jet, with nine porthole windows on each side. The jet was unmarked except for a sequence of letters and numbers that he assumed were its equivalent of a license plate, P4-AQA, on the engine housing, and a small "Bombardier Global Express" near the nose that looked like it could either be the company that owned the jet or the one that built it. He typed the name and the registration letters into his phone and signaled a foreman over and motioned for his clipboard; all those years bossing people around worked, because the man came over and handed it to him. He saw the same letters and numbers at the top of the sheet, and copied down all the information he could onto his phone, including the large letters CGK, which was the only thing that looked like an airport code, pretending he was checking this against other information he had. He gave the man a job-well-done nod and handed back his clipboard. He feigned searching for a box, grabbed one at random, allowed the man to find it on his list and check it off, and then walked it back to his car. As he turned the key in the ignition he noticed that his hands were both shaking. He drove past the guard, who kept an eye on him as he passed, but really, that was just his job, right? He hit the main airport road and took the exit for rental car return.

The rental clerk went over his paperwork, asked if everything was OK, since Frank had rented for a week and was returning after less than a day, and he said yes, fine, change of plans. He asked her if she knew what CGK stood for. She said it was the airport code for Jakarta. He took the shuttle bus to the terminal, toting his bag and the pilfered box, and looked at the big board. The next flight for Jakarta was on China Airlines in four hours. He went to their site on his phone and bought a one-way ticket.

He checked his bag and took the box to a restaurant — he hadn't eaten since he got off the plane the day before. He set the box on the chair next to his and opened it, and as he suspected, it was full of files. Most seemed to be records of random financial transactions, none of which meant anything to him. He was aching, tired, dirty, and woozy from traveling and sleeping on the floor, but buzzing with suspense, feeling like he'd been dropped into a spy movie. Why was Prabam moving boxes in the middle of the night? Why were boxes of Credit Lyonnais records in Dmitry's apartment? Why was Yuli fleeing to Jakarta? It made sense for her to run to her family after Dmitry's death, but to pack up and move all her belongings in a matter of days? And why do it under the cover of night? Obviously she was scared. Obviously she needed help. Then, in one folder, feeling a rush of good fortune, he found a number of documents with the name Yuli Serang, which he assumed was her maiden name, and that gave him greater hope of finding her family's compound in Jakarta, the one with the sloping white walls and swords over the mantelpiece.

He used his phone to google things, since he had clumsily left his laptop in his checked bag, and the internet was so slow he kept dozing off in his chair waiting for the next page to load, awakening with a panicked start, afraid he had missed his flight. The Bombardier Global Express was a brand of jet. They sold for around sixty million dollars, could go around the world with only one refueling stop at a maximum speed of 600 mph.

The jet would clearly be in Jakarta before he would.

Then it hit him: she may have been on the plane. He may have been standing within a few yards of her. He imagined a bedroom in the back of the plane, a large bed.

What an idiot. Maybe she was on her way now, and if he had just waited…

But maybe not, maybe this was a follow-up flight, maybe she'd been gone for days, weeks, months. He knew nothing. He was deeply, deeply tired.

The flight was longer than he expected, a little over five hours, and he slept the horrible old sleep of the economy seat, his head snapping to every fifteen minutes — one trip on business class and he was ruined. He had booked a room at the Ritz Carlton over the phone before getting on the plane, something he wouldn't normally splurge on, maybe because he yearned for a good shower and good bed so badly he couldn't take any chances, maybe because the $478 a night seemed like a bargain compared to a sixty-million-dollar private jet, maybe — well, whatever the reason, he also had them send a car. After immigration he skipped the baggage carousel and let the Ritz's driver show him to the car and go back to grab his bag. He sprawled across the back seat and fell asleep until he was at the hotel. It was appropriately ritzy. He was shown to his room, tipped the guy a couple of American dollars, and stepped into the shower. He looked briefly out his window at the city's seemingly endless array of new and unfinished glass buildings, many adorned with Dubai-like sails and curves, dozens of them brightly lit top to bottom — another Asian powerhouse city, sprinkled with fifty-story cranes and rigid concrete accordions waiting for their fascia. Many stories up in the air but still many below him, the Ritz's impressive rooftop pools and gardens looked like something out of *Metropolis*. A stark, five-hundred-foot monumental tower stuck out of a park to the east and an oversized mosque here and there reminded him where he was. He was between worlds.

He had never been so happy to feel clean sheets in his life. He was asleep in seconds. If he dreamt he had no recollection of it.

Waking up in the black night, he got out his laptop and googled "Yuli Serang" and "Serang Indonesian minister" and found very little, none of which was helpful. Finally "Serang obituary" got him there: "Juwono Serang, Undersecretary of the Interior, Dies." It was dated May 2009, and noted that he was survived by his wife and three daughters, Amarya Serang, Lastri Serang, and Yuli Heald. Why hadn't he thought to google "Yuli Heald"? He tried that and the sisters' names.

Yuli and Lastri had various job-related notices, but nothing turned up an address.

He would go to the Ministry of the Interior. He found a website and an address and started getting dressed. It was the middle of the night. He would have to wait. He fell back asleep for a couple more hours.

He hit the dining room as they opened the doors at 6am, ate, went back to his room, brushed his teeth, called for a cab, and set out for the Ministry. The traffic was light — a family of five going by on a motorbike, trucks making early-morning deliveries, the buses running only one-quarter full. He saw a couple groups of dirty kids that seemed to be waking up on the street, and as he moved through the city, its contemporary mall-face would pull back here and there to reveal the garbage-strewn canals and narrow alleys, the corrugated tin patchworks of the shanty town within. An additional hundred cars, motorcycles, bicycle-rickshaws, moto-rickshaws, trucks, and taxis were thrown into the street every couple minutes, and the daily gridlock was about to take hold, the grey haze of untreated exhaust starting to colonize the air.

No one was at the Ministry except a couple of soldiers in an exterior guardhouse, but it was still before seven. He sat on a concrete bench and watched a flock of schoolchildren walk by, all in white long pants and white smocks, the girls with crochet-trimmed *jilbabs* covering their foreheads, the bottom half tucked under their chins like a Dominican nun's habit. The majority of women wore a headscarf, some old-fashioned, like the schoolgirls, some updated, almost Grace Kellyish, looking like TV stars or Muslim fashionistas, with here and there an uncovered woman in a suit — businesswomen, he guessed. A few of the lower-class men wore a sari, or whatever they called the skirt, but most of the men walking by, in that part of town at least, were in jeans or khakis or business suits. This was not a boisterous people, and the pedestrians made no notice of each other or of the foreigner watching them, eyes to the ground in front of them for the most part, intent on their various morning missions.

Twenty minutes into his vigil, a man approached the front of the Ministry. The guards recognized him and nodded, one of them hopping up to unlock the door. Frank ran towards them, making the guard put his second hand on his rifle.

"Excuse me, sir?" Frank said. The man at the door was in his sixties, probably had been a colleague of Yuli's father. He had a sizable paunch and deep purple bags under his eyes.

"Yes?"

"I'm sorry to bother you," he said, and the man nodded, agreeing that Frank was bothering him. "I am a friend of the Serang family. His daughter —"

"That old son of a bitch."

Frank wasn't expecting that.

"If you say so, sir, I never met him —"

"I thought you said you were a friend of the family." This was not a guy to let you finish a sentence.

"A friend of his daughter's."

The man had been inching into the building, waiting for the least excuse to close the door, but now he stopped and gave Frank the hairy eyeball.

"Which one?" he asked suspiciously.

"Amarya," Frank blurted out, maybe out of some protective instinct.

The man lost interest again, but before letting the door close between them, gave him one last chance: "What do you want?"

"The address. The family house."

"I don't know!" he fairly shouted. "Out the Pangang road." And with that he was gone, the door solidly closing.

Frank debated whether to wait and sandbag someone else, but he was too edgy. At a taxi stand, with the help of a few other drivers, eventually he made it clear he wanted to start down the Pangang Road — a little like asking a cab to take you to Sunset Boulevard or Broadway, because it went on for miles. He regretted not renting a car again as they wound out of the city center, down streets lined by painted white-and-black-striped curbs, meticulous workers in blue coveralls sweeping them clean. The parade of modern high-rises was punctuated by wooden gingerbread colonial buildings, stretches of unreclaimed freelance bricolage, homemade buildings with hand-painted signs, fruit vendors and food stands on the sidewalks. Occasional fortified estates were surrounded by concrete fences topped by coils of razor wire.

And then, twenty minutes out of the city, eight-foot-high, white-plastered walls came into view as the road curved, and somehow Frank knew this was it. The walls seemed so familiar he felt he had been there before. He had the cabbie pull over and, from his window, asked a gardener tending to some shrubbery along the road, "Serang?" The man nodded yes. His nod might mean he had no idea what he was being asked, but the walls did slope and Frank got out and let the cab go.

He decided, out of some misplaced sense of manners, that he couldn't ring the doorbell until at least nine, and so wandered the neighborhood. A block away a teashop had outdoor seating, and in the early morning, the temperature only in the low eighties, he sat facing his quarry, sipping a cup of coffee. A line of trees rose behind the tall walls, and the house, set back in the lot, could only be seen in tiny patches. It was huge. It didn't look like the kind of place you bought on an undersecretary's salary, so perhaps Serang and Dmitry had a lot in common. He imagined Dmitry standing outside the wall, shouting *But I LUV her!* to the heavens. Probably he did love her. Aside from that story, though, Frank had never seen any particular indication of it.

At a few minutes before nine, the front gate opened, and a car came out, a big black Mercedes. He started walking toward it and saw that an Indonesian driver, not Prabam, was in front, and in back a young woman. His adrenals had already released a flood of hormones before he could see that it wasn't Yuli at all, but in all probability one of her sisters. The sister didn't look up, although the driver couldn't help but notice his interest — a frenzied, poorly shaven white man didn't peer into his car every morning. Frank decided it was time to ring the bell, before anyone else left.

He walked up to small guardhouse flush with the front gate. A man in a blue uniform greeted him.

"*Selamat pagi*," the man said, looking confused.

Frank didn't even have the wherewithal to repeat it.

"Hello," he said. Was that the best he could do? The guard looked blankly at him through the booth window. Inside there was a surveillance station, four screens, each apparently hooked to three or four cameras, switching every one and a half or two seconds. It was a big property.

"Do you speak English?"

"*Saya tidak mengerti*," he said, whatever that meant. He reached for a phone, said something else in Indonesian, then handed Frank the phone.

"Hello?"

"Can I help you?"

"Yes, I am here to see Yuli."

"I'm afraid Mrs. Heald lives overseas. I'm sorry."

His disappointment was a punch in the gut.

"Can I speak to Ms. Serang?" He figured that would cover the mother, the other sister.

"May I say who is calling?"

"My name is Frank Baltimore. I've come from Los Angeles." It was possible, he thought, that Dmitry had mentioned him. There was silence for a moment. Probably not. Probably he was never mentioned. Why would he be?

"I'm afraid Mrs. Serang is not available."

"I am a very close friend of Dmitry Heald's, and I came across from America as soon as I heard of the tragedy. It seems somewhat rude," and as he said this he started to get a bit hot, "to keep me outside the gate speaking to the butler, if that's what you are, through an intercom

— I might expect this from the prime minister's office, or the police, but not from the family servants of a friend." He didn't know where that little reserve of *noblesse petulance* came from, but he was kind of impressed by it, and he hoped the butler was. From his "One moment, sir," it was hard to tell.

After ten seconds of silence, long enough for him to notice that none of the security cameras ever lit on an actual person, the grounds completely empty, the butler came back on and said, much less aggressively, "If you don't mind, sir, please hand the phone back to the guard." The guard took the phone, listened to his boss, hung up, a buzz sounded, and the gate sprung open.

Frank walked down a red flagged pathway surrounded by large, foot-wide shiny green leaves, trumpet vines overhead supported by a trellis, pink and red hibiscus, and a frenzy of yellow and white frangipani flowers. The tunnel of lush vegetation dropped the temperature ten degrees, making it more like a miniature, manicured rainforest, or an exhibit in a botanical garden, than a pathway to a private home. The city's noise immediately sounded miles away. The impressive nineteenth-century house rose up in all directions. He reached the front door, which opened just as he arrived, the butler bowing him in.

"Please, sir," he said, his outstretched palm up and away, motioning toward a large sitting room to the left. The entryway was at least two stories high, with a tessellated floor, massive columns fifteen or so feet apart, and tapestries on the walls. It looked like an ad for an expensive hotel in the Algarve.

He motioned Frank to sit. The relation of servants and masters was something he had very little knowledge of, but he recognized that the power in this relationship was not his. He sat.

"Can I get you anything, sir?"

"No, thank you."

The butler bowed, withdrew, and Frank looked around. Over the mantle of a white fireplace the two cutlasses — or what did he call them, scimitars? — were crossed. Frank wasn't sure if the wave of nostalgia he felt was about Dmitry, or simply about the merciless passing of time. He sat wishing that Yuli's sister hadn't left, or hoping that the other was still home. He had no idea if he would be able to talk to the mother, or if she was even alive. The room was elegant but straightjacketed, and he remembered Dmitry calling it Buckingham Palace. It wasn't quite that grand, but was more like a museum than a place to live, the Louis the This or Louis the That chairs more like sculpture than furniture. He moved onto a couch that was modestly more comfortable. Freshly cut flowers adorned as many surfaces as one would expect at a mortuary and tchotchkes filled any leftover horizontal space. The scimitars looked to have been polished five minutes ago. He wanted to walk over and see if one had been welded back together.

The house was as silent as only an old double-walled house can be, the masonry deflecting the outside noise, the internal wood framing and plaster soaking up anything from the inside. Thick wooden doors kept sound from traveling between rooms, upholstery, heavy drapes, thick rugs, tapestries — the place was almost engineered for sound absorption. Maybe that's why he didn't hear her enter.

"Franky." It was Yuli, standing in the doorway. She had somehow reminded him, the day they met, of Jackie Kennedy, and now she did again, stoic, appropriately grim, slightly shaken yet composed. She wore a simple white t-shirt, jeans, and heeled sandals, perched somewhere exactly between vulnerable and invincible, innocent and world-weary, ethereal and solid, unconscious and hyperconscious, exotic and familiar, elusive and straightforward. Again, he stopped himself, thinking: *what the hell is wrong with me?*

"Yuli," he finally got out.

"It was good of you to come." It was all he could do to stop himself from rushing and taking her in his arms like the fool he was.

"I'm in shock," he said. "How are you holding up?"

"Some moments better than others," she said, with a sad smile. "It is so strange to speak to you now, after only knowing you through Dmitry all these years. We didn't get a chance to talk when you visited in Taipei, but Dmitry talked of you so often I feel I know you."

"And the boys?" He was stupidly overjoyed that she remembered meeting him.

"They are safe."

"Yes…" he said, slightly puzzled by that response. But then it dawned on him: they *did* need his protection, it hadn't all been wish-fulfillment fantasy. She motioned to two chairs, facing each other, and as they sat down his hesitancy made her meet his eyes — he could see she wasn't sure how much to confide.

"They are with their nannies and the rest of the Taipei staff at one of our houses, on an island. Very few people know of it."

"He said he wanted an island," he said. "And a jet."

"Yes," she said solemnly, "and he got both." She didn't have to add that the price had been too high.

"I want to do anything I can," he said, feeling awkward, knowing his sincerity was disingenuous, his motives duplicitous, his position false: he was a love-sick wolf in a sheep suit, and every attempt to contain himself inflamed him more. Berating himself for being a snake, he gazed upon her ankles. He wasn't even able, as discombobulated as he had become, to hide it, and all but unconsciously leaned toward her. He felt like an imbecile.

She gazed at the floor, her perfect hands folded on her perfect lap.

"I'm sorry, Yuli, I truly am. Please excuse my too-full heart." Christ, where was this stilted language coming from? Had he lost his mind? "I don't know what to say."

"Forgive you? Please, Franky. We have both loved Dmitry. This puts us in a very tiny club, perhaps a club of two, or four counting the boys. He was never, for most people, an easy person to love. Most people preferred to judge him, or despise him, or envy him, or all of these."

Her saying this impressed him; it seemed even wise; it made him love her more. It also snapped him from his trance, made him conjure Dmitry. He sat back, knowing finally that if Yuli needed him, she needed him to be neither a bonehead nor a child. And since it was an adult she needed, he decided he should try to act like one. "What can I do to help?"

"Help?"

"Well, do you need to talk about arrangements, or legal issues? Can I help with logistics, money, arrangements, insurance, pick up the laundry?"

"You are so kind," she said, smiling, reaching across the coffee table to put a hand on his knee, turning his entire body into a hormonal free-fire zone. "I mean it, Franky, very kind. But I worked in arbitrage. I have a degree in economics and an MBA. And servants! We can handle all of that — but I can't tell you how wonderful it is to have you here, someone who not only has known Dmitry but has always really understood him." She smiled again as she said this, warmly.

"I wonder," he said, "if I really did."

She looked at him then with what seemed like added respect. "Yes, well, that is what I mean. To know him included wondering whether you did. But *he* always felt you did." She stood up, and he followed suit. The butler immediately opened the door. "Have a drink, Franky, won't you, so I can? I realize it is the morning, but there is some acceptable option, isn't there? Something that wouldn't be too pathetic: a mimosa or Bloody Mary?"

"I would love either."

"We'll have Bloody Marys on the terrace, Setiawan, with a light brunch."

"*Ya, Ibu Yuli*," he said, starting to leave.

"English, please, while Mr. Franky is here," she said.

"My apologies, sir," he said, scowling.

She stood up and held her hand out to him to come, and as he walked toward her she took his left arm in her right. His chest swelled with the momentary coupling, and as he felt her firm, tender warmth against his side he thought, *I have arrived, however briefly, home, home, home.* She walked him out large French doors to a tiled terrace, roofed by trellised vines, a mister around the edges keeping it cool. The house might have been some British tea baron's place in the 1870s, enormous teak beams providing the skeleton, the exterior with a lot of wood — painted clapboard siding, jigsawed trim along the soffits and eaves, oversized gingerbread giving it, from a distance, the appearance of a colonial building half its size, like an exploded, inverse scale model. The interior was all stately columns and arches, smooth plaster and colonnades, with the wide, sweeping staircases of a presidential palace or an Astaire-Rogers movie set. A lot of man-hours. A lot of square feet. A lot of foot-wide, elaborate molding.

"Please tell me you will stay with us," she said, "at least for a few days. I can send the driver to get your things, if that doesn't feel too intrusive. Where are you?"

"The Ritz-Carlton. I would love to. But won't you be going to join your boys?"

She hugged his arm tighter, and leaned her head, very lightly, against his shoulder. "For right now, I think, it would be... well," and she hesitated. "It would be better for me to take care of things here." He assumed she was about to say it would be safer, not better.

They had Bloody Marys and tumpeng, a cone of rice surrounded by piles of savory curry stuffs that were as hard to identify as they were fabulous. They spoke very briefly and tentatively about the bombing, which she clearly didn't want to discuss. There still was no official word of any kind about who was responsible, nothing. She asked about Frank's life, his work. He prattled on, aglow in her attention.

"How did you think to come here?" she asked, then. "And how did you find us?"

"I followed Prabam to the airport," he said. "And took one of the boxes."

"Ah!" she said, "the solution to the mystery of the missing box."

Huh. She knew about that. "In it I found your name. Googling you I found your father, his obituary, actually, where you were mentioned, and then, this morning I went to the Ministry, and got a rough address, well the neighborhood, at least."

"Ah! A detective," she said, and this was either mocking or concerned or neither. "Who did you speak to at the Ministry?"

"I didn't get his name, but he wasn't a fan of your father's, it seemed. He looked like a morbidly obese lemur." She smiled at this, but not happily. "For some reason, I don't even know why, I said I was a friend of Amarya's."

This seemed to relax her. He would try to figure out why later.

"Amarya? How could you possibly know about Amarya?"

"She was mentioned in the obituary. And I remember Dmitry telling me she was your messenger during your courtship."

"Courtship!" she said, now truly smiling. "My imprisonment, you mean!"

Two maids had been serving them, but now the butler reappeared at the door without saying anything. "Excuse me a moment," she said, "and let me take this call." She left the room, and he sat wondering about life with servants, communication so well-oiled that you can know you have a call without being told. He also wondered about his own state of mind, realizing that he was unaccountably, inappropriately, and quite contentedly happy. The Bloody Mary was warm in his blood. When she returned they talked for another half hour or so, she socially skillful enough to avoid and deflect anything difficult. She talked about the work she had done before the children, in renewable energy finance, which she still dabbled in, kept up. He talked to her about solar heat and hot water, heat pumps, insulation, absorptive surfaces, refractive surfaces, gray water recycling — the home construction end of the ecological equation — and how hard it still was to talk people into doing the right thing.

"It's not just my social conscience, Franky, I hate to admit: when I got in, it was an emerging market, and still is. There is money to be made." He saw her then, the hard-ass businesswoman, the high-flying MBA. It worried him of course, since it reminded him she was really out of his league; if she was going to shop for a new husband, a moderately successful contractor from LA probably wouldn't be where she'd settle. Someone on a museum board or two…

"But in any case, Franky, we are on the same side," she said, and they had one more drink, exulting in their shared interest in ending the horror that was climate change as if nothing else in the world was amiss. Then she stood. Instantly Setiawan appeared.

"Yes, thank you Setiawan, please have Mr. Franky shown to his room." She took Frank's hands in hers and held them to her chest. "I am truly glad you are here."

"Mr. Franky," he said. "Sounds ridiculous."

"It is custom. I am Mrs. Yuli, not just here, but at a state dinner. If you are introduced to the President, it would be as Mr. Franky."

"Mr. Frank, at least, hopefully," he said. She looked at him with a quite shrewd glint in her eye.

"But we have always known you as Franky!" she said, and it wasn't the last time that he wondered if she was privy to every conversation he had ever had.

In his room, his bags had already been delivered, his laptop set up on a desk the way he had left it at the Ritz, everything arranged in the bathroom exactly as he had left it there, toothbrush and toothpaste to the left of the sink, deodorant on the right. He had never actually agreed to this, and while he felt minutely taken care of, such an invasion of his privacy felt alien. It was like discovering people had been reading his diary or watching him sleep. He felt exposed, unsafe. And although everything about his belongings was the same, the two shirts hanging in the closet, his toiletry bag on the sink, his books on the bedside table, two things were missing. His dirty laundry, which he assumed was out being cleaned. And the box of files. It had been reappropriated.

He guessed that was only right. It wasn't his.

The day and evening before, he had slept the sleep of the beat-up air traveler — necessary, desperate, incomplete. But after the Bloody Marys and so much uncertainty resolved, he lay down in the middle of the afternoon and slept in peace for many hours. He woke up in the dark, except for the slight glow from a nightlight in the bathroom, and noticed for the first time that his room, although quite large, had no windows. Wondering if that was a bunker-mentality design decision from colonial times, he ambled into the bathroom where there was a window, and saw that it was indeed night. He had fallen asleep with the light on and wondered: was it on a timer? Or did a servant actually come in and turn it off? Since he had thrown off all of his clothes and just dropped on the bed, he felt exposed again, literally this time.

He rustled his phone out of his pants pocket and saw it was only midnight. The world was upside down.

He turned on his laptop, went back to the bathroom, peed and brushed his teeth, came back and checked for a wireless connection. The wireless system was working, and, he could see, password protected, which meant someone had opened his computer and entered the code. He had that creepy feeling again, like he was living in East Berlin under the Stasi, a disquieting combination of guilt and resentment, or, given all the luxury, like a king waiting for the revolution. He pulled up his email, which held nothing of note, and realized that this was his first trip since Isa left, that for the first time there was no one in the States wondering about his daily being, nobody that cared that he was gone. His quasi-step-kids had their own proto-adult lives, Kennedy with a year to go at University of Iowa, of all places, Lulu a freshman at Mount Holyoke. They both claimed they loved talking to him but could rarely find the time, and of course their interest in him was complicated by the monthly checks he sent. If he went two or even three weeks without calling, they didn't seem to notice. The business in LA was singing along without him. He felt liberated. He was free. It was not altogether pleasant.

He looked at the ceiling and indulged a strong, full-sense memory of exquisite Yuli — he couldn't help it, that was how he always thought of her, *exquisite Yuli* — hugging his arm as they walked through her house. He knew, extremely clearly, that this was what he wanted for the rest of his life. Or at least for as long as humanly possible.

He knew how crazed that was. She was in mourning, and he was a friend of her dead husband. He needed to move slowly, he found himself thinking. Fool! He needed to not move at all, he needed to keep this stupid fantasy life to himself, respect her grief! He needed, he knew, to get a grip.

He sat down at the laptop to tour the Asian papers and could see that the news cycle had started to purge talk of the Taipei bombing, with no new information to be found. He checked on a Scorpio 72 he had bookmarked, berthed outside of Taipei, and saw it was still for sale. Maybe that would be his new home. He'd sell California, start living.

The Serang house was dead silent, which meant nothing. He dropped back in bed, propped up a couple pillows, and flipped on the TV. He maundered through hundreds of satellite channels, marveling at the strangeness of the American content, the peculiar Japanese stuff, the time-warp Eastern European variety shows, the new slickness of Chinese

TV, feeling throughout like a Martian ethnographer cataloging the varieties of human media experience. American shows he had forgotten existed were in syndication: *Simon & Simon, St. Elsewhere, Alf*. He dozed off again and woke up at 2.30am. It was going to be one of those nights.

Should he drink the tap water in the bathroom? He decided to venture out to the kitchen. He threw on the silk robe that was hanging in the closet and opened his door. The hallway had low lights and he felt like a thief as he padded through the carpeted hall and down the stairs. He jumped as he came around the corner and saw Setiawan waiting for him in the foyer, fully dressed.

"Can I help you, sir?"

"I'm sorry, Mr. Setiawan, you startled me. I was looking for some water."

"The tap water is fully filtered, sir, but I can fill an ice bucket for you if you'd like."

"Thank you, that would be great." He had no real desire for ice, but it felt better than slinking back to his room empty-handed.

"I will have it sent up to your room straightaway, sir." Frank got the distinct feeling that he was being told to go back to bed like a child.

"OK, thank you, Setiawan," he said, as if reasserting his position by not calling him 'Mister.'

Just then a soft bell tone sounded and Setiawan looked slightly nervous.

"Good night, then, sir," he said, staring at Frank, ignoring the bell, clearly waiting for him to leave. Frank started back up the grand staircase and Setiawan went to the front door and waited another few seconds for Frank, who had purposely slowed down, to get up the stairs. The bell went off again and Setiawan gave up and opened the door.

"*Selamat jalan, Nona Amarya,*" he said, as a young woman entered. Amarya, the younger sister, Dmitry's early confederate.

"Wait!" she said, ignoring him, "Is that Franky at the top of the stairs?" She came bounding up the stairway. "I heard you were here!"

She was not the girl he saw leaving in the morning. She was a spitting image of her sister Yuli, some years younger, not much past twenty, and, it seemed as she darted up the stairs, a little drunk or high or both.

"Amarya," Frank said. "Forgive me, I'm not exactly dressed," suddenly extremely self-conscious in his thin robe and bare feet.

"He knows my name!" she trilled. "How adorable!" She came to the top of the stairs, grabbed his right hand with her left, and started dragging him back down. "Come down and have a drink and let me get a better look at you!" she said. She stopped suddenly halfway down so that he bumped into her. She fell back into his arms, and pronounced, almost in his chest: "They didn't tell me you were cute!"

OK.

"I'm cute, too," she added, turning and heading down the rest of the stairs. True enough. "Dmitry talked about you so often!" she added. That surprised him.

He was torn between letting himself be pulled wherever she wanted and going back and putting on some clothes. As he saw Setiawan's disapproving face his embarrassment won. "Let me throw some clothes on, at least," he said.

"Nonsense, Franky!" she said. "You're practically family, and I'm hardly dressed myself!" She was gotten up, it was true, for a night on the town, in a very sheer club dress, cut low and high and clinging to everything else. She saw him notice and laughed. "You see what I mean! It's *outrageous*, isn't it? Us young girls these days!" She laughed again and turned to Setiawan. "Have a tray of drinks sent into the parlor, will you, Setiawan?" she said. "And don't be a sourpuss — that will be all for the night." To Frank she said, "It will just be the basics: gin, whiskey, soda, ice, is that OK?"

"Yes, of course," he said. Setiawan bowed, frowning, and left.

"I *swear* he is something out of *Dickens*," she said. "Sit down!" She gave him a slight push onto a sofa and plopped down next to him, revealing a — whoa! — yes, outrageous stretch of inner thigh. She again noticed his glance and laughed. "I see that you and Dmitry were kindred spirits," she said.

Then, with an abrupt emotional reversal, she threw herself into his chest, weeping, moaning in grief. "It is so, so, so, horrible!" she said, quietly. He was conscious of being in nothing but what amounted to a silk scarf with sleeves, conscious of her superb form in even less, conscious of her vulnerable state, conscious of it being the middle of the night, conscious of his own increasing arousal. What a monster! A maid entered with the tray of drinks, as if Setiawan was too disgusted to see them again, while Amarya stayed cuddled against his silk-robed chest, his arms having somewhat automatically encircled her. The maid didn't look at them directly as she set the tray down, but he still felt more awkward than he thought it possible to feel. Amarya took no notice of the maid, and he wondered whether she had passed out. For some perverse reason, that increased his state of arousal. The only thing that could have added to his consternation would be if Yuli walked in.

He needed to stand up and get out of there, but as he tried sliding out from under her, she turned over, squirming farther onto his lap, and threw her legs out across the sofa, kicking off her heels, leaving at most an inch of silk covering whatever she might be wearing under her skirt. And that showed him he was wrong, there was something that could add to his consternation. As she squirmed getting comfortable, his now-engorged penis throbbed against her back like an obnoxiously loud knocking at the door. In his defense, it had been quite a long time since he had had sex, and he did, immediately, try to extricate himself and stand up. She put a finger up to his lips, in the international signal for "don't say a word," rolled toward him again, and threw her arms around his waist.

"Please don't leave me," she said.

He now felt her breast hard against his thigh, his erection cupped in her armpit, and her latest squirm had left the thin line of a thong across her hip exposed. It was too damn much.

He lifted her off, stood up, tried to straighten his robe, and as discreetly as possible, which wasn't saying much, used the robe's belt to minimize his comic outline, strapping his hard-on against his stomach just as Yuli was coming in the door.

"You've met," she said, without the slightest trace of disapproval, even amused, walking up to them, putting a hand on his arm. Frank wondered if Setiawan had summoned her. "You could at least have allowed him to dress!" she said to Amarya, but again with a light tone, almost teasing, and full of kindness. "These days of adjustment after that flight, sleeping at the oddest hours, they are so difficult," she said to him. Amarya had gotten up and gone to Yuli, hugged her, and remained with her arms around her, her face resting on her sister's perfect shoulder. "And Amarya, the dear," she said, "has a very fluid sense of personal boundaries. Your jetlag will be her jetlag."

"Shut up," Amarya said, petulant but playful, the words muffled, as her face was now buried in Yuli's neck. Then she kissed Yuli on the cheek, stood up straight again, turned to Frank with a huge smile, and said, cheerfully, "Let's have that drink!"

The jetlag that hits you going from the US to Asia can be as strong as psilocybin, throwing you into several days of a fugue state. Amarya passed him a gin and soda, and he floated through the rest of the night, remembering little of the conversation, except that every few minutes he became aware in an awkward flash of his thin robe. Then he would forget everything and bask in the glow of these two magnificent women, or this magnificent woman and magnificent girl.

He drifted through the days and nights that followed as unaware of how he seemed to people as any volunteer subject at a hypnotist's show, compounded by the fact that Amarya began to slip in and out of his room at all hours and in all sorts of undress — he knew that it made him a terrible, terrible person to let her. He had abandoned any notion of his own future, and not just the near future — he had no idea what he would be doing not just in a day, two, three, or a week, but in a year, a decade, two. Yuli and Amarya seemed unconcerned as well, and he supposed this was how the Zen people and sadhus would like us to live, moment by moment, no future, no past, although perhaps they would suggest doing it without servants. The third sister, it turned out, didn't live in Jakarta, but in Bali, where she owned a resort. She had been heading to the airport when Frank saw her. The mother, they explained, had been shuttled off to join her grandsons on the island, and this news gave him one of his few brief jolts of reality. It reminded him that they were in an ongoing state of at least potential siege — why else hide the boys? As Dmitry had warned, some people would be wanting their money back. The only question was whether they knew to look in Jakarta. He should talk to Yuli about those accounts in Tokyo, ask if he should go find them and transfer them.

In the morning, though, just as he came down, a phalanx of police arrived at the door. Amarya was gone, and Yuli looked panic-stricken when Setiawan announced them. Frank suggested he go talk to them alone, but she came with.

"*Selamat pagi, Ibu Yuli,*" the man in charge said.

"May we please speak in English? My friend and counselor," she said, motioning to Frank, "does not speak Bahasa Indonesia." Counselor.

"I wanted to ask same," the man said in English. "I have two colleagues here from Taipei. They do not speak our language also."

"Please, sit down," she said.

Three of the policemen peeled off from the group and followed them into the parlor. These must be the detectives, or the ones who spoke English. The other four stayed by the door.

"My colleagues of Taipei have some questions."

The main detective from Taiwan had a gentle face and bowed. "My condolences, Madam, for your loss."

Yuli nodded but said nothing.

"Perhaps you could explain, Madam, your sudden departure from Taipei after the bombing?"

"So it was a bomb?" Frank said.

"Excuse me, sir, no, I misspoke. We have not made finding yet. But, Madam, you hurry why?"

"It was not sudden," she said, "Only coincidental. We had been planning to move back to Jakarta for some time, were already moving when —"

"I see," said the detective. "And was Mr. Dmitry Heald also moving back to Jakarta?"

"Yes," she said. "He was planning to retire."

"Retire?" the detective said, and flipped through his notebook. "But he is only thirty-five years old!"

"Yes," she said. "But very successful. And thirty-one. His corporate biography added a few years." Not defensive, not boasting, just the fact.

The detective wrote in his notebook. He had not expected this and was stymied, for some reason. His colleague, taller, with tiny eyes and a head of hair that was all cowlicks, stepped into the breach.

"Please excuse my English," he said, and it was pretty atrocious, English sounding like "egg dish." "But where Dmitry Heald?"

At this Yuli threw her hands to her face and started to whimper. Frank stood up, the big hero.

"What kind of thing is that to ask?"

"He is here?" the cowlick asked, undeterred.

"No, he is not here," Frank said. "He is dead!" He managed not to add *you cad!*

"Yes," the first detective said, rallying. "This is one assumption."

"What other is there?"

"He is alive and fugitive." This made Yuli shudder.

"Tactful, aren't we, detective," he said, realizing immediately that sarcasm was tough to get across in such a situation and wondering how much English you have to study before you get to 'tactful.' But then he asked: "Fugitive?"

"He is wanted for questioning, like everyone else who worked in the building and did not die."

Frank couldn't help it. It made him curious. "What makes you think he didn't die?" he asked. Yuli looked up to hear the answer too, red-eyed and wet-faced. Frank couldn't tell if it was also hopeful.

"Please, sir, what is your connection?"

"I am a friend of the family."

"Your name?"

"Frank Baltimore."

"Franky," the detective said, writing in his notebook.

"Frank." Was that a mistake?

"Madam, you know why we come here. No remains are identified. We want to decide what happened. Have you heard from your husband since explosion?"

"No."

"Is something else you can tell me?"

"I can't imagine what," she said.

"We would like search house," the Taiwan cop said to Yuli.

"See here," Frank said, again having that odd sensation he was saying lines someone else had written, and written in the 1940s. "Is that necessary?"

"No, Franky, it's fine. Please," she said to police, holding out her arm in welcome.

The detectives said something in their respective languages to their patrolmen at the door, who then spread into different parts of the house.

"Setiawan," Yuli said, and he miraculously appeared. "Unlock any doors that need unlocking."

"Yes, ma'am."

The detectives asked for a download from the security system and she had Setiawan load it on a drive they provided.

Eventually all four of the other policemen came back empty handed.

"Thank you for time," the Taiwanese detective said.

"We may need to speak with you again," the Indonesian detective said. "I'm sure you want to help discover those responsible. Please let me know if you are leaving the city." All four detectives then awkwardly, in eight handoffs with a lot of crossing of arms, each gave Frank and Yuli one of their cards.

The affair with Amarya — it was hardly that, in a way, since she seemed to take it as lightly as ordering a pizza — convinced him that his obsession with Yuli was something more than infatuation. Even *he* assumed, with part of his brain, that the whole mirage of love was based on the fact that Yuli had the ideal body, was exotically different, too young, and extremely beautiful, but Amarya had and was all of those things as well, and although she was enormously exciting, she didn't move him in the same way at all. His love for Yuli was epic, his desire for Amarya wonderfully, beautifully mundane.

Amarya also was, thank god, a made-to-order safety valve. Every night or morning that she came to his room gave him the strength to get through another day without spilling his guts and making a fool of himself with Yuli. He still had to strain to keep himself from dropping to one knee or both when he was with her, but it also helped that, as he played out various scenarios, the film scripts always went awry, and none of them gave him any succor. Most ended with him on a plane home, tail between his legs, heartbroken and dreamless. He wasn't sure if he was biding his time until he could arrange his perfect future, or simply delaying his inevitable despondency.

One day in the parlor, as the three of them had a cocktail under the withering eye of Setiawan, this time at least at an internationally recognized hour for such things, he took notice of the books in a glass-doored bookcase, and with a shock of recognition realized that a couple shelves were devoted to classic novels, all of which were among his favorites: Brontë's *Wuthering Heights*, Chandler's *The Big Sleep*, Melville's *Typee*, Greene's *The Third Man*, Ellison's *Invisible Man*, O'Connor's *Wise Blood*, James's *The Ambassadors*, some Conrad and Kafka, Library of America volumes of Faulkner, Fitzgerald, Hawthorne, Cather and Wharton. Patricia Highsmith. Some Freud and Nietzsche. And Marx.

"I wondered if you would notice that," Yuli said. "The Baltimore Public Library, he called it."

"It looks like every book I ever mentioned to him."

"He would do a running commentary for us about each book," Yuli said.

"It was infinitely boring," added Amarya.

"I believe it," he said.

"Hardly," said Yuli, and then did a credible Dmitry imitation: "*In marginalia now housed in the Special Collections of the Bodleian Library at Yale University, Yuli*," he would say to me, "*the esteemed Exchequer of the Horseguard and internationally renowned flugelhornist Franky B.* — he often calls you Franky B. and gives you outlandish titles — *noted that Henry James's* Ambassadors *is the first novel to take seriously the modern phenomenon of advertising, and to chart its relation to age-old moral conundrums regarding rumor, sexual deception, and the relativity of cultural value* — Dmitry talks this way, too, sometimes, so maybe these aren't your words? — *while insisting that renunciation of our desires, rather than gratification, was the only way to forestall the inevitable alienation into nothingness* — I'm sorry, I'm losing the voice." But she was quite a good mimic, and they all felt his presence for a moment, her reversion to the present tense — *he talks this way* — heightening it.

"I can tell you, in fact," she added in her own voice, "what you thought about many of these books." There was a challenge in it.

"So could I," Amarya said, rolling her eyes.

"I was never sure if he was listening," he said.

"Not one to miss a trick," Amarya said, with perhaps a hint of bitterness, and not for the first time he concluded that she had slept with him, too.

He fell into silence. He was touched that Dmitry had not only heard these ramblings of his and remembered them, but seemed to have felt they were worth repeating — even if, as was clear from the impersonation, he was being mocked as well. Even if Dmitry was making him out to be a bit of a pedant. A bit of a fool.

One day bled into the next, and he felt, oddly, like they were at an Edith Wharton house party in the country, no one the least concerned with work except the servants, some mild intrigue — a man in love with his friend's widow, dallying with her sister — and thus the tempest in the teacup impending, but also a larger, unnamed tragedy looming. He took to rereading some of those old favorites from the Memorial Library, starting with *The Ambassadors*, and when Strether turns to Little Bilham and tells him to *Live all you can; it's a mistake not to*, he recognized he had to take a chance. He looked up from the book to see Yuli coming in.

"I have been realizing, Franky," she said, as if she had picked up Dmitry's very syntax, "that I don't know how we shall go on without you." She must have seen how this had made him, involuntarily, hang his head, because she added, immediately, "Oh, no! Please don't think that is a hint for you to leave!" The passion with which that came out surprised both of them, it seemed, and he got up, went to her, and stood close. They leaned toward each other until their foreheads were touching, and calmly held each other's hands.

They didn't say a word, but some new understanding had arrived. He didn't know what it was, but it was something.

"You don't like to talk about this," he said. "But Dmitry, I know, was in trouble. I know that some of his dealings were illegal. I know that some of his money came with enemies. And I want to help. I want to make sure that you are safe, that you —"

He paused to see if she was OK.

"No, go on," she said.

"That you and the boys are safe. I think I should go talk to these policemen, that I should find out what they want, what is at stake, who is pushing, and for what reason."

"Please," she said. "Please don't."

He felt, again, the astonishing simplicity of these last days, the deep bath of affection he had been in since he arrived. He wanted to return it. Besides, if she wasn't ready, he had to respect that.

"OK," he said. "Don't worry. You let me know when. I just want to help."

She looked at him with real gratitude.

"He also put some money in an account in Tokyo for you, money in my name. I could run and get that…"

"Not yet," she said. "I have to assume the police are watching us, and I wouldn't want to give them any ideas."

"No," he said.

She knew about the Tokyo account? And what ideas?

He spent a little time each day checking in with the office and his crew chiefs, but they all seemed more than happy to go on without him. He negotiated a couple new deals on the phone. He wasn't needed back home. Was he needed here? Maybe.

Amarya was gone a good part of every day, supposedly going to university, but she never seemed to have books or notebooks or projects due. Yuli had daily rounds that included tennis, the gym, lunch with old school chums, and classes in calligraphy and classic noir cinema, which she admitted she signed up for as a way to stay busy, to take her mind off things, but which she was not much invested in. She sometimes forgot to go, sometimes intentionally played hooky. She was often gone for hours with no explanation, and although she did not want to talk about it, she was, she said, managing her ongoing projects in the energy sector. Both she and Amarya continued to deftly deflect any attempt he made to bring up the future.

Whenever they were both gone, he had taken to snooping around the house, at least in part because discovering Dmitry's bookshelf had made him curious about other nooks and crannies. One day he discovered a stairway to a third floor or attic and went up to see what he could find. Part of it was set up as a living space, with a bed and dresser, and a curtained-off set of bathroom fixtures, he assumed for one of the staff. The rest of it was typical attic storage: boxes, old furnishings, junk. One pile, though, was clearly newer than the rest, and it included the box he had commandeered and then lost. The other boxes in that pile were taped closed with clear packing tape. They looked to be the boxes from the Taipei house.

He went downstairs and asked Setiawan to call the car so he could go to a hardware store. Setiwan tried to get a shopping list from him instead, but Frank insisted he needed to go himself, holding out until the butler relented. As he was driven from the compound, he saw a man, a white man, stand up in the café down the street. As they drove by he came toward the car, much as Frank had done, that first day, already some two weeks ago. This man was plain, very pale, in square casual clothes, maybe fifty-five or sixty, with a middle-class look, trimmed grey hair and bit of a tight beard, accountant glasses. He peered into the car as it got close, and Frank ducked. He wasn't sure why, but he didn't want the man to see him. Maybe, he thought — maybe it's starting in earnest, maybe this guy is Interpol — does Interpol still exist? He'd have to Wikipedia it when he got back. Or maybe he's a hired gun, a hit man. Don't they sometimes pose as nerds? He bought a roll of clear packing tape at the hardware store and a retractable knife. The driver returned him to the compound, and he noticed, as they passed, the European or whatever he was still sitting at an outdoor table, facing the compound. Back in the house, he made his way to the attic, careful to not let anyone see.

He opened one of the boxes and it was, as expected, all files. He tried to get a sense of what they were about, but had no idea how to read them. They were records of transactions, clearly, and, as far as he could tell, stock purchases. They weren't balance sheets, but records of transfers of various kinds, most with no names, just account numbers. A few had shocking sums attached to them, and he snapped some pictures with his phone, then taped the box back up.

He cut open another and this one had names. He didn't recognize most of them, but about halfway through he saw a file titled Than Shwe. He couldn't place him (her?), but it sounded vaguely familiar. He snapped pictures of at least part of all the other files. Khin Nyunt. Thein Sein. Soe Win. Norodom Ranariddh. Norodom Sihamoni. Joice Mujuru. That one sounded familiar, too. Bouasone Bouphavanh.

He opened a third box, noted names, and saw a file with "Franky Baltimore" written on the tab. It had a list of transactions as well, all in his name, huge sums, tens of millions. He was in the middle of a criminal conspiracy, had been for some time without knowing it. He started to sweat, and wiped his hands so he wouldn't stain the boxes. He took pictures of as many pages as he could before his panic took over. He taped up the open boxes, looked out the door to see the coast clear, and snuck back downstairs.

In his room he started googling the names. Nyunt, Sein, and Win were all current or former ministers in the military government in Myanmar, the famous dictator-generals. Ranariddh and Sihamoni were sons of the notoriously corrupt King Sihanouk of Cambodia. Bouphavanh the head of the Laotian politburo. Mujuru a Mugabe lieutenant. What would he find in the other boxes: Laurent-Désiré Kabila? Omar al-Bashir? Fujimori? Charles Taylor? Maybe Mugabe and Putin after all. And what would he do with this knowledge? Was this the raw material for the retributive exposure Dmitry had threatened? If so, who would expose it? Given such an over-the-top gallery of evil miscreants, who might be responsible for the bombing? He wandered around in the mystery, going in circles, only to realize that once again, he knew nothing, nothing at all, and might never know.

Yuli, he then realized with a start, knew about the boxes.

Someone might merely have told her that a box of files had gone bafflingly missing, which wouldn't necessarily mean she was cognizant of the contents, or that she was aware of Dmitry's business in any detail. Maybe, as in the case of his prostitutes, she both knew about it all and didn't — knew in principle, but no specifics. Maybe, on the other hand, she knew everything. The boxes hadn't been opened — except by him — since arriving, unless someone else had cut them and retaped them shut. No, he would have noticed that, he thought, and then, with the realization that anyone else could probably see that his had been cut open and retaped, he went into another panic.

But who was he afraid of? Dmitry, on the slim chance that he was alive somewhere?

Why did the thought of that unnerve him so much?

He had known the amorality of his friend already, known how deep he was in the evil of the world, hadn't he? Or had he only been half believing it all these years, assuming there was some braggadocio involved?

Who else cared? If it was Yuli caretaking the boxes, was she only following his directions, like Frank was going to do with the Bank of Tokyo money? Speaking of which, since she now owned the private jet and the private island and untold other assets, did she even need the Tokyo money? He knew nothing, he knew nothing. He was face down in his pillow, feeling his heart, sure it was palpitating irregularly, and, even if not, beating way too fast.

"The future," he blurted one day. Her face composed, immediately, into pure kindness. How could she possibly land on exactly the right expression so quickly? She forgave him, reassured him, thanked him, comforted him, and all with a single catching of his eye. "I'm sorry," he continued, "I know you can take care of yourself, as you told me the first day, but you must miss your sons, and I need to know, or at least I would love to know, what you are thinking. I feel hamstrung otherwise." They sat, in almost the same arrangement they were in that first day, across a small coffee table from each other.

"The boys — I miss them, yes. It comes with being a mother of my station in this part of the world. I will spend time missing them. They will go away to school, as I did, in Europe first, then America. I don't know what the opposite of helicopter parenting would be — submarine parenting? That's what we do here. But I'm glad to talk to you about anything Franky, because in fact I could use some advice, and it is silly of me, but there are some things I can't bring up myself."

He started, then hesitated, was lost, because of course, he couldn't say what he wanted to say. She leaned over and touched his knee, encouraging him. "Have you thought," he finally asked, "about having a memorial service?" He was concerned that Yuli's denial would keep her from healing, from moving forward. And he wondered: Was she too scared to have a funeral? Did she know more about what was threatening them than she had so far admitted? And who was he kidding with the *moving forward*?

"I think not," she said.

"I know," he said, "but why?" He looked up to see Setiawan walk in the door behind her, surly as ever. He thought, absurdly, that the butler might run to the mantle and grab a scimitar.

"Let me take this call," she said.

He hadn't heard a phone ring, but he never did.

"And thank you, Franky," she said. "We will talk about this, about everything, soon."

He didn't see her again that afternoon.

He slipped away to the attic, whenever he could, spending every possible minute going through boxes of files, taking notes, taking pictures. When too many people were around he spent time in his room researching the names he came up with. He found Bosnian war criminals, African dictators, Russian oligarchs, Arab and American and French arms dealers. Dmitry had become the money launderer for every piece of bigtime and smalltime scum on the planet, it seemed. Frank wasn't surprised, since the unscrupulousness was certainly broad enough: Dmitry would have only sincere respect for any man who could stage a guerilla war, take over a country's government, and proceed to pillage every red cent the country managed to produce for the next five or ten or forty years. His was a simple world, untrammeled by the common good.

What surprised Frank the most was his own response. Even though investing the ill-gotten gains of genocidal maniacs, and thus in effect refinancing them, was contemptable, despicable, he felt a slight sense of anticlimax. There was something so quotidian and ignoble about it. Rather than an Armageddonish Bond villain, Dmitry was turning out to be a functionary, a bookkeeper, a handmaiden to the fraternity of international dickwads. And it made Yuli's dilemma much harder to live with, since there was no telling which of these madmen Dmitry had ripped off, or how many of them knew it and were out for revenge or restitution. What danger lurked? How many dangers lurked?

The white guy at the café had set up shop. Both Yuli and Amarya had seen him sitting there, sipping coffee or tea, waiting. He could be plainclothes police or he could be an assassin. Not a particularly clever version of either, since they had all seen him clear as day — weren't the criminals and undercover cops supposed to remain hidden, unidentified? Maybe the guy was an insurance adjustor, staking out the house before paying a death claim. Yuli hadn't made a claim, as far as he knew, but maybe the bank had — many corporations these days take out life insurance policies on their employees. Maybe he was a freelance investigator working for one of the aggrieved investors. It occurred to him that, clumsy as the man was, he still might know more about everything than Frank did.

He went upstairs and asked one of the maids, a girl in her late teens from the countryside, where he might be able to see the café from a window. She took him to a room, which she gigglingly explained was her room, and sure enough standing on a chair looking out her window he could see the café. The man was there and seemed to be studying the compound with a set of binoculars. He backed away from the window and looked at the maid, a hand covering her smiling mouth, her eyes demurely down, still giggling a little. Did she think he was really there for something else? It seemed that if he was, he was being given permission. What a life Dmitry had led.

He thanked her and left, resolved more than ever to help Yuli move on with her life. Things couldn't remain in limbo forever.

He made a decision.

He was going to go have a cup of coffee.

He walked out the front gate, realizing it was the first time he had done so under his own steam since he arrived — his only other exit and reentry was the hardware store trip with the family driver. He headed over to the teashop. At 11am the sun and vapor were already high enough to make for an instant sheen of sweat. As he approached the café, not only could he see the spy, he watched the guy take a picture of him. Not subtle.

Maybe not a spy.

Frank had originally thought of nonchalantly ordering a coffee and watching the man surreptitiously, but clearly the jig was already up, so he walked right up to his table.

"Should I join you?" he asked.

The man was a little flustered by this, but he half stood and mumbled, "Right." A Scouser, like Dmitry. This cannot possibly be the way spies run their business.

"You're watching the Serang house. Why?"

"I'm sorry," he said, quietly. Sorry?

"Who are you?"

"George Heald," he said.

George Heald. "Good lord! You're Dmitry's father?" This had brought Frank to his feet, which confused the waiter who had just arrived. He sat back down. "Cappuccino, please," he said.

"Yes, sir," they both said. George Heald waited. His average grey hair, his nondescript, close-cropped beard, the glasses — all seemed to hide his face more than adorn it. Frank couldn't think of what to say. They looked away from each other, awkwardly. It wasn't long before they had been quiet for longer than was conscionable.

"I am so sorry for your loss," Frank finally thought to say.

Heald may have flinched slightly at that — or maybe he nodded. Frank intuited some bodily response, though none verbal. Again they waited, as if expecting some third member of their party to arrive and properly introduce them.

"Why...?" Frank wanted to ask why he didn't come to the house, but again, Dmitry was right, it was very difficult to ask the man a direct question. He appeared so intensely meek that asking him anything difficult seemed cruel, almost violent.

"I'm Frank Baltimore," he said, instead. "Dmitry worked for me in Connecticut years ago."

"Franky," he said softly, as if to himself.

"Yes."

Again they were quiet. This time he waited.

"They haven't had a funeral," Heald said at last.

"No. Yuli isn't able to admit yet, I think even to herself, that he's actually — you know they haven't identified, well, as of yet there are no remains." He felt like a marauding Hun stuttering out the barest facts.

"Does Yuli know you're here?"

"Yuli is his wife?"

"Yes, don't you know her?"

"We never met. I was a bit hairy at the heel there. His mother met her once."

"Once? In Liverpool?"

"Right."

"Did you and Dmitry have a falling out?" he asked. "Were you estranged?"

He winced. "We haven't seen each other in many years. I'm not sure what happened."

"Did you two fight?"

He looked up, surprised by the idea. "No. He stopped coming by."

"And you didn't try to get in touch?"

Heald was silent. Frank's eyes, he realized, kept wandering elsewhere — he watched the waiter talking to the cook inside, looked at a three-story concrete building across the street, saw that the setups on the table next to them were slightly unsymmetrical. But looking back up he saw tears streaming down Heald's face; his features were otherwise quite still, with none of the muscular contractions of anguish or grief, but his eyes were leaking.

"I should have grasped the nettle…" he said.

The traffic was intermittent, and the two of them were the only customers, except for an Indonesian man on the far side of the café, reading his paper. A slight breeze and the café's large green umbrellas kept the heat from being too oppressive. A tiny bird fluttered to the edge of the table looking for crumbs and then dashed away. He wondered what the hell he was going to do with George Heald.

On the table in front of him was a beat-up old paperback, a pulp Western with a cheesy cover, titled *The Brave Rider of Santa Palo*. He must have noticed Frank looking at it, because he pushed it toward him.

"This was his," he said. "When he was young. He loved this book." Frank picked it up, opened the front cover. On the title page, in a boyish hand, it was inscribed "Dmitry Heald." Heald took it from him, opened it to the last page, and handed it back. The inside back cover had, in pencil, a series of dates, starting in 1990, when Dmitry must have been around eight. Next to each date was a number, preceded by a £. In 1990, he apparently had £1, and planned to make it £5 by 1991, £25 by 1992, and to keep quintupling it each year. He was scheduled to hit around £2,000,000 by the age of seventeen, and over a billion by twenty-one. That was where the chart ended. He hadn't hit any of those benchmarks, but he passed them by thirty-one. Now that he was dead, it looked like a pretty pathetic, arbitrary set of goals. His father seemed proud of it.

"I'm sure Yuli would like to see you," Frank said finally.

"Oh, no," he said.

At first this seemed a simple fact of his retiring nature.

"No, really," Frank started to suggest, noticing that he was imitating the father's quiet, dispersed speaking into the air instead of addressing him directly. He was going to say that she would very much want to see him, without knowing if it was true. But it seemed like the least one could do for a man whose son had just died.

Heald absentmindedly, sounding more like he was talking to himself than to Frank, said, "I don't trust them."

"What?"

"The Muslims. They stick together."

"What?"

"I know them, you know. I worked with them. In North Africa. Sneaky. Conniving. Murderers. As soon kill you as look at you. The whole world is seeing it now, finally giving it some stick. I've always known. And now they've killed my son."

Seriously? Could he actually believe that?

Heald's left hand fidgeted over the book cover, as if petting the Brave Rider's horse. His tears had dried and Frank searched his face for some resemblance to Dmitry. He could see none. What was he going to do with this guy? His quiet, diminished rant felt less like the derangements of grief than the continuation of lifelong muddles, like some inanity he had repeated every afternoon in his pub for the last forty years. Frank realized he simply couldn't ask him another question.

"I'm pushing for a memorial service of some kind," he said, getting up, leaving some money on the table for his coffee. He looked at Heald once more but his gaze was immediately distracted by the bill he had left on the table, fluttering in the breeze. He moved his empty cup and saucer over to weigh it down.

He was going to ask Heald where he was staying, but decided not to. He would be here at the café. Or he wouldn't.

Walking back toward the house, Frank realized that he hadn't actually said goodbye. He turned and waved. Heald was looking through the binoculars again, but apparently not at Frank. He didn't wave back.

Frank flashed back to Dmitry's story about his sister, the one he told him in the tent. Years later, he had asked him what had become of her.

"You know, Franky, you're the only one I ever told about that. I do think it had a large influence over me." Frank thought so too, that it was the reason he was such an addict, the reason he was constantly drawn to illicit sex. "I do believe it is why I am in Asia. I once read, Franky, that men with shoe fetishes develop them as toddlers, fixating from floor level on their mum's heels. And it makes sense to me that one's earliest experiences help set the dials on one's sexual machinery. Some Asian women have the kind of pubic hair — sparse, neatly contained — of a

fourteen-year-old British girl. I really do believe it is that uncomplicated."
This struck Frank as batty, as grotesque oversimplification or a sad excuse
for introspection, and, yet, perhaps not entirely wrong.

"Simple? Huh," Frank said. "And your sister? What happened to
her?"

"It's sad, really, Franky," he said. "She has gotten horribly fat — I
mean dreadfully fat, the kind of person who has rolls and rolls of *fat*,
not your average, even American-average overweight fat, but freak-
show fat, *National Enquirer* fat, extra chins, saddlebags on her *arms*,
Franky — she has two fat nasty kids from two loser guys — nice word,
that, loser, isn't it? Remarkably descriptive for such a simple little word
— *looozer* — as is, I hope I made clear, the word *fat*. She lives like a sorry
old who-er in a council flat in Liverpool. Sad."

"Do you see her?"

"No. Every couple years. Less."

"She doesn't visit."

"Hey, yeah, no, really!" he laughed. "She isn't capable of getting her
corpulent ass into London, much less Asia." He paused for a moment,
then said, "Maybe I should let her live in the mansion in Liverpool with
her delinquent boys and whatever brain-damaged meth addict she's
fucking this week, eh, Franky? In that room with me mum."

Up until that point, it was the cruelest thing Frank had ever heard
him say. What a hateful bastard he was.

He walked back through the gate, back down the rainforested front
path, and into the house. Yuli came in from the pool wearing a simple
sarong, her hair freshly toweled and still wet. She looked so burnished
and scrubbed, so spry and delicate, so damned exquisite, it was all he
could do not to prostrate himself like Troilus.

"We have to talk," he said, which sounded more like soap opera than
courtly romance.

"Yes?" she said, slightly alarmed by his tone.

"The man at the café?"

"Yes?"

"He's Dmitry's father."

"His father."

"Dmitry was right, he's impossible to talk to. But he wants a memorial service, and I agree. I think it's time." She waited, instead of responding, still looking him straight in the eye, looking as if she knew this second shoe would drop. "And I've been reading through the files in the attic," he said.

Now she looked at the floor.

So she did know.

"You know what's in them," he said.

"Not exactly," she said.

"It seems Dmitry was doing a fair amount of investing for war criminals. He made money for dictators, death squads, terrorists, mass murderers. The worst of the worst. I always knew he was fundamentally amoral, but still, I'm kind of appalled." She seemed appalled, too, stricken. "But that's not important. Except that there are a lot of them, and they are very bad people. Any one of them could be responsible for the bombing. Any of them could come looking for you. So I need to know. Did he double-cross any of them? Is there anything else I should know? Is there anything else you should be telling me?"

She stayed staring at the floor for a minute, but then, of all the answers she might have made, of all the things she could have done, of all the reactions he had thought possible or could have imagined, he didn't expect this — she kissed him on the mouth, firmly, in promise, and walked down the hallway toward her room.

"Wait right here for one minute," she said over her shoulder. He stood on the spot, wondering what had happened, what was happening.

A minute or maybe two later — it seemed much longer, but he was aware that time was crawling — she came back. Without saying a word, she took him by the hand and led him down the hallway, into her room.

As they entered, she shut the door, locked it, and turned back to him. In a single motion she allowed her sarong to drop to the floor. "Now you know all," she said, and stood, facing him, unafraid, glorious, absolutely perfect.

He had worried, on and off, the way people do, what it might really be like if his dream came true. The absurdity of his obsession, his irrational, unwarranted, unfathomable fixation — could any reality live up to it? Would he, as seemed to be happening with Amarya, start very quickly to bore both himself and her? Is this where love would die forever? Would he measure up — and of course he wouldn't in one particular — as a lover? Would that one particular be a dealbreaker? Would they like the same kinds of things in bed? He was experienced enough to know that if someone was a tie-me-up-and-hurt-me person, not as a once-in-a-while experiment, but as a steady diet, there was no jollying them out of it.

And what if he didn't like the way she kissed? There was a woman once he had a fling with, a very large woman, which was unusual for him. He had always otherwise been attracted to the petite types, but this woman was built like Serena Williams, had thighs practically the size of his waist, and was as tall or even taller than him. Nonetheless he found her astoundingly hot, as well as amazingly sweet, and they were really hitting it off. Then they started making out. Every time they kissed, her tongue plunged into his mouth like something from a horror film, this surprisingly large and sinuous muscle ramming its way towards his tonsils. Nothing he did made any difference, no hints or kissy counteroffers modified this natural expression of her passion, and that was that. They drifted away from each other. Would his splendiferous love for Yuli rip aground upon equally stupid shoals?

And his most sincere fear was that she was acting out of distress, that he would come to find that he was a simple stopgap, a paltry port in her storm, a temporary fix. Or worse, a poor stand-in. Would he be always upstaged by her memories of Dmitry? He wasn't sure he could bear that.

Or maybe he could. All his fears evaporated as she stepped toward him, unbuttoned his shirt and helped it fall off his back, unbuttoned and unzipped his khakis, all slowly, tenderly, without a trace of anything lascivious or crass or hurried or desperate. He stepped out of pants and boxers and sandals and they stood, touching but barely, electric, nothing but crackling ozone between them. In the past he'd gone to bed the first time drunk, gone to bed high, gone laughing, gone crazy passionate, guilty, romantic, paranoid, bored, heroic, stupid, hesitant, heedless — just about every way, he thought, you can make that first tumble. But he'd never approached it with this combination of solemnity and tenderness and purpose, never with eyes wide open, heart full, all perils at bay, all the angels of heaven hovering, the very universe ahum with a bliss too luminous to be mocked or questioned.

The first time was without any further preliminaries, but so slow that just entering was a kind of extended foreplay. He had heard about the tantric stuff all his life and had tried versions of it at times, staying tense and still for as long as possible, but this was different. They never stopped moving, and yet rushed nothing, poised halfway between maximum bodily tension and pure relaxation, as if somehow they were inhaling and exhaling at the same time. They seemed to agree there was plenty of time for everything, plenty of time to explore, to discover, to experiment, to indulge, to have fun, to goof around. This time, the first time, though, was the unadulterated undulation of nature, man, and woman in their resplendent essences — oh, he knew it sounded like sappy bullshit and he could imagine the knowing smirk any such talk would elicit from Dmitry — and even from himself on many days. But if ever love had found unblemished incarnation, he felt, even as it was happening that afternoon in Jakarta, that this was it.

"You might not believe this," she said, a couple hours later, "but you are only my second real lover."

"Really!"

"Really. I was a good girl until Dmitry got hold of me. He ruined me."

Ruined? "Oh, yes. You were pregnant before you were married. Nobody cares."

"Not that," she said.

"What — I mean — did you have affairs?"

"Oh, God, no!" she said with a little laugh. He wasn't sure why it was funny, but it struck him that Dmitry would have laughed the same way if anyone suggested he *didn't* have extramarital lovers.

"You knew that he —" Frank started to say, but paused. It was stupid to bring it up and stupid to stop halfway. What patently false gallantry! She knew that, too.

"Had sex elsewhere? Of course. He was a normal man in Asia. We accept this."

"But women are not allowed."

"No, but —"

"But, what?"

"Nothing."

"What."

"You won't like it."

"Try me."

She looked at him. What a great poker player she would make. Whatever was going on inside made a clear impact on her eyes, face, or body, but one that was impossible to read.

"You know these trips he took to Thailand."

"Yes."

"I sometimes went with him."

"*What?*" It came out faster, and had more heat on it, than he had hoped.

"You see, I told you you wouldn't like it."

"No," he said, making a conscious effort to sound much more at ease than he felt, "go ahead, it's fine. Tell me."

"I went with him sometimes. To a hotel in Bangkok. He would get a girl or a boy, or both, delivered to the room — I know, it sounds horrible —"

She looked at him for a reaction and he did his best to shake his head no, no, not so horrible, rather than nod yes, which is what he wanted to do. "No, not horrible," he said. "I want to know." He wasn't sure he did, or why he didn't just say, *hey, we all have pasts* and let it go, didn't know why he had to pick this particular scab.

"I told myself it was Dmitry's show, he was the director, that I was reluctantly playing a bit part, but it wasn't true. The idea that it was all him — this was a silly ruse, I know, but there it was. It let me live with it."

"And so?" How perverse was he being? He gestured with his chin for her to go on.

"He would have the Thai boy go down on me — God, it sounds so squalid — it is squalid."

"No, I get it."

"You do? Sometimes Dmitry would fuck me while the boy sucked on my shoulders — you know, those places you found already. My only rule was nobody penetrated me but Dmitry. Why was that the rule? I don't know. Why anything —"

"And the girl?"

"You see how easy it is to get drawn in? But you knew that already." Did he? "The girls? Oh, you know, the standard things — she would lick his balls while he was doing me. He would 'call a conference' once in a while and all three of us would go down on him." She laughed.

"You know how he was. He kept things light. Fun. Most of the time it all seemed more silly than nasty. And sometimes, I don't know, it seemed so, so *human.*"

"I think I know what you mean."

"He was a big voyeur, as you must know, and sometimes, when we were momentarily sated, he would have the boy and girl, or the two boys, the two girls, whatever he had ordered up, have sex in front of us. And at first I could hardly watch, but after I got used to it a little, after it became normal, I thought, one night — this is the same as watching actors kiss in the movies, and unlike pornography, they are right here, we are all being nice to each other, it is all very affable, nice, warm, even. There were no cameras — unless Dmitry had set one up — but still, no lights, no bored crewmembers, no microphones. It was all so much more friendly, more chummy, more human than pornography."

"Huh."

"You think I was rationalizing? Maybe I was."

"No, I think you are the most wonderful person in the history of the world and I think you are absolutely right. But I would probably think anything you said was absolutely right. Everything you tell me makes me crazier about you. I am almost ready to make an Aztec sacrifice of myself, rip out my own heart and hand it to you."

"Please don't," she said, and laughed. "It's the thought that counts." That made him love her more, too, but at the same time he noticed that she had said nothing, made no sign, after what was unmistakably a declaration of love. Was she ignoring it on purpose, the most polite way to suggest he shouldn't repeat it?

He was about to get depressed, but instead found himself reaching down between her legs, where the slightest throb greeted his palm, and moments later he felt again, against his middle finger, the sublime parting, the wet, swelling answer to every question. It brought a mirroring tear to his eye. After all of the women, all of the great and not-so-great sex in his life, there he was, feeling like he had discovered the real thing for the first time.

As they went through the night, making love over and over, dozing off for a while only to re-engage, he felt like he was eighteen again, and more than that, he was finding reserves of sexual ingenuity and dexterity and adroitness, an improvisatory genius he had never thought he possessed. He was under no illusions — it was she who made him a better lover, she who had the reins — but it didn't matter. It worked. At one point having willed his ten fingers, lips and tongue to do the combined work of a man, two Thai boys, and a Thai girl, she cried out, right after she came again, "My God wow! Franky! Why? Why you didn't tell me you can do this!" her perfect syntax crumbling in orgasmic delirium. Through it all he remained in awe of the incredible sweetness and tenderness in her eyes, at her body's flawlessness, at the endless parade of pleasures they served up for each other.

He couldn't help it. Despite her silent suggestion to the contrary, he couldn't stop it, and he declared his love again, and declared it again. He told her he wanted to write songs about her, write poetry, paint her portrait, recombine her DNA, teach her to fly, elect her prime minister, canonize her, cast her in a movie, put up a statue of her in the main square. To his eternal delight, she loved his goofy chatter. She soaked it up like light loam takes in the rain, and that made him go on and on and on.

"I want to make you forget everything you've ever known," he said at one point, kneeling over her and grazing his fingers lightly up and down her stomach, "I want to make you remember everything you have ever forgotten." She jumped up, threw her arms around his neck, kissed his mouth hard, and then said, into his neck in a whisper, "That is the loveliest, most beautiful thing anyone has ever said to me." And *that*, in turn, felt like the most lovely and beautiful thing anyone had ever said to him. They were on the mountain. They were in the clouds.

"Promise me," she whispered to him, again straight in his ear, "that you will always feel that — that whatever happens, you will accept who I am, and know that this is real."

He promised. Of course he promised.

He woke up in the early morning light and had the aching sensation of being the luckiest man alive. Yuli was stretched across the bed, wrapped in wisps of white sheet, and as his eyes watered again in appreciation, she took on an actual halo. He leaned in, kissed her neck.

"I suppose I should slip out."

"Don't," she said, and reached for him. He luxuriated in her arms for a while.

"The servants? Amarya?"

"Trying to keep things from the servants, you'll learn, is impossible and usually causes more trouble than not. Amarya said from the first she was planning to enjoy you until you finally 'grew some balls' — her words — and got up the courage to come and get me." That set off a flurry of kissing.

"You certainly are an openminded group," he said.

"You don't know the half of it," she answered, and they went another round. He hadn't had a fifth orgasm since he was in his twenties. This one knocked him out and when he woke up again she was already up and dressed, taking a last look at herself in the bathroom mirror. He hopped up, came and stood behind her. She looked at him in the mirror in a way he couldn't read, then turned and kicked the bathroom door closed, threw her head against his chest and wept.

"What is it, baby?" he said, and wondered if that idiom was too far off. She didn't answer at first. "The boys?"

She nodded.

"I miss them," she said, calmly.

"Dmitry?" He was being masochistic, but also gallant.

"All of them."

"Come back to bed. Let me hold you."

"No," she said, but not coldly, wiping her eyes dry and turning to face the mirror again. "I have to run a few errands. Go back to sleep. I'll see you at lunch." She walked out, closing the door behind her. He made his way back to the lazy bed and stretched and indulged himself, replaying image after blissful image of the night. Eventually he pulled himself up, put on yesterday's clothes, and headed to the attic. Only two boxes to go, and even if he wasn't going to learn anything new, he figured he should finish the job.

He got up the stairs, pulled on the light and looked at a patch of bare floor. The boxes were gone.

All of them.

As he headed down the stairs, Amarya was headed up.

"Don't speak to me," she said, blowing past him with a 'talk to the hand' arm in the air.

Christ. Downstairs he heard commotion. Setiawan was speaking heatedly to two men straight out of *Men in Black*, sunglasses and everything, two white guys, one tall and skinny, one short and skinny. Setiawan was asking them to leave. Frank came down the stairs and asked, as he got close, what the problem was. It was the first time Setiawan seemed happy to see him.

"We're looking for Dmitry Heald," the shorter one said.

OK, Frank thought, here we go.

"As I'm sure Mr. Setiawan informed you," he said, "Mr. Heald is recently deceased."

"He did *not* tell us that," the tall one said. "And we're not so *sure*."

Frank turned to Setiawan. "How did they get in?"

"They seem to have come through the gate when Miss Amarya came home," he said.

"So they are trespassing."

"Don't get cute," the shorter one said.

"Cute? Where are you from?"

"East coast," he said.

"Me too," Frank said, "long time ago."

"What are you doing *here*, then?" the tall one asked.

"Helping my friend's widow manage after the tragic and horrible death of her young husband. And I'm helping in part by keeping people like you out of her face. Please leave or I will call the police."

"*Dude*, we *are* the police," the tall one said.

These guys gave him the creeps — he couldn't figure out if they were inept or stupid, but either way that made them dangerous. And who did they work for?

"The police do not call people dude," Frank said, with more confidence than he felt, and started walking out the front door.

"I don't know how deep you are in this, Hollywood," the shorter one said, starting to follow him out. "But you don't want to be deep."

"Hollywood," he said, noncommittal, heading down the walkway toward the front gate, hoping they would follow. "So you know who I am." This was not good.

They were torn, it seemed, not wanting to leave the house, looking over their shoulders, but unwilling to lose Frank as he walked toward the street. They finally chose to follow.

"Yeah, yeah, we know who you are. We also know Dmitry Heald took a lot of money that didn't belong to him. Things are going to get rough all around if he don't give it back."

"Wow, a threat," Frank said, pretending nonchalance. His vague plan was to get them out in the street and then run back into the compound. He didn't like the image of himself running in fear — the whole ploy was more Bugs Bunny than badass — but, what else could he do?

"That's *right*," said the tall one, catching up to Frank and falling in step, dropping his sunglasses an inch so Frank could see his eyes, grey and scary. "And you're *right*, we're *not* the police. You *wish* we were the police. We are *not* the police so we don't have to *play square*. The only reason they flew *us* in is because the *local* guys apparently didn't know how to be *rough* enough."

"And listen, pal," said the short one, "we can give you a significant finder's fee if you help us recover these funds."

"So you guys do 'good not-a-cop, bad not-a-cop,'" he said. "Swell." A little surprised that his fake insouciance was sounding almost natural, he noticed that talking that way made him feel much calmer, more in control. "But too bad for you. I told you: he's dead."

"Money don't die, Hollywood," the shorter one said. "It's alive and well in an account or two or ten. Let us know where, and you get to keep a big chunk of it, like a rebate."

By then he had them on the street.

"So who do you guys work for?" Frank asked, the heat already making them sweat.

"Don't be a chump," said the short one. It was if he learned to speak from watching James Cagney movies.

"How do *people* stand this *heat?*" the tall one asked. He was starting to drip.

"You learn to go careful," Frank said. "Walk slow, take it easy. Take off your jacket and tie for starters. Don't wear black." He wasn't sure they could manage without their costumes, and neither made a move to take off their jackets. "Listen, maybe I can help you, maybe you can help me. But not if I don't know who you are. I've been trying to figure this all out, too."

"You *have?*" said the tall one. "*How* have you been doing *that?*" Down the street, he could see Dmitry's father, taking pictures of him and Smith and Jones. A white woman stood next to him, also looking their way. The Indonesian from the other day was again reading his paper.

"Is that your competition?" Frank asked, pointing with his chin. They both turned to look at the café.

"No, that's Dmitry Heald's *father*," the tall one said.

"That's Heald's mother next to him," the short one offered. So she was here now, too? "The father sure hates the Muslims, don't he?" Frank must have looked surprised, because he added, "We know you've talked to him. We've been around for a couple days. This is the first time we got past the guard and that damn butler."

"Damn *butler*," muttered the tall one.

"Look, kid," said the short one. Frank was maybe five years older than him. "Let's say we work for a detective agency, and let's say we're on spec, as it were, for the various stakeholders involved, people you don't want to know."

What the fuck was he doing, talking to these men? Were they as hapless as they seemed?

"Alright," Frank said. "I can tell you this. The wife knows nothing."

"Hard to believe, Hollywood."

Every time they called him that he felt a little spike of terror.

"Yeah," the tall one said. "*She* was in the business too. She worked for the *firm*."

"Yes," Frank said, although it hadn't occurred to him in this way. "But only briefly, and years ago. She was just a kid, really." Did he sound as transparent as he felt?

"Looks all growed-up to me," the short one said.

That made Frank boil. Anger, it seemed, was what he needed to have a proper self-protective response. He turned around and went back through the gate, fast but not running, into the compound.

"Don't let them back in," he said to the guard over his shoulder, more for their benefit than the guard's, since he didn't speak a word of English.

"*Think* about it!" the tall one called to him from the street. Then he heard the little one say, quietly, to his colleague, "The idiot has no idea. He's a dead man."

When he got back inside Setiawan was waiting.

"I think it best you have a word with the man at the gate, and make sure something like that doesn't happen again." Dead man, he thought.

Setiawan winced a little. "I believe I know my duties, sir."

"I wish I knew," Frank said, shaky with adrenaline, thinking the guy had no right to get huffy, "what they all were."

"And yet I will always appreciate, sir, any advice you have to offer," he said in his High Snideness mode, putting Frank in his place but managing to keep all the resentment below the surface — what a pro. The most unimpeachable "fuck you" he'd ever heard.

"They say they work for powerful, scary people," he said. "But who knows." He was talking to himself.

"Very well, sir." After a perfunctory bow Setiawan headed out to the front gate. Frank ran to Setiawan's office and rifled his drawers. After long ticks of the clock finding nothing, he chanced on a key ring hanging in plain sight on the doorjamb. He grabbed it, ran up the stairs, found a key that unlocked one of the two doors that were always locked, assumed it was the master key, and sure enough it unlocked the other. He ran back down, without looking in the rooms, hoping to get the keys back before Setiawan returned. He heard the front door open as he reached the office. He jammed the keys back on their nail, jumped in the kitchen and opened a large refrigerator.

"Can I get you something, Mr. Franky?" Setiawan was suspicious, no question, and Frank worried he was red in the face. He was breathing hard.

"I guess I was a little shaken by that encounter," he said. "I wanted a gin and tonic."

"Allow me, sir," he said, still pissy. "Where can I bring it to you?"

"The library, thanks." he said. "But perhaps a whiskey sour, instead." That would take longer.

"As you will, sir."

He walked out of the kitchen, and ran up the stairs. The first room was a man's bedroom, maybe Setiawan's. He checked the closet. The boxes weren't there. He pushed the button on the inside knob to lock it as he left and crossed the hall.

He opened the door to the other room. Bingo. The boxes were stacked against the wall inside.

But that was the least of it. The room was lined with monitor screens, a much more elaborate security station than the one in the guard hut out front, maybe twenty screens in all, some big ones monitoring a dozen cameras each. As he scanned them, four more or less in the center of the wall caught his eye. It took him a while to process what it was, but once he did it was clear: four different cameras focused, from four different angles, on the bed he had slept in, and did everything else in, last night.

He didn't have time to think about it, because he saw, on another screen, Setiawan coming up the stairs. He slipped out of the room, pulled the door closed quietly, and ran across the hall toward his room, realizing too late that he had left the door unlocked. He got almost to the end of the hall and did a U-turn to be on the right trajectory by the time he met Setiawan, as if he was coming back from some errand in his own room. Everything looked normal, he hoped, except for the fact that he was breathing too hard again, flushed, and altogether looked severely seasick.

"Your whiskey sour is in the library, sir."

"Thank you, Setiawan," he said, hoping he had left the mixings for a couple more.

As he walked down the stairs, that marvelous stone-clad, sweeping, movie-set stairway, he held his hands in front of him. Each finger seemed to jump at a different speed.

"The thing that astounds me, Franky," Dmitry had said to him, it seemed like a lifetime ago, as they sat in that Hooters in Santa Monica eating a pile of fried food and drinking beer, the night before they went to visit Dwayne, "is that we have an entire economy that is fundamentally based on the notion of risk, and yet people are terrible, *terrible* at assessing risk. Even me, although I'm better at it than almost anyone." Dmitry had researched the area bars to locate one carrying a closed circuit Ultimate Fighting championship bout, and this was it. He was already working out with his fight club then, studying and sparring, although he had only competed a few times. For some reason, this fight was, in his fan world, an extremely important one. Frank was sure that before long he'd hear why.

The Hooters waitresses were distracting — they are hired to be distracting — and so was the crowd, Ultimate Fighting aficionados full of confused testosterone. Frank was keyed up. Dmitry was his usual relaxed self.

"It is impossible to say who will win this fight," he said. The two fighters were in the ring, and it looked like a real mismatch to Frank. One, named Hughes, was built like a Bowflex ad, muscles everywhere, tight as a drum, with a soccer hooligan's lunatic intensity. The other was B. J. Penn, who Dmitry adored. Penn was a baby-faced, skinny-looking guy with no discernible muscle tone at all. Dmitry had explained that he was coming out of a two-year retirement, and it looked as if he had skipped the gym that whole time. "B. J. Penn, Franky, is perhaps the best fighter in the history of the game. He received a black belt in Brazilian jiu-jitsu after studying only three years — it usually takes ten — and four years after that he won the UFC championship. The championship bout was with this same guy, Hughes, who was the reigning champion, and B. J. won it in four minutes. Then — and this is the most astonishing thing, Franky — during the title ceremony, the minute they handed him the championship belt, he held up his hand to quiet the crowd and announced he was retiring from the sport! He said all his goals had been met and handed the belt over to Hughes, who thus immediately became World Champion again. B. J. won the belt, gave it back, and simply walked away. Later he said it was all too easy and pointless and he was going spend his life meditating instead."

Dmitry thought this not just astonishing but glorious; Frank couldn't quite follow the storyline, nor could he understand why, if Dmitry agreed with B. J. Penn that it was all pointless, he seemed so invested in the sport to begin with. As the two fighters came forward to bump fists, the crowd on TV cheered, the crowd in the Hooters went berserk, and the referee started the fight.

The match was fascinating in part because Penn's limbs looked like they were made of rubber. He could slink and slide his arms and legs in and out of Hughes's grasp like they were four independent-minded snakes, all with preternatural calm, expressionless. The oddly archetypical pair — very Tortoise and Hare, David and Goliath, Grasshopper and Ant — were not just equipped with different fighting styles, they embodied two fundamental, eternal principles: Hughes, the insistent, muscled striver against the slithery wraith Penn, yin vs. yang, the fierce angry dog up against an almost supercilious cat, idly sharpening its claws. For much of the fight Hughes seemed to be battling a phantom, Penn slipping through his fingers and disappearing from holds, Hughes's punches and kicks seeming to pass through him with no effect. And the fact that Hughes had been disgraced twice by Penn, first by losing the title and then by having it handed back to him as worthless, all in one day, made the fight seem more like Hughes's own internal psychodrama than a real bout, as if he was, indeed, punching a ghost.

Eventually, though, Penn got trapped in some position that allowed Hughes to bring down his forearm from over his own head, and ram it, full force, into Penn's face, over and over again. It was a horrific, bone-crushing thing to watch, on the order of a baby seal massacre. Penn never showed an ounce of desperation. He kept trying to maneuver out of range, moving more slowly with every shocking, soul-destroying crack to the face. An American boxing match would have been called twenty blows earlier. Penn's head was starting to wobble with each new strike, and his eyes were beginning to dim. At long last the referee called a halt.

"I am very disappointed, Franky," Dmitry said, pointing their empty beer pitcher out to the waitress. "The real finesse of the sport resides in the jiu-jitsu elements, and it is always disheartening when the striker wins. Plus, the story isn't as good." The fight, the fried food, the beer, the pimply repression of the fans, the waitresses working the marks like so many hot-pantsed, buxom carnies: all of it gave Frank vertigo.

"This was a very hard fight to handicap — the risks were equally distributed and incommensurable. That always makes calculation impossible, in finance or in sport — there, there, Franky, he'll be all right, buck up, it's just a few *wallops to the kisser* — try to focus. The real wild card, for handicappers, as always, was personal. Would the most magnificent act of humiliation in the history of sport make Hughes a better fighter, his eternal, shameful fountain of anger fed by that mortification, or would it make him a worse one, impetuous and lacking calculation?"

"Hughes was much stronger, physically," Frank said. "You could just see that."

"Oh, Franky, you can't really believe that's what this is about, can you? The mind beats the body every time. Did I ever tell you about my skydiving adventure?"

Their next pitcher of beer came, Frank once again distracted by the waitress.

"Franky, shall we find out when she gets off work? You look like one of those cartoon wolves whose tongue hits the floor and then unrolls like a carpet while his eyes pop out of their sockets." He did a quick appraisal. "No, of course not, you're a good boy these days." He was living with Isa then. "I decided to go skydiving, Franky, because everyone talked about how thrilling it was, and it seemed like a reasonable skill to have if you fly as much as I do. You laugh, but I sometimes use quite unconventional carriers in some dicey airspace. So I did the training, learning how to roll when I hit the ground, how to pull the ripcord, the emergency pull, the emergency chute, all that, how to turn around and face the wind in order to slow down for landing." He sipped on his beer. "She does have quite a nice little bum, doesn't she, Franky?"

"Don't you ever get tired?"

"Yes, but then in roughly thirty minutes, I'm ready to go again. So we went up in the plane to 10,000 feet, which doesn't look that high from below, but when you get up to the open bay door in the middle of the rusty albatross they use for such things, it hits you, with a preposterous burst of nausea that this jumping out of airplanes is a formidably stupid idea. Luckily they were used to such hesitation and they quite forcibly pushed me out. The wind slapped me in the face with real violence and instead of waiting the ten seconds I was supposed to wait, I pulled the ripcord *immediately*. Somehow I expected everything to calm down, and dump-dee-dump-dee-dum, I'd just float gradually down and enjoy the scenery. But it wasn't that kind of parachute, Franky, not the World War II big balloon-like affair, but the little, fast kind, a single rectangular strip of silk, which I guess is better for maneuvering, but does not slow you down nearly as much. I kept plummeting toward the Earth at an alarming rate.

"Then, out of nowhere, I saw in front of me the big X in the field, our landing zone. We were told to watch our altimeters, strapped to our wrists like watches, and when we got to 1000 feet we were to turn 180 degrees into the wind, which would slow our fall and our forward motion. We would lose sight of the X for a while, they told us, as we floated backwards with the wind, but not to worry, we would land in the right place if we just followed instructions. Very simple. The chute had two handles, and if you pulled down on the left one, it turned left, the right one, right. *Piece of cake*.

"But as I came to 1000 feet, I was directly over an extensive woodlot. It was late fall and the leaves were gone, and all I could think of was getting multiply impaled on the lethal branches, poking up at me by the thousands, and a voice in my head started saying, *I am not going to land in those branches, I am not going to impale myself on those trees.* Meanwhile, on the ground, the head of the jump school was on a megaphone, shouting up to me, *OK, wonderful, now turn around and face the wind*, and when I didn't respond — I couldn't Franky, I just kept saying over and over, *I am not going to land in those branches, I am not going to die on those trees* — the man tried again, and I could hear the urgency in his voice as I hit 800 feet, 700 feet: *Alright now, no need to panic, everything is OK, just turn around*, now, *and face the wind!* But you've heard that phrase, right, paralyzed with fear? My entire body was rigid, all four limbs locked, and I don't think I could have moved them if I wanted to. *It's not too late!* the man on the megaphone screamed, *TURN AROUND AND FACE THE WIND!* I went sailing over his head, still a couple hundred feet up, still doing thirty miles an hour. There weren't even any trees anymore, but there was nothing I could do, nothing. The man with the megaphone was now running along the ground. *NOW! Turn around and FACE THE WIND! FOR FUCK'S SAKE!* I tried to look back over my shoulder. *That's right, but more, MUCH MORE!* In turning, stiffly, to look at him I had pulled down on the left handle and changed direction slightly. *TURN AND FACE THE WIND, you PILLOCK!* he shouted, very perturbed. I wanted to say to him, *don't worry, it's not your fault, it's simply human error.* Once more he tried, *TURN AROUND and face…* but tailed off, and then gave up. A moment later I smashed into a farmer's field.

"Luckily for me, the ground was newly turned and therefore unusually soft, so I got off easy. I broke both my legs just above the ankles. The people from the flight school were really pissed. They had to come out with a stretcher and carry me across a quarter mile of freshly plowed earth, and every jolt, as they stumbled, sent shoots of pain like I had never, ever known. They were so mad at me I believe they started stumbling on purpose. The megaphone man was muttering about his insurance, and I tried to explain. The best I could do was to keep repeating, *It was only human error*. I don't know why. *Human error*. They told me to shut up.

"I say all this, Franky, as I'm sure you're already aware, to make a point about risk assessment. When I did the risk-benefit analysis of skydiving, I looked at the numbers of accidental deaths at skydiving schools, which approaches zero, statistically, lower than you'd think. Then I factored in, as benefits, what I erroneously thought was going to be a thrillingly good time, along with the marginal utility of being able to save my own life at some statistically improbable point in the future. But what I did *not* figure in was the possibility of that particular form of human error. I did not factor in my own culpability. People rarely do.

"Where will human error manifest? That is always the question. Would B. J.'s ambivalence toward the sport, his Buddhist nonattachment, continue to make him undefeatable, or sap his desire to win? Would Hughes's white-hot anger enable or disable him? These are considerably more important questions than relative muscle mass. It's the human factor that you can never predict. The human error." Dmitry watched their waitress walk by once more. "I've decided that the phrase is a redundancy, human error. Either word will do. In my case it was double casts in a wheelchair for six weeks, crutches for another ten."

He remembered that story because there he was, trying to assess what the risks were. If Dmitry was alive, and the locked voyeur's playroom was evidence he was, that was one thing. If dead, another. Smith and Jones must have guns, and Dmitry's father, too, for that matter — these anti-Muslim whackjobs always have guns. At what risk was he putting himself? And Yuli? The whiskey sours weren't helping him think any straighter. He went upstairs — someone had already relocked the door to the security room — and went to his own room and lay down. He realized he no longer cared where Dmitry had got the money, didn't care how dirty it was, only what kind of trouble came with it. He wanted Yuli to have the money, but without the trouble. He wanted her to — well, he wanted too many things, but Yuli should have the money. The Indonesian police wouldn't care, and the Taiwanese police couldn't touch her here. And him, Frank? Smith and Jones had no reason to kill him. Dead man? Him? Why? Who was he a risk to? He walked back downstairs — the house seemed empty, Setiawan missing — and poured a third whiskey sour from the shaker, a little watery with melted ice. It was barely noon. He was cracking up.

The four cameras on the bed. That was creepy. Setting it up was just Dmitry being kinky, but anyone with that key could watch it now. Creepy, creepy, creepy.

He grabbed the retractable knife he had bought and went straight to Yuli's room. He found each of the cameras — they were all in plain sight, but tucked into corners of the very high ceiling, white against the white plaster — and he dragged a dresser under the first one, put a bedside table on top of it, and on top of that a chair. He teetered on this improvised scaffold and cursed the whiskey sours. He snipped the wire on the first one, then went to each corner, disabling them all without killing himself. There must be a recording of him doing this — first on four cameras, then on three, then on two, then on one. In other circumstances he'd find that funny. He put the furniture back where it belonged, went to his room, and flopped onto his bed.

After his nearly sleepless night, he crashed at once, and dreamt the dreams of the devious.

He woke two hours later, showered, and wandered downstairs once more, neither drunk nor sober.

He was surprised not to be intercepted by Setiawan, whose absence made the house feel abandoned. Remarkably abandoned for early afternoon.

"Hello," he said. No response. Frank saw an envelope in the silver mail tray on the foyer table, a tray that had always been empty. It said "Franky" on the front and was sealed.

He opened it.

He knew what it would say before he read it.

> *Franky,*
>
> *Please forgive the suddenness of my departure. I needed to run to my boys. They were coming to repossess the plane, and it was my last chance. All is lost here, the banks have taken everything. I can't tell you where we are, it wouldn't be safe. But I know Dmitry told you about Tokyo. Go there. I know you'll do the right thing. I can't —*

The letter just stopped, had no signature. Stunned, he turned to see Setiawan, who had silently appeared. He was a little self-satisfied, but maybe a little sympathetic as well. Frank didn't care. He was too staggered to care.

"This is for you also," he said, not unkindly, handing him another envelope.

"Where is she?"

"I cannot tell you, most obviously."

"I'll have you arrested." Inside the envelope was a ticket to Tokyo.

"As you wish, sir."

"Tokyo."

"For you, yes, Tokyo."

"And you?" he asked, knowing he would get no answer.

Setiawan waited.

Frank couldn't stand the idea of staying in the house another minute. *I can't*, she had written. Can't what? Can't be with him, obviously. It was over.

What had he expected? Happily ever after?

Why had she stopped mid-sentence? Why no *love, Yuli?* What would that have cost her?

And what was he supposed to do in Tokyo? She had taken the jet to the island, and now was without a fortune. Maybe. Or maybe she was there with Dmitry and he had metals and currencies and accounts strewn across the globe. Why did she want Frank to go to Tokyo? Was she going there, too, keeping it a secret from Setiawan? Maybe there was a safe-deposit box for her as well.

"OK then, Mr. Setiawan, the airport."

"There is a taxi waiting. I'm afraid the chauffeur and the rest of the staff have been dismissed. You will have to gather your own things."

He went upstairs, packed his stuff, pulled his email up to see if there were any old ones from Dmitry with details about the Tokyo bank and its safe-deposit box. There was an email from his business manager titled FYI.

"Isa is getting married," it said. "She is pregnant and very happy. I thought you should know." It was signed with a little heart icon.

He didn't love the idea that Isa had shared this with his employee but not him. She didn't owe him anything, he supposed, but still. He searched and found the one email in which Dmitry mentioned Shinjuku in passing, nothing else. Then he remembered him saying Bank of Japan, because he thought at the time: if you were trying to remember the name of a bank in Japan, what easier one was there? He took care of the few other things his business manager had emailed about, told her he'd be going to Japan for a few days, that he'd get her the flight info when he could, and that she should send his congratulations to Isa. He sent chatty notes to his step-kids. He broke down and wept — not for the last time, he suspected.

His email pinged with a confirmation of his flight. It was in two hours. Fuck it, he thought, either she'll be there or she won't. He looked around one last time, checked to make sure he had everything, and went downstairs with his bags.

Amarya was posted by the front door.

"Leaving so soon?" she asked, angry.

"I'm sorry, Amarya, I didn't mean to hurt you."

"You and every other man I've ever met. Isn't it interesting how few people ever mean to hurt anyone?"

"Please, Amarya…"

"Pfff…" she said, dismissing his plea. "Really. You are so fucking clueless."

"I am."

"Yes, you are." They were standing at the door, both taut, unmoving.

"I'm sorry."

"Yes, you're sorry. And you're a fool."

"I know, I know. Where are they?"

"No, you don't want to know where they are, and you never will, unless they want you to, and if they ever do, all the worse for you." They? And what happened to the sweet little sister? "You know nothing," she added. "They're using you."

They. He was alive.

He wondered if she was somehow spinning a romantic novel in her head, the way she did with Dmitry and Yuli when she was sixteen.

"Using me how?"

She shook her head, looked away.

"All you need to know is this: you don't have a clue. Go home. Protect yourself."

"What about you?" he asked.

With that, she threw herself into his arms, tears in her eyes, gave him a serious kiss on the mouth, turned, and left.

He watched her half-run up the stairs.

The taxi driver — with some sixth sense? — opened the door and took his bag.

Frank had hopped on the plane without getting a hotel, so when he arrived at Narita he went to the Tourist Information booth and asked for one in the Shinjuku neighborhood. They said the Park Hyatt would send a car so he let them call for him. He sat on a bench outside. He was not in Kansas anymore, or in Jakarta, either. Everything about Japan — every advertisement, every structure, every piece of packaging, every bench, every sign — was meta-designed. The seat he was on had the precise amount of curve to make it impossible to sleep on, or set a drink on, or even a backpack. It was for people sitting and sitting only, an anti-loitering bench. He got a can of something called Pocari Sweat from a vending machine by pushing a button with Brad Pitt's face on it. When the car arrived from the Park Hyatt, a white-gloved driver picked up his bags. Plastic bottles of cold water sat in insulated cup holders. White crocheted liners covered the seats and the armrests. It was as if a high-end Manhattan limousine service had mated with your grandma's doilies. The city went by in alternating slabs of grey concrete and wild bursts of color.

When they arrived at the Park Hyatt a room was $916. Plus tax. He could hear Dmitry in his ear saying, "It is not good value, Franky." He told the clerk he was sorry, paid for the car service and walked out with his bags. He checked into a hotel in the next block called the Sunroute, hard to say what that meant. It was two hundred dollars and change. The room was the size of a walk-in closet, or a berth on a submarine. It was so cramped he worried he would feel like he was getting a CAT scan all night. Instead, he ate an Ambien and slept like he was already dead until the morning sun blasted through the magnifying glass of his tiny window. It was already 10am.

He jumped up, headed back to the lobby, and pulled up Google maps. The road names were in Japanese. He grabbed a map from the front desk with transliterated street names and went in search of his bank.

The science-fiction, parallel-universe feel Tokyo produced was enhanced by the odd costumes of the various youth subcultures — Bo-Peep dresses on the teenage girls, the boys in matching boyband outfits — and by the excess neon signage up and down tall buildings. He found a Bank of Japan branch on the main drag and went in. He showed his passport to an English-speaking bank officer, a classic salaryman in what now looked — after the kids outside — like a cosplay version of a suit instead of a suit. The banker looked on a computer and told him his box was at a different branch. If I were him, Frank thought, I would have found this a little suspicious, but if he did, he made no indication. The man gave him directions to the correct branch, six blocks away, and bowed. Frank bowed back, hoping it was the right thing to do.

At the second branch, he was taken by a grey-sheathed young woman, another cosplay office-worker, past a man in a security guard costume, to a room lined with deposit boxes. She opened his box for him and then left him alone with it. Inside were a dozen envelopes, which he opened one at a time. Several felt empty and were, but five of them each held a bankbook, a plastic debit card, and a sheet of paper with PIN numbers and security questions for internet access. A sixth held a British passport. Everything he had wanted to find in the box was missing: any information about what had happened, a little note from Dmitry explaining things, a confession — yes, he stupidly had thought Dmitry would have wanted to disburden himself to his old confidante, share whatever the trouble had been. He had even half hoped, illogically, to find a note from Yuli, explaining her disappearance. But instead of answering any of his questions, the contents of the box created more. That sterile room, lined with polished-steel doors, was designed to give a feeling of complete security, with its gleaming marble floor, multiple scanning cameras, and antiseptic, unscratchable surfaces. He felt the opposite. He felt at the mercy of forces he didn't in the least understand.

The bankbooks were from five different banks. He opened the one from the Bank of the Cayman Islands, and it had his name, with all his data — passport number, date of birth, name, address — and had been opened with three million dollars three years ago. The information sheet with it had a PIN code, all his biographical data, including his mother's maiden name, his father's middle name, a security question (favorite song: "Born Slippy"), phone numbers, address, social security number, driver's license number, all correct. The second was from a Swiss bank and it had been opened within a day or two of the Cayman Island account, also with three million Swiss francs, which were worth almost a dollar a piece, if he remembered right. It had the same information on the sheet, the same PIN code and slate of security questions and answers. The third was from a bank in Cyprus. It had opened with a million and a half Euros. The fourth was from the Bank of China and had, as of a few days ago, over ninety million yuan. He wasn't sure what yuan were worth, but ninety million of anything was a lot. The fifth was from the Bank of Japan, and had started with three billion yen. Thirty million dollars. The bankbooks seemed anachronistic, from a time before online banking, and he wondered what the point was. Had someone walked in and out with suitcases holding millions of dollars in cash? The Bank of Japan deposit was from 2007.

He couldn't stand not knowing and pulled up the browser on his phone. Eight yuan to the dollar: eleven million bucks. A lot of disposable income. Fifty mil all told.

He pulled out his phone and signed into the account online, using the password on the sheet. The account was getting drawn down by ten million yen a day — the outside limit, he guessed — every day for the last twenty days. It was now worth only ten million dollars and change.

Someone was taking Yuli's money.

The passport was in the name of Quentin Compson. It had his passport photo, his date of birth, and an address in Liverpool. Folded into the passport was a picture, printed from a computer, of a Scorpio

72. When had that been added? Who had he talked to about the Scorpio 72? He couldn't think — maybe Isa? He had bookmarked several of them on different yacht sales sites. Was someone monitoring his internet browsing? Or *had* he mentioned it to Yuli? He had told her about wanting to buy a sailboat, about wanting to take her sailing, her and the boys, maybe take a trip together — had he mentioned the Scorpio 72? If it was Yuli who knew, who had *she* told? Had Dmitry left instructions for someone to do it, or was it him, still very much alive, still scheming? If Yuli had been to Japan, it was mere hours ago. But she could have told someone to put it there, someone who had access to this box, and had been in it recently.

The name "Quentin Compson" was all Dmitry — although Yuli knew the Faulkner novel too. Frank couldn't figure out what the name was supposed to mean. Was it some reference to the fact that Dmitry had slept with his sister? Was it some dig at him, Frank, being a depressive romantic, a dimwit prizing fuzzy ideals over money? And why the name change? He looked back at the bankbooks. The Swiss and Cayman Islands accounts were in his name. The Bank of China account was in Quentin Compson's name, again, with the same Liverpool address as the British passport, and again, all Frank's personal details. If some of the bank accounts could be in his name, why not this largest one? What was going on? Amarya was right. He didn't have a fucking clue.

He put everything in his pockets and stepped into the street. Then it occurred to him: maybe this was an elaborate practical joke, some taunting by Dmitry from the grave. He went back in the bank and up to a teller's window. He handed over the passbook and said, in English, that he wanted five million yen, a bit more than $50,000. The teller bowed to him and went to get her supervisor. He came over and asked Frank to write down the amount he wanted, nodded and walked away with the bankbook and his passport. Might as well go down for fifty thousand bucks as a few nickels, he figured.

The supervisor came back with a small bag and his bankbook.

"I have taken the liberty to update your bankbook, sir," he said. "I hope these denominations are suitable." In the bag were ten neat, matching bundles of bills, which set off a huge shot of adrenaline.

"Thank you," he said, and thought to himself, this must be what high blood pressure feels like. High finance. Like jumping out of a plane.

He left the bank and got in a cab. The cabbie turned and looked at him, waiting for an address. Frank pointed to the Bank of China bankbook; the driver looked confused, but then nodded and took him to a branch. Frank went in, waited briefly in a line, and then asked the open-faced teller if he might make a withdrawal of five million yen from his account. She took his Quentin Compson passport and the passbook and walked over to talk to a guy who looked like a manager. The manager came over and asked how much he wanted. He told him five million yen. The manager took him over to a desk and explained he could only withdraw three million a day. Frank said OK, no problem, and they filled out some forms. He sat wondering at the strangeness of it all. The man signed off on it and walked away with the teller. He felt like a hundred security cameras were trained on him, but he reckoned there were only a dozen or so. His adrenals kicked off again when the teller returned with three million yen in six bundles of 10,000 yen notes and receipts for him to sign.

"Thank you," he said, trying to keep his hand from fluttering as he put everything in the canvas bag the Bank of Japan had given him.

"We are glad to be of service, Mr. Compson," she said. "If you have a minute, our manager would like to speak with you."

OK, here we go, he thought, and considered running. But it was too late. The manager and another man in a suit had come up, bowed low and motioned him toward an office. He walked in and took the seat they offered.

"Mr. Compson," the man who appeared to be in charge said. "We noticed that you have withdrawn very large sums in recent days, and we just wanted to make sure that you were pleased with our service, and whether there was anything we could do in the way of investment management for you." He felt like singing. "We very much appreciate your business, and would hate to lose it." He looked at the bankbook the teller had updated and saw that the ninety million yuan had grown, over the last several years, to ten times that, but that in the last weeks it had shrunk back to some forty-two million, less than five million bucks. The dozens of recent withdrawals had been electronic. Each of the last withdrawals had been for three million yuan each, and were happening every day.

Someone had electronic access to these bank accounts, someone who, right then, was sucking the majority of the funds out.

"Yes," he said. "You can help. I'm superstitious. I want to start an entirely new account, and transfer the remaining money into that account."

"Right away, Mr. Compson." He bowed and came back with a form to fill out. Frank did, and five minutes later Quentin Compson had a new account, a new VISA card, a new PIN number, and a new first pet: Fishy.

"There is a maximum for transfers?"

"That is for interbank transfers, sir. For same-bank account transfers there is no limit."

He asked the man if he could use a computer in the bank, guessing a millionaire had some perqs, and the manager took him to a small, unoccupied office, opened the computer to a browser, and left him alone. Using the information from the different envelopes, he went online and started opening new accounts at each bank, transferring the maximum allowable in each case to them, and setting up new passwords and security questions. The Cayman Island bank was very quick and easy. The Bank of Japan as well. The Cyprus Bank account showed withdrawals of ten thousand euros a day for the last three weeks or more. There were still some six million left, but the bank would let him transfer just a million a day, and he set up recurring transfers for the following days. When he got to the Swiss bank, it was empty, some twenty million Swiss francs moved only minutes earlier. Someone else was moving money. He pulled up the Bank of Japan account. Empty. Thirty million dollars, maybe more, of Yuli's money, lost forever in minutes. Someone had already figured out what he was up to. Someone out there was watching.

There was a shredder in the office and he fed the defunct bankbooks into it, the cards and information sheets. He kept just the Compson passport, his new account book, a debit card, and the cash. His accounts for Yuli were worth over $50 million. And he had $80,000 in his pocket — well briefcase — they had brought him a briefcase while he was working and had called him a limousine. He thanked the manager, who along with a half dozen minions bowed almost to the floor, and walked out into a fearsome Japanese sun.

He got in the limo, but asked the driver to stop and got out a block later. He couldn't go straight to the hotel. He walked south out of Shinjuku, with its commercial bedlam, its peak neon, its elaborate maze of advertisements plastered over every available surface, and headed toward a green patch on his hotel's map named Yoyogi Park. He wanted a moment of quiet. But first he stopped in a shop and bought a small backpack. Walking around with a briefcase felt conspicuous — he wasn't dressed for it. He transferred the cash into the backpack, and left the briefcase, open so nobody would think it was a bomb, on a windowsill.

A hundred yards into the park he passed under an enormous torii, an ornamental gate made from two perfect, round and straight tree trunks that must have been sixty or seventy feet high, with cross beams above, the top one sweeping up toward the heavens on each end, the bottom one decorated with three golden disks. Hard to say how such a simple structure could be so beautiful, Frank thought, but it was.

Families walked the park's paths, which wound off at random angles through fat old trees. A large Meiji temple complex in the middle was just what the doctor ordered — it kept him from obsessing, and he immersed himself in a simple appreciation of things Japanese. Like the kids on the streets, the Tokyo temples were all of one recognizable type or another, and all were acutely manicured. This temple had bonsai trees, purposely stunted, every twig redesigned, placed around the grounds. All the details accomplished what they were orchestrated to achieve: he felt lifted out of the trials and tribulations of his life. He felt peaceful, calm. For a time, he thought about nothing.

But that couldn't last. Confused images of Dmitry and Yuli and Amarya and the Men in Black and the police and the dictators swirled. Whoever else had access to the accounts had taken what, hundreds of millions of dollars or more out of them since the bombing? Who was it? The resurrected Dmitry? Somebody in his office? One of the bad guys? The Cambodians? Russians? Chechens? Were they the same people who blew up the building? Was "his" $50 million safe? Or did he need to change banks a couple more times to erase the traces?

If Dmitry was still alive, he was in hiding. On his island. Was he monitoring the accounts and grabbing the money from there? Did he blow the building up himself? Not likely, he didn't cook his own food, clean his own house, or even drive his own car. Did he have someone do it?

Would Dmitry have innocent people murdered? He was piggish and misogynist and had no conscience, but could he kill a hundred of his own co-workers, on purpose, cold-blooded, like that? Frank thought not. He knew him. No.

Besides, Yuli would never have let him… He tried to imagine her as an accomplice, but he couldn't. No way she could have faked the connection they had, no way she could have whispered into his ear such precious, munificent words, and not meant them. He refused to believe it. If Dmitry was a murderer, she didn't know it.

Walking through the park, on automatic, he found himself back in front of his hotel. The thought of sitting in his room taking stock — allowing the worry and doubt and fear to creep back in, stewing about what to do next — kept him moving.

He stepped into a restaurant a few blocks away, chosen because it had pictures on the menu. He ordered a sashimi dish with a whole small fish on a skewer. When it came, the five-inch fish had been filleted, and the cartoon skeleton — the head and tail intact, a set of bones in between — was curved decoratively by a skewer and served as a theatrical backdrop for the pieces of sashimi that had been mined from it. He looked up to see, eight feet away, an aquarium with a few dozen fish exactly like the one he was eating swimming around. His fish had been schooling with them just a flash of the chef's knife earlier. What was he to make of this? That we murder to live? Eat or be eaten, one creature's death another's dinner, death simply another transaction? Is this the way he would become Dmitry, coming to such conclusions?

Seeing his dinner's brothers and sisters swimming around flatlined his appetite, but with the help of a large Sapporo he managed to finish eating it. He walked out of the restaurant into Shinjuku and let the never-ending weirdness of the Tokyo streets distract him. He must have walked three or four miles by the time the sun was setting, slowly circling back toward his hotel. A small park with a temple, set in a nook in the busy city, drew him and he tried his new contemplative skills again. They worked for a half hour or so, but then he got antsy and had to move.

The money he had saved for Yuli and the boys would turn a million and a half dollars a year in a very safe portfolio. Whatever the hell was going on, she was rich enough. Not private-jet secure, but secure.

As for himself? He was just lost.

On the far side of the park he stumbled into an odd little neighborhood. Everything about it was the opposite of the neon ultramodern shopping extravaganza a block or two away. It was almost a shanty-town, unlike anything he'd seen in the city, the place hand-sewn together, single-story, low-tech, with a spaghetti of wires here and there, and a general look of dilapidated impermanence. A cobweb of alleys, too narrow for cars, ran through the warren of rickety buildings, which seemed to house nothing but tiny bars. He poked his head in one and saw a half-dozen middle-aged, bohemian-looking men occupying all the available seating. They weren't actively rude, but they were far from inviting, so he kept going.

Through the curtains of another bar, under a small blue sign, cracked and faded, with one Japanese character and a big question mark, he saw no one but a young woman behind the bar. He went in and said hello. She said hello back, and her English turned out to be pretty good. He ordered another large beer, wanting to blur out. She was an actor, she said, which made him feel back at home in Los Angeles, where all the bartenders were actors. She told him the neighborhood was called the Golden Gai and was one of the oldest neighborhoods in the relentlessly modernizing city, unimproved since it was thrown up after World War II. By the 1960s, rents low, artists, prostitutes, intellectuals, and other fringe types moved in, and it became the center of Tokyo's social, political, and artistic radicalism, the Japanese Greenwich Village. Guidebooks talk about the place, she said, so tourists ramble through during the day snapping pictures, but the same guidebooks warn tourists that the neighborhood bars don't welcome Westerners, and that there is more crime than in most other parts of the city. It was very rare to find a tourist anywhere in the maze after dark — he was her first.

He was carrying eight million yen in a backpack.

The bartender was very interested to hear anything he had to say about LA and Hollywood. Her dream, just like the LA bartenders', was to someday act in a Hollywood film. He answered her questions and recited the requisite celebrity encounters that every LA resident is forced to disclose when out of town, although as usual, even here, anyone he had a work relationship with was off limits, offering instead Drew Barrymore reading a script in a coffee shop, Ted Danson at a Pottery Barn, Jack Nicholson in a men's room. By the time he finished talking to her he had had a couple beers, and had a significant buzz going. He thanked her, stepped back out into the alley, and felt quite drunk.

The alley had a noir feel, criminals lurking in the shadows, no one else to be seen. The bars, despite open doors with only bead screens, were disturbingly quiet. After a block or so, he decided, OK, maybe the guidebooks are right, maybe it's dangerous. He made a U-turn to follow his steps back out of the neighborhood. As he did, across from the Question Mark, a short red-haired guy popped out of another bar. When he saw Frank, he made an awkward swing away, and with the deliberate yet wayward step of a stoned person on a mission, started down the road ahead of him. How odd, Frank thought, that the only other person in the Gai was a foreigner. The man kept forty paces ahead but was starting to slow down. Frank had lost track, watching him, of his own route home, and something started to seem suspicious, almost as if the guy was keeping track of him. He stopped, and the man slowed down and stopped, too, swaying as if drunken, but listening. Frank was poised to run in the opposite direction, maybe back to the Question Mark, at least get off the deserted streets. The guy turned. A cold shiver whiplashed him. It was the Irish guy from Dmitry's office, the guy who tried to pick a fight with him at the brothel.

"Hey!" Frank shouted, motioning to him with his chin, but without getting any closer, like gunfighters in the Old West. "You worked with Dmitry at Credit Lyonnais."

The guy did a big show of looking over his shoulders, as if to see who Frank was talking to, hand to his chest, eyebrows raised. He wore a heavy metal band's black t-shirt and jeans, like a sailor on shore leave, but Frank was pretty sure it was the same guy.

"Me?" he said.

"Yes, we spent that crazy night in some brothel in Taipei, the day the new guy, the guy from Hong Kong who had lost all the weight, the night he came to town. I'm Dmitry's friend from California."

"Sorry, mate," he said, with what sounded like a fake Australian accent. "Wrong bloke." He started to walk away.

"You're kidding me!" Frank said, maybe a little too loud. The guy turned back around. The glint of the sociopathic streetfighter returned to his eye, the very glint he remembered, making him even surer he had the right guy. "That's right," Frank said, "Don't walk away," imitating someone whose threats should be taken seriously. It had worked for him with the Men in Black.

That brought the guy closer. Looking Frank in the eye, he said, "OK, mate, then *you* walk away." They stood like that for a minute, a cheesy standoff, until Irish shook his head and added, "You have no idea," turned, and walked away.

"So I'm told," Frank said after him.

The guy ducked into another bar. The sign outside was green but said "Orange." Frank followed him in. There were two small tables and three seats at the bar. An old Japanese beatnik was playing acoustic guitar. Two guys sat drinking beer and smoking cigarettes. A pretty woman was behind the bar — that seemed to be the norm. She was wearing a t-shirt with a picture of a woman with half her face ripped off, the muscles and veins exposed. The little Irish guy was standing near the bar, but facing the door as Frank came in. The other four people in the place took no explicit notice of the newcomers.

"Talk to me," Frank said. The guitarist kept playing and started to sing. It might have been 'All Along the Watchtower.' It might have been in Japanese, but maybe English.

"It's amazing you're still alive," Irish said.

"I try not to take it for granted."

"Seems to me you do."

He spent some time thinking about that: a threat? His second death threat in as many days? Hm. It slowed him to a stop. The Irish guy walked over to him and he heard a metallic whoosh and click and looked down to see a large, gleaming switchblade pointed at his belly. The guy leaned next to his ear and said:

"Go pick up your fucking boat and get out of here. Go home. Go anywhere. But go the fuck away."

With that he walked past him and left Frank staring at the place the knife had been. The old beatnik kept playing — now it sounded like some other Dylan song. He finally looked up, still trying to process what he had just heard, to see the bartender watching him — he could see now the woman on the shirt was ripping her own face off with her right hand, elbow raised. None of the other patrons looked at him. He made his way back into the ramshackle street, where there was no trace of the Irish guy. The old man's sour voice and tinny guitar leaked into the street and then stopped. A door closed. The green "Orange" sign blinked once and went out.

Frank made his way back to the hotel. The Irish sociopath: *he* had put that picture of the sailboat in the safe-deposit box — how else would he know about it? Bumping into him was no accident — he'd been following Frank and accidentally got caught when he turned around. Was he doing this alone? Monitoring Frank's every move? Had he been the one emptying the bank accounts? He had all the same information Frank had, since he'd been in the box. Who else was part of this? Setiawan? Why? The beer wasn't helping him think clearly. The knife had briefly scared him straight, but now he was feeling woozy again.

Was Irish executing some prearranged errands for Dmitry? Is he the guy in charge of the exposure and everything else? He, Prabam, the Men in Black, Amarya, and everyone else said the same thing: Frank had no idea what he was up against, and they didn't want him to know more than he did. Why *go home*? And if *go home*, then why the ticket to Tokyo? And why the boat? Didn't that say *stay*?

If Irish had access to the safe-deposit box, why leave all that money for Frank, why not take some of it for himself? Maybe he had, maybe there had been stacks of cash. Maybe he emptied the other envelopes of their bankbooks and passwords when he dropped the boat picture off, and that they had even larger sums. If he was stealing Dmitry's money, no wonder he wanted Frank to go away. And what about the knife? If he wanted to knife him, why didn't he? He wanted to scare him away, not kill him.

Had the Irish guy set the bomb at Credit Lyonnais? He had wanted to fight Dmitry that night — did he kill him? And if so, had he kidnapped Yuli? That would explain how she could leave him after a night like the one they had, and why her note was unfinished. Then again, maybe the Irish guy was doing Yuli's bidding, maybe she was trying to protect Frank, and give him what she could — the boat, some cash — and keep him safe: the bad guys were afoot, and Frank needed to get out of town. The only way Irish could know Frank had been snooping around is if Yuli had told him, so that must be it, he decided: *she* must be trying to protect *him*. Irish was his shadow bodyguard.

He somehow found his way back to the Sunroute, and in his room he looked through his bag and found the cards of the two Taiwanese detectives. He didn't want the sour sidekick, he wanted the moonfaced guy in charge, but since he didn't know which card went with which guy, he just flipped a coin. He didn't know what to say, either, what he wanted to say, or what he ought to say. He would just have to wing it. It was earlier in Taipei, but already way after office hours. He'd leave a voicemail.

A man answered right away, which was surprising, and in Chinese, which was not.

"Is this the detective investigating the Credit Lyonnais bombing?" Frank barged ahead in English.

"Yes," the man answered in English.

"This is Frank Baltimore."

"Yes." Apparently he got the sour one.

"I don't really know how to begin."

"Where are you?" he asked.

"In Tokyo."

"Japan."

"Yes." Is there another one?

"Good."

"Good?" What did that mean?

"Sir."

This was getting nowhere. "I have reason to believe crimes have been committed," Frank said, wondering if he was still drunk. "I want to report a crime." Crime?

"In Tokyo?"

"No, well, yes — I know who did it."

"Please, I tell you, sir," his voice got quieter. "There is warrant for you in Taipei. Accessory after fact. Money laundering after bombing of Credit Lyonnais building."

"Me?"

"Yes. Franky Bal'more. With warrant we arrest you at airport." Frank sat trying to figure this out. He was a wanted man. How incongruous.

"At airport, Taipei," he repeated, as if he, too, had limited English.

"Yes, Taiwan only. Stay away Taiwan."

So he couldn't go to Taipei. OK. Did he care?

"It was another Credit Lyonnais banker, the Irish one," he said into the phone. "He is alive. He is here, in Tokyo. He did it."

There was silence on the other end. When the detective spoke, it was low and ominous.

"Franky Bal'more not safe."

He tried to understand this as a warning, but it didn't work. It was a threat.

His mind was too slow, but it gradually dawned on him that the police themselves were somehow involved. He had just accused the Irish guy of blowing up the building, and the cop agreed and then threatened Frank. Silence. The cop could stand a lot of dead time on the phone.

"Why are you telling me this?" he heard himself finally ask, still with some nagging need to understand more.

"Mr. Dmitry Heald have many friends in police," he said, almost whispering. "I am friend."

"Have…" Was he just not using the right tense?

"Thank you for information, Mr. George," he said, suddenly loud, for somebody else's benefit, and hung up.

The hotel room felt doubly claustrophobic. Warrant for his arrest. Money laundering. He felt like a puppet. Every second he sat in the room it seemed smaller. The walls were closing in. He was having trouble breathing.

None of it made sense. *Had* the cop agreed to the idea that the psycho-killer Irish punk was the bomber? Or was Frank just over-interpreting his silence? Had this cop been paid off by the Irish runt? Why, then, had the cop and his colleague come to Jakarta? Maybe one got paid off and the other hadn't. Maybe he got paid off after the trip. But why and by who? What did it have to do with Dmitry's *many friends* in the department? Maybe they're right. Maybe he should get out of there. Let the crooks kill someone else.

Then he got it. Like he was slowly making his way through a mathematical proof, he put it together. Not only did the Quentin Compson passport make it possible for him to fly to Taipei and pick up his Scorpio 72, somebody had known that it would. And wanted him to go back to Taipei not as Frank Baltimore — and make a mess of things — but as Quentin, wanted him to buy his boat and sail away. Whoever arranged for the extra passport knew that he would need it, and wanted no part of Franky Bal'more, known associate. And of course Quentin Compson couldn't go to the police or the embassy — how good was that passport, anyway? The hotel room was now torturously small.

"Fuck it," he said out loud. He stood up, packed his bag, checked out, walked across the block, and checked into the Park Hyatt with his Quentin Compson passport. He was a freaking millionaire after all. He was shown to his overlarge room, cracked a beer from the mini-bar — bad value — and flipped open his laptop, thinking everyone was corrupt. Everyone. Among his new emails was one from a woman he had dated a month or so earlier. It seemed like a different life, but seeing her name gave him a little shot of warmth. He opened it. The subject line was "thinking about what happened between us." She wrote:

> *Dear Frank,*
>
> *I realized that I just wouldn't feel right about it all unless I said, at least in an email: fuck you.*

OK. Sweet.

He shut his email, pulled up Google. Typed in "Tokyo, escort service." He was drunk and depressed and surly and lonely. And rich. The Miss Platinum escort service charged 200,000 yen before tip. $2,000. He had a pocket full of cash. He browsed the available women. He picked one. He picked up the phone. She would arrive, he was told, within thirty minutes. They insisted on a credit card, and he rifled through his pockets, found the debit card for the account in Cyprus, and read off the sixteen numbers, the expiration date, the three-number code on the back. He put the phone down and grabbed another beer.

An incoming email popped up. It was from you-lee22@gmail.com. He opened it. It had only two words:

Come back.

You-lee22. Yuli. That answered the question whether he really wanted the call girl. It also, at least for now, answered the question of what he was going to do with his life.

He hit reply and typed: *I'm on the next flight.*

He checked back out of the hotel fifteen minutes and $1,121 later — $40 for the two beers — and went to the airport. He called the escort service from the car and canceled. They would keep a 50 percent service charge. Sure. What did he care? He got to the airport and was on a redeye to Jakarta within the hour.

When he arrived in the morning, Yuli's driver was waiting for him in the entrance hall, apparently not fired after all. On the ride from the airport the glass between the front and back seats was closed, leaving Frank free to imagine his reunion with Yuli in a hundred different ways — all of them a little fraught, none of them quite right. Had something happened to bring her back so soon? Did it have anything to do with the Taiwanese cop? Or the Irish guy in Tokyo?

Maybe she loved him. Maybe she needed him. Could he stand to entertain the thought? No, no he couldn't. Not just for the obvious reason, that if he got crushed again, he'd have to tie an iron to his foot and jump in a river. Something was gravely wrong with the whole picture, something so not right that love could not possibly be at the center of it.

Still, despite all such nauseating conjecture, when the driver dropped him inside the gate, he trotted up the path, anxiety replaced by anticipation, surprised to realize — and then surprised that he was surprised — that he was ecstatic at the idea of seeing her again.

The front door, as usual, opened just before he reached it. He smiled: he was even going to be happy to see Setiawan again.

But it wasn't Setiawan at all, of course.

It was Dmitry.

Of course it was Dmitry.

PART FIVE

2013

"I should really like to say, *Hey, no, you look like you've seen a ghost!* but I have a feeling, Franky, you mightn't be in the mood to find that particularly amusing."

"You're alive." As if he could continue deluding himself, as if he had ever really thought Dmitry was dead. All of a sudden he realized that everyone could see it — he hadn't even pretended to mourn his friend's passing. He hadn't tried to find out who had killed him. Why would he? Dmitry was alive.

"You sound so disappointed." His trademark goofy grin looked more like a smirk than ever.

Frank didn't know where to start. "Robert Mugabe?" he blurted out. "You dedicated your life to helping Robert Mugabe?"

"Ah, so that is what is bothering you?" Smirk. They remained standing in the foyer.

No, it wasn't the main thing bothering him, not by a long shot. "It doesn't bother you?" he asked anyway. He wanted to cry. Instead, he continued down the wrong path, like Dmitry skydiving, unable to turn. "Don't you ever think about the fact that you're helping the worst men in the world stay in power, and get more powerful?"

"OK, I'll pretend for the moment this is what you are upset about, Franky. Do you think I should have refused and let Citibank manage Mugabe's money, on the off chance they would get a worse return, thus weakening, by half a percentage point, his hold over the Zimbabwean people? That is a silly way to understand the world."

Frank wondered: did he care about Dmitry's crimes at all? Why was he talking about them?

"And I must say before we go any further, that your brand of resentment, this peasant hatred you have for the rich, it really clouds your judgment about everything, since the rich *are* like you and me — in fact they are identical. You are, even before my largesse, among the top one percent of wage earners on the planet, and, exactly like me, you make your own quite comfortable living off people even richer than you. Having a home recording studio, when you aren't a musician, Franky, is a rich person's sport."

Did Frank tell him about the actor? He couldn't remember. Dmitry was alive. Frank's world was dead.

"Cat got your tongue? I suppose not believing myself that I was dead, I have a hard time realizing that you really bought it — I had an idea you'd seen through all this. In fact, you did, didn't you, right? Ah, here is Setiawan finally."

Setiawan came in with a tray of Bloody Marys, handed one to Dmitry and one to Frank.

"I thought you didn't drink," Frank said.

"Mine's virgin. Yours has a little kick to it. I thought you might want it. And a nice bookend, right? You had Bloody Marys your first morning here, if I'm not mistaken." He walked into the parlor and sat. Frank's knees being weak, he followed suit. His glance went to the scimitars.

"I don't know where to begin," he said. And he didn't.

"Well, let's get rid of one source of your apprehension: my days as handmaiden to the rich are over, and yours, too, if you want — we neither of us need to do that anymore, do we? And I *am* interested to see how my little accidental experiment will work, Franky — will you turn over all those ill-gotten gains to a charity, or the SEC? Or will you do what normal people do with money, use it, enjoy it. I am predicting a solid ten percent goes to charity and that you develop a very good and highly ethical rationale for why you will keep the rest. Then, upon finding yourself a rich person without any plausible deniability, you will have no choice but to hate yourself."

He laughed at this and Frank didn't. Instead he drank half his Bloody Mary in a long draught.

"But since I digress," he went on, "allow me to digress further. You have it all wrong about Mugabe and the others. I never worked *for* those men. People make this mistake all the time, and obviously the error has almost always been in my favor — people think their broker is their friend, a person who wants to provide a service to them, one who cares about their financial wellbeing. But that couldn't be more specious. Your broker is not your friend. Your broker is never your friend. Your broker is, in effect, your opponent. You want to invest your money, make money with your money. Your broker wants to use your money, too, your capital, in order to make money for himself, and he keeps you on the hook by releasing dribs and drabs — one of those great phrases, eh, Franky? As far as I can tell of unknown origin — by doling out minor parcels of the profit, just enough to keep the capital pump primed. The singular goal, for the broker, is to make money for himself, period. The client is no more or less than a pack animal in the caravan, carrying his or her load of capital across the financial desert, and only a stupid caravanner doesn't feed his camels. Mugabe, the rest of them — they are my camels. I don't help them; they help me. I *use* them."

Frank looked at him. Dmitry was calm, and preoccupied, as if unhurriedly trying to remember where he put down his keys. The keys to his Bombardier Global Express.

"And don't you have to admit, Franky, that, having pulled some fifteen billion dollars out of the system, I have inadvertently joined your crusade to change human nature, your redistributive revolution? I have, in fact, not grown the money supply of the bad, bad people who run the world, I've shrunk it. I have made the world a better place by extracting money from their pockets and putting it in mine own."

He will be leaving here to join her on his island, Frank thought. In his jet. There was nothing he could do. He couldn't follow them. And what would he possibly follow them *for*? He had lost the ability to think. He was an open mouth, an outstretched palm, a beggar's bowl.

"Fifteen *billion* dollars?"

"More, actually, and yes, quite astounding, isn't it? I always wanted to amass a trillion pounds, Franky, ever since I was a wee lad — that's impossible, as we know, but I have now, at least, made over a trillion yen! If my wealth were not so damnably well hidden, I would end up just ahead of Carl Ichan on the *Forbes* list. But really, Franky, my *crimes*? How can it be a crime to give money to those men and it also be a crime to take it from them? You have always allowed an unconscionable level of contradiction in your moral philosophy."

Frank knew if he stayed silent, Dmitry would just go on, and besides, his tongue didn't seem to be working.

"I would add, Franky, that the parade of people waiting to help these men manage their money is long and deep, anyone could do it. But stealing fifteen billion dollars *from* them? Not many people, Franky, could do that, only thirty or forty of us in the world. It takes quite a clever man to do that."

Frank was sprawled on the same couch where Amarya had first kissed him, the same couch where he sat with Yuli evening after evening, in his brief days of bliss. He downed his Bloody Mary and Setiawan immediately refilled his glass.

"Yes, it takes quite a clever man to blow up a building," Frank said, his mouth having taken over the argument without any brain involved. "As a business maneuver! A clever man to walk around with the blood of hundreds of innocent people on their hands."

"There *are* no innocent people. But that aside, I do regret the carnage, Franky, more than you can know."

"So you did do it." He finally admitted it to himself: he hadn't quite believed it.

"Oh, very good, Franky, that was a bluff, was it? Well done. I thought you actually had figured it out. Regardless, my little *Oirish* colleague claims that the size and timing of the blast was unintended; we had agreed on a much more contained conflagration and at night. Then again, he is probably lying since, as I'm sure you can see, he is a bit of a sadist. Still, like the man said, *for thirty years under the Borgias, they had warfare, terror, murder and bloodshed, but they produced Michelangelo, Leonardo da Vinci and the Renaissance. In Switzerland, they had brotherly love, they had five hundred years of democracy and peace — and what did that produce? The cuckoo clock."*

"Nicely performed." He was an utter, callous brute.

"You gave me that book, Franky."

"That speech isn't in the book. It's in the movie. Orson Welles wrote it on set."

"And as you also showed me, there is something absolutely beautiful about useless information."

"You remember when Welles says it, right? His friend has found out he isn't dead, and so have the police, and he's about to get caught." He finished his drink again.

"Yes, Franky, why else would I have quoted it? Try to stay on track." He winked and smiled at him. "But, hey, really, how can I *get caught?* There is no crime. There are no fingerprints — didn't they have fingerprints in *The Third Man?*"

"Faking your own death is an admission of guilt. I'll let the cyberpolice take it from there." He didn't think he was drunk, but he felt like throwing up.

"I never faked anything, Franky; this is a very different story, is it not? I was in shock and feared for my life, and in hiding — someone had just murdered my colleagues! We had no memorial service, we collected no insurance, I came back to my family's home, all completely normal and understandable. I've been here the whole time, as you know, since you spent some hours in my little attic room, and as the servants will testify. The police report, which will be released shortly, will explain that the blast was the result of a gas leak — no bombs involved. And this is interesting: we calculated the length of time it takes people to stop caring about traumatic events, based on how many people die, and the cause, and came up with a date about two weeks from today. And in any case, Franky, no crime, no evidence, no nothing. A pity that so many records were destroyed in the blast. Oh, and the copies I had? The ones you were so assiduously nosing through? They are all digitized and shredded now. And the encryption is done by Assange's people. Neither you nor anybody else can possibly see them, unless I decide you should."

"Maybe I should just turn you over to the other side, let Robert Mugabe and Omar Bongo and Han Sen and Vladimir Putin get their revenge."

"My goodness, Franky. Delusions of grandeur. Even if they were in the slightest bit interested, how would you manage that?"

"Just let them know you are alive and where you are."

"You must love her very much."

Frank didn't have much to say to that.

"Did you really think, by the way, old man," he asked, again with the Orson Welles smirk, "that you could make her forget everything she's ever known?"

Frank had never understood, until that very moment, what it meant to want to murder someone. He started to get up, but Smith and Jones, on some signal of Dmitry's, had stepped into the room.

"What up, Hollywood?" the short one said. Dmitry gave him a look and they both took a step back.

"Frick and Frack," Frank said. "They're yours."

"Good boy! Yes, they're mine. Charming, aren't they? So American. Like from a movie!"

"All those cops, too?"

"No, one of the Taiwanese detectives was really after me, the other on my payroll. And the Jakarta cops, well, they wouldn't have been a problem if it came to that."

For some reason Frank remembered that horrible loud POP of an elbow snapping out of its socket in Fullerton. He felt stiff, could barely move. He sat down, drank more of his replenished Bloody Mary — he hadn't notice Setiawan come back — thought of the first one he had had with Yuli. Maybe he dropped a tear.

"Atta boy, drink up! But there is something you *must* understand. The men you mentioned — whatever their alleged crimes — they are all in a very small club, and that club is also now my club. I don't need to do business any more, I really don't, but I don't want to become persona non grata in the various places you know nothing about but where I will now spend most of my time. The rumor that I somehow ripped these people off would definitely make it difficult to renew my membership in that club, as it were, and it would be untrue. I didn't rip them off."

"Yes you did — where else did you get the plane and the island. You just said you got them with Mugabe's money."

"Mugabe, Mugabe, why this obsession?" He turned to the short man in black. "Erase the security system mainframe and leave it off — I'm fine here." They stood there a moment too long, Kafka's assistants, but then left in unison. Dmitry turned back to him. "Franky! Zimbabwe's entire economy rolls not much more than thirty billion US per annum; he rakes off one or two percent, has to dole out at least half of that to his cronies to keep himself propped up, and ends up with pretty small potatoes — one hundred million US a year or so. He invests half of that with us and we get a return of ten or twelve percent, of which the company takes one and I skim maybe two. In my five years with him he was worth maybe a million US a year, no more. Real money, but not *Forbes* money."

Frank tried to get up, but couldn't. He couldn't feel his legs.

"Credit Lyonnais," he said. "They have better people than Mutt and Jeff there. I'm sure *they'd* be interested to know you took their clients for twice what they were getting."

"Such a hedgehog, after all, Franky! But again, don't be silly — would you be hearing any of this if it were documentable? The accounting software was modified to hide much more than that, company-wide, and we modified it back in time for the blast. Everything we did along those lines is thoroughly untraceable, unfindable, vanished."

"Along those lines."

"Very good, Franky, you're paying attention. The real money came from the access all these relationships gave me. A new oil refinery in Angola? I buy bundles of the contractor's stock through complicated strings of holding companies, passing through the countries that make a living being lax about such things. The contract is announced, the stock jumps, my people sell it. The Indian government hires a French company to build a dozen nuclear reactors? I am in Areva stock a week before the announcement, out of it a week or even a day later. The Angolan interior minister and the Indian undersecretary of energy get large payoffs, but the payoffs are a minor business cost as well as great insurance against exposure. I couldn't have done one fiftieth as much without the highly irregular temporary use of massive Credit Lyonnais assets, but they were all returned safe and sound. Thankfully, there were no major disasters — one always has to worry about a new war breaking out in Angola or some democratic or religious madness in India. But we had no unrecoverable losses, and all the working capital is back where it started, no regulatory agency the wiser."

"Then why do you have to hide? Who is still looking for you?"

"Ah, Franky, I'll admit that one thing that still puzzles me is the question of how much of your ignorance is willful. You can't pull down a few billion dollars a year without people noticing — and any number of people, some for good reason, some with no reason at all, believe that they should get a taste of that money. Some of them feel, unjustly in my view, that because I was so much more successful than they were, my practices were somehow unfair. That I violated some unspoken pact amongst us thieves."

"Honor," he said. "Honor among thieves." He felt stupid, and his tongue had now followed his legs into dullness. He might have said theivth.

"Yes, but these are not just thieves, they're pirates. The government ministers, the CEOs, the fixers: they all look at my pile of money, and like all pirates everywhere they are willing to destroy a lot of people to get their hands on it. Not because it's mine — they feel the same way about any pile of money they see. They wouldn't be who they are if they felt any other way. And when we're talking this kind of loot, things get murderous quite easily."

"I thought you said your 'pile' was all hidden in different people's names and that kind of thing," he said, again slurring a word or two. "How do they even know it's there, how do they know enough to covet it?"

"'Covet'? — really, Franky? So biblical, and your Freudian slip is showing." He was right. Frank was not in control of what he was saying. "But to answer you, it's a small world. I retired at thirty-one and bought a sixty-million-dollar jet, took a half-dozen very profitable small- and mid-cap companies private, and bought quite a lot of real estate on several continents. Everyone in my business can do that kind of math. They may not know any of the details, but the central story may as well have been printed in the *New York Times*. They won't know whether I put together five billion or fifty, but they know that is somewhere in that range. They have less, and think they should have gotten a taste. I think not."

"And they are willing to hurt you to get it. Show — I mean so — you are putting yourthelf and everyone you know at rithk by reappearing now."

"Touching of you to worry about me, Franky!" he smiled, patronizing. "And who could you possibly be referring to with 'everyone I know'? Maybe you mean our Irish friend. He will be so moved to hear of your concern." He laughed. Frank didn't bother responding.

Heckle and Jeckle returned. Dmitry nodded to them and they went out the front door.

He rolled one shoulder. "Do you think I'm getting too old for jiu-jitsu, Franky? I seem to take longer recovering after a good scrimmage these days." Frank let that stand as the rhetorical question it was. "To be clear, though, I'm not sure I *am* reappearing quite yet, although I am itching to reenter international competition before I really do get too old. It's a question of staying out of the limelight long enough for everyone to save face, to not look like I'm flaunting things. This is more a leftover business courtesy than anything else."

Frank was hardly listening to him. Thinking about Yuli caught him up. She had known all along that Dmitry was alive. *He* must have told her to take Frank to bed. *She hadn't cared about me at all*, he whined to himself. *I am an unmitigated idiot who will spend the rest of my life bereft. And her? If someone asked her if I was blond- or brown-haired, if I had a mustache, would she even know?*

Meanwhile, he was on the verge of passing out — was he going to faint? Dmitry blathered on and on.

"Franky, are you there?" Dmitry asked and waited as Frank zoned back in from unconsciousness. "If I have your complete attention, nod." Frank couldn't move his head. He blinked. He was drugged. Something in his drink. "As I was saying, these people may want to break my legs, but if you go shooting your mouth off they'll break yours first. You're a bigger threat to them than I am. They know I'll keep my mouth shut." God, that smirk. Frank wanted to punch him in it. But he couldn't move his arms.

"I wuv Wuwi." He heard himself saying it before he realized he was going to say it.

"Of course you do, Franky. She is exquisite, as you told her so many times the other night."

"You don' de-zuv huh." Aglow with rage, unable to move, his tongue a mess.

"Deserve her, hm. I'm not sure we have time for rehashing our various arguments about just desserts, Franky. The Jews didn't deserve the Holocaust, Mickey Rourke deserved an Oscar, I don't deserve my life — let's agree to agree that people don't get what they deserve and move on."

Nothing Frank said appeared in his consciousness until it was already said. He tried to say *You humiliate her. Make her do things, cheat on her*, but the consonants were smushed and vowels disappearing — *megadofings*, *cheenr*. He wanted to say something else, but couldn't remember what it was. He mumbled a version of *gynecologist…*

"Well, if you are going to start impeaching my sexual conduct, let's review for a moment, shan't we? You couldn't grow up in time to stay with Tracy, you've recently sent that poor little girl Isa packing — she really loved you, Franky, you know that, don't you? — when all she wanted was a child, a child you could well afford, even a nanny or two, no nappies for you, no work — but no, after selfish Franky takes poor Isa off the marriage-and-children market for her five most sellable years, he dumps her off at the Goodwill when he's done. You've been having sex with desperate older women and confused younger women in Los Angeles without a thought to their happiness *or* their financial wellbeing, and as you know, I am the opposite — I do take some pains to see to everyone's finances, helping to support many women on a daily basis. And let's not forget, closer to home, my home, that is, you slept with your good friend's grieving widow, not only before the corpse was cold, but before it had even been found. Oh, and sleeping with her sister, too! Tacky!"

Frank realized he was paralyzed. The drug in his vodka — was it lethal or just incapacitating him?

"I'm a sexual criminal because I help pay their rent? Please."

Dmitry stood up and Setiawan came in and took their glasses. Frank's head fell sideways toward his shoulder, and he couldn't lift it back up. Was he drooling?

"Ah, I see the drug is achieving its full result. I thought you'd appreciate the Chandleresque effect. And I wasn't sure how far your misplaced chivalry might take you. Even if this does kind of make me the Fat Man."

"S'Hammett, na Shandler," he mumbled. He was definitely drooling.

Setiawan, the driver, and the Blues Brothers were going by, loaded down with suitcases.

He wasn't sure why, but Frank started remembering a certain evening in Connecticut, at dusk, as they were taking their baths in the pond, he and Dmitry — he remembered it fondly, odd as he knew it might sound, the sun setting, his body aching from a long hard day, sinking into the water, chilly at first, but regulated by the sun and the Earth to be the exact temperature the local beasts might find amenable, the grime of sawdust and cement dust melting away, the magic of immersion doing its work, and he thought of the Ganges and the innumerable watery rituals of birth and rebirth the world over, listening to the katydids in the trees among the myriad insect sounds and frog burps and birdsong: primal, pastoral, pacific. Was this part of their perverse bond? That particular night they were washing up as usual, which meant one guy soaping up for a while, handing off the bar while the other rinsed, then handing it back for the other to do his hair or whatever since they used the same soap for shampoo, and in the course of things Dmitry, absentminded, handed him the soap directly after rubbing it around his genitals and the crack of his ass, straight from his ass to the handoff.

"The fuck the fuck the fuck, Dmitry!"

"What, Franky?"

"You just had that soap in your crack!"

"Well, truth be told, Franky, that particular bar of soap has been in both of our cracks every day for a week or more, twice on Sunday."

"At least rinse the damn thing off."

"It's not necessary, Franky, it's soap."

"It's soap with your asscrack gunk on it."

"Don't be neurotic, Franky," he said. "Soap is by its very nature clean, cleaner than what it comes in contact with. Otherwise it couldn't work."

He wasn't sure why this memory seemed to sum things up for him, but, at that moment, debilitated by whatever was in his drink, devolved into a junky nod, it did.

"I should thank you for taking such good care of my wife, and frankly, Franky, we have enjoyed everything so far — quite a good show the other night, by the way — much more acrobatic and inventive than when you fucked my girlfriend in Connecticut — although, as I'm sure you can appreciate, a tad sappy for my taste in the verbal department."

Dmitry looked at him for a moment with pity. Then the smirk returned.

"As we know, though, all good things, etcetera, etcetera, etcetera as the king says, and you are starting to make people nervous. Our petite Irish friend. My policemen. Even the normally unflappable, always exquisite Yuli. So. Our revels now must end. Go home, or go to Taipei and buy your boat. Enjoy my money. Turn around and face the wind."

Yuli came out, as if on cue, wearing a bright yellow sleeve of a dress, seemingly made of leather.

Frank was not sure if he was weeping or not. "Don't leave me," he said, and then thought, again: how stupid! Could not even this night dampen his colossal illusion? At least it sounded like *dahlimi*, he thought — maybe nobody caught it.

She walked over to him and framed his face gently with her hands. She kissed him tenderly on the forehead, straightened his head out and then kissed him once on each cheek. She looked him in the eye, and he thought maybe she teared up a little. "You are a very sweet man," she whispered in his ear, "and you made me feel as good as I have ever felt, ever. Nothing he can say or do will ever change that." Then she kissed him on his numb mouth and turned and walked toward the door. It was — well, it was a smart thing to say, a way to keep him loyal to her. Yes, smart. She was a smart woman. Was that all it was? He didn't know and didn't care. He felt ridiculously grateful. Dmitry kept smiling.

"Don't forget to give Setiawan cash for the movers," Yuli said to Dmitry as she reached the front door, without looking back, and he felt like Caraway, seeing Tom and Daisy in their familial mode — he felt betrayed by their domestic chatter. Then she left. Forever.

"I shouldn't say this, Franky, but I can't resist."

He took a wad of cash from his pocket, and counted out a number of bills.

"I am a bit disappointed in you. I had always fancied you behaving like a Henry James character in such a grand moment, renouncing your own gratification, careful to get nothing for yourself — your favorite line, yes? I always knew that in the small ways you were as selfish as the rest of us, but you were always so preachy — do you remember the night you said loudly to all my colleagues that Wilcox, the new guy, was a 'prissy fucking tool'? He remained 'P. F. T.' around the office until his untimely death in the blast; not nice of you, Franky, however accurate. You are not altogether, in your great solemnity, kind. But I thought providing you such a splendid stage, such a magnificent set-up for a renunciative declaration, you might finally live up to it all. It occurs to me that 'renunciative' may not be a word. Pity. Should be."

"'S'fur," Frank said, trying to say *it was for her*.

"Cat really does have your tongue now! But yes, Franky, you have let me down. You could have left my gifts in the safe-deposit box. You could have thrown them in my face. You could have said at any moment, or even now, that you would not take such blood money, such a bribe to buy your silence and absence. But you didn't. It confirms to a T my assumptions about human nature, but it saddens me a little that you didn't, after all, prove to be the last upright man you so would like to think of yourself as, and as I, I'm sorry to admit, was counting on myself — your rectitude was the final frontier for my cynicism. Now there's no one left for me to look up to. I feel it as a loss. My guess is you will too. Is that what I wanted? Perhaps…"

He stood up, rolled his shoulder once more. Frank could no longer even move his eyes in their sockets.

"Oh, and one more thing. The money in those accounts? I thought that putting some money in your name would somehow repay you for the land yacht fiasco — pushing that thing down the hill *was* awfully callous of me, I'll admit, exposing you to charges of insurance fraud and negligent homicide and all that, and I did feel bad about it at the time. So the accounts were penance. But the first of it came in before I had perfected the art of laundering, and it is traceable — in fact traceable to a Chechen pipeline deal, a deal Credit Lyonnais financed and that went belly up. Once you came over and started mucking things up, it occurred to me that I had a way to insure your silence."

Yuli was gone forever.

"For a while I despaired of you ever doing it, and so had to bring Frick and Frack, as you say, in to goad you — which still didn't do it! — forcing me to stage the kidnapping of my own dear wife in order to get you to finally do me the favor of physically, in person, posing for the security cameras at Bank of China and Bank of Japan as both yourself and Quentin Compson. Moving money into new accounts — thus cementing your ownership — and your criminal impersonations of fictional characters put you in the bull's eye instead of me. Your gallantry, running off to claim the money for your exquisite Yuli, makes you, forever, the most exposed unindicted co-conspirator — unindicted only because as of yet there are no indictments.

"I reclaimed the majority of the money, as you saw — it came to a tidy half-billion or so — all except that fifty-two and half million you so ingeniously transferred into new accounts — brilliant, that, and welcome to it. I am sorry in advance if any of this catches up with you, Franky, but I assume knowing how things stand will help you to *lay low*" — it was the least funny use of his gangster voice ever — "and help you *keep your trap shut*."

He paused as if he had lost interest and started to leave the room. Then he turned and stopped.

"Listen, Franky. If any further misplaced gallantry prompts you to come after me, you will lose that fifty million, because I will expose it, inform the IRS and tax services, you will be a target of various government agents and much worse people, and you will go to jail or die or both. So let's call it even, yes?"

He was halfway out of the room.

"I must say, it does seem, especially given that you slept with my wife, a fitting risk to saddle you with."

But you wanted me to sleep with her, he tried to say. "*Buchewwannamseepher*."

Dmitry walked out of Frank's range of vision. Since Frank couldn't turn his head, he couldn't tell what he was doing.

"Ah, Franky," he said from somewhere behind the chair. "What do any of us really want?"

He walked back into Frank's line of sight in the foyer, looked around the room as if seeing whether he had forgotten anything, grabbed a black attaché case from the hall table, and handed the cash he had counted out earlier to Setiawan, who had, once again, thaumaturgically appeared.

Dmitry said something in Bahasa, and Setiawan came over and moved Frank's head so he could see the door. The puppet master setting up his own exit.

Dmitry's driver, Prabam, opened the door from outside and Dmitry turned to face Frank one last time.

"Do not try to contact me or Yuli again," he said, "will you, old man?" And then, with a last smirk, he was gone. The lights went out.

2017

And so.

Frank had christened the Scorpio 72 *God Sees Everything* — pretentious, maybe, but *The Big Sleep* was worse, and too morbid. As the cyclone season approached, worse and worse it seemed to him with every climate-changing year, he liked to pull into Rangoon, where the dry dock and refitting charges were quite good value, and where people kept his ship seaworthy. He took a covered skiff up the mighty Irrawaddy, a couple days' journey, and wandered among the pyramidal temples strewn across the plains of Bagan.

An inn there, all but empty in the rainy season save an occasional throng of Chinese businessmen, passes for a luxury hotel in the middle of nowhere. He found a local woman to cook for him — the hotel restaurant was horrid — but sometimes he would go down to the patio and order a lemonade and listen to a man play the *saung*, a Burmese harp, his daughter adding some finger cymbals and singing in that high East-Asiatic whine, which he first found grating but then came to feel expresses the basic human plaint.

Once a week a marionette show featured the classic characters of Burmese *commedia del arte*. The marionettes he found uncanny, the way the slightest waggle of fingers by the manipulator resulted in full body movements of the puppet, the way she could make them dance, give them emotions, have them do convincing double-takes, experience moments of ecstasy. And there was no end to the complexity — on one puppet each eyebrow could be raised independently. The manipulator — a woman very young to be so accomplished — worked from behind a waist-high curtain, and at times her hands and arms were a flurry of activity, throwing strings one way and another, moving six or more control bars at once, roaming behind the curtain to move multiple puppets back and forth across the stage, faster when she made the horses gallop. At times like that she always smiled. Some of it had become rote, but at the edge of her game she was pleased by her own skill, her own dexterity, her power.

It always made him miss his work, this non-sailing time, made him wonder what he was doing. Out among the islands, he pulled whatever strings the sea let him, and exulted in his new prowess as a sailor. Was that what Dmitry was after in all his double- and triple-dealing — the thrill of skill, the feeling of mastery, the exercise of capacity? Maybe. But maybe that was giving him too much credit.

He had, he knew, given him too much credit. He chalked some of it up to youth: youth loves a narcissist, which is why young people love rock stars and movie stars — everyone dreams that maybe, somehow, they will learn the narcissist's secret, learn how to be both fully self-contained and the center of attention, the secret of how to not care about anyone or anything other than one's own pleasure and profit. As we get older, he decided, we see narcissists for what they are — they are the death of love, the death of beauty, the diminishment of the world around them. Narcissists smell of possibility to the young, they smell of death to the old. They suck up all the possibility in the room. They leave us with nothing.

Except, in this case, fifty million bucks. Once the typhoons had done their worst, he'd drift down the 150 miles to Rangoon on the still-rain-swollen river, collect the spruced-up *God Sees*, and wander off to wherever his whim might take him. Last year he went all the way to Papua New Guinea. This year, he decided, he's going to Bangladesh. He's never been there. Perhaps he'll hug the coast all the way around and down the subcontinent to Sri Lanka.

People told him it was crazy to sail these seas, what with all the pirates, but so far, so good. He had everything he needed, and kept his passports, a hard drive, and some significant cash in a waterproof safe that he could chuck overboard and find with a SCUBA tank and a GPS device. And he opened safe-deposit boxes in a dozen cities with some wads of cash and all the bits of paper and ID he would need to get set up again if he lost everything. Needless to say, there's more money than he will ever need. He sold the Nichols Canyon house, sold the company to a group of his employees at a bargain-basement price. They were happy, he was happy. He would have had enough for a nice life even without Dmitry's money. He gave around 60 percent of it all to charities of various kinds — mostly environmental, anonymously — and kept the rest in bonds, metals, and money markets, with a certain percentage in the hands of younger versions of Dmitry, the next generation of thieves, the whole pile tooling along at six or seven percent. He gave away 60 percent of that million and a half, too, and still spent a fraction of what was left. He'd leave some tidy millions for Lulu and Kennedy, for Isa and her kids, and for a half dozen nonprofits, when he was gone. With no mortgage, no car, no taxes, no debt, and no reason to save, he could afford to be an extravagant gift-giver, a magnificent tipper. He was never sure if it was because of the guilt or the loneliness. Or — and this was without question part of it — the vanity.

The ship was everything he dreamed she would be. Incredibly seaworthy, luxuriously comfortable. He went ahead and bought a new one, because why not? In it was everything that was his except his investments and safe-deposit boxes. It was preposterous how aphrodisiacal the ship was for Western women, and his rich Americanness had the same impact on everyone else. He was always happy to meet people, the women often more interesting to talk to than the men, while most couples avoided the weird single guy. If the women started to act interested, he told them right away he was still, four years later, too brokenhearted to play, and he was. He had come to see that every romance in his life, from the big loves with Tracy, Isa, and Yuli to his briefest encounters, had all been fueled by a bathetic and finally exploitive desire to validate himself, to feed some need for an approval he was unwilling to give himself. His love was a burden he gave to people who didn't, and shouldn't, want to carry it. Celibacy was a way to stop the endless death and rebirth of his own self-regard.

He told himself, sometimes, that he should relent, that a dalliance or two would help keep the purity of his love for Yuli alive. He told himself all sorts of things. He even wondered if, to paraphrase Flannery O'Connor, nobody with a 72-foot ketch needed to be justified — or that nobody who has given $30 million to help save the earth from the Anthropocene needed to be justified. That is, maybe whatever recognition, or justification, or approval he sought in sex and romance had been obviated by this pile of good luck fallen in his lap, and he was now ready to just be a decent companion to someone.

Still, he knew he would never marry. He would never fall again. He could no longer pretend, or be party to pretense. Nor could he use any of Dmitry's loathsome excuses. He helped people pay their rent, but not in exchange for sex. He knew this was only a tiny step toward a morally defensible life, one less rife with contradiction than his life had always been, but it was a step.

He quit drinking, and he sometimes wondered if he hadn't made these decisions, if he had chosen, instead, to lose himself in alcohol, or in the pleasures of the flesh, or if he had returned to LA and turned into some version of Phil Spector, snorting coke and picking up girls on the Strip, he might have shuffled off the deck already. He also sometimes wondered if the events that led him to Yuli, and then away from her forever, and the solitary life he had chosen since, had so molded him to himself that he was not entirely in his right mind anymore. Who could know? There was nobody close enough to register it.

He thought about Yuli often, and about Dmitry too. Once in a while he emerged from some deep memory and — hence the worrying about his right mind — felt that she had been right there with him. He snapped to from these waking dreams surprised to find himself on a boat, a thousand miles from anywhere she might be.

He sent Lulu and Kennedy each a check for a house down-payment, and they were both grateful, but also, he could tell, a little embarrassed. They didn't think of him often, and were abashed at his interest in them. So he kept what he hoped was the right distance. He called on their birthdays, and let them know he had their backs if they ever needed anything. Isa, Margie and Paul, the journalist, Catskills, Trog, the Heals, Tracy, Amarya — he had no idea. They were either dead or they were alive. He had no reason not to assume the latter. He hadn't seen them in the flesh, or anyone else from his past, for that matter, since that last noir nightmare at the Serang family compound.

When he had come to from the drugged drink that day in Jakarta, having slipped out of the chair onto the floor, the house was empty. His suitcase stood at the front door. He took a shower, put on fresh clothes, and walked through the miniature rainforest and away from the empty house. For the first time there was no driver, and no guard at the front gate. He walked over to the café, rolling his suitcase with him. He sat down at a table with Dmitry's father and mother, a new guy, and the Men in Black.

"So we meet again, Hollywood," the short one said.

"I'll have a cappuccino," Frank said to the waiter.

"Who is he?" the new man, also a Brit, asked the rest without looking at him.

"Who are you?" Frank asked in return. He looked like Uncle Toby from *Tristram Shandy*.

"Sam Bert," he said. "Dmitry's uncle. Come to straighten this out and take everyone home."

"*The Ambassadors*," Frank said. Maybe the drug hadn't worn off yet. Sam looked at him funny. "It's a novel — they send someone to save the son, then someone to save that person, then —"

But Sam had stopped listening and was back to watching the compound. He was the kind of guy who, if he didn't understand what you were saying, immediately decided you were not worth listening to.

"You *leaving*, Baltimore?" the tall man in black said.

"You're Franky?" asked Dmitry's mother, swinging around.

"Yes, Franky Baltimore," said Dmitry's father.

"Gotten pretty chummy with the infidel, have you?" Bert said, with a sour face.

"Yes and no," Frank said. He noticed, at a table across the patio, the same Indonesian man pretending not to listen that had been there the day he met the father. He looked even more like a cop.

"Who's the shadow?" he asked the Men in Black. They looked over at him and shrugged. Could they be that incompetent? Dmitry's father, mother, and uncle all continued to gaze straight ahead at the front gate of the compound. He thought about whether or not to tell them that the show was over, that the family was gone, everyone was gone, it was all gone gone gone. But he didn't. He didn't see the upside.

"Can you call a taxi for me?" he said to the waiter when he brought the cappuccino.

"Yes, sir."

"You can't leave yet," Dmitry's mother said. "Trog is on his way over."

"Trog? Why on Earth?"

"He's also had experience with Muslims," Dmitry's father said, while the new man nodded in agreement. "This won't be giving the donkey strawberries, I warrant."

Dmitry's mother shook her head at that line. She looked directly at Frank. She seemed sane enough. "I originally thought Trog might help me get George to give up this madness and come home," she said, her eyes wandering back to the front gate. "But now I'm thinking maybe he's right. Trog may be just the man. He dealt with some desperate characters in North Africa. Maybe he can help."

"Help do what?" Frank asked. It came out more flummoxed than he intended, but it didn't matter. None of them seemed to hear him, deep in their vigil. What could they possibly expect to happen? What could anyone have possibly expected to happen?

"I seen both cars went out," said Bert. "They leave you all alone?"

"You could say that," he said.

A cab arrived, and he assumed it was his. He put down a bill for his coffee, finished throwing the searing tar down his throat, and stood up. But it wasn't his cab, it was Trog's. Looking more than ever like Tolstoy's pissed-off brother, he got out, and the driver put his duffel on the walk.

"Somebody pay this guy," he said, all gravel. "I've got no local currency." No hello. No howdy do.

Bert handed the cabbie his fare.

"I thought you were on the inside," Trog said to Frank. "What a fucking flight that was. I'm a million years old."

"No," Frank said. "I'm not on the inside. I never was."

Everyone looked at him. He motioned to the cabbie and pointed to his bag. The driver stuck it in the trunk, and Frank told the waiter he could cancel the other cab.

"Where are you going?" Trog asked. "I just got here!" The Indonesian man leaned over to hear what he might say.

"I have no idea. Why are you here?"

"Cathy said George and Henrietta needed sense talked into them. This is craziness. What do they think they're doing?"

Well, that was a good question. "You tell me. Working out their grief? Defending civilization? You should send them home. Dmitry is alive and long gone. The whole family. Gone." He couldn't get himself to say her name.

He followed their eyes. "That the family manse?" he asked, motioning to the entrance.

"Yes, but they've all left," Frank said. "Like I said. For good. Go home. Dmitry staged the whole thing. These clowns work for him," he said, nodding to the Men in Black. With their sunglasses on it was unclear whether they reacted.

George had handed Trog his binoculars, and he was scanning the white walls.

"Looks like nobody's home," Trog said. "Guardhouse empty." He made no sign he had heard Frank.

OK. He walked over to the cab and opened the back door.

"You're not going to stay and help?" Dmitry's mother asked him, as if she was hurt.

"Trog's your man," Frank said. "He has experience with Muslims."

He turned to the odd septet. They kept staring at the house. He got in the cab and shut the door.

"To the airport," he said to the driver, his voice a bit wobbly.

He was going to Taipei. As Quentin Compson. If he couldn't have anything he really wanted, he was at least going to have his fucking boat.

He tried sometimes, out on the open sea, to figure out what it all meant, why so much of it seemed to be scripted from things he had read, whether that meant that he had more to do with engineering the whole thing than he thought. Sometimes he replayed Dmitry's last speech and thought, really? Could that possibly have happened?

This story, this mess: he couldn't see inside, he couldn't see the bones — exactly what he loved about framing, the 2x4s all in a perfect line, all square and plumb, the joists arrayed against the heavens, the fresh fir rafters on their elegant angles, the doorways and windows with their jackstuds and headers, all leading nowhere and everywhere: he always felt like he was seeing into the mystery of human achievement, the animating design itself. So clean.

But with this he couldn't see any design. The beginning, the middle, the end — he wasn't sure how they fit together.

Every once in a while he thought about going home, back to the States, considered resuming some kind of normal life — no one is immune from homesickness, not even those who have no home — but he quickly abandoned the idea. He might be ceaselessly borne back into the past, but not that past. Once in a while he checked into some swank resort for a few days, one of the $3,000 a day joints that dot Southeast Asia, the kind of place he assumed Dmitry and Yuli and the boys stopped, where among the guests were undoubtedly a certain number of the arms buyers and arms dealers, the dictators and dictators' henchmen he saw in Dmitry's files. The people he met in such places were invariably boring, with their abortive elations and short-winded sorrows, ambassadors from a land he had left forever, a land where people care about status, accumulation, winning. He once did, but he didn't anymore — easy as that was to say for him, what with the millions in the bank.

In the Aman Resort on Phuket, watching cable in his room — his only contact with media was in these places; otherwise he stayed away from TV and computer screens, even newspapers and magazines, and did email only when he was paying his monthly bills — he saw on C-Span one of those bizarre fragments of media surrealism, a fancy banquet in Qatar, the guest of honor Al Gore, speaking to a bunch of Arabs and Westerners about alternative energy, and on the dais with the Emir and George Soros and George Clooney and King Abdullah II of Jordan and his lovely wife, Queen Rania, was, yes, none other than Dmitry Heald and his quite extraordinary, exquisite, lovely wife, Yuli Serang. The speakers were Gore, Clooney and Serang — Dmitry was the plus-one, it seemed. This sent Frank to the business center, where he googled Dmitry and found that he had re-emerged as "former financier" Dmitry Heald, now CFO of something called the Asian Energy Study Group, a corporation building major green energy projects — tidal installations many miles out on the continental shelf off the Philippines, wind generators in the Gobi desert, new-generation nuclear plants in South Africa and India, oil-spill and ocean plastic and greenhouse gas recovery technologies — and that the visionary founder and CEO of the company was Yuli Serang. Since Trump's election, the rest of the world had embraced renewables like never before and AESG's stock quadrupled in value in the six months after the company went public. Yuli served as an advisor to UN commissions and governments, and Google had an endless parade of grin-and-grip pictures of her with the heads of dozens of countries. He stared at them as if they might tell him, finally, the truth. Why? he asked himself and the eternally dumb photos, why?

She would be easy to find, now. He resisted looking up AESG's website, where they might have posted the next conference she would address. He could just show up. But again, why? Tracy had said to him, during one of their falling outs, *they call it being partners because you're supposed to be in it together — it's not about feelings, it's about life.* But he had continued falling in love under the mistaken impression — and here he felt his books had steered him wrong, too — that his strength of feeling was the only measure of love, that and the torque of his lover's emotions. It had worked with Isa until it didn't. How odd that of all the couples in the world, this one — the peculiar union of the vile amoralist Dmitry Heald and the exquisite environmentalist Yuli Serang, perhaps evil and amoral too, but more likely a wonderful, well-meaning, open-minded pragmatist — showed him what partnership was. He had never been anyone's partner. Even though Tracy had told him, all those years ago, what the score was, he'd never figured it out for himself, never figured out how not to be alone.

All in all, he knew he shouldn't complain. His life was full of marvels. Thousands of pristine islands managed to glide by his days. As he tacked against the current, salt spray from the open sea painted his cheeks like sweet tears. Sometimes he docked and had a driver take him inland to sit surrounded by the august ruins of Angkor Wat, or let the booming gongs and clashing cymbals of Gamelan fill his ears in Ubud. A couple months ago he leased a slip for *God Sees Everything* amongst the junks in Halong Bay and took the slow, light gauge overnight train from Hanoi, up the lazy Red River, with its fishermen in conical straw hats poling their thin boats in the early morning haze, to the frontier town of Lao Cai on the Chinese border. He rented a rugged jeep and drove it up into the Tonkingese Alps, high amid the stone-terraced rice fields and little mountain towns and the Hmong and Dao and Dai tribes with their elaborate dress and embroidery and bangles, all living close to the dirt and rice-giving mud. He arranged to spend the night in a house a mile or so off the road, in a small Red Dai village, a big indoor cooking pit releasing some of its thick woodsmoke out a hole in the peak of the roof, the man of the house toking on enormous spliff after enormous spliff.

He joined the man at some point in the evening, and after countless hits, unidentifiable beasts appeared for moments in startling reality, and then vanished. He stayed a second day, smoked for breakfast and entered a Carlos Castaneda-like alternate universe, striding the glowing mountain trails, hopping rivers in unconscionable leaps, sitting improvised Zazen for hours, sharing meals and smiles with his momentary family, and then, for a transitory, enchanted moment he knew, *knew* that he had had revealed to him everything. Everything. These tribes had not changed for two thousand years, not changed their dress, not changed their agriculture, not changed their lives since long before there was a Vietnam. They never blew up each other's buildings. They never embezzled each other's funds. They never strove beyond the deep labor of bringing in rice and firewood. They adorned themselves into works of art. *They* held the secret. They had never lost their capacity for wonder.

It took a week or more to return to some sanity and realize that all of that was, again, easy for him to say, that few of the Hmong would not trade their dirt floors for his yacht and his bloated, excessive disposable income, his limitless freedom from want (minus one). And, yes, he knew they had to be, on average, as corruptible as anyone else. Probably some of them had taken more than their share of the communal milk. Probably some of them had slept with each other's husbands and wives. Their dreams took them, as all of our dreams take us, dictated by the nature of human yearning, to somewhere not exactly home.

Never careful about what he wished for, Frank found himself living a dream that had once been his, catching glimpses of his receding orgiastic future in the blue trees of Laotian jungles, in Ratchaburi's floating markets, in the stilted fishing villages of Kukup, in the peek he still managed to get, now and then, into the life he might have made.

If he learned anything from his odd, misshapen triangle, from his consterning decade and a half with Dmitry and devastating year falling for Yuli, it was simply this — that the heart is a cruel organ and there is nothing to be done about the past except sigh it all comically, all tragically away.

Oh, and if pressed, he'd admit that he learned a few other things as well. He learned that if you don't like the way people eat you better not come to the table, that you needn't worry about the first note since you never know when the last note will sound, that an even chance is one thing you never get, and that one day you just have to accept that no matter how far you sail across the water, you are still in it, and that no matter how badly you want it to be otherwise, the sea will never be entirely empty and blue and serene again. Never.

Repeater Books

is dedicated to the creation of a new reality. The landscape of twenty-first-century arts and letters is faded and inert, riven by fashionable cynicism, egotistical self-reference and a nostalgia for the recent past. Repeater intends to add its voice to those movements that wish to enter history and assert control over its currents, gathering together scattered and isolated voices with those who have already called for an escape from Capitalist Realism. Our desire is to publish in every sphere and genre, combining vigorous dissent and a pragmatic willingness to succeed where messianic abstraction and quiescent co-option have stalled: abstention is not an option: we are alive and we don't agree.